Happy Birthda

# THE CASE AGAINST FILI DU BOIS

*A stray child, an unsolved crime, a precious legacy*

by

Barbara Mutch

Copyright © 2024 Barbara Mutch UK Ltd

All rights reserved. No part of this publication may be reproduced, stored in a retrieval system, or transmitted, in any form or by any means without the prior written permission of Barbara Mutch UK Ltd, nor be otherwise circulated in any form of binding or cover other than that which is published and without a similar condition being imposed on the subsequent buyer.

Book ISBN: 979-8-32-013123-8

The moral right of the author is hereby asserted in accordance with the Copyright, Designs and Patents Act 1988.

All characters in this publication, other than those clearly in the public domain, are fictitious and any resemblance to actual persons, living or dead, is purely coincidental. The organisations and events portrayed are either products of the author's imagination or are used fictitiously.

To my Family – near and far

## Author's Note

This is a work of fiction. Apart from recognised historical figures, the names and characters in the novel are the product of the author's imagination. Any resemblance to actual persons, living or dead, is purely coincidental. While the wine farms and towns of the Western Cape are a beautiful reality, Du Bois Vineyards is a product of the author's imagination.

# PROLOGUE

### The Cape, South Africa, early 1990s

*I remember the day I was left behind. After all, how could I forget?*
*But I can't remember my mother, however hard I try. Instead I see the light, a dazzling, shifting presence, as if a torch had swung down from the sky, rousing me from infant sleep and allowing no rest as I lay where she'd left me. They said I was wrapped in a shawl, quite a pretty pink one, and laid in a cardboard box which was itself wedged into the ditch that ran along the rear of the church grounds.*
*Why? Why did she leave me? All I needed was her.*
*And why did she choose that particular church?*
*Perhaps she believed - literally - the sign fixed to the side of the building:*
*Baby drop off, it said. Ages up to 3.*
*I've tried to make excuses for her, but I can't. Surely she could have kept me until I knew her voice, recognised her face, grabbed her finger with mine...*
*How can I love her when she never kept me?*
*Would you?*
*The shifting light, I realised when I was older, was the sun. Not at full strength - I'd have died in its direct beam - but deflected and tempered by the leaves of the red flowering gum trees overhead. She probably reckoned I'd be shaded from the heat of midday but still kept*

*warm when the sun fell down at sunset, though she must have expected I'd be found by then.*

*Or maybe not. Perhaps she changed her mind, rushed back, searched the ditch, but I was gone.*

*And so my earliest memory is not of her but of brilliant, probing sunlight. It creeps across my face and drenches my sleep. I wake in my bed, screaming.*

*Only the gum trees save me.*

*I hide in their dappled shade.*

## CHAPTER ONE

The first trees planted at Du Bois Vineyards were red flowering gums.
Do you suppose God intended such a neat coincidence?
I've often wondered whether Mum and Dad knew about my saviour gums but I've never asked them. If I'd done so, or blurted out a question about my birth, it might sound like ingratitude - and Mum and Dad don't deserve that. If they happened to see the church and its sheltering canopy, I like to think the leafy connection with Du Bois persuaded them to take me. Surely a child left under trees they were familiar with, might be a child they could love?
Whenever one of our Du Bois gums died of old age, another was planted in its place.
"For continuity," Grand-mère Nanette liked to murmur, as she stroked my hair. Grand-mère smelled of lavender and wore black ever since Grand-père died. "Tenure."
"What's tenure, Grand-mère?"
She put her silvery head to one side and thought for a while.
"It means time, *chérie,* and ownership. The right to stay in a place you've made your own."
I stared at the orderly, green vines pressing against the wild veld. Surely any demanding ancestor, peering down from heaven, would be pleased with our tenure? He'd still be able to spot his gums even if so much else had changed. A lot can happen in three hundred years.

And while there may be more beautiful trees on the farm, the gums talk to me. They toss down strips of curling bark that crunch, satisfyingly, under my feet when I run along the avenue towards Franschhoek. They float crimson blossom through the air like a drawn-out sigh. Perhaps it was to honour their surname that the family decided to plant trees along with the vines they brought from France. Or maybe they felt compelled, as Grand-mère was suggesting. Newcomers, after all, have to assert their rights, like diamond diggers putting a stake in the ground. If they don't, someone else might come along and steal their claim.

"Look," the Du Bois could say. "We planted these gums at the start, they're our mark of ownership."

Or, less politely... *Get off our land!*

Apart from flowering gums, we have stately oaks grouped around the house, shivering poplars set against the sky and a pair of lime green camphor trees that mark the point where the garden gives way to the vineyards. If a shortage of sons should ever cause the family name to disappear, the towering *bois* will still be all around us. But when Mum and Dad didn't have a baby of their own they decided to rescue me from the box where I'd been wedged, and brought me to the farm and raised me here to be a Du Bois. I wonder why? Weren't there any boy babies?

At first, I didn't know the facts about my start.

"Our very own baby!" Dad often used to whisper when I was small.

I didn't understand why he said so, over and over, but Mum clearly did, for she would hug me a little harder and nod and stroke my dark curls. It took me several years to notice the difference between me and Mum and Dad. It seems strange to be blind for so long but perhaps love makes us that way? It stops us seeing what might harm us if we understood sooner.

"Why don't I look like you?" I asked boldly one day, when my discrepancy couldn't be put off any longer. We were on the verandah, dressing a doll who was also different from me. But that was because dolls aren't born like humans but knitted or sewn from a pattern, or made in a factory. For a moment, an expression of panic crossed Mum's face. She smoothed her blond hair. "We're all different from one another, Fili. Think of the proteas you know. None are the same, are they?"

I stared out into the garden. It was true: some were tipped with charcoal beards that I loved to tickle, some looked like the yellow pincushions in Grand-mère's sewing box, others had feathery blooms that spread to the size of dinner plates.

"See," Mum held up my doll, "isn't Dolly lovely in her dress? You'd look beautiful in a dress like this."

"But Bo looks like his Mum and Dad. Everybody else matches except me."

Mum put down the doll and drew me onto her lap and held me fast against her. Beyond the rambling garden our vines marched across the land with certainty, like they knew exactly where they'd come from and what they were meant to be. I could feel Mum's heart thumping against my body. I'd never felt it that hard before.

"You match your mother, Fili. But she couldn't take care of you so Daddy and I became your parents. Now you belong to us, and to our family."

I wriggled upright, fear stabbing my heart. "Why couldn't she take care of me?"

Mum hesitated, then patted my face. Her normally brilliant eyes were clouded, as if they couldn't see clearly enough to find the words she needed. "She wasn't strong enough, Fili."

"Do you have to be strong to look after a baby?"

"Oh, yes! And your Daddy and I love you so much!" Mum's expression cleared and she picked up Dolly again, "you choose the next dress. How about the pink one with the lace?"

I twisted off Mum's lap and ran into the garden. I don't know why I didn't hug her even harder for loving me when my real mother couldn't, and for helping me understand why I didn't look like her or Dad but rather like someone who was once my birth mother before I was rescued. I don't know why I wasn't more grateful in that moment.

"Fili!" Mum shouted, her voice snatched away by an eddy of wind, "come back! Come back!"

The roses were breathing out their perfume into the breeze. I knew their names: Peace, Just Joey, Fragrant Cloud... like I came to know the name for what had happened to me. It was called adoption.

Dad and our ridgeback, Blaze, found me later that afternoon among the rustling vines. He carried me home, my tear-swollen face buried against his neck, Blaze loping at his side.

"We love you, Fili," he murmured. "Only you."

Dad always knew what to say. And how to say it in the fewest possible words - or maybe that was because mothers talked more, so fathers didn't get as much chance.

"You're our girl. Always."

The southeaster whipped my shirt like it wanted to punish me for being too strong for my real mother.

"Always, Dad?"

"Yes. Always."

Grand-mère, at first, wasn't so sure.

"Sweet enough at this age, Martin - *adorable* - but what about later? We know nothing about her origins -"

I've always wondered why grownups don't realise children have good ears, especially for picking up whispers. We may not understand what we hear at first – like the word 'origins' - but we can always store it up until we do.

"Fili is God's gift to us," Dad said firmly, reaching for Mum's hand, "and we'll give her a future."

Philemon Sammy, our brown Coloured foreman, wasn't sure either. But he kept quiet when I began to come by to play with Bo, his son. Philemon's round wife, Shenay, was more encouraging – *welkom kindjie!* – welcome child! - and gave us lemonade and syrupy *koeksusters* when I turned up at her door. The other grownups in the village went back into their neat cottages, muttering among themselves. *Who is this child*, they would say. *Where did she come from? Who is she to us? To Du Bois?* I think my arrival also surprised neighbouring owners like the van der Weydens, but they patted me and brought soft toys for me to play with and said how brave Mum and Dad were. They failed to say I was brave, which I thought was unfair given how much everyone stared.

"Truly uplifting!" declared Mrs van der Weyden gaily, while her husband stood by with folded arms and a set face. I didn't know what she meant by being uplifted either, or why my arrival should attract curiosity. Maybe it was simply because I wouldn't ever look like my parents. It turned out that people who were strangers were the most approving.

"Such a lovely child!" they'd say with real smiles when I was out and about with Mum and Dad.

Perhaps it was easier to be generous if you were an outsider and had no stake in the ground.

"Are you afraid of me, Bo?" I asked one day when I was eight years old and we were climbing the oak that overhung our thatched roof. The house was not French Huguenot, as you'd expect from our ancestors, but Cape Dutch. It had a high white gable, dark green shutters and a gleaming yellowwood floor. Those old Du Bois, chased out of France because they believed in a different kind of God - so Grand-mère said - stopped at nothing to make sure they fitted in. It seemed to me that fitting in was something that had to be worked on, whatever you looked like.

"No..." he said slowly, fingering a twig, his face turned away from mine. Bo was two years older than me and he surely knew more about the world outside of the farm than I did. He had soft brown eyes and stiff brown hair that stuck up in tufts from his head, and thin legs that could run further than mine.

I picked a leaf and tore it carefully down its splayed veins.

"Is it because I was adopted? Because I don't come from here? Because I don't belong by blood?"

"Shoo, Fili!" Bo almost fell from his perch. Blaze, capering below, broke into a volley of barks. "You say very silly things!"

Maybe Bo didn't know as much as I thought. Or maybe he didn't want to say what he knew.

Dad knew everything about everything, what fitted in and what stood out.

"See," he said, hoisting me into his arms one autumn day when the poplars were turning gold and the winds were veering from the usual southeaster, "the world alters every season, honey. Yet underneath those changes, it remains the same. Year after year. We depend on that."

I warmed to his reassuring, crooked grin, meant only for me. It was unlike the grownup smile he gave Mum, or the tender warmth for Grand-mère. And Dad was handsome, far more handsome than Mr van der

Weyden whose face might once have been good-looking before he became permanently annoyed. I don't know why, because he had a beautiful farm and a pretty daughter called Petro who was my friend.

"But our own *terroir*," Dad went on, gesturing across the rolling vines, "is truly unique, Fili. The soil, the angle of the slopes, the weather over the mountains – it's what makes our wine special." He gave me a little squeeze. "Quite unlike the Steyns further down, much better than the van der Weydens across the valley!" He chuckled and swung me lightly to the ground, as easily as he shifted crates of bottles one moment or delicately swirled wine in his glass the next.

I stared beyond the quilt of vineyards, the glint of our farm dam, and on towards the grey mountains folding around the end of the Franschhoek valley. They were like Dad's arms when he rushed into my bedroom to stop me crying from the nightmares beneath the yellow sun. Luckily, he and Mum and Grand-mère were now my sheltering gums. If I was a faithful daughter and grand-daughter, the underneath world would hold steady through the seasons and the yellow dreams might give up and leave me forever. That's what I told myself to believe.

"Grand-mère says the *terroir* gives the vines *l'esprit de la vigne*," I twisted my tongue around the French. Grand-mère had spent time in France as a child and still spoke the language. "It's our heritage," she'd look at me with appraising eyes, "and part of our future. Nothing in life is ever wasted, child."

I reached out and fingered the soft vine leaves and traced their pointed outline.

"Dad, when can I help you make wine?"

It could be my chance, my route to belonging forever, a sure way to quieten any of the remaining surprise and chatter. Bo and I and the village children were allowed to stamp on the damaged grapes at harvest-time, our legs running with the juices and our hands stained with the delicious mess, but the choice bunches and the serious matter of turning them into wine was out of bounds.

I tugged at his hand. "I want to help, Dad!"

Whenever Bo and I stood in the cellar doorway, the oak barrels gave off a sweaty, yeasty scent that rose from the dark cavern and tickled my nose and throat deliciously.

"It's our great-uncle Baantjie," he would whisper from behind me. "He fell into the wine and drowned, my Pa says he walks between the barrels at night -"

"There's no such thing as ghosts, Bo!"

"It's true, ask your Granny Nanette!"

When I did, Grand-mère raised an eyebrow and said that folk could be 'wilfully superstitious'. On the other hand, she went on, no-one doubted that wine was a vital, breathing force. "It gives life and it takes life away. Birth to death, child."

Dad folded my hand in his large, calloused one. "Next year, Fili. But you must promise you'll only go into the cellar with me or with Philemon." He knelt down to my level. "Never on your own."

"I promise."
Perhaps Dad had seen great-uncle Baantjie, too.

"Martin," Mum whispered later when she thought I couldn't hear or see them, "are you sure? We can't impose, she may prefer something else, a different vocation, it's too soon to tell -"
Dad ran a hand through his fair hair. Grand-mère's hair must once have been the same, but now it was the colour and velvet feel of the silver trees that I stroked when we walked on the mountainside. Sadly, silvers didn't always stay healthy. No-one knew why they suddenly tarnished and died. I think it was out of boredom, from being admired too much.
"She's keen, darling. Why shouldn't she learn? It'll be hers one day."
I gasped from my hiding place behind the door and felt my heart swell. I peeped through the crack. Mum was looking away from him and smoothing down her skirt. She liked to wear pastel colours that matched the roses she picked or, in winter, the rusty shade of their fallen petals.
"Now don't be foolish," Dad murmured, getting up from the kitchen table where he'd been writing up his notes. He took Mum in his arms. She rested her face against his chest. They fitted together, Mum and Dad. Just like I fitted with them even though we didn't share blood. We matched in the parts that mattered.
"Yes, but what if..." Mum's voice trailed away.

"We tried," I heard him say in a low voice, "but it wasn't meant to be. And now the world's changed around us. Remember, Ray, we pledged to look forward rather than back?"

## CHAPTER TWO

Each winter our vines turned dark red against the resting earth. The swallows fled north, leaving the sky clear for jackal buzzards to circle and wait for their prey to show themselves against newly-bare ground. The Franschhoek peaks glittered with the first snowfall while, lower down, icy rain drove across the valley floor. Our avenue gums swayed in the gales and shed spare branches across the road, ready to trip you up or tangle in the underside of the farm *bakkie*.
"*Hayi!*" Philemon would wrench to a stop and we'd have to pile out to free the car.
Blaze dozed in front of the fire in the lounge all day, and had to be forcefully nudged to join Dad for his evening check of the boundary. Mum cut back the roses and picked fronds of red-tinged conebush for her vases and waited for the winter proteas to flower on the mountainside. For me, the thrashing trees brought a chilly anxiety. Dead leaves eddied about my feet as if trying to warn me of something I couldn't yet know. Grand-mère picked up on my mood and shifted it to the next season's wine – and the belonging that might, in time, flow from it.
"If you want to learn, Fili," she said on one of our cold vineyard walks, limping along slowly in her voluminous black dress, me at her side, holding her hand and helping her over the uneven ground between the rows,

"then you need to start with the soil. Even now, when it's ready for winter rest."
"The soil?"
She bent down with difficulty.
"Careful, Grand-mère!"
She waved me away and scooped up some earth and rolled it between her fingers. I knelt down beside her. Her fingers were gnarled like the vine's twisted trunk.
"Here, feel. And smell."
I rubbed the earth in my hand, but it was wet and greasy and smelled, disappointingly, of nothing special. Nothing like the rich bouquet that Dad let me sniff from an opened bottle.
"This special dirt, " said Grand-mère, her tiny blue eyes glowing in a web of wrinkles, "will decide which cultivars we plant, whether we make a sauvignon blanc or a merlot that glows in the glass like a sunset. This, *chérie*, is the starting point. The essence of what will come after."
I dribbled the soil from my hand. It fell around the roots at my feet.
"I'm going to learn, Grand-mère. I'm going to make wine. Then I'll be a true Du Bois."
I stood in front of the mirror in my bedroom that evening. Huge black eyes gazed back at me. Matching dark hair, cropped short, hugged my face. Different from Mum. Different from Dad.
Yet one day my sort of eyes and hair might be seen as true Du Bois.

*I'll make you proud!* I whispered fiercely to the ancestors who might be listening. *Watch me.*

And the rest of the valley did, from the moment I came to Du Bois as a baby. It started when Mum and Dad went to church every Sunday morning. I think they went because, as Dad had said, I was God's gift and they wanted to be sure to praise Him for that. So church was the place where I was most watched. I used to sit on Mum's lap, looking up at the roof soaring to heaven, and then over Mum's shoulder at the curious eyes in the pew behind. Some people smiled, some nudged one another and whispered but I couldn't hear what they said because of the low murmur of the organ or the preaching of the minister.

"So brave," Mrs van der Weyden declared to Mum. "And look how well Petro and Fili play together!"

Maybe she meant that I was brave not to cry because sometimes Petro would pinch me and say I was lucky my parents took me otherwise where would I have ended up? Especially as I wasn't given to the orphanage for adoption but left in a ditch. Later, I joined the Sunday School where we learnt about Jesus who was not fussy about matching families and loved everyone He happened to meet. He also turned water into wine which was a hard thing for children from wine farms to understand.

"Why, you have to believe, young Fili!" my teacher exclaimed. "Some things can't be explained."

"But -"

"The Lord moves in mysterious ways," piped up Evonne Newman. "It says so in the Bible."
"Indeed it does."
"Can we play outside?" asked Petro. "We can pretend to be Jesus, with the water."
We flung our bibles down and ran outside into the church courtyard where a small fountain gurgled.
"I don't believe it!" giggled Petro as we dabbled our hands. "It's a fairy tale!"
"It was a miracle, Fili," Mum explained later, stroking my head. "That's why we worship Jesus so much, because he could perform miracles. Remember the loaves and the fishes?"
Maybe, I thought to myself as I stared over the vines, if I learnt to do something miraculous, then people would forget where I came from and only see what I'd made.

It seemed to take far too many years of growing but when I was thirteen and we had climbed well into the new millenium, I got my chance. Dad announced that I could make my first vintage for Du Bois Vineyards. It would be a cabernet, a famous red grape with hints of blackcurrant and cherry, and a liking for several years' rest in oak barrels that had come all the way from France.
"But I'll have to wait so long for it to be ready!" I protested. My wine would only reach its best when I was grown up. I'd be old. Eighteen or even more -
"Maturity," observed Grand-mère with a glint, "is wasted on the young."

And maybe that was Dad's point all along: to make me wait; wait until I'd built up thirteen years of belonging to Du Bois - and then choosing a slow cabernet rather than the quick reward of a sauvignon or chardonnay. He was teaching me the value of time yet also, conversely, showing those around us that, at thirteen, I had a stake in the ground sooner than they might have expected.

"Bo, look!"

My fingers shook as I pointed out the tiny buds on the vines, showing in the first flush of a windy, showery spring. Our swallows had recently returned, swooping through the gusts and searching out their old, caked nests beneath the eaves of the cellar. But Mum's roses and Grand-mère's lavender stayed wrapped in their winter hibernation until one day the skies cleared, a watery sun appeared, and the sap across the farm stirred in earnest. I watched as proud coots led bobbing trains of chicks across the dam while pied kingfishers hovered and dived in an orgy of fishing. Tendrils of lime green began to sprout. Bo and I raced down the enlivened rows until my heart threatened to burst in my chest. I stumbled over an exposed root and caught myself from falling.

"Slow coach!" Bo yelled over his shoulder, skipping ahead.

"Dad, have you seen?" I ran over to where he and Philemon were bending over my cabernet vines.

"Too wet, sir," Philemon scratched his head and squinted at the sky, and felt the moisture in the soil and wondered about a late cold snap. The snow had not long melted from the tops of the mountains. "We need sun, sir."

But the vines didn't want to wait any longer. It was as if they sensed my eagerness and couldn't hold back either. Defying the risky cool, the tendrils became infant bunches and the infant bunches grew into darkly jewelled trusses. Far above the swelling rows, the jackal buzzards yelped and searched for food with extra urgency. "They'll have babies already, Miss Fili," Philemon said, pointing up the mountains. "They don't need the sun as much as we do. A fat young *dassie* will taste just as good, hot or cold." Philemon was careful about titles. He called Dad 'sir', and Mum was 'madam' and Grand-mère *'ou missus'*. After I grew out of babyhood, I was 'miss'.

Some weeks before that showery spring I turned fourteen years old. Fourteen seemed to be a signal for my body to grow in a new direction without me telling it, because I suddenly became rounder. Bo and my classmates and the farm workers began to look at me with fresh eyes.

"Quite the young miss!" cackled Tannie Ellie, one of the village's senior women, to Philemon's mother, Mary Sammy. "Who'd have thought?"

My school friends also began to change. Petro started to wear more dresses. I hate dresses, they stop you running and Mum says you must be sure to sit with your legs squeezed together otherwise you will show your knickers and that is not polite. Evonne was less interested in clothes but spent ages in front of the mirror curling the ends of her hair, which made me laugh. I wanted straight hair rather than my curls, she wanted waves.

"We need to look at your wardrobe, Fili," said Mum. "You need some frocks now you're a teenager."

"But I don't like frocks!"

"My!" exclaimed Mrs van der Weyden, running her eyes over me when we met in town, "you're turning into a beauty, Fili!"

"Just as lovely as Petro," said Mum swiftly. "But perhaps not as tall."

"Indeed." Mrs van der Weyden took Mum by the arm and strolled ahead of me but not so far that I couldn't overhear. "I've such high hopes for Petro. University, of course. A good marriage. I'm sure you want the same for Fili -" she hesitated.

"We'll meet that when it comes. She's only fourteen! Shall we look in here?" Mum disengaged Mrs van der Weyden's hand, turned back to me and pointed at a nearby shop.

"Of course," Mrs van der Weyden kissed Mum and waved at me. "Good luck!"

When we got home, I took off the new dress and stared at my changing body. My breasts were budding like young grapes. And while the rest of me was curving, my face was thinning and could sometimes hold a blush that stained my skin more pink than usual. Even though I understood why I didn't resemble my parents in looks, perhaps Mrs van der Weyden was hinting at a further obstruction when she wondered if Mum was worried about my future?

To mark the decision to grant me my first vintage, Dad had promised to include *treize ans* somewhere on the wine's label even if it was only in the tiniest possible print. "But you'll have to earn it, Fili," he warned. "We walk the vineyards every day without fail. Can you manage it with school?"

"After homework," corrected Mum swiftly. "Fili's education comes first. More cake, Martin?"

"Of course," Dad went on with mock seriousness, handing over his plate for an extra slice, "if you can't do arithmetic, you can't calculate yeast concentration, the length of fermentation -"

"But she will," murmured Grand-mère, placing her hand on my arm. "She will."

Grand-mère is no longer unsure. She loves me for who I've become.

"Lucky fish," whispered Bo when I ran down to his cottage with cake, "your own wine, *nogal*!"

My teachers at school soon noticed a distraction that they put down to teenage daydreaming.

"Petro van der Weyden?"
"Present."
"Evonne Newman?"
"Present."
"Fili Du Bois?"
Silence.
"Fili Du Bois?"

Petro nudged me.

"Present," I said, pulling my focus back from sugar content, phylloxera, cellar temperature...

"Why do you bother?" asked Petro later as we ate our sandwiches in the school grounds. "I can't bear all the wine stuff. So messy!" She bit into an apple. "I want to go to Cape Town as soon as I grow up. Don't you?"

"No. I'm going to stay at Du Bois forever."

Petro raised a thin eyebrow. She'd begun plucking hers into arches.

"What if they don't want you to?"

I gasped and searched her face. I'd started to believe that fourteen years of faithful daughter-ness had cemented my place. I laced my fingers together and made a double fist.

Petro thrust the half-eaten apple into her lunch box, shrugged, and sauntered off.

\*

"Darling?" Ray Du Bois came to the cellar late one afternoon. "Elaine van der Weyden thinks Fili may struggle later -"

"Why?" Martin looked up from inspecting a row from the previous year's vintage. "Fili's brighter than Petro."

"She wasn't talking about cleverness. It's about the future. Marriage prospects, for instance -"

"Because she was adopted?" Martin gave a laugh as he lifted a random bottle from its place. "What nonsense!

Fili's a delight - quite aside from her cleverness. She'll be fighting off suitors!"

"Her teachers are also concerned," Ray persisted. "They say she's obsessed with this vintage." She caught hold of his free arm. "You're pushing Fili in a direction she may not be fit for, and feels she's obliged to succeed! She may think she has to make wine, otherwise -"

"Relax, Ray," Martin replaced the bottle and turned to her. "Fili will find her own way. If she wants a career away from the farm, of course I'll support her. Why are you worried about this now?"

He reached down and kissed her lightly but she edged away from him.

There were times, Martin acknowledged as she left the cellar, when Ray latched onto something and wouldn't let it go. In most instances he would let her have her way. After all, the disappointment at being unable to have a child had nearly crushed her – and nearly destroyed their marriage. But since Fili arrived, those fads – insecurities? - had all but disappeared.

It was Fili who'd restored them, who now held them together.

Fili, who was integral to their future.

And perhaps that was, in fact, the source of Ray's fear.

For all her desire to protect her adopted daughter from a predestined role on the farm, maybe what she really feared was that Fili might indeed escape… and leave them, and their marriage, once more bereft?

## CHAPTER THREE

Every day after school, Bo and Blaze and I walked the rows of my soon-to-be *treize ans* vintage. Vineyard walking was not a stroll, it was exacting work. We checked every vine, felt the swelling grapes, looked under the leaves for the scourges Dad taught me about, and measured the bunches against previous years.

"Slightly smaller," I said, writing down the numbers in my notebook. "They'd better fatten soon."

I glanced up, willing the sun out from behind ramparts of cloud. A *bokmakierie* hopped from a nearby row, glanced at me as if to ask why I couldn't conjure up brighter weather, and launched into a piping *bok-bok-mak-kik* before flying off in a flash of yellow-green feathers.

"There's some strangers, black strangers, on the other side of the fence by the avenue, on Du Bois land," Bo said, his feet scuffing the damp ground. "They want to work here."

I stared at him but he didn't meet my eyes.

"How do you know? Maybe they're just passing through?"

"No," Bo ran a hand through his tufty hair. "They want to stay. And Pa says there'll be more, there's no jobs where they come from," he gestured to the east beyond our protective mountains, "and we won't be able to turn them away."

I nodded. Where a row got less of the reluctant sun, the bunches were even smaller.

"Are you alright, Fili?"

"Yes." I bent to pat Blaze. "Just tired. Home, boy!"

But I wasn't tired, just surprisingly anxious. A different kind of anxiety from the winter one.

"This is too much for her, Martin," Mum protested over supper, mistaking my silence for weariness. "Fili's schoolwork mustn't suffer -"

"I'm fine, Mum," I roused myself. "I have to learn."

"One step at a time," Dad gave me his special, crooked smile, "you can't learn everything at once."

"The land gives up its secrets slowly, *ma chérie*," Grand-mère murmured from her rocking chair outside her cottage, a short walk from our gabled home. "It won't be rushed. Every year you understand a little more, sometimes the *terroir* changes a tiny bit, too. In all of life, we must adapt to the new." For Grand-mère each growing pain, each fresh discovery, could be mirrored in the journey from grape to glass. "Wine," she patted my head comfortingly, "can be your teacher, Fili."

Philemon agreed. "If you understand the vines, Miss Fili, then you'll know the world for sure."

With him, as with Grand-mère, we usually started out talking about grapes but often ended up someplace else, like my start at Du Bois Vineyards – when I was a stranger, too. I wonder if the people on our boundary were also left behind, like me.

"Do you remember when Mum and Dad brought me to Du Bois, Philemon?"

"*Ja.* Shenay and I waited outside the house to greet you, Miss Fili."

He bent down to check the drip irrigation. Each vine received its own dose, but only rarely otherwise it wouldn't fight for the water hiding in the soil. Lazy vines, Philemon would say, don't make good wine. I watched his brown hands, steady and deft, unlike some of our villagers whose hands shook whenever they tried any finicky work. "It's the drink," Grand-mère sighed when I asked why. "Our fault, Fili. Our forefathers used to pay the workers partly in wine. The *dop*. Now some can't live without it, and they sadly pass the tendency along."

"Was I crying, when they brought me home, Philemon?"

"No! Fast asleep!" He straightened up, chortling, and took off his cap to air his head. He was bald, so Bo's lively hair must have come from his mother. "I don't know why you didn't wake up with the extra shouting across the valley and the dogs barking. Even the doves *skrikked* from their *werk sta-dig, werk sta-dig*, work slow-ly, work slow-ly! But you slept through it all, Miss Fili!"

I'd heard the story many times before. On a dusty road beneath a mountain ridge speckled with bearded proteas, a man had walked free from prison the year before my arrival. Nelson Mandela raised his voice that day and began to change the world. My Du Bois parents liked what they heard and decided to adopt an abandoned child as their particular vote of faith in the future. One year later, people gathered on the same

dusty road to chant and demand an election in which everyone would have a vote, whatever their colour or wherever they came from – even if they had no place of their own. It was their shouting, and the dogs' barking across the valley, that had somehow failed to wake me.
"All done," Philemon twisted the tap and reset the timers, then mopped his face with a creased cloth. "We'll check again tomorrow."

Over the next few weeks the sun hammered down as if to make up for its tardiness. The mercury in the thermometer outside the kitchen door rose into the late thirties and remained there. There was no talk about the black people on the other side of the fence, or the possibility that they would settle there, and what that would mean for our tight community. Yet I know strangers can disrupt, especially if they stay. Instead, Dad began to worry about excessive heat but my grapes lapped it up and swelled to a purple lushness. Each morning, before breakfast, I threw on shorts and a shirt and ran out to make sure no heat-drunk *goggas* had eaten my beauties overnight, or attacked the chardonnay and sauvignon grapes that grew on different slopes.
"Where are you going, Fili?" called Mum from the kitchen.
"To check -" I shouted over my shoulder, "for bugs!"
"You'll be late for school!"
And each evening, after Mum and Dad had kissed me goodnight and imagined me safely asleep, I climbed out

of my window in my pyjamas and ran past the roses to stare at the vineyards beyond. I'd seen harvests since I was a toddler but this one was different because it was mine. And along with ownership came a needling voice in my head to say that I was responsible if it went right - but also if it went wrong. Especially as I wasn't yet a true Du Bois.

*Be strong!* I hissed into the darkness.

*Make a miracle like Jesus!* Water, soil, and *terroir* into wine...

"Only we can judge the right moment to pick, Fili," Dad murmured, watching over the rows one sweltering day. "It doesn't matter what everyone else in the valley's doing, our sugar must be in range, our grapes ripe but not past their prime." He plucked a berry and crushed it between his fingers, tasted it, and examined the colour of the pips left behind. "It's a science, honey, but also an art. A balancing act. And then there's the weather -"

I'd lie awake in bed and listen for a warning gust of wind that might herald a storm that would destroy my bunches before we could even gather them in; or a downpour to soak the ground, seep into the roots and travel upwards to dilute the precious juice so close to its best.

"What if we wait too long before we pick, Dad?"

"Ah," he gave a wry smile, "then we risk a cooked wine with too much alcohol. We don't want that for our cabernet."

"You must be patient, Miss Fili," insisted Philemon. "We look for the right sugar readings."

"Ten years ago," Shenay muttered, staring out of the kitchen window, "we waited too long."

One afternoon, as fat clouds poked ominously above the eastern horizon, I ran to see Grand-mère.

"How often does a harvest fail, Grand-mère?" I wiped at the sweat in the crease of my neck. "How often have we got the balance wrong?"

She shifted in her chair and peered over the heat-shimmered land. The Drakenstein mountains reared brown against a glaring sky. An orange-and-blue paradise flycatcher swooped above Grand-mère's lavender, snapping up flies on the wing.

"Not often, child."

"But what if there's a storm?"

The clouds bunched higher, their purple bellies swollen with rain.

"Ah," she dabbed at her forehead with a lavender-scented handkerchief, "then you must hope that the Almighty steers it towards our competitors."

"Grand-mère!"

Finally, when it seemed that the grapes could get no plumper and the heat must surely collapse into a frenzy of thunder and destruction, the Balling meter showed the correct sugar levels. The news rushed through the vines and eddied into the village on the back of a rising berg wind.

"Harvest!" declared Dad. "From tomorrow. Spread the word, Philemon. I'll call around. Early start."

"Harvest!" our workers shouted and clapped their hands. "Harvest!"

"About time!" yelled Tannie Ellie to Mary Sammy. Her grandchildren began to dance and chant on the swept ground outside her cottage, "Har-vest! Har-vest!" Even the blacksmith plovers at the dam caught the mood, clinking and piping non-stop.

"When I was young," Grand-mère nodded from her verandah, "we had to go on instinct. Your father's sugar readings tell us better these days."

I was allowed to stay home from school.

"Lucky you," whispered Petro reluctantly, from behind her hand in class. "Maybe I should adopt a vintage, show a sudden interest."

"They're your grapes, Fili," said Dad, sweeping aside Mum's protests about missed lessons. "You've patrolled them, you should be here."

\*

Ray Du Bois told herself that she wasn't being difficult. Just realistic.

It was Martin who was manipulating reality. Attempting to fashion the outcome he hoped for.

She bent down to sniff a perfect rose bloom. Glorious. In the distance, the mountains cut sharp silhouettes against the baking sky. It wouldn't do to stay outside for too long in this heat. She could already feel the onset of a headache.

At the orphanage, they'd been encouraged by staff to consider taking a black baby...

There were so many infants in need, the government was legalising transracial adoption, they would be doing their bit for the future of the country by building a rainbow family...

Yet imagine if they had!

The difficulties Fili was experiencing in trying to fit in - not to mention the comments she, Ray, was having to field - would have been magnified a hundredfold.

Be that as it may, it was necessary to acknowledge Fili's unknown heritage even though she shared their colour. And she and Martin ought to recognise that they had no right to impose a future on the child. Or encourage her in any particular direction.

Equally, Ray admitted privately, being honest about Fili's unknown background would allow Ray to point to that fact if her daughter ever turned contrary. Ray could simply shrug and say they'd done their best. Given her their all. Put any indiscretions or shortfalls down to nature rather than nurture.

She and Martin had intended to adopt a baby boy but Fili had been the most adorable child on offer.

She'd lifted her arms to them in appeal, and they'd looked no further.

## CHAPTER FOUR

Dawn was breaking when I proudly tolled the old brass bell, as our ancestor Du Bois had done to rouse their workers for the first ever harvest. Blaze, kept inside the house, barked in frustration and I ran back to give him a consoling pat. The clang of our bell travelled far in the morning stillness and dust clouds soon rose above Gum Tree Avenue as pickers from neighbouring farms tumbled off the back of arriving trucks. "If you help to bring in my grapes," Dad used to say at farmers' meetings, "I'll help bring in yours." And now the whole valley was converging on our ripe acres.

"*Môre!* Morning! Join the queue!" Dad called, as a chattering crowd gathered in the courtyard. Philemon raced about, organising the handing out of baskets and instructions for where each picker should go. Families shouted to be chosen together, snatches of harvest song rose above the throng.

"*Môre!*" I repeated, standing up to my straightest at Dad's side as the pickers came forward, and ignoring the surprise in the eyes of those who didn't expect a teenager to be in a prime position. "Thank you for coming!"

Dad must have noticed their surprise, too, because I felt his hand on my shoulder from time to time. To mark the occasion, I'd dressed in my best new shorts and blouse even though they'd soon get dirty. Dad had taken trouble, too, and was wearing pressed khaki trousers and an open-necked white shirt. It was important to look neat, he insisted, to show respect.

"For ourselves?" I wondered.

"No, for our workers, Fili. To show we respect their part."

The sun broke above the mountains and flooded the courtyard with warm light.

"No pushing," yelled Philemon as the queue surged. "There's work for everyone!"

In the kitchen, away from the crush, Mum and her helpers were assembling mountains of sandwiches and filling endless bottles of water to keep the pickers going all day.

"Clean picking! Clean picking!" went the refrain from one person to the next in the queue.

"Boss!" someone shouted. "Boss!"

Blaze, capering behind the kitchen window, began to bark with greater frenzy.

Dad looked up, then glanced at Philemon. He touched my arm briefly. "Stay here, Fili."

A group of three black men were standing on the edge of the courtyard. They looked poor and their clothes hung loosely off their bodies. I felt the mood of the crowd change.

*Blacks here? This is Coloured work! Coloured land!*

I followed Dad, pushing through the crowd.

"We've come for work, sir," the tallest one called out.

"Fili!" Mum shouted from the kitchen doorway, her voice higher than normal. "Come back!"

Shenay tried to lead me away but I wriggled and stood fast near Dad, Shenay alongside me.

"We're good workers, sir. We do heavy work if the others," the man gestured, "don't want to."

Dad nodded, and then he reached forward and offered his hand.

A swell of outrage rose around me, sweeping towards the poor, hopeful men.

Their leader hesitated, and then extended his own hand.

The ground began to tremble under my feet.

Our workers weren't just shouting, they were stamping on the beloved *terroir*, hurting it as if it was responsible for something that went beyond making wine.

"Dad!" I cried, but he didn't hear.

Slow, defiant clapping joined the thud of bare soles on hard earth. Shenay's grip on me tightened. The warm sun suddenly turned hungry, burning my face like in my nightmares. The trees were too far away to shade me -

"I'm sorry!" Dad shouted over the din, "it's the harvest. We're very busy, I can't help you today."

The shoulders of the men dropped but they remained facing Dad.

"Another time," their leader called out, not as a question, but as if there was no alternative.

"Our work!" a woman yelled back. The chant went up, "*On-se werk! On-se werk!*"

A bumble bee whizzed past my face on its way to a nearby hibiscus. Red petals trembled as it dived towards the centre of a bloom. Couldn't it sense danger? The crowd was heaving forward like a swarm about to break around Dad, lost amid the noise and dust of those pounding feet.

Should I wrench free from Shenay?

Run forward to tell the strangers they weren't needed right now? But maybe later?

"Martin!" Mum's high-pitched voice broke through. Dad glanced around sharply and hurried to her side. The bumble bee hoisted itself out of the flower and lumbered off. Mum held out several packets of sandwiches. "I'm sorry we can't help," she called to the men, "but we can give you some food." Dad nodded and took them from her and went back to the men.

The leader glanced at his companions. For a moment I thought he might be insulted, grab the gift and throw it to the ground. That would have been the spark. *How dare you!* I could imagine our Coloureds screaming, as the swarm broke and they rushed forward. *How dare you toss away Mrs Ray's kindness*? The man seemed to be weighing the same possibility because he looked over the angry crowd and said "Thank you, Sir," took the sandwiches and turned away. The others hesitated, then followed him towards the drive.

Shenay released me. My hand ached from where her nails had been digging into my flesh.

"Martin?"

"Not now, Ray."

Dad turned back to the bunched crowd of pickers. "There's no need to be alarmed," he shouted.

"*On-se werk!*" came the chant once again. *On-se werk!*

One of the departing men turned around and stared, but he was pulled away by the others.

Dad wiped his forehead and held up his arms for quiet but there was no halt to the chanting. Where his short sleeves fell back from his raised arms, the sunburnt skin gave way to muscled paleness. I'd never seen him both strong and weak before, I'd never known him to be ignored on his own land.

Mum rushed across from the kitchen and bent down to embrace me.

"Thank you, Mum," I cried into her throbbing neck. "Thank you for giving them food!"

"Please! Listen!" Dad kept his arms raised. The noise abated slightly. "We have a harvest to get in!"

The black men rounded the curve in the drive and disappeared.

"I'm relying on you," Dad went on, "Du Bois is relying on you - as we always have!"

But no-one was moving back into the queue. They were huddled together, wondering whether to begin stamping again. If their hearts weren't in it, our harvest would fail as surely as if a storm had destroyed the grapes on the vine. I broke free of Mum and ran to the pile of baskets. The air prickled with heat and the whiff of sweat mixed with fear. I picked up a stack - heavier than I expected - and hobbled back to put them at Dad's side.

"Thank you, honey," Dad gave me a strained version of his crooked smile. "Here," he found a smaller basket and looped it round my shoulders, "here's yours, Fili!"

I blinked back sudden tears.

"What's this now?" He bent down and put an arm around me.

I squirmed out of his embrace, ashamed, but for some reason the pickers were looking at me with respect. And the rage in the courtyard was over. Philemon began to hand out baskets again.

"Stay close to Dad or Philemon, don't speak to strangers," Mum ordered, into my ear, before she and Shenay went back to the kitchen.

"Off you go and pick, Fili!"

I led the way out of the courtyard.

Afterwards, I told Grand-mère that harvests were about more than grapes.

"*Bien sûr!* Now you're learning!" she said, surveying the bustling vineyards from her verandah. "As complex as a fine bouquet - and rarely predictable, child."

As a young girl, Grand-mère had also gone onto the land to work alongside the pickers.

"To learn their rhythm, Fili. To prove my worth. To seal my place."

Yet while the farm rang with the traditional songs - *Daar kom die Alibama* - and the deep growl of tractors carrying the newly-picked crop, I could still taste the courtyard rage as surely as the pips in a crushed grape. Nothing was said in front of me, but I sensed its lurking whenever the singing stopped or when groups of pickers gathered to go home at the end of the day. I'm alert to shifts, to moods, in a way that people who belong by birth are not. Grand-mère still hobbled along the rows in the late afternoon. I wonder if she noticed? Had the ancestors noticed? They'd stamped their mark on the farm in gum trees and grape vines, as had our faithful brown workers over many generations of harvest. Mum and Dad took a risk and stamped the land with me even though I wasn't truly theirs. And now there were newcomers on the farm who wanted to make their presence felt on the land, too.

Towards the end of the picking, as we stretched out in the shade of a willow with our sandwiches, Bo's mother introduced me to a group of Coloured girls from a distant farm.
"Say hello to Fili," she said, patting me on the arm while I blushed. "These are her vines!"
"How come?" asked one curiously, a pretty girl older than me. "How come they're yours?"
"I was adopted by the family," I said. "They wanted to give a stray child a chance."

## CHAPTER FIVE

"Hold off, dear Lord!" murmured Grand-mère, casting a glance at the darkening sky as she prowled the trestle tables set up in the courtyard to receive each load of newly-picked grapes. This was the first sort, to remove random twigs and soil and damaged berries; it was the particular task of the senior women in the village, whose backs might no longer manage the picking but who could still run experienced hands through the grapes before they were crushed.

"Beautiful, *neh ou missus*?" Tannie Ellie held up a perfect truss, and gave a defiant sniff. "And we didn't need help."

"Indeed," Grand-mère smiled and patted her shoulder. "Not this time."

"Never!" snorted Ellie, with a quick glance at me.

I felt a shudder in my heart. What if I'd been a black, adopted baby? How far would Tannie Ellie have gone to rouse the village against me? The pickers in the courtyard had been on the edge of mutiny, ready to attack the black strangers. Was a future without bias possible - or only a shimmering, temporary dream hovering over the vines and then dissolving?

I helped Grand-mère down the stairs into the cellar.

A distinct, earthy aroma tickled my nose and I remembered her words about the soil holding the promise of what would spring from it. *This special dirt*, she'd called it.

"Stand back, Mum! Fili!" Dad shouted. Mounds of ruby grapes poured down the chute into the de-stemmer and crusher. One moment Dad was picking grapes alongside the humblest worker, the next he was in the cellar being strict with each fresh cargo. *Learn every task*, I whispered, storing away the wisdom, *talk down to no-one.*

"Here, Fili," he scooped a sample of the must into a beaker, sniffed, and handed it to me. "Your raw material - perfectly grown!"

"Thank you!" I reached up and hugged him. "Thank you!"

Every day I searched Dad's face for any disappointment in my own performance or any sign he'd detected the unease hovering among the vines or beneath the gossip around the sorting table, but he gave nothing away. Or perhaps there was no time for him to think about anything other than the grapes pouring in day after day – firstly white chardonnay and sauvignon, then my red Cabernet, a small harvest of merlot...

I watched as the must was led into a steel tank for fermentation.

"Remember the yeast we chose, Fili?" Dad said, performing the crucial inoculation that would turn my grapes' natural sugars into alcohol. "This variety is designed for the mix of blackcurrant and cherry we're after."

I imagined the yeast swirling into the liquid, bubbling and hissing as it did its work.

"We have to keep the skins in contact with the juice at all times," Grand-mère mouthed into my ear, over the roar of the de-stemmer. "If they sit on the top, then we lose colour and flavour. So we work for the next few days -"

"To knock down the cap! I know! Dad's shown me how it's done."

"Just so," Grand-mère beamed.

"It's all about the right heat to ferment the must," Philemon rushed back from the crusher to adjust the dial, "between 25 and 28 degrees, Fili. Five to seven days. Bo? Bo! Tell Ellie and her crew less *skindering*, more sorting! I want no bad berries!"

Bo was hanging about at the top of the stairs even though the lights were on and the place was filled with people. I ran across and stood next to him and took his hand. Bo's arms and legs have filled out but he's still afraid of ghosts.

After two long days my cabernet grapes were picked. The sun struck low across the block of vines, now shorn of fruit and ready for their winter rest. A pair of sacred ibis, more elegant than their hadeda cousins, flapped to their roost by the dam, their black-tipped wings etched against the sunset. We'd dodged the weather - I glanced up at the mountains where streaks of cloud were slanting – and it was almost time to celebrate. There were only some late grapes to harvest if the hungry berg winds did not dry out the last, lush bunches before they could be picked.

"After all those months of patrolling," Dad murmured as we walked along the rows, "it's quiet time in the cellar that makes great wine, Fili. Now we must coax nature to perform a miracle."

"That's what Grand-mère says - and what Jesus did, when he turned the water into wine." I grabbed his hand. "He can't have, can He? Not really?"

"Think of it as inspiration, honey," observed Dad with a fond smile. "A lesson for what's possible if we have faith. Your grandmother goes even further. She believes wine takes on a life of its own."

"Do you believe that?"

Dad stopped and stared over the land.

"When we get it right, yes. A perfect alliance of man, nature and God. You can taste it."

I eased out my fingers, stiff from the days of picking, and touched a gnarled branch and rubbed the crisp, green leaves. They had done their job. They'd taken the sun and turned it into energy that plumped my grapes to their best. Now it was up to me.

"Come," said Dad, putting an arm about my shoulders, "it's getting late."

Shouts and laughter drifted down from the Coloured village. The *dop* might have been outlawed but that didn't stop all liquid celebration, especially after a hard day beneath the beating sun.

"What are you going to do about those men, Dad? On the boundary?"

Maybe he was hoping they'd simply move on. But what if more arrived, like Philemon expected? "Are you sorry you shook hands?"

"No," Dad's voice was firm. "It was the right thing to do."

The matter of what to do next, though, was not as simple as the handshake that had started everything off. Dad's reaching out was still causing anger in the village, and disquiet among our neighbours who saw the potential for trouble on their own farms. Grand-mère, who hadn't been in the courtyard but still knew what happened, took the long view.

"We were immigrants once," she shrugged. "Local people gave us a chance. Better to make an accommodation," she glanced at Dad over her evening glass of red, "than refuse all contact."

"But we can't help everyone who turns up!" protested Mum, giving Grand-mère a surprisingly cool look. "Don't you see, Martin? It'll only encourage more to come!"

It turned out that Mum's clever defusing of the situation with her sandwiches had made her less keen to be helpful in the future. I put my hand up to my face and imagined, again, the wild throbbing of her neck against my cheek. I'd been proud of her that day, but perhaps generosity sometimes, oddly, springs from fear? Petro says her father will chase squatters off his land with a loaded shotgun, Evonne says her father is waiting to see what happens at Du Bois. Both my friends are frightened of people who don't look like them.

"Only offer a small amount of heavy work," suggested Grand-mère, rearranging her shawl. "They may move on to look for easier labour elsewhere."

Dad shot Grand-mère an amused glance but Mum wouldn't let it go.

"I know we're privileged," she said to Dad after he'd returned from walking Grand-mère to her cottage in the fading light, "because we have a home of our own. But this settlement is an invasion of our lives. Our privacy. That land - even though it's on the other side of the fence - is Du Bois land!"

I watched from the shadows. Dad was silent.

"Martin," Mum reached over and gripped his arm, "please be sensible. You feel guilty - so do we all in this country - but think of the consequences if we don't stand firm. Our property taken over! Our safety threatened! The police are reluctant to clear informal camps -"

I stole away to my bedroom.

I've learnt that guilt makes people do things they don't want to because they feel they must, or because others are watching - or because they truly want to make a difference. But should guilt over apartheid, a policy I know Mum and Dad opposed, extend to allowing strangers to settle on your farm without being invited?

Dad didn't answer Mum that night. Yet I knew the situation gnawed at him.

When harvest was over, we dressed up - Dad in a suit and tie, me uncomfortable in a pink gingham dress that Mum insisted on - and went door-to-door in the Coloured village, delivering harvest bonuses and greeting the members of each extended family as had been the custom since Du Bois was founded. Dad seemed extra solicitous, extra careful to greet everyone who had helped.

"*Dankie*! Thank you for your hard work," he said, at each doorway. "Is this the latest baby?" sweeping the infant into his arms, and ruffling the hair of the young children.

"These are for you," I said, following behind with roses from the garden for the Grannies like Philemon's mother, fierce Mary Sammy, who still picked grapes despite arthritic knees, or nosy Tannie Ellie who watched from her doorstep and missed nothing. Bo said she wasn't watching me but rather looking out for her nephew, Blake, who'd run away to Cape Town to live a life of drink and loose girls. "*So mooi met die rokkie!*" the old ladies cried, admiring my itchy gingham. "So grown up!" They clapped their hands and hobbled off to find vases for the roses.

"Our workers are our partners, Fili," Dad said as we left. "They share in our profits. Remember that."

While the farm baked beneath the late summer sun, I ran into the cool of the cellar after school every day. The grape-skin cap was being slowly pressed to extract the last of its goodness before being recombined with the juice.

"We need the tannins, Miss Fili, for flavour and colour, but not too much. We ferment the malic acid to lactic, but that works better if we do it in barrels after the first fermentation and pressing."

"Where did you learn all this, Philemon?"

He grinned, and drew a sample from the base of the tank and held it up to the light.

"From your Pa, Miss Fili. And he learnt it from his Pa before him."

"It's a balance, *chérie*, all the way through," said Grand-mère, appearing out of the shadows. "We add yeast, we press gently, we taste and monitor and watch, we clarify and filter before bottling - a balancing act between doing too much and doing too little. Above all, we respect the grape! This vintage will have its own signature - isn't that so, Philemon?"

"*Ja*," Philemon nodded, "and the *ou missus* has tasted more vintages than anyone."

While we watched and waited in the cellar, the poplars shaded to gold outside. The berg winds gave way to cool breezes out of the north. Rain fell at last. Brazen hadedas strutted across the lawn, plunging their scimitar beaks into the grass for worms. I picked the best of the Victoria plums on the bush outside Grand-mère's cottage and she and I made a thick purple jam for winter. And I began to linger on Gum Tree Avenue after school, at first well away from the fence but slowly approaching closer each time. It wasn't about anxiety, it was more about curiosity: I wanted to see what an unrescued life might look like.

Wouldn't you? If you'd been me?

"Miss!" shouted a tall black man one day from the far side. He was the one who'd taken the lead in the courtyard. I approached warily. Petro van der Weyden's father muttered that all unemployed men - black or any other colour for that matter - could never be trusted.

"Has the farm got jobs for us?"

A teenage boy, several years older than me, sidled up to the fence and grabbed the strands of barbed wire and shook them.

I stepped back.

"No, Kula," said the man and directed a stream of Xhosa towards him.

"You'll have to ask my Dad," I said, staring at the boy.

"Your father?" the boy scoffed.

"Yes," I said, lifting my chin. "I'm Fili Du Bois, and I belong here. Mr Du Bois is my father. He adopted me. And this is our land, on both sides of the fence."

The boy, Kula, smirked and turned on his heel.

The man shook his head and said thank you and that they were ready to do whatever work there was, and would I please ask my father, and then he returned to where four plastic-sheeted shanties crowded together. Despite their unkempt appearance, they looked permanent to me. Washing flapped from a line strung between two trees. They must be drawing water from the stream nearby that we used for irrigation. Several gum saplings, seeded from our avenue, had been cut down for firewood. You could see the roughly-cut stumps poking up from a swept area in front of the shacks. A length of hose dangled over the limbs of a bearded sugarbush protea.

*Get off our land!* those early Du Bois might have said...
Yet who, I suddenly found myself wondering, had the true right to this patch of earth? Does God give ownership to the people who were here first, in the earliest of times? In that case, this was not Du Bois land - or black land either. It belonged to the *strandlopers* and the *San*, who first hunted and gathered and fished at the foot of Africa, long before black tribes migrated south or white men sailed across the oceans.

I turned away and ran home.

"Where have you been, Fili?" Mum asked, eyeing my breathlessness and mistaking it for trespass of a different kind. "You haven't been going into the cellar on your own, have you?"

I hesitated. Dad, scrubbing his hands in the sink, turned and raised an amused eyebrow. Mum didn't know how much he was allowing me inside. I loved to be alone with him and the quietly simmering vats - no ghost of Uncle Baantjie so far - while low light played across the oak barrels where my wine would one day rest.

"No," I said. "I was speaking to the squatters."

There was a beat of silence.

"In their camp! On your own?" Mum gasped and reached for her chair to sit down, angry colour staining her pale cheeks. Mum hadn't been well lately. She lay down most afternoons, saying it was the heat. I would bring her cold lemonade instead of tea, on a tray laid with a fresh rose. Shenay wrapped ice in a flannel for Mum's forehead.

"Fili, it's not safe being out there! You're an attractive young woman! Martin -"

"I'm not on my own, Bo's always with me. Or Blaze."

That was a lie. Blaze would have leapt up at the fence. And the last place Bo would go would be the camp. The villagers hated the squatters.

"I forbid you to go back there, Fili," said Dad, frowning. "Do you understand?"

Mum got up and took me in her arms. I felt the wild beating of her heart, the heat of her cheek against mine. I've learnt that Mum's fear has several faces: sometimes it shows itself as generosity, sometimes as anger or denial. "If we encourage them," she released me and glanced at Dad, "more will arrive. We can't help everyone in the world, Fili, however much we'd like to. "

I wriggled out of her arms and looked from her to Dad.

"Please can you give them work, Dad?"

He stared at me as if he was noticing my difference from him and Mum for the first time since he'd held me as a newly-acquired Du Bois. As if it mattered, now, more than it did then.

"There'll be trouble if we employ squatters, honey. You saw what nearly happened in the courtyard."

"Your father's right, Fili!" Mum clasped her hands together. "I don't want to hear any more of this!"

I said nothing.

I wanted Dad to do what he used to do when I was little: lift me up to see the autumn-tinged poplars, or hold me close to banish the yellow nightmares. Then explain that the soul – the *terroir* - inside each of us is what makes us special, not how we look on the outside.

After that, Mum began to fetch me from school instead of letting me catch the bus which used to drop me at the entrance to Du Bois on Gum Tree Avenue.
"Why does your mother collect you?" asked Evonne, tossing her gleaming hair from her face. "Does she think you'll get off the bus and run away?"
"Or be kidnapped," giggled Petro. "How much will they pay to get you back?"
She and Evonne collapsed against each other in gales of laughter.
I felt my hands curling into fists. I want to fight back. It's happening more and more. Perhaps these clenched fists come from my birth mother or father. Will they strike out one day on their own?
And I don't understand my friends. Maybe it's part of growing up, to say hurtful words to get a reaction; or maybe they recognise that I'm unlike them in a way that can never be erased.
I should tell them what it's like to be considered an outsider. Perhaps that would halt their unthinking laughter.
But I tell myself that it doesn't matter because I know I'm loved at home.

Mum and Dad forbid me from doing certain things only because they care so much.

## CHAPTER SIX

You may think me sly, but I like to listen to what grownups say to each other when I'm supposed to be in bed. I don't eavesdrop often, only when there's tension in the air between Mum and Dad, or Mum and Grand-mère. In the past, the tension was sometimes about me and I'd try to understand what I should do to be a better daughter. Or a better friend.
Nowadays it's mostly about the farm.
And the matter that Mum doesn't want to hear about anymore.
"How are you going to deal with this?" she demanded of Dad as they sat on the verandah one evening after dinner. I was up the oak tree by the side of the house. A nightjar whistled its distinctive call over and over - *Good Lord, deliver us... Good Lord, deliver us* - from Gum Tree Avenue. "If we offer them jobs, Martin, there'll be an entire community on our doorstep before we know!"
As I've got older, I've noticed that grownup love can ask questions that may not have answers, questions that could end up separating you from the one you loved at the beginning. And Mum was hard to counter, furiously lovely in flowing, pale pink silk. She always dressed for an argument.
"I don't want to feel unsafe in my own home!" She twisted her hands in her lap.
"That's exaggerating somewhat, Ray," Dad reached across to untangle her fingers. "I've been to their camp.

Four shacks only. And no women or families. That's a sign they don't intend to stay for long."

"But look what's happened around Cape Town, Martin! No respect for private property, huge informal settlements, rampant crime -"

There was a new note in Mum's voice these days, a tremor that made her run out of breath before the end of her sentence. And I could imagine her heart beating like it did in the courtyard.

"Also," she gathered herself, "Nanette's being totally unrealistic - give them difficult work, for goodness sake! You know we don't have any work for them."

*But we do!* I wanted to shout from my hiding place. They could dig out the new vineyard, remove the stones, turn the soil. Philemon says his people don't want to dig, it's much harder than their usual work. And they'd want more money, Bo says.

"Especially now." Mum's voice shook again. She straightened her full skirt. I'd never be able to wear such a pale skirt, I'd make it dirty in no time.

"What do you mean, Ray?"

The nightjar's call broke off abruptly. I strained into the darkness. Dad and I regard nightjars as our chance evening alarm. They settle on quiet roads and only move when disturbed, so their warning comes when their call stops. Dad heard the cut-off cry too, because he cocked his head and then looked at Mum with a trace of impatience. I could tell he wanted to collect Blaze and check the avenue, make sure there was no break in the fence, no new intruders on Du Bois land -

"It's happened at last!"

I peered at Mum, whose face had taken on a radiance I could see clearly from my perch. Dad stared and then, to my surprise, he stumbled from his chair and knelt in front of her, his normally steady face ecstatic. He seized her hands in his own huge ones and kissed them.

*Dad*, I wanted to yell, *what about the warning? What about the bird's warning?*

"My darling! How far?"

I thrust aside the oak fronds. Mum was crying.

"Four months!" Mum wiped her tears. "I didn't want to say anything 'til I was certain."

"Oh, Ray!" Dad kissed their clasped hands again. "What does the Doctor say?"

"He says it's because I haven't been worried! Once we adopted Fili, I relaxed." She breathed deeply, and then continued. "He says I'm doing well, and the baby's fine."

I grabbed a nearby branch. A splinter bit into my palm.

"My God!" Dad muttered. "I've been so worried, you haven't been yourself lately. You should have said something, let me help you -"

"Now do you see, Martin? I need to be calm, I need to feel safe."

Dad got up and went around the back of Mum's chair and bent over and embraced her. She held his arms against her chest. They gazed into the distance where the vineyards' straight rows were merging into the soft inkiness of night. Dad kissed the top of her head.

"My dearest, how extraordinary. After all this time."

Mum leaned back against him. They remained like that for some time, and then she began to speak again. I strained to pick up her words.

"What about Fili?"

"What do you mean?"

She twisted round. I could see her face, the radiance now overlaid with caution.

"With the new baby -"

Dad stood up and went to stand at the front of the verandah with his back to her. It was a moonless night and, even if you were a stranger to our valley, you'd be able to divine the sweep of the mountains where they blotted out the stars. I shrank into the tree. It seemed that he stood there forever and when he turned back I couldn't tell what he was thinking. I don't think Mum could, either, because she said "Martin?" in a kind of strangled voice.

Dad knelt down in front of her once more.

A single bark sounded from the direction of the farm dam. A caracal wild cat. Pointed ears twitching, calling for its mate. Or hunting for prey. Every creature on the farm was disturbed, on the prowl -

"Fili is our daughter." Dad's voice was firm. "We vowed to bring her up as a Du Bois. Our new child will be her brother or sister but there'll be no change in her position, darling. When the time comes, she could take over management of Du Bois if she's fit to do so. And if she wants to."

It was a long speech for Dad. I clung to my branch. A trickle of blood seeped down my hand.

"But Martin!" Mum's voice rose into a stifled cry, like the animal neither of them seem to have heard, "we'll have a biological child!"

He caressed her cheek and spoke clearly, as if he didn't mind his voice carrying beyond the verandah and into my bedroom, or even as far as Grand-mère's cottage.

Grand-mère! Whose side would she be on?

"We'll treat both children the same, and change our wills accordingly. Come," his tone softened, "this isn't something to be worried about right now."

"Isn't it?"

\*

Martin made sure all the doors were locked and Ray was in bed before he put Blaze on a lead and headed through the courtyard towards Gum Tree Avenue. The night was still, and he played his torch down the gravel road and into the motionless, overhanging trees.

Nothing. No sign of intruders.

He allowed himself to relax, to revel once more in the surge of joy that had welled up at Ray's news. It filled him with warmth - but warmth with a chill.

Fili...

The distant hoot of an owl made Blaze prick up his ears. Martin patted him and the dog relaxed.

Fili must never feel her position was being usurped. He recalled her excitement at her first vintage, the dedication of her vineyard patrolling, the earnest focus on the chemistry of turning grapes into wine. She had an affinity for the process and the *terroir*, no doubt about it.

But what if the new child had these qualities as well? Or even more so?

They'd raised Fili with the understanding that she would be sole heir.

Blaze growled as they approached the camp. It was in darkness save for the faint, wavering light of a candle inside one of the shacks. No sign of any new dwellings. No-one wandering about.

And then there was Ray -

Blaze whined and strained at the lead.

Martin whirled around. The teenager, the one called Kula, was standing in the shadows, watching.

"Everything alright?" Martin called.

The boy just stared, then turned away and disappeared into the dimly lit shack.

**CHAPTER SEVEN**

Adam Mfusi was hopeful.
Du Bois had not chased them away.
It was close, after the courtyard, but it hadn't happened.
And Mrs Du Bois had given them food, a sign of some understanding.
Not all white people were villains and oppressors, as his son, Kula, liked to believe. It would just take time for them to get used to sharing. Mandela had preached something he called reconciliation, and Adam could see that no good would come from more selfishness.
Hopefully whites could see that, too.
The brown Coloured villagers were a different sort, though. Suspicious, protective of their position.
Yet Adam could understand why. If he had a secure job and a cottage, he might be the same. Especially when they now feared they might fall not only behind whites but behind blacks, too, in this brave new South Africa.
But these were matters for men more clever than him to deal with.
For now, his goal was work, food and shelter.
He, Adam, had told Abraham and Peter and Kula how it would be: if they remained quiet, if they caused no extra trouble with the Coloureds, if they did not take too much water from the stream or cut down trees for firewood but collected only fallen branches, Du Bois might give them jobs.

Jobs that might last.
But it had to be soon.
Otherwise they'd have to move on to find work, and pitch their plastic shelters there.
The small pretty girl, the one called Fili, seemed kind.

## CHAPTER EIGHT

"Your poor hand, Fili!" Mum turned my palm upwards at breakfast the next day.
I'd washed it in the basin but the cut was clear to see, snaking across my skin.
"How did you do this? Playing with Bo?"
"Yes," I lied.
"Just as well we got your tetanus injection." She turned away to the cupboard and came back with antiseptic and cotton wool. "Silly girl," she scolded, cleaning the wound and then covering it with a plaster, "you're getting too old to be racing about and climbing trees."
Later that afternoon I ran to check the fence that lined the far side of Gum Tree Avenue. There was no break, even near the squatter camp. And the caracal and the nightjar made no more interruptions during that long week as I waited for Mum and Dad to break the news. I told myself that the wild cries must have been in my imagination.
Our roses began to droop. The vines turned red.
The baby would be born when the new season's buds were unfurling.
*We'll treat both children the same.*
*This isn't something to be worried about right now.*
"Fili," said Dad one evening after supper, "we've got something to tell you."

He and Mum were sitting side by side on the sofa. I was pretending to read on a cushion beside Blaze's slumbering form. "We're -"

"I'm going to have a baby, Fili!" Mum interrupted, her voice shaking. Dad clasped her hand and smiled at me. His eyes, warm for Mum, were anxious for me.

I gasped, to show surprise. "You must be so happy!" I got up and ran into their arms.

Blaze lifted his head, turned over and went back to sleep.

We hugged each other, a tight group of three.

"Nothing will change, honey." Dad moved aside to let me sit between them. "You're still our girl."

I smiled at him. No-one ever believes children might understand more than grownups, do they?

No-one ever believes children might detect what grownups most try to conceal.

"The only difference, " Mum said brightly, "will be a little brother or sister to play with!"

She smoothed her hair, her eyes brilliant. Dad put his arm round me and gave me a squeeze.

Will their love wane, a quiet, steady retreat to match the fading of the vines this winter?

"When, Mum? When will the baby be born?"

"Spring-time. It'll be new life all round," she looked at Dad over my head.

"So it will," said Dad, stroking my hair.

The news travelled swiftly around the valley. Most people struggled to say what they felt to me. The stares returned, and I became a subject they had to navigate around or avoid altogether. In private, though, there was talk. Tannie Ellie, up in the village, sucked in her breath and muttered to Mary Sammy that there'd be trouble, mark her words. You couldn't mix up blood from different families and expect a smooth dessert. Evonne came up to me before school and said she was sorry she'd been horrible about the bus, especially now my mother wouldn't have as much time to spend with me. The Steyns down the valley offered congratulations and brought soft toys, while Mrs van der Weyden pretended that nothing had changed when I went to their farm for the afternoon.

Only Petro was blunt.

"Is it really true? I thought she couldn't, you know," she gestured to her own belly, "so that's why -"

"It was a surprise," I interrupted before she could say words like 'they took you'.

We were in her bedroom trying on dresses, or rather Petro was, and I was adjudicating.

"Fili? Do you like this one with the frill?"

"It's lovely. Really suits you."

"Well," she pulled the dress over her head, "you're sunk if it's a boy. Mum says you won't inherit. Now try this one on," she held out a spotted shift dress, "it will make use of your new curves."

Bo wasn't as forthright, and he looked away from me when he spoke.

"Do you mind, Fili?"

"No," I said. "I'm happy for Mum and Dad. Nothing will change."

"*Ja*, but -"

"But what?" We were walking between the rows. I still patrolled the vines even though it was the dormant season and the red-gold leaves were falling. Blaze raced ahead in the hope of surprising a sleeping *dassie*.

"Well, you know -" Bo waved his arms, instead of saying the words I knew he was thinking: how will you feel if you're pushed aside. Yet how could I be so selfish as to deny my parents a child of their own? Bo stopped and looked at me. He was sixteen, and in the months since the harvest he'd grown taller than me. He ran to his local high school every day but he hated it and wanted to leave and work alongside Philemon.

"Will you always be my friend, Bo? Whatever happens?" He nodded and grabbed my hand. His skin was rough against mine. I reached up and did something I'd never done before. I kissed him on the cheek. Then I turned and ran back to the house. Grand-mère was waiting for me on the verandah.

"Walk with me, Fili," she commanded. "I've just seen your father. We'll have tea together."

I linked my arm with hers, and she used her stick to help her as we made slow progress up the slope towards her cottage. Dad had offered to buy Grand-mère a buggy, but she dismissed the idea. She'd walk, she told Dad, until she was put in the ground and covered over.

"Do you know what a *laatlammetjie* is, child?"

"Yes. A late lamb, a baby born long after all the others. Lots of families have them."

"That's so. Your mother's baby isn't strictly a *laatlammetjie*, though, because it's her first child."

Grand-mère stopped and gazed over the vineyards. "But, in another way, it will be. Nature sometimes gives older women one last chance, one final triumph."

"It's wonderful for Mum and Dad," I replied. "A proper miracle."

"Indeed." Grand-mère shot me a glance and set off again. "But maybe not so wonderful for you?"

I said nothing. The breeze lifted Grand-mère's grey hair and blew it about her face. Wind rarely disturbed my curls. She stopped to nip off the heads of a late flush of lavender. "You have to clip it to keep it blooming, Fili. Otherwise it gets too woody to flower." She rubbed her fingers and held them to her nose, and then to mine. "Heavenly."

We climbed up the steps to the cottage.

"Put on the kettle, *chérie*. I must rest for a moment."

I laid a tray with Grand-mère's favourite French china, bought on a stay with Du Bois cousins whose ancestors had hung on in France through the Huguenot crisis. I remembered her stories about our pioneering South African Du Bois: their devotion to continuity, their desire for tenure. I thought I'd done enough to win mine, even without shared blood.

"Here, Grand-mère," I said, putting the tray down on the small wrought iron table.

"Thank you, child."

We drank our tea and ate some of Shenay's shortbread speckled with orange zest that she made regularly for the *ou missus*. Grand-mère liked a little tang.

"Your mother was told she couldn't have children, so this baby is doubly unexpected."

I stared out over the vineyards. Sometimes I came to sleep in Grand-mère's little side room and we cooked omelettes for supper and she spoke about how her older brother, Jean-Pierre, had left to fight in the War and never returned.

"We Du Bois know about loss, Fili, and about cherishing the next generation." She laid her cup down with a decisive click. "You are that next generation, child. You will be loved as much as ever. There will be no lessening."

"But they won't need me anymore, Grand-mère!" I cried. "They'll have a real family instead!"

And maybe, a voice in my head whispered - the same one that told me I'd be blamed if my harvest failed - maybe they might even come to regret taking me.

"Now listen here, Fili Du Bois!" Grand-mère leaned forward and grasped my arm shakily. "Do you hear me? I called you a Du Bois! This is your home, we are your family. Always!"

*You're our girl. Always.* Dad's words to me, when I first learned about my adoption.

But he'd said nothing about how I would fit in with the new baby.

Maybe, like everyone apart from Grand-mère, he didn't know what new words to use, to avoid me feeling I was

about to be sidelined. Mum, fluttering about in vibrant colours rather than her usual pastels, was the opposite. She couldn't stop talking joyfully about the little one, as if life at Du Bois was about to change for the better. Maybe - I balled my hands into fists – I had never been enough? I opened my palm and looked at the place where I'd cut myself when I heard the news.
"No-one speaks to me like you do, Grand-mère. I think they're afraid to."
"You're unique, Fili," she gripped my hand. "Like our *terroir*. So embrace it, child! Don't hide."
I gathered the cups and took them to the kitchen and washed up.
When I went back outside, Grand-mère had fallen asleep. I sat beside her for a while, watching the mountain cliffs change from blue to purple, listening to the shrill *clink* of the blacksmith plovers down at the dam, and trying to make sense of what was to come. Grand-mère and Dad still embraced me but Mum saw only a new, pristine Du Bois on the way. Petro believes much depends on the baby's sex, Evonne has skirted the subject, the villagers pretend in front of me that nothing has changed, and the rest of the valley shies away from talking about it when I'm in the vicinity.
I stood up and covered Grand-mère with a shawl and left a small plate with an apple and a knife on her side table. Blaze would be wondering where I was. Come sunset, he'd put his head down and sniff my scent up to the cottage. I should go home. Our gabled house waited

for me, nestled between the oaks and camphors, fragile with new life.

## CHAPTER NINE

It was either guilt or distraction that made Dad agree to employ Adam Mfusi and two others from the informal camp. Or maybe it was because the summer fell into an early autumn, shrouding the land in cloud and drizzle and disinclining our Coloureds to venture from their cottages. The jackal buzzards keened in disappointment from the heights, the coots on the dam tucked their necks in and hid from the rain. In the cellar, my wine progressed on its journey. One damp weekend, all of the required indicators aligned. Rich fumes filled the air as I watched the ruby liquid being led into a series of barrels lining the cellar walls.
"Well done!" Dad called from where he was supervising. "You're on your way, Fili!"
I clapped my hands and ran over to hug Bo at the steps.
"Fili!" he flushed and shot a look at Philemon but he was occupied with the gurgling pipes.
"We'll have to delay the new vineyard until next year," Dad said to me later, as we peered into the rain from the cellar door after the barrels were secure and Philemon and Bo had left, "what with the weather, and the baby coming."
I glanced back into the darkness. The lingering aroma of my vintage sharpened the air. *Aroma*, Grand-mère liked to insist, only gives way to *bouquet* once aging is complete.
"We could ask the squatters. They'd take any work."

"You haven't been there again? To their camp? Why, Fili?" Dad's face showed bewilderment. "Why are you disobeying us?"

"I feel sorry for them."

But it wasn't sympathy. I didn't want to feel sorry for them. I wanted to turn my back and be loyal to my adopted world. Yet something made me go and see them, an urge inside of myself that I couldn't resist. "I know Mum's frightened of them and the Coloureds hate them, but I was once without a home -" the words tumbled out of my mouth before I could stop them.

Blaze whined and pressed his nose into my hand.

Dad stared at me, his forehead creased. Just then, a squall blew in and the rain beat on the ground like the pickers' feet stamping on the courtyard earth, or the rhythmic chants of *on-se werk, on-se werk.* Dad remembered, too, because he glanced towards the spot where the men had stood when they asked for work.

"If it isn't a success," I pressed, "at least we tried. You always tell us to look forward, not back."

Still Dad hesitated, his large hands fidgeting at his side.

Maybe - I felt a cold clamp on my heart - his silence wasn't about me and the squatters at all, but about me and the coming heir, a child of his own blood. Maybe he and Mum had spoken in the privacy of their bedroom and I was already surplus.

"Dad?"

*Please, Dad, say it won't be like that! Tell me I'm still yours, forever... that I belong...*

"What if it causes a riot with our Coloureds, honey? Worse than last time? What then? We can't risk our regular workforce, they're crucial to Du Bois." He paused. "You know that, Fili."

I swallowed, and arranged the words carefully in my head.

"We must help them if we can, Dad. Like you helped me."

His gaze softened.

"And we could do what Grand-mère says. Only offer work that our people don't want."

Bundled up in jackets, Dad and I detoured around the fence and headed for the camp that very afternoon. I thought he'd want to think it over first, consult Grand-mère and Mum, but it seemed he'd made his decision. So I hurried alongside him before he could change his mind and before I could scold myself about where my loyalty ought to lie and what the consequences of my persuasion might be. Rain coursed down the plastic shelters and carved channels across the clearing the squatters had made in the summer. The remaining eucalyptus saplings drooped. One end of the washing line trailed in the mud. At first we thought they must have moved on because there seemed to be no-one about. They'd left their plastic structures and gone.

A woodpecker shrieked from Gum Tree Avenue into the dripping silence.

"Wait," I said to Dad as he turned away. "Kula!" I shouted. "Mr Mfusi!"

"You know all their names?" Dad turned an astonished face to me.

"Yes. Mr Mfusi is Kula's father. He's very polite. But Kula doesn't like me."

"Fili," Dad muttered, his forehead creasing, "what else haven't you told me?"

Mr Mfusi pushed out of one of the makeshift huts and came towards us. He had no protection from the downpour and his tattered trousers began to darken with the rain. Of course, I thought. The first law in any informal settlement: if you can't dry your clothes, you can't afford to get them wet so you'd better stay under cover. Dad must have come to the same conclusion because he edged closer and held his umbrella over the now shivering Mfusi. Thunder rumbled from the direction of the Franschhoek pass. There was no sign of Kula.

"Good afternoon," said Dad. "I have some work for you, hard but honest work. It will take three men. When the weather's better," he gestured at the leaden skies, "come to the entrance gate and I'll show you what we need done."

"It's for our new vineyard!" I broke in.

Adam Mfusi said nothing. His face was thinner than the first time I saw him in the courtyard. He looked ill, or maybe he was just cold. What was he eating? How do you feed yourself - and your son - when you have no income?

"Mr Mfusi?"

"The Coloureds," he asked, rousing himself. "What do they say?"

"This is not part of their work," Dad said carefully. "They have other duties."

"They don't want to do it - what you're going to do," I put in.

"Fili, hush!"

A flicker of amusement crossed Mfusi's rain-streaked face.

"Thank you, sir," he said, "thank you, miss. We will come. The next dry day." He went back into the hut, pulling the plastic closed behind him.

"It wasn't supposed to be like this," Dad said, as we began to slosh our way back home. He stopped and pointed to where the mountains held back the vast plains of the Karoo. "We knew people from inland would be drawn to towns and cities because they thought there'd be more work. But no-one, not even Mandela, expected this many. Cape Town's squatter camps are huge."

"Mum wants to evict Mr Mfusi and the others."

"She's worried about security, Fili. Especially now."

"Because of the baby?"

"Yes," Dad allowed himself a fond smile. "And you, too. That's why I don't want you coming here alone. I don't want Mum worrying about you."

I remember when I ran into the vines after Mum told me I was adopted. She shouted for me to come back, but I didn't. I needed to be alone to accept the reality of not being of the same blood. Ever.

"I'm sorry, Dad. I'll take Blaze next time."
"Ah Fili," he sighed and put his arm around my shoulders. "A mind of your own. Just be careful."
We reached the driveway. The rain had stopped and mist was beginning to lift from the peaks even though it would soon be evening. From behind us on Gum Tree Avenue came the incessant squawk of guinea fowl heading for their roosts. I wondered if the men had ever tried to catch one. A guinea fowl would make a good meal if you could gather enough dry wood to keep a fire going for long enough to cook it through.
"You go inside, Dad. I'm going to see Bo -"
But it was Philemon I needed to see.
"Don't you want to come inside and dry out first?"
"I won't be long," I called over my shoulder.
The village was quiet. Smoke curled up from several chimneys. No children played on the grassy pitch and even Tannie Ellie had been driven from her step by the weather. I picked my way along the path in front of the line of cottages. Most were brightly painted, which gave the village its character.
"Philemon?" I rapped on their door.
There was a scuffling inside and Philemon appeared, rubbing his eyes. "Miss Fili?"
"Can I come in?"
"Bo isn't here. After we finished in the cellar he went to town with Shenay, Miss Fili."
"I came to talk to you, Philemon."
"Sure, Miss Fili."

He opened the door wide and I wiped my boots on the mat and followed him in. All the cottages were of a similar design, with a combined kitchen and sitting room, leading to two bedrooms and a family bathroom. A dying fire smouldered in the grate and Philemon threw on a fresh log. Crocheted cushions were piled in a corner of a sturdy couch. I'd interrupted Philemon at his Saturday afternoon nap.

"Can you help me, Philemon?"

"Is it the cellar, Miss Fili?" He looked about for his jacket. "Has the temperature gauge gone again?"

"No, nothing like that. It's about the squatters."

He frowned and passed a hand over his bald head. He, Philemon, didn't want to talk about the squatters, Shenay never stopped complaining about them, and Bo said Miss Fili had visited them.

"Dad has offered them work clearing land for the new vineyard. I want you to help us stop any trouble from the village. Can you do that, Philemon?"

If I could persuade him to give the black men a chance, especially if it was heavy work, the rest would follow Philemon's lead. He sank down onto the couch and reached behind him to push aside the cushions. Rainwater began to drip off my jeans onto the floor. I knew Philemon liked me. I was Bo's friend, after all. And, though he wouldn't say so out loud, he realised he'd better like me anyway because I'd be an heir to Du Bois one day. Or maybe not -

"Why should I do that, Miss Fili?" Philemon's voice was rough. "Blacks will work for lower wages. I can't tell my people they'll also have to take less if they want to keep their jobs from now on -"

"No!" I broke in. "It's only for the new vineyard. Casual work. And it wasn't Dad's idea."

"It wasn't?"

"No." I hesitated. "I talked him into it. I said we needed to help them because they've got nothing but plastic shacks in the bush. You must help me, Philemon." I crouched in front of him. "Please."

Philemon stroked his fingers across his lips and then sighed, like Dad had sighed earlier on.

"Why, Miss Fili? What are they to you?"

What, indeed? Is it all down to shared abandonment?

"It will be hard, Miss Fili," Philemon went on. "Our people won't like it. You know that."

"But will you try? They listen to you. Even Tannie Ellie listens to you."

The fire crackled as the fresh wood caught.

"You must go home, Miss Fili. You'll catch horrible cold if you don't change your clothes."

I stopped on the step outside the doorway and felt my hands tightening. But Philemon doesn't deserve my anger. He's closer to me than any birth parent.

I took a breath and tried to calm myself.

"I could have been like them, Philemon." I paused. "Without a proper home."

Philemon shook his head and closed the door carefully behind me.

Dad told Mum he'd offered the squatters casual work with no long-term promise, and Mum was so taken up with the baby swelling her body that she didn't protest with her usual force. Maybe she also told herself that if they remained out of sight and didn't come down the avenue to bother the house or the village, she could pretend they weren't there.

Mrs van der Weyden agreed. "You don't want to dwell on unpleasantness, Ray - think of the baby! And they'll leave soon enough, surely? Casual work isn't any sort of commitment."

"But if there's trouble," Mum remarked to Dad as she hung a bumble bee mobile above the cot waiting in the nursery, "you must promise to call the police and get them evicted. Now, isn't this pretty, Fili? I love the way they twirl! I found it in a craft shop in Franschhoek."

I stared at the spinning bumble bees. A real one had buzzed past me in the courtyard near-mutiny.

Dad's offer wasn't casual work. Even though I'd said otherwise to Philemon, I knew it wasn't. And Mrs van der Weyden was mistaken. Once we gave them jobs - however hard, however short-term - the squatters would stay and hope for more. They'd strengthen their shelters, clear saplings and string up the washing line again. Mr Mfusi might even send for other family to join him. Grand-mère might have made a light suggestion, but I'd taken it further with Dad. I'd persuaded him into a grownup kind of rescue. At night, when the caracal barks down by the dam, I tell myself to face the truth: Dad probably agreed because he wanted to be especially kind to me before the new baby arrives. He suspects I'm about to be displaced. But does he realise the full extent of the shift he's set in motion across the farm?

In the cellar, an equally unpredictable force was at work. After several weeks, the next fermentation that Philemon had taught me was complete. My vintage was siphoned back into a tank to free it from the dead yeast that had done its bubbling work, and then returned to the barrels for maturation. Not too much malic acid, not too much tannin, no unexpected surge of rancidity that would have meant us pouring the precious stuff away. I checked every day after school, resting my hand on the wood, willing the dark liquid to age with distinction, to honour the *terroir* it carried inside itself.

*Be strong!* I whispered each time. *Be my miracle!*

"Look," Dad inspected the sample he'd drawn and held it up to the light, "see the colour?" He swirled the wine around and watched it settle. "And smell -" he held the glass out to me.

I sniffed. Blackcurrent? Cherry?

"We're on the right road, honey."

But Dad wasn't to know that, for me, this was not a road but a tightrope, like the one I'd walked between my ripening grapes and the approaching thunder storms; or between the tannins that were good in small concentrations or fatal in abundance. Or between being an heir or surplus.

For my wine, success would depend on years in the barrel - and a dose of luck: would my dark liquid feel inclined to transform itself into a wine that would tell the world I was worthy of being a Du Bois? Worthy of a permanent stake in the ground? In the meantime, while it was deciding, a new vineyard would be prepared, and an heir would arrive where before there had only been me.

"*Bonne chance!*" whispered Grand-mère, placing one be-ringed hand on the barrel, and the other on my shoulder. "*Bonne chance!*"

I held her hand and helped her up the cellar steps.

Grand-mère, I reflected, was right about wine and life: they both hover on the edge. A vintage could be lost by a burst of rankness in the cellar as easily as by a flash of lightning in the vineyard. And a child might be gathered up with the best of intentions and then overlooked when the world turns.

## CHAPTER TEN

Ray settled into her seat on the verandah and put her feet up on the stool Shenay had brought out.
The doctor was insistent she should rest, feet up, for at least two hours in the middle of the day.
"We can't be too careful," he liked to say while taking her blood pressure, "given your history."
And Ray was happy to oblige. Indeed, if he'd suggested doing handstands or swinging from the oak tree, she would have done his bidding. Anything to bring this baby safely to term.
But physical rest did not necessarily translate into mental respite.
Ray feared her blood pressure was probably more volatile than the doctor realised. However much she tried, she could not calm the excitement she felt at impending motherhood, something that a male doctor would surely not understand. Yet, amid that excitement, and perhaps stirring it in some way, was guilt over Fili, the child she and Martin had brought to Du Bois as the substitute for the child now growing inside her.
What was to be done about Fili?
And how would she, Ray, be able to divide her love equally?
Even in the womb, the new baby was claiming every ounce of her being, a private infatuation that she knew would only increase when he – she already knew it was

a boy, but Martin didn't and she'd sworn the doctor to secrecy – was born.

She kept telling herself that Fili would simply have to adjust to her altered status; adjust to being second in line, even though Martin was insistent there'd be no change. It must be something to do with father-daughter sentiment, the bond that fathers feel with a child of the opposite sex to themselves. As if they can't quite believe they have fathered a girl. And although Fili was not his, strictly speaking, he clearly couldn't bring himself to disappoint her.

Martin was also more soft-hearted than was good for him; his continued deference to Nanette, for instance, who by this stage should be humoured rather than relied upon for serious advice.

There was an equivalent mother-son sentiment, she admitted, watching the sun paint the far mountains.

Especially now. Especially for a son so desperately sought.

A son she could shape, one whose blood was known.

A son for Du Bois.

## CHAPTER ELEVEN

Bringing on a new vineyard is a slow process, like waiting for your body to grow into its final shape or holding on for a cabernet to develop its true bouquet - or waiting for a baby to be born. None of the steps can be rushed, each unfolds in its own time, and the eventual outcome cannot be predicted.

In the case of the vineyard, a lot of sweat has to be committed early on.

Dad had begun the process by turning over the land with a digger at the end of the previous autumn, since when it had lain uninvitingly churned up and pooled with water all winter long. Snow-white egrets, attracted by the wet, flew in from time to time to step delicately through the mud, searching for hidden frogs. And then summer arrived. The channels that had been wet, now baked as hard as concrete until the rains returned once more to soften the soil.

"We start by clearing the rocks and stones," Dad said to Adam Mfusi and Abraham Phillips and Peter Choba who were waiting at the end of the drive on the first dry day. "It will be hard," he went on, "and it will take time. I'll pay you by the week, with a bonus for how much you do by each Friday."

"We're used to hard work," said Adam Mfusi with a shrug. "Some of us were in the mines."

His two companions nodded. They could understand English but didn't speak much and would leave any negotiation to Adam. At least this work was in the open, not underground where men could die of heat or explosions in the search for gold.

Dad named an amount, Mfusi agreed, and the men nodded again.

I stood a little way off, holding Blaze on a lead, peering towards our village.

Evonne said their Coloured villagers had chased a black family off Newman property just a week ago.

"Stones were thrown, Fili!" Evonne whispered. "That's never happened before. Someone was hit!"

I found myself flinching, but it was only a glint of emerald green darting over my head - a malachite sunbird, pointy-tailed, lightning fast, heading for the protea-rich slopes beyond the vines. The police had raced to the Newman's farm but because there were no witnesses who were prepared to testify, and the black family had fled, there could be no arrests. The police left, saying they could take no action. Mrs Newman visited Mum for tea the day after. "What will you do, Ray, if there's a confrontation? Violence? Does Martin carry a firearm?"

I stared at Dad as he shared out a pile of hessian sacks between the men. I couldn't leave him alone. If the Coloured swarm broke like it had so nearly done in the courtyard, or as it had done at the Newmans, I could be a witness. Blaze and I could even rescue him if he found himself pinned down. I pressed my hand against my chest. Mum's heart beat wildly when she was upset. I seem to have picked up her trait even though we're not related.

We set off towards the land on an indirect route that avoided the village. Mr Mfusi wore shoes but the other two were barefoot. Yellow-and-black butterflies, fragile and exquisite, fluttered up from the track in front of us and Blaze snapped half-heartedly at a couple that drifted too close.

"Hey!" came a shout from behind. I turned back in panic. But it was only the young man, Kula, strolling towards us. Blaze growled. Mr Mfusi watched his son's tardy approach, and turned and muttered to the other men. "Sir, he addressed Dad, "my son can also work."

Kula arrived and stood, hands on hips, on the edge of the group. He had lost none of his attitude and stared at Dad as if he was a bad smell rather than a potential employer.

"I only want willing workers," said Dad evenly.

"I can be willing," Kula replied after a moment, "if I'm paid."

"I see. If there's any trouble, young man, your father and his friends will lose their jobs. It's up to you."

Kula shrugged.

"Well then," Dad said, pointing to the stretch of churned earth, "I suggest you each take a row and work forwards. Adam, you start here. Next will be Abraham, then Kula if he wants to, then Peter. When you've filled a sack, drag it to the side and we'll fetch them with the tractor. Any rocks must be rolled aside, or if they're still in the ground we'll need to get some picks to break them up. Any questions?"

"What about lunch?" It was Kula. His father muttered to him in Xhosa.

I glanced at Dad. We never provided food for our workers. They went home for lunch.

"We will buy some bread," said Mr Mfusi hurriedly. "We will bring our own."

There was a further mutter, this time from the other men. I caught my breath as I realised our error. We were assuming they had enough money to buy food until Dad paid them. But maybe they had none. They couldn't afford to buy their own lunch.

Kula's attitude might be down to hunger, not rudeness.

"No need!" I interrupted, coming forward. Blaze tugged on the lead. Dad raised his eyebrows. "It's my school holidays. I'll make you sandwiches until you get paid."

One of the men placed his hands together as if in prayerful thanks.

I felt a jolt of shame. Kula turned his head away.

"That's a good idea, Fili," Dad smiled. "Thank you. You head home, then, and tell Mum."

If Mum was annoyed at this extra inconvenience, she covered it up. But Shenay pursed her lips and bustled about the kitchen in a put-upon way. I insisted that I would make the sandwiches and deliver them to the vineyard every midday - and not just for the first week, but for as long as my holidays lasted. "Take Blaze," Mum called each time from the verandah where she rested before lunch. "And your new phone, Fili, for an emergency. Don't hang about, come straight back. Why don't you invite Petro over? You've hardly seen any of your friends this holiday."

But there was no emergency, at least not one that I told her about. Instead, on my sandwich-delivering trips I discovered that the men sang as they worked, yet differently from our pickers at harvest time. They sang songs from the mines, like *Shosholoza,* imitating a steam train taking migrant workers far from home.

*Sho... sho... shosholoza.*

Or they chanted. A low, sad chant that made me think of loneliness and people left behind.

"Thank you, Miss Fili," Adam Mfusi said on the second Monday. "You are very kind."

I turned to look at Kula, who'd grabbed his lunch and was eating a little way off. He ignored me, just like he ignored the villagers who sometimes walked by in groups, staring and muttering behind their hands. I noticed that Adam Mfusi always made sure to nod and say good morning. If I happened to be there at the time, I'd call out "Hello, Mrs Sammy!" or "Hello, Tannie!" and run across the partly-cleared land to talk to them so that if they intended to throw stones at the men then the stones would have to hit me - hurt me - first.

And there was a stone, and nearly an emergency. I told no-one about it.

Perhaps it was not intended for me, but it whistled past my ear.

The men sang and chanted, unaware.

I whipped around and stared into the adjoining vines but I saw no-one.

Afterwards, Dad said that the success of the new vineyard was built on my sandwiches but I know it was more about the productivity of the men and their careful politeness to those passing by. Philemon, who patrolled often, ready to criticise their work, admitted to Dad that the four of them - even the rude boy - were doing the job of ten men. I don't know if that helped him convince the villagers that the men were less of a threat, or if it had the opposite effect: making our Coloureds more worried by competition that was not only black but also efficient - and perhaps oiling the hand that threw the stone. I must be alert.

"Miss Fili's even feeding them," sharp-eyed Tannie Ellie snapped to Philemon's mother.

"My Granny says you should stick with who you know," said Bo with a hurt expression when we were walking the rows. "She says you'll get in trouble. She says you must decide who you're for. What side you're on."

"I'm just helping Dad," I hedged.

"Don't you like us as much as you used to?"

I bent down and picked up some soil and rubbed it between my fingers.

"We all have to learn to share, Bo."

"We don't want to share Du Bois!" Bo shouted, sprinting away. "Not with outsiders!

He stopped after a couple of strides and looked back.

"And I don't want to share you!"

The new vineyard was half-cleared and the first buds were swelling on the established vines by the time my brother was born. Petro said that a boy baby would at least put an end to my uncertainty. "You'll know where you stand, Fili. Then you can go your own way. Listen," she tapped the button on her radio to turn up the sound. "Michael Jackson. Vintage cool."

*But I don't want to go my own way! This is my home, my only home.*

A week later I waited with Grand-mère, who'd come down to the house to be with me while Mum and Dad were at the hospital. *God is testing me, forcing me to be patient. Like Dad tested me with my slow cabernet. But now I want Him to nudge time onto my side so that the days pass faster for my vintage but slow down for this baby, and pass without trouble - or stone-throwing - for the squatters so they won't need to sing sad songs for too much longer.*

"Babies follow their own sweet routine, child," Grand-mère cautioned, as I kept peering for the tell-tale cloud of dust that would mean they'd turned off the Franschhoek road onto Gum Tree Avenue. *She mistakenly thinks I am suddenly eager for this child.* "These things can't be rushed."

"They're coming, *ou missus*!" Shenay bustled out of the kitchen. "I hear the car!"

Blaze raced off amid a volley of barking.

Grand-mère smiled and glanced across at me. I helped her up and we walked out onto the driveway. Puffy clouds sailed across a sky of the palest blue. A black-shouldered kite, smaller than our buzzards, hovered in mid-air, its wings beating while its body stayed motionless, gaze fixed on the ground where a mouse or a lizard must be sunning itself. The dust cloud was taking ages to advance. Dad was driving more slowly than normal. From the direction of the new vineyard came a low chant and the repeated strike of a pick on rock, like the *clink clink* of the plovers at the dam.

"Ah," said Grand-mère, fanning herself, "here they are."

Dad got out of the car, and opened the rear door for Mum who was hugging a well-wrapped bundle close to her, like I'd surely been held close on the day they rescued me.

"You're a Du Bois," Grand-mère whispered in my ear, "so act like one! Darlings!" She opened her arms for her new grandchild. "*Félicitations*! And what do we have here?"

Mum pulled down the shawl to reveal a tiny face, button nose, tightly-closed eyes and rosy lips.

"Here he is, Mum," said Dad, his face ecstatic. "Your brand-new grandson. And Fili," he turned to me and swept me into his arms, "this is your brother!"

I held on to him, drawing strength. I wanted to stay there, right there, and never leave.

"And what will you call him?" murmured Grand-mère, stroking the velvet head nestled in the shawl.

"Jean-Pierre," said Dad, releasing me. "After Uncle in the war."

Grand-mère turned away for a moment.

"Come, Fili," said Mum into the pause, "say hello to Jean-Pierre."

I stared at the infant. By the time my *treize ans* vintage was approaching its best, I'd be ready to take my place on the farm as Dad had once said I should. By that time, too, Jean-Pierre might already be old enough to want Du Bois for himself.

"You can hold him if you're careful."

Mum placed the bundle in my arms, holding on until she was certain I was secure with him. Grand-mère turned back, wiping tears. I stared down. The baby was surprisingly heavy although maybe it was because of all the wrapping.

"He's beautiful," I found myself saying. And he was, creamy skin gently flushed from being born, one tiny fist escaping from the blanket to flex delicate fingers. I touched the down on his head, as soft as the fluff on the leaf of a silver tree. A phantom mother rose up before me, her child similarly wrapped. How could she have left me...

"Let's go inside, Fili," Dad said, "out of the sun. Mum must rest."

I'd filled their bedroom with Fragrant Cloud roses, and created a nest of pillows to make the bed comfortable for Mum when she fed Jean-Pierre. I'd laid out fresh nightclothes for her to change into.

"Thank you, Fili," Mum stopped at the threshold and breathed in the perfume.

The dust cloud had been spotted by others, too. The remainder of the day was taken up with visitors from the village, tip-toeing in to see the baby and leave behind knitted gifts of matinee jackets and booties, or gaily wrapped parcels of rusks for the family.

"*Foeitog*, so precious, Ma'am," Bo's fierce Grandma put on her glasses to smile at the little one, "a gift straight from the Lord, *neh*?"

"Yes," Mum smiled. "After all this time."

I took the old lady's present of a felt rabbit with button eyes and laid it next to the other gifts.

"Thank you, Mrs Sammy."

"You must come to us whenever you want," she muttered with a knowing glance backwards at Mum and Jean-Pierre. "Your Ma will be busy now there's a baby in the house."

Mrs van der Weyden and Petro arrived, bearing a knitted romper suit and a large basket of fruit.

"Marvellous, Ray!" gushed Mrs van der Weyden. She turned to me. "You must be thrilled, Fili!"

Petro rolled her eyes at me behind her mother's back.

"Fili," Mum said a little later, "I can't see any more visitors for now. I must feed Jean-Pierre. Will you tell them thank you and they can come back tomorrow?"

Blaze, lying just outside the bedroom door, raised his head, growled, and rushed outside.

"Oh, not more," Mum said wearily. "See who it is, Fili."

There were two village women by the kitchen door waiting to see Mum. Blaze paid them no attention and instead tore across the courtyard to where Mr Mfusi was standing by the gate.

"Blaze!" I shouted at the capering dog. "Down, boy! Down!"

I'm ashamed that dogs seem able to distinguish by colour. The van der Weyden's dog was the same. But maybe it's more about familiarity. We smile at people we know but we frown at strangers, so the dogs mimic us in the only way they can. And yet Mr Mfusi is no longer a stranger.

"Can I help you, Mr Mfusi? Dad isn't here. He's taken my grandmother back to the cottage."

The Coloured women began to edge away.

I stared at them and then back at Mr Mfusi.

*Shoo!* I could hear the women quiver. *Such foolishness to allow black squatters to stay! And what greater foolishness to be so honest!* For I'd just told a black man that my father was not at home. Blaze was the only barrier between Mr Mfusi and me, my mother and her new baby.

He was standing completely still, hands at his sides.

I glanced up the path leading to Grand-mère's. If Mr Mfusi had turned wicked and wanted to rob us he could walk into the house and I wouldn't be able to stop him. Blaze, for all his capering, would protect Mum and me, but not our possessions. If Mum could see through the bedroom walls, she would order me to grab my phone out of my pocket and call the police. But they'd never get here in time and in any case this was Mr Mfusi. I knew him. I'd fed him.

"Mr Mfusi?"

Blaze growled and paced. The kite from earlier reappeared above the avenue gums, swooped down, then clawed its way up again to resume the hunt. I should be sensible, go back inside, lock the doors, wait for Dad.

"Why are you afraid, Miss?"

"I'm not. Why should I be afraid?"

"I don't know, Miss. I don't want trouble." He shrugged. "I brought you something."

Slowly, watching Blaze carefully, he took a package out of his pocket and laid it on the ground, then turned around and walked away.

"Blaze, come here!"

The dog loped back to me and nosed against my leg. I bent down to pat him. My hands were trembling. They never trembled when I visited the vineyard with my sandwiches even after the random stone throw. Or maybe it was because out on the land the risk was only to myself whereas here, amid the polished spread of our Du Bois home and the new life it guarded, there was much more to protect. Much more to lose.

The women were gone by now. The story would be around the village in no time.

*That black squatter came into the courtyard again, bold as brass!*

*Only the dog saved the klein missus...*

I picked up the small package wrapped in brown paper, opened it and drew out the contents.

It was a rattle.

A rattle made of thatch reeds carefully plaited and woven so there were no sharp ends to hurt a baby. Inside, half a dozen shiny, orange seeds gave a lively clatter when I shook it. Lucky bean seeds. Blaze cocked his head and sniffed at the black man's gift.

I sat down in the courtyard, on the bare earth, and wept.

## CHAPTER TWELVE

Can you understand that I'm caught in a tug-of-love?
Or maybe, if I'm truly honest, it's more like a tug-of-war... a hidden battle that will go on until there's a winner and a loser even though Petro says I've already lost. "Give up!" she shrugs. "You can't compete. It's not your fault, it's just bad luck. Look beyond Du Bois. And play up your good points, Fili, you're pretty if you ever bothered to notice!" Boys are indeed starting to look at me with more interest. Evonne says it's the contrast between my pale skin and dark hair and eyes.
But no-one sees the struggle -the tug - beneath, the moment when my fists clench. Not even Dad. And while Mum tries to be fair, she can't help the way her eyes drift away from me and towards Jean-Pierre, imagining her own child claiming sole inheritance as a genuine, blood-born Du Bois.
And me?
I am torn, which is why it is a tug of both love and war. I adore my baby brother but I'm jealous of what he represents. I love Dad but he's increasingly distracted by Jean-Pierre and a restive workforce. I love Mum but she no longer notices me or sees my value to Du Bois. And I can't look forward, as Petro advises, because this battle is too finely balanced to be able to predict my future. Evonne, who is kinder these days, says that if I'm good to Jean-Pierre, my parents will still love me. "Don't ever argue with him, Fili," she urges, "let him have his way."

Then there's Grand-mère, who believes in me even though she should be saving her wisdom and her diligence for her grandson. And, as if that isn't enough, I continue to feel a nagging duty towards the men who lurk beside Gum Tree Avenue, unnerve our villagers, and thank me every day for their chance to work. "We like it here, Miss Fili," Adam Mfusi said to me. "It's quiet, not like the bigger camps. We're grateful, Miss, that we can stay."

"You're crazy, Fili," sniffed Petro when I took her past the camp and showed her how Mr Mfusi and his group were now living under corrugated iron rather than plastic sheeting. "You've all been addled by this baby. You're not thinking straight since Jean-Pierre arrived. Why don't you get the men evicted? My Dad says Du Bois is sending the wrong message. Mum agrees."

"And what message is that?"

Petro threw up her hands. "That squatting is somehow okay. That anyone can pitch up on your land and make a hovel -" she broke off. Kula Mfusi had come out of his shack and was standing in the clearing, watching us. He was better-dressed, these days. His eyes, even from a distance, had a peculiar penetration. And he could stand still, like a statue. Watchfully still.

"Let's go," Petro tried to pull me away. "Let's go."

"Don't you believe in Mandela's rainbow nation?" I hissed. Petro was wearing a dress that probably would have kept the squatters in food for months. My voice rose to a shout. "These people have nothing but they're still humans like you and me!"

Petro tossed her head and began to march away. She rifled in her pocket for her mobile phone. I stared across at Kula. He must have heard. I wish he would acknowledge me. I wish he would admit, with the faintest of smiles, that I'm trying to help him and his father. But there was no expression on his face, just those piercing eyes. He turned back to the shack.
I ran after Petro.
"And what about me?" I yelled. "Do I belong here, or do you think I'm also squatting?"

After that, it wasn't a surprise that my school friends turned away from me, too.
I'd crossed a line.
I'd said words out loud that marked me as a traitor to my adopted community.
I sat on my own during break-time. Even the boys who once whistled at me by the school gates because of my newly-interesting face and body, now turned their backs. My only refuge lay with my *treize ans* cabernet in the cellar, and with Bo who was always pleased to have me to himself and, surprisingly, with my brother.
When Jean-Pierre began to speak, his first word was not 'Mama' or 'Dada' but 'Thili'.
"Clever boy!" I picked him up and hugged him, loving him more than I ever believed possible. He became my little shadow, following me into the garden to watch the orange-and-blue paradise flycatchers or up to Grand-mère's cottage to be cuddled on her lap, or to the

Coloured village to see Bo who'd hoist him on his shoulders for a ride.

Jean-Pierre saved me when others looked away.

Yet maybe Petro was right?

Maybe the arrival of my brother, with his lisping and cuddling, had indeed driven sense from all our minds. Or distracted us sufficiently so that when the seasons turned, the squatters remained.

Their camp became permanent despite the urging of our neighbours to have it declared illegal.

"I told you it would happen," Mum said with a furious glance at Dad. "You wouldn't listen!"

The evening breeze stirred her skirt against her legs as they sat on the verandah one evening after dinner. It had been a while since they'd sat outside. A crescent moon hung low on the horizon, a brilliant scratch against the silk of the night. I was watching from behind the lounge curtains and Jean-Pierre was asleep in his cot in the nursery. If anything, Mum was more lovely now than before he was born, with a vividness to her that hadn't been there in the past. It was a glow that mostly bathed Jean-Pierre, but I couldn't begrudge it. A mother should surely glow for her firstborn, shouldn't she?

"There's been no trouble, Ray," Dad protested mildly. "They've done the heavy work, they're willing to clear a second parcel of land in due course, and they haven't interfered with our Coloureds."

"So far."

Dad took her hand in both of his and gave it a squeeze. "Fili was right, darling. She said to me one day," he stopped and searched for the words, *"'We should help them if we can. Like you helped me.'"*

"She has no idea," Mum exclaimed, pulling her hand away, "she's only a child! But we're storing up trouble. Elaine van der Weyden says Fili was rude to Petro!"

I wiped my palms on my pyjamas. There was a dark side to Mum's vividness, a fresh impatience with Dad and me and the world... although perhaps it had been brewing all along. It took the arrival of Jean-Pierre to bring it into the open.

"Then consider this, Ray. I think the squatters respect Fili."

"What nonsense!" Mum put down her wine glass with an impatient click. "It's madness to believe that would stop them robbing us. And what about the risk to Jean-Pierre and ourselves? They might spare her, but we'd be of no consequence."

I felt the rise of the old courtyard alarm.

"What's happened to you, Ray? Why are you so negative, darling?"

Mum stood up and made to gather the glasses.

"No, sit down. Please." Dad's voice took on an unexpectedly formal tone.

I edged closer.

"I don't want us to be in dispute over this, but I must make decisions for the good of the farm. Nanette is in agreement. We've reached a working relationship with the squatters. They're useful and reliable and," he held up his hand as Mum made to object, "the land they're clearing will enable us to start several new vineyards, and add to our profitability."

"What about the villagers?"

"Their jobs aren't at risk, neither are the senior families' share in the profits of the farm. They know that. Listen Ray," Dad leant forward, "this isn't just about money, either. We have to be brave. We did so by adopting Fili and making her our daughter. This is another version of that bravery. One day, the council will build houses and the men will leave. We'll have helped them on their way."

He reached across and touched Mum's cheek. She didn't pull away but averted her head slightly and his hand dropped. He tried again. He drew Mum to her feet and gathered her in his arms and kissed her gently. But Mum gave nothing back. She refused to allow her body to melt against his like she used to do after previous arguments, and turned away too quickly when he released her.

"I'll check on Jean-Pierre, Martin. You go ahead to bed."

Their quarrel rippled through the dark house like a wraith, hiding in the corners until Mum chose to call it up again. Something had changed inside her, and nothing was ever going to be the same again.

Not for Dad, not for me.

## CHAPTER THIRTEEN

"That Fili came to look at us," Kula muttered to his father. "She brought another girl who laughed. I want to make them pay. More than the money."

"Miss Fili is good, Kula. You will respect her!" Adam tried to keep his voice down.

Abraham and Peter had so far put up with Kula, put up with his moods, but it wouldn't take much for them to tear down Kula's shack and tell him to go before he messed up the only steady jobs they had found since the mines.

Out on the land there had been some shouting from the Coloureds when their foreman wasn't around, and one day Adam found a tear in one part of his shack and a large stone inside, so they needed to be on guard. He didn't want a fight. He and Peter and Abraham wouldn't be able to take on the Coloureds, there were too many of them.

But Kula, with his sudden rage, could start something that he wouldn't be able to stop.

That would help no-one.

He, Adam, thought of saying something to Du Bois about the stone and the shouting but then thought it might make Du Bois more likely to tell them to leave. After all, the Coloureds were more important to the farm than he and Peter and Abraham. So he kept quiet. But he told Peter and Abraham that they should be watchful. And he placed the large stone in the centre of the swept area in front of the shacks. Anyone spying on the camp would see it, would know that he knew.

While he was prepared to keep quiet about the first stone, he might not do so if it happened again. The mines had taught him to be prepared. Wherever he went, he separately buried a part-stick of dynamite, a cap and fuse. But could he ever bring himself to use them? Never for himself or Peter or Abraham, they had already lived much of their lives. No, he'd only use it if his son's life was at risk. It might mean arrest and prison, but a child – even one as troubled as Kula – deserved to be defended. Or avenged.

He turned back to Kula. "If you don't want to work here, then you should go."

Kula shrugged. The girl, Fili, was not bad. He knew that. He'd like to talk to her, but his English wasn't good enough yet, and she couldn't speak his language so he didn't know how to be friendly after being mostly angry, most of the time.

He would leave.

But not just yet, not before he knew more about this place and these people.

What it took to make a farm like Du Bois work and make money for its owners.

## CHAPTER FOURTEEN

"Do you ever think of your real Ma, Fili?" asked Bo one day.

We were in the cellar where he'd once feared to come because of the ghost of Uncle Baantjie. But Bo was more confident since he'd left school and started to work permanently on the farm and earn a weekly wage - and since I kissed him on the cheek in the vineyard. These days Bo touches me, too. I don't mind, I like the way he puts his hand on my bare arm without thinking. And he doesn't stare at my body like some of the boys at school do when they think I can't see them. Petro and Evonne preen when that happens, but it makes me uncomfortable.

I shot Bo a quick glance. We'd never talked about my mother before.

"Sometimes I think about her." I poured away the sample I'd taken and rinsed out the test tube.

"Do you want to find her?"

I gasped.

"Sorry," Bo gestured awkwardly. "Shouldn't ask you that."

I looked about the cellar, deceptively quiet despite the must fermenting, and my vintage steadily accumulating its bouquet. This cellar, Grand-mère, Jean-Pierre, Dad... my shelters, now. Would it help to find her? Or would it enliven the parts of me that make me want to fight?

"Maybe," Bo squirmed, "when you do all that stuff for the squatters, you're really thinking of her, and doing it for her."

The villagers may agree with Bo. They may believe the reason squatters are being employed by Du Bois is down to guilt on my part for my good fortune in being adopted, a guilt that has infected my father and encouraged him to offer work to the outsiders.
And their dismay goes further.
*Who will be in charge one day?* they mutter amongst themselves. *Miss Fili, who feels sorry for the black men? And even if young master Jean-Pierre takes over - will she talk him into replacing us?*
*Who is this Fili we thought we knew?*
"You'd better be careful," Bo warned as we sat by the dam and watched a grey heron stalking the shallows, "they know you persuaded my Pa to agree the squatters could clear the new vineyard. But that was supposed to be all. Now they're doing other work. My people think they'll stay for years."
The heron elongated its neck, aiming its beak towards the water.
"Look," I breathed, "it's found something!"
It struck, then re-emerged, neck bulging with its catch, droplets cascading off smooth feathers.
"Why must I be careful, Bo?"
"They wonder who you're loyal to." He picked a piece of grass and examined it. Bo always found things to do with his hands when he didn't want to look at me.

"I'm loyal to Mum and Dad. To Du Bois. To you and Philemon and all the villagers -"

"I know that. And I know you help the squatters because of your Ma. But some people think you've changed sides."

"There are no sides," I cried. The heron took off with laboured grace. "Not anymore!"

"That's what you say, Fili. That's what Mandela said, what he hoped - but maybe he was wrong?" Bo finally met my eyes. "And maybe you're wrong, too."

He got to his feet, touched my shoulder and loped off.

The courtyard rose in my mind's eye: the weight of the past driving the stamping of feet, the glimpse of a better future seeming to tremble and vanish in the heat...

But Dad doesn't believe that.

"I'm proud of you, Fili," he said, hugging me one evening in the cellar. "You were brave, you showed us that we could reach out. And, to add to that, you'll be the youngest winemaker in the country! Du Bois could be a model for the future, honey."

"It was a gamble, Dad," I murmured against his shoulder. I live for Dad's hugs now that Mum's are saved for Jean-Pierre. "Like with me."

He released me and glanced down. Despite the low light, I can read Dad's face more easily here than I can in the kitchen, or on the verandah when he's with Mum. Just for an instant I caught a flicker of sadness - or was it more than that?

*No!* I wanted to scream, *don't regret me!*

*Only regret this tug-of-love, this uncertainty until my future becomes clear!*

"Purely as a business," Dad recomposed his face, "Du Bois should be free to recruit anyone we choose for extra work. And it shouldn't matter who does it as long as it's done properly."

I thought again of the courtyard, how Dad had seemed at that moment to be both strong and weak; how our farm - our lives - could look both prosperous and vulnerable depending on where you were standing and which way you looked.

"But are we trapped, Dad? Trapped into having them on our land forever, like Mum says?"

"I doubt it! One of these days, they'll realise they can get factory jobs that pay more and they'll be off. In the meantime," he smiled, "we'll have done a good deed - and they may have given us an edge over our competitors."

I stared at him. Those men weren't going anywhere. Factory jobs these days probably needed more skills than they possessed. And Mr Mfusi said the men liked working in the open, rather than underground or inside. Did Dad know less about the world than I thought he did?

"Mr van der Weyden wants them gone. He'd be furious if he heard you."

"So he would. Now Fili," Dad's voice hardened, "I don't like to hear that you and Petro aren't friends anymore. This is a small valley. We all need to get on."

"I asked her if she thought I belonged at Du Bois. Or if I was a squatter, too."

Dad looked angry for a moment and then he threw back his head and began to laugh. And he laughed until he was shaking all over, as if I'd said something so outrageous that laughter was the only response. I joined in even though I found myself crying. The cellar reverberated, stirring my vintage, surely even rousing Uncle Baantjie. I can't tell my father that I'm jealous of his son, the brother I love -

"My dearest girl," Dad wheezed after a while, mistaking my tears for mirth, "you need to learn something called tact. Go see your Grand-mère. She'll teach you *la politesse*."

"I'm sorry," I called to Petro, as I waited outside the school in the shade of a pepper tree. A pair of dusty sparrows grubbed about in the dirt near my feet. She was a few metres away but I knew she could hear me. "I was rude to you, Petro."

She tossed her blond hair and looked around. Some boys nearby cast covert glances.

"Yes, you were! Especially when I've been your friend from the start!"

I leant back against the low wall that flanked the main gate. Even though we've attended the same school and lived a similar life, Petro and I look at the world differently. My particular view isn't something she can understand or forgive. If I want to stay friends, I must hold my tongue.

"Listen," Petro relented and came to lean next to me, "I was nasty as well. But you must decide where you stand, Fili. You can't live in a big house and run about with poor people. It doesn't work."

"I don't want to run with them, " I replied quietly, "I just want to help them."

"But you can't!" she rolled her eyes. "You're rich, they're poor. It's not about their colour. I don't care what colour they are. But even if you help them, they'll still be poor and you'll still be rich. That's the way it is in Africa. They have to find their own way up."

"But if those of us who are rich don't help them, who will? How will they have a chance?"

Petro shrugged. Petro often shrugs, it's her version of her father's folded arms and set face.

"They'll find a way. People always do. Now," she tapped my hand and turned her back on the nearby boys, "I've seen the perfect dress. Evonne's brother asked me out. First date!" she giggled. "We're going to a party in Stellenbosch."


"Have I made a mistake, Grand-mère?" I asked later that week, as we sat on her verandah. Turtle doves crooned *werk sta-dig, werk sta-dig* in the nearby oak. The harvest was over and the vines were turning. "Have I caused trouble by wanting to do the right thing?"

"Whatever do you mean, *chérie*?"

"Everybody thinks I favour the squatters. That I've changed sides."

"And have you?" Grand-mère raised an eyebrow.

"No!"

"So what will you do, child, to prove your allegiance?"

I stared at her. Grand-mère and Dad are co-Directors of Du Bois Vineyards. She must know I persuaded Dad to give the squatters work. Just like she surely knew what the villagers were saying and what the van der Weydens were saying. Grand-mère's ears are as close to the ground as Bo's.

"I could talk to both sides!" I jumped up and crouched by her chair. "On the same day, Grand-mère! I'll go to the village and tell the Coloureds I'm still loyal to them. Then I'll take Philemon and we'll go tell the squatters that I'm loyal to Du Bois and the village, while trying to help them. I'll say there are no sides anymore!"

"And if the villagers don't believe you? Or Philemon refuses to go with you? What then?"

I gazed out towards the clouds swelling above the mountains. The world that Mandela fought for, and the atonement I tried to make for my real mother seemed like rain falling on arid ground, seeping away to leave no trace.

"I - I don't know."

"You should always have a plan." Her purple-veined hands grasped mine. "A clever girl like you doesn't go out on a limb without a plan, or a way back along the branch if it starts to fail."

"I suppose I could give up," I muttered. "Ask them to leave after they've finished their latest job."

"And why would they do that? You and your father have given them work and shown them respect. The world

outside is far colder. They'll only leave if their chances are better elsewhere. That may take some time."
Grand-mère is being diligent on behalf of her ancestors. She wants to make sure I'll make good decisions, that I'll be a worthy guardian of Du Bois land if it comes my way. I understand, but -
"So why did you encourage Dad to help them?" I cried.
Her hands loosened on mine and she stroked my face.
"Because it made economic sense, Fili. And because your father is a good man, a man who looks to the future. That's why he adopted you." Her rings were cold against my skin. "And that's why he gave those people a chance. Because of you. And because of their pitiable circumstances."
*And Mum?* I wanted to ask. This new, loose order was too threatening for her. I could tell she was forsaking the vision she once shared with Dad, a vision that had also brought me to Du Bois. But I said nothing. Grand-mère had recently started *la politesse* with me, and I knew this was a moment to be quiet. I should not question the loyalty of the only mother I've ever known.
"You could try a different route, child. A middle way. Less confrontational. More gradual."
"What do you mean, Grand-mère?"
She smiled, as if reminding herself of a memory from long ago.
"In the bush, where the country is still wild and not tamed like it is here," she spread her arms to encompass the farm, "you find a bird called a honeyguide. It's brown and not especially noticeable,

nothing like our bright sunbirds or flycatchers. But it has a particular skill, Fili. It calls and flutters in front of a human hunter," Grand-mère waved her hand in the air in imitation, "and flies towards a hive, leading him to the prized honey."

"I don't understand."

She leaned forward and fixed me with her sharp eyes. "The bird is a go-between, *chérie*. It talks to the hunter and it talks to the hunted. It beguiles both, although the bees may regret it!" Grand-mère chuckled. "You're perfectly placed for that role."

I stared out over the vines. A go-between. Cultivating all sides. Accepted by all sides?

Or a target...

A stone aimed directly at me.

## CHAPTER FIFTEEN

Ray lay on her side of the bed and listened to Martin's steady breathing.
Did nothing stop him from getting a good night's sleep?
She sometimes wondered if she loved him anymore. How could it have come to that?
They were happy, outwardly, he still called her darling, but when she tried to offer matching endearments they sounded increasingly hollow.
What had gone wrong?
This should have been the most idyllic, rewarding period of their lives. The birth of Jean-Pierre, the increasing prosperity of the farm, Martin's recognised leadership role in the valley...
Yet all was being sacrificed for a motley bunch of people on their fence!
And then there was Fili. A smart, dark-eyed girl who should have been engrossed in teenage fancies yet was, instead, tying herself in knots over a supposed duty to strangers who reminded her of when she herself had been discarded.
The odd thing was that she, Ray, had no real objection to blacks – she was no racist - they could be attractive in an exotic, muscular kind of way. But only if they were educated, civilised individuals.
She shifted the pillow beneath her neck into a more comfortable position.

The whole business was tiresome; an unwelcome distraction that had gone on for far too long.

As far as she was concerned, the safety and security of the entire farm and its inhabitants was at risk, despite Martin's belief that the individuals were not a danger.

The situation even had the capacity for making her ill.

Martin seemed unable to see sense.

She wished to be loved for who she was, and respected for what she believed in.

She was still beautiful, after all.

Her blonde looks still drew attention in town.

## CHAPTER SIXTEEN

The Du Bois squatters did not seek factory jobs and move on as Dad had hoped.
The valley shook its head and chased off new arrivals on its own farms swiftly, before they could create similar settlements. If you acted as soon as the first shacks appeared, the poor folk were easier to dislodge. Trespass was still a crime. So far none had made a stand to stay, none had defied the law to claim a stake in the ground but no-one knew when this would change, or if guns might appear on one side or the other, and blood might be spilt. Just like no-one knew how much force it would take to remove the small, established settlement on our land. Adam Mfusi, Peter Choba and Abraham Phillips kept their place well-swept, their shacks were sturdy, and they stayed out of the way of our village workers. I noticed that he and the men were able to afford shoes. And Kula had taken to nodding at me when he saw me.
But they did not leave.
"I told you!" Mum would repeat to Dad when she thought they were alone. "You didn't listen! You only thought of putting them to work. You swapped our safety for a new vineyard!"
Again, her words chased through the house, hiding in corners, and then re-emerging with every fresh disagreement. Dad would reach out to her, Mum would contrive tiredness or a pressing chore.

The cellar became a place to escape for Dad, too.

In its dark calm, my vintage approached the end of its ageing. Each barrel had to be tasted separately and then we made a practice blend to see if the combination carried the right notes, the distinct flavours that would turn an ordinary wine into something special.

"This is it, Fili," Dad murmured after the final tastings and blendings. "We're there."

I found myself clutching my head, blanking out the voice that came at night and whispered of failure.

"Ready?" Philemon shouted.

The men positioned along the length of the pipe gave a thumbs up. The computer was set. Dad, our ringmaster, cast a final look at both ends of the connection and then at the attentive cast. The performance couldn't start until wine, man and machine were synchronised.

"It's all yours, Fili!"

I grinned at Bo, hovering nearby, and pressed the button. A vibration filled the air. First a trickle and then a flood of red cabernet filled the pipe and splashed its way into the first bottle. I watched the liquid rise up to the required height.

"Good fill!" I called.

The flow halted briefly as the bottle moved off to be corked and the next one took its place.

Philemon sprang at a tap to adjust it slightly. Dad confirmed the setting on the computer for the rest of the run. The flow resumed with a gurgle. The second bottle was full. I ran to my position at the end of the conveyor. The first bottle was there, already sealed. I picked it up and slotted it into a crate. The second one approached. Bo was ready at my side. When the crate was full, he'd carry it to the deepest part of the cellar. And so we'd continue the performance until the tank was empty. Then we'd lay down the bottles on special shelves for the next part of their maturation. It was getting closer -

"Happy birthday to you," Dad began to sing over the noise.

"Happy birthday to you!" Philemon, Bo and the rest of the workmen joined in.

"Happy birthday dear Fili," they roared as my cabernet flowed steadily, "happy birthday to you!"

"Thank you!" I shouted over the clapping and blew them a kiss. "*Dankie!*"

"Ah," Grand-mère struggled down the steps and across the cellar on Mum's arm. "Your sixteenth birthday and your first vintage bottled, *chérie*! Perfect timing. Well worth waiting for!" She arched an eyebrow at me, then picked up a bottle and examined it with a practised eye.

"I must get back to Jean-Pierre," Mum waved at me. "Will you take care of Grand-mère? You know how Jean-Pierre shouts when I'm here and he's not allowed in!"

It took hours to complete the bottling of my Du Bois cabernet.

True to his promise, Dad had included *treize ans* on the label, below the distinctive picture of our Cape Dutch homestead amid flowering gums. Grand-mère stayed to watch, resting on a wooden stool. Shenay brought us iced lemonade when we took a break half way through.

"Well, Miss Fili. Your *eie* vintage! And on your birthday, too!"

"The first of many, we hope!" Grand-mère added.

"*Ja, ou missus*. This is Miss Fili's place," Shenay clattered the glasses back onto the tray.

Grand-mère inclined her head. Shenay headed back to the kitchen.

"A go-between, courted by all sides, " Grand-mère said, leaning towards me.

"I'll try, Grand-mère."

But Grand-mère's wisdom isn't able to address a vital contradiction: how can I influence all sides when I might already be surplus to the one that matters most - Mum, Dad and Du Bois?

"Happy birthday, Fili!"

Bo placed a cardboard box in my hands, one of the ones we use to hold six bottles of wine.

"Bo, you shouldn't have!"

I lifted the lid. The internal dividers had been removed. Something soft brushed my hand. I reached inside and lifted out a delicate object, a posy made of long white egret feathers interspersed with the fluffy grey of *werk stadig* doves, the burnt orange of a paradise flycatcher's tail, a brilliant wisp of malachite sunbird and the charcoal gleam of a buzzard's wing...

"You're beautiful too, Fili. Small but beautiful."

"Really?" I stroked the bright, fragile feathers, surely gathered over many months.

Whoops came from the nearby workmen who hadn't gone outside for a smoke. Grand-mère clapped her hands. I reached up and kissed his cheek, and Bo closed his arms about me.

The feather bouquet made Mum raise her eyebrows when she saw it on my dressing table.
"Very sweet, Fili. You're being careful not to raise his hopes, though, aren't you?"
"What do you mean, Mum?"
"Well," she tilted her head, "do you want to take up with a farm boy?"
I stared at her. Mum had never spoken about Bo like that before, as if he was inferior to me.
"Bo isn't just a farm boy -"
But she'd already left the bedroom.
For her part, Shenay pretended not to notice her son's present when she flicked a duster around my dressing table. She must have seen it, though, a precious gift that went further than the *koeksusters* and lemonade of a shared childhood. Yet maybe she thought it was just a trinket, not a declaration of love, and therefore not worthy of comment. Instead, she liked to scowl over my shoulder as I sent messages to my friends via my computer, a device she regarded with suspicion.
"Why do you do this?" she puffed her cheeks. "You'll see them all at school in the morning!"
Shenay only trusted what and whom she could see and touch, even if she chose to ignore what her son had given me. Or perhaps she had more pressing concerns.

"You know that pumpkin, Ma'am?" she announced in the kitchen some weeks later. "It was ripening right there on the roof, just like every year. And now it's gone!"

"Gone," shouted Jean-Pierre as he drove a toy plane in circles on the floor. "Gone! Gone!"

"Have you checked with your neighbours?" Mum glanced up from where she was arranging the last of the season's roses.

"Yes, Ma'am. Tannie Ellie says she saw it safe and sound on Friday and now it's gone."

Mum adjusted the blooms so they were evenly spaced in the vase.

"Pitty thlous!" burbled Jean-Pierre.

I smiled from the table where I was doing my homework. He still couldn't say his rs or fs.

"I'll buy you one when I'm at the shops in Franschhoek," said Mum. She took off her gloves and waved them at Jean-Pierre. "And who loves Jean-Pierre? Who loves him the best?"

"Thili," he cried. And then, "Mama, Dada, Ga-mere!"

"But that's not the point, Ma'am, it's theft!"

"Who do you think took it?" Mum asked.

"Why, the squatters," Shenay pursed her lips. "There's no-one else."

Mum picked up the vase to take it through to the lounge. She paused in the doorway. "I told my husband from the start there'd be trouble. But these days it seems you can't evict people without going to court. The Steyns discovered that last week when they called the police to clear squatters who refused to move off their boundary. If they're stealing, though -" she looked across at me, then left the kitchen, followed by Jean-Pierre and his plane.

Shenay filled the sink noisily and began to wash up the lunch dishes.

"I'll ask Adam Mfusi if he knows who stole your pumpkin, Shenay."

"Thank you, Miss Fili, but it's not safe you going to that place." She lifted a dripping plate onto the drying rack. "Your Ma doesn't like it. We don't like it."

"Why, Shenay? They won't hurt me. They need our work."

"But we don't need theirs!" She smacked a second plate into the drying rack and scurried over to the table to hiss in my ear. "We've managed all this time for your Pa and the *ou missus!* I tell Philemon but he won't listen to me!"

Dare I tell Shenay that Philemon has seen the value of black muscle power? "They cleared that land so quick, Miss Fili, I couldn't believe it," he'd muttered to me. "Mfusi said it wasn't half as bad as gold mining."

This is where I need Grand-mère's tact but I don't know how to use it. I can't tell Shenay that there's a private agreement between Philemon and Dad that the squatters will be tolerated so long as they don't cause trouble and don't out-earn our villagers.

Just like I can't tell Mum that Bo and I are becoming more then friends.

No amount of tact can obscure that reality.

Shenay marched back to the sink and plunged her hands into the soapy water. I looked down at my fingers. Shenay loved me, she'd held on to me when the strangers first appeared in the courtyard. She'd held on so hard that there were still crescent shadows from her nails on my skin.

"My friend," Shenay went on, scrubbing vigorously, "the one that works for the Newmans, she heard Mr Newman say that there's nothing to be done, that squatters can settle where they like. They've got no respect, Miss Fili. And the government lets it happen."

She hauled out a casserole dish and turned it upside down to drain.

"And that Kula, Miss Fili. You watch out for that Kula. He may be handsome but I don't like his eyes."

## CHAPTER SEVENTEEN

The missing pumpkin was never found. And no-one confessed to the theft. It was, officially, a mystery although village gossip implicated the men on our boundary, in their well-established shacks. Now, you may think that a stolen pumpkin is an inconvenience but to our villagers it was a crime, and a portent. Who knew what would be taken next? And, in retaliation, who knew when a well-aimed stone might hit its target? Bo said there was talk of villagers going down Gum Tree Avenue at dead of night armed with rocks -
"Careful, Fili," Grand-mère warned when I told her about the theft, "go-betweens only point the way. They don't dispute robbery of the hive or identify the thief. Or rebuild if it's plundered."
In another unexplained turn, my nightmares returned.
Why now, I asked myself, wiping the teary sweat from my face when I woke. What have I done?
There was no reason I could pinpoint, the yellow dreams simply decided to push into my sleep, bringing the familiar heat and rising panic. I don't scream anymore but I toss, searching for the gum trees that are always too far away to shade me. And I can never see my mother, she's just out of sight. Like the church where I was left.
"*Do you want to find her?*" Bo had asked me. Yet if I managed to, she might choose to haunt me even more, rather than let me go. But then again, I've started to

realise that everything I do - every impulse that makes me who I am - springs from that moment of being left behind. There was a less risky option, one that might meet Grand-mère's advice of a middle way in all things.

"Can I see the church, Dad? Just once? Then I'll be able to put it behind me."

The act of visiting in daylight might defeat the yellow-scorched nights, and bring some sort of closure. Otherwise, I might start to blame my rescued life for the nightmares and that wasn't fair.

One Saturday we drove over the crest of Helshoogte Pass, just Dad and I. The peninsula reared ahead in jagged profile with Table Mountain emerging from a tablecloth of swirling cloud. Below, to our left, stretched Stellenbosch, with its historic university spread along leafy streets. In a year's time I'd be going there to study viticulture.

"Are you sure, Fili?" Mum had asked, but I could tell the question was really directed at Dad: why should I be encouraged to pursue a degree in wine if it might only lead to false expectations?

"Ignore opposition, *chérie*," Grand-mère murmured to me privately. "Build credentials."

"We'll be classmates," Evonne announced. "You must help me, Fili! I don't know as much as you do."

Petro said I was crazy not to study something that would give me a career away from the farm. It was clear to everyone in the valley that Jean-Pierre would take over from my father. What was the point in trying to cling on? I should break free, go my own way.

"I've told Ray she has to spell it out," Mrs van der Weyden apparently declared over lunch to Mr van der Weyden. "Jean-Pierre is the true heir. Fili's a sweet girl but she must concede."

Indeed, it would've been easier if Mum and Dad had chosen to tell me - and the world - that Du Bois would no longer be mine. A careful, considered disownment, despite Dad's speech to Mum on the night the caracal barked. My lesser position, as proposed by Mrs van der Weyden, would be clear. I could still study wine-making but my skills could be used someplace else. There was, I told myself in the wakeful hours after a nightmare, no shame in accepting second best. I'd still be far better off than if I'd been left in the ditch.

I must be careful, don't you think? Ingratitude will cripple my heart if I let it take root. And then I might say or do something with my fists that can never be forgiven.

"You're very quiet, honey," Dad glanced across at me. "Yet perhaps you're right to visit. This church is part of you. Part of your heritage."

It took us an hour to make our way along the peninsula, past sprawling townships ringed by vast squatter camps hard up against the side of the highway. Ragged children played in the dirt outside shanties improbably festooned with television dishes.

"There's pay-as-you-go electricity," said Dad, "so they can get TV. People want to see a better world even if it takes their last cent."

I craned out of the window. Maybe these settlements started like ours, with only four shacks? I found myself gripping the door handle as a child waved at the cars whipping heedlessly by. The townships eventually gave way to wealthy, ordered suburbs that girdled the mountainside or shared the lush valley with historic wine farms like *Groot Constantia, Uitsig* and *Buitenverwagting*. We laboured up *Ou Kaapse Weg* - the Old Cape Road - and took a last look at the vineyards spread below, then twisted through Silvermine's stands of yellow pincushion proteas.

"Like ours, Dad!" I pointed out, eager for some connection.

Finally we slipped down into a broad plain on the edge of the Atlantic.

"Your mother and I only drove past, " Dad warned when we were a km or so away. "We don't really know the place. We first met you at the orphanage."

"There are gum trees. Like we have at home."

"How do you know, Fili?"

"I just know."

The church, set on the outskirts of a shopping complex, turned out to be a modern design. I hadn't expected that. I'd imagined a traditional structure similar to ours in Franschhoek, with pristine whitewash and intricate stonework, and a spire leading straight to God. Perhaps even massed beds of roses like at the Huguenot monument where we went every year to give thanks for the sanctuary of the Cape. Surely only a church that was both handsome and elderly could have lured my mother to do what she did? But this church was plain brown brick, set on a square of thin lawn, and with a squat tower at one end. It certainly had no fountain like the one where my Sunday school friends and I had tried to turn water into wine.

"Fili," Dad sensed my disappointment, "you don't have to go further if you don't want to."

I climbed out of the car. Seagulls cawed as they swooped over our heads. A stiff breeze - salty, I realised, from the nearby sea - whipped across the open site. My mother would surely have known that taste on her tongue, just as I knew the aroma of the cellar on mine. I ran around the back. Dad hurried after me. The building didn't matter as much as the trees.

"Look!" I pointed.

And there they were: a line of tall, rather scraggly gums forming the boundary. At their base, a furrow ran along the ground, sparsely covered in grass and weeds. There were tufts of fresh growth here and there where someone might occasionally have directed a hose. At the end, where the gums petered out, the furrow became a narrow ditch.

"Fili?" Dad placed a gentle arm around my shoulder.

"That's where she left me."

"Surely not? They told us you were left at the church."

"I wasn't left inside, Dad."

"But how do you know, honey?"

I slipped out of his clasp and bent to touch the rough grass, then stretched out on my back at the side of the ditch. The ground was hard under my shoulders and hips. A tracery of branches and leaves unfolded in the canopy above.

"Fili?"

I closed my eyes and felt the familiar pattern imprint on my eyelids. The shifting foliage. The relentless sun. My heart began to race. I waited for the next explosion of light on my face, the desperate need to get away, to scream -

I opened my eyes.

Dad was staring down at me. "You were left here?"

"Yes." I sat up and brushed the earth from my hands. "In the ditch."

"So this is where the nightmares come from?"

"Because of the sun," I felt my throat contract as I gestured upwards. "It burns -"

"My darling girl," Dad's voice broke and he sank onto the ground beside me and pulled me into his arms. I buried my head in his chest. "Do you think," he whispered after a while, rocking me to him, "that you'll be better now, having come back?"

"I hope so."

This could become my new memory, a ditch-side embrace to overwhelm the yellow horror. I could reach for it in the night and hold on to it until I fell asleep again.

"Do you have other nightmares, Fili?"

I lifted my face to him and searched his eyes. "Sometimes I dream I've lost you, too."
"No!" Dad shook his head and clasped me harder. "I told you once that you were our girl. That will never change."
"And Mum?" I asked, recklessly. Grand-mère would say, in her lessons on *politesse*, that I should never push for an answer that can't be given and, in any case, may be best left unsaid. *Some questions are not for asking, child.*
"Mum loves you just like I do. You must believe that, honey."
I nodded. The sea breeze began to blow harder. Over Dad's shoulder I could see cloud pouring over the nearby peak in silent, braided waterfalls, like the wraiths of Mum and Dad's past arguments about me. It wasn't my place to dispute them, even when I was in their path.
Shouting came from the side of the church.
"What are you doing?" A man in a grey shirt and white dog collar rushed towards us, waving his arms. "Leave that girl alone!"
Dad and I scrambled up.
"Forgive us, Reverend," Dad wiped his hand on his trousers and held it out. "I'm Martin Du Bois." He turned to me. "This is my adopted daughter, Fili. We're here because this is where Fili was left -" he gestured at the ditch and the sheltering trees, "before she came to us."
"I beg your pardon?"

"I was left in the ditch," I pointed at the spot. "Seventeen years ago."

The minister gaped at me. The trees tossed above our heads. A hooter blared from the car park.

"Then you're the one!" he exclaimed. "Praise the Lord! You're the baby in the pink shawl!"

I smiled. Maybe I needed this, too. A witness to my beginning. It seemed that the minister understood, because he reached for my hands and began to speak rapidly and impatiently as if, like me, he'd held on to the memory for far too long.

"We found you in the afternoon, Miss Du Bois. You must have been here for several hours because you were crying and hungry -" He paused for breath and glanced at Dad. "I took you inside and called the police. For the next few days we sent people into the neighbourhood to look for your mother - a young woman who'd had a baby - but no-one came forward. There weren't many mobile phones in those days, so we had to go door-to-door."

He slowed down and sighed. "We didn't want to make trouble, we only wanted to help her. And to help you. Every child deserves to know her mother. But no-one came forward. Or ever has. I'm so sorry -"

Dad rested his hand on my shoulder.

"After a week," the minister glanced at Dad again, "we'd had no luck. So we contacted the adoption services. They came and took you away and we never heard what became of you."

The gums thrashed above our heads. Sun and shadow chased one another across the ground.

"I was lucky," I said. "Mum and Dad rescued me. I became their baby."

"Ah," the minister smiled and released my hands. "Praise the Lord indeed!"

Furious hooting sounded from the shopping centre's car park. If my mother was too poor to care for her child, she would've been too poor for any kind of transport except her own two feet.

"Why do you think she left me here, Reverend. At your church?"

He regarded me for a long moment, as if unsure whether to be honest or not. I wonder if ministers are obliged by God to be honest - even if it means being reckless or tactless like I often am?

"I wondered that, too. In the end we decided that there might be a logical explanation. Come with me." He led us around the side of the church. "Look up there," he said, pointing to an area on the church wall that seemed lighter in colour than its surroundings. "We used to have a sign up there but we took it down after," he glanced at me, "what happened."

"What did it say?"

"It was for a free creche for needy mothers. It said," and he gave a sad smile, "*Baby drop off. Ages up to three.*"

## CHAPTER EIGHTEEN

Ray peered into her bathroom mirror and realised she was developing frown lines, all the more noticeable in the morning light.

She'd warned Martin repeatedly but he wouldn't listen.

And now the storm that had been slowly gathering over Du Bois was breaking.

The squatters, the thieving, Martin's stubbornness, Fili's intransigence...

Hopefully this trip with her father to the church would settle her down, although it might simply stir up more uncertainty, more confusion. Ray had committed to love and care for Fili but it was becoming harder. Friends like Elaine van der Weyden had warned of teenage moods but Fili's quirks were of a different sort, and carried awkward consequences - like her continuing obsession with the men on the fence in some sort of compensation for her mother's choice to give her up.

And now she wanted to be Bo Sammy's girlfriend!

It was utter foolishness. She and Martin weren't giving Fili every opportunity in life in order for her to throw herself away on a youngster with no secondary education. And how would their relationship be received in the village? Across the valley?

And what about her dearest boy, who should be sole heir to Du Bois? Jean-Pierre, bless his heart, idolised Fili who believed herself to be co-heir and whose cause was championed by Nanette and Martin!

Maybe she, Ray, should change her will? It would be a step, no-one need know…

She reached for her brush and swept it through her blond hair.

Suddenly, through no fault of her own, Ray was finding herself on the wrong side of key family decisions, and looked at with pity or light scorn by friends who would never have allowed the same situation to develop on their property or in their own homes.

Bizarrely, she'd recently encountered the young man, Kula, in the supermarket car park.

He'd appeared out of nowhere and offered to help load her groceries into the boot. At first, she refused. But he simply went ahead and she let him do so. He smiled at her before he walked away.

The encounter had left Ray confused.

She'd painted the squatters as thieving invaders – particularly the youngster.

She smoothed the lines on her forehead and turned away from the mirror.

Martin still reached for her at night in an attempt to quell the discord between them.

But Ray's energy seemed all used up by the end of the day. She needed a kind of restorative therapy, an interlude where she could see a new horizon, experience a different view, perhaps travel to a place where some passion might be rekindled.

## CHAPTER NINETEEN

I spoke to no-one about our Saturday morning trip to my birth church. I said nothing about the breeze spiced with salt from the sea, the cawing of gulls as I lay down beside the ditch, or the diligent minister who'd searched in vain for my mother. Did he look any further than the immediate neighbourhood? Possibly not. But the word would have reached the wider community. A young mother who didn't want to be found could have closed her ears.

I understand more, now.

My mother chose to leave me at a place that promised to look after children for free, for a couple of hours. Did she truly misunderstand the sign? Or did she reckon that a place which was temporarily generous, might be generous for life? Petro would have laughed if I'd told her, and then perhaps even posted the story on facebook, her latest craze. She would have suggested there was a fair chance of finding my mother via the internet, if I truly wanted to look for her.

Do I want to find her?

And would she want to be found, all these years later?

Before we left the church, the minister kissed me on the cheek and told me he would pray for me.

"But why, sir?" I asked, taking a last look at the ditch and the trees. "I've already been rescued."

"We can rise above our past as you've done, Miss Du Bois," his eyes met mine kindly, "but we can never free ourselves from it entirely. I will pray you make peace with that."

When we returned home, Mum didn't speak to me about the trip other than to say, irritably, that Jean-Pierre had missed me while I was away and that she'd searched for the shears in the workshop but not even Philemon knew where they were, and did I?

Grand-mère must have known where we'd gone but she always chose to wait rather than push for an early confidence. *In a long life, child, a delay is a small scratch and not a wound.* The only time she'd pressed was after Mum and Dad told me about the coming Jean-Pierre. Then she wasted no time in seeking me out and reassuring me of my place.

I didn't find my mother at the church.

And I didn't cry for her, as I thought I might, when I learned how hard they'd tried to locate her. No search can find someone who doesn't want to be found. She'd been determined to give me up. Yet it was a comfort to have met the gums once more, and to receive the prayers of the kind minister who found me. And to hug Dad beside the ditch from where my new life sprang, and hope that the nightmares would leave me forever in favour of the new memory I'd made.

The day after we got back, I went down to the dam hoping to see Bo. Since the posy, we'd started to meet every day aside from our usual vineyard patrols. Sometimes we held hands, sometimes he kissed me and our hearts raced in time. Was it defiance of Mum? All I

know is that while Du Bois seemed, at times, to be ebbing away from me, Bo remained fixed: keen, tufty-haired, afraid of ghosts but in love with the land like I was. And in love with me. Today I wanted to tell him he was right about my mother even though I hadn't found her: that, underneath the resentment, I've always wanted to pity her - and the only way to do so was to transfer my pity to the poor black men by the avenue and try to help them as she, perhaps, had never been helped. But there was no sign of him at the dam. Or the pied kingfishers that caught tiny fish and beat them against a nearby branch to break their backbones. "Not to be cruel, Fili," Dad reassured me when I was a child, "but to make them easier to eat." Instead, a pair of swallows were performing loops above the water, snapping up insects in their path, cleaving the air so sharply it seemed to quiver in their wake.
"Fili Du Bois?"
I twisted around.
"Kula? What are you doing here?"
He sat down at my side. I shifted away. There was an unspoken arrangement that the squatters would only go to and from their areas of work and not roam the farm at large.
"I come here all the time."
I didn't often see him close up. He was bigger than Bo and several years older as well, surely twenty by now, with sharp cheekbones and those piercing eyes. He was looking at my face in a way that might have been rude if his eyes had been focussed, but they weren't. His

English was better than before, though. Or maybe it always had been but he couldn't be bothered to use it or he chose not to because it was the white man's tongue. And his clothes were less ragged. Du Bois wages were clearly helping him.

"I've never seen you here before. I didn't know you liked the dam."

"You're always at school. Or running after that Coloured boy."

"Bo's my friend."

"He's not mine."

"You don't make it easy for anyone to be friends with you."

"I don't need friends," he muttered. "They let you down. You know that."

"What do you mean?"

"That girl you brought to look at us. Like we were animals in a zoo."

"No! I don't think that -"

"She isn't your friend!" he snapped. "She laughs at you. I've seen her and her ugly father. They want to kick us out. Your mother wants to kick us out. And the Coloureds throw stones."

My hands were suddenly icy, like Mum's had been that day in the courtyard. Does the body draw blood away from your end parts when you're frightened? I thought it was the opposite: that blood would pour in to help you escape faster than normal. I forced myself to wait, as Grand-mère had taught, even as every sinew screamed to run. Kula liked to say things that shocked.

If you didn't react, he might stop. If you stood your ground before a charging lion, it might back off.

And so it seemed.

He rolled on his back and closed his peculiar eyes. A swallow launched into a spectacular dive, its beak ripping the water, its feathers glinting like hard, polished steel.

"I know there are people who don't like me," I said eventually into the silence. "When you're adopted, there's no map to show you where you came from. Or where you should go."

My words hung on the air. He didn't stir. He wasn't wearing shoes and his feet were broad and strong. If I ran, he would catch me. And then?

"Mrs Sammy's pumpkin was stolen from her roof last year. Do you know who took it?"

His eyes flew open. "You think I did?"

"I don't know. But if you did, will you put one back in its place?"

With cat-like speed, he launched himself up onto his haunches.

"Don't call me a thief! Don't tell me what to do!" he shouted, his eyes inflamed, devouring me.

I jumped to my feet and ran hard up the hill, away from the dam. The slope was steep and the ground was soft from rain the night before. I slipped and cried out as I felt my ankle twist. But the blood that was now pounding through my body didn't fail me. It hauled me up and propelled me on. At the top, I looked back, my

chest heaving, my hands crusted with soil. The vineyards flowed in calm green waves across the land.
He was gone.
And my ankle wasn't twisted, just sprained. Even so, I struggled to walk normally so no-one would notice, especially Petro and Evonne who could spot a new lipstick or a slight limp with equal speed.
Kula disappeared from the workforce after that.
"Totally unreliable," Dad said in passing. "His father doesn't know what to do with him. In fact, I'd prefer it if he left altogether. Now, honey, would you like to try your hand at next summer's oaked chardonnay? For your eighteenth birthday? It's time to move on from reds." We'd recently taken delivery of the latest batch of oak barrels, beautifully made by coopers in France and shipped to us for when the old ones had given up all their flavour. Grand-mère says we use oak like a chef uses spices. "We want notes of apple or pear, leaning towards citrus" Dad went on. "Lightly oaked."
But Kula didn't leave Du Bois for good as Dad had hoped.
After some months he came back, his brooding presence on the land silencing his workmates from their *Shosholoza* and echoing the muted skies of winter. Then he began to work less for us, so he must have found employment elsewhere. One day I found a sealed note addressed to me pushed under our front door after I got back from school.
*Im sorry. Im sorry I made you fal.*
He had come to the house in broad daylight.

*Why didn't Blaze bark?*

I crushed the scrap of paper and threw it into the bin with trembling fingers before Mum could notice. And if he could calm Blaze, he could also come at night while we were sleeping, and peer through the windows left open to catch the breeze. Had he watched my nightmares in the past? Heard me cry out?

A few weeks after the note under the door, two cans of petrol that we kept for the tractor as emergency fuel, disappeared.

"Please, Martin," said Mum at supper. "First it was the pumpkin, then the shears disappeared and now the petrol. We can't ignore it any longer. We must take action."

"Naughty Daddy," crowed Jean-Pierre over his scrambled eggs. "Action! Action!"

"Not now, Ray," said Dad, inclining his head towards the boy. "We'll talk later."

"I don't think there's anything to discuss. They have to go!" Bright spots burned on Mum's cheeks.

"I'll ask Mr Mfusi," I put in. After all, I was the farm's go-between, as Grand-mère envisaged. "I'll tell him we think someone's stealing. Maybe his son?"

"You'll do nothing of the sort, Fili. It's far too risky. Tell her, Martin!"

"Don't get involved, Fili. I'll speak to them tomorrow."

"I talked to Kula once before, Dad. I told him he must return Shenay's pumpkin if he stole it."

Mum gasped. Jean-Pierre banged his fork on the table. Jean-Pierre is indulged by Mum. She can't bring herself to teach him that he isn't always the centre of attention."

"I'll deal with it, Fili," Dad's voice hardened. "Adam Mfusi knew from the start that if there was any trouble, they'd all lose their jobs."

"What is this?" Mum muttered as we were clearing the table. "This interference? Haven't you done enough harm encouraging your father to employ them? Dragging Petro along to see them?"

I ran up to Bo's straight after supper, climbing out of my window so no-one saw me go. Flocks of sacred ibis were heading for their roosts by the dam, their black-tipped feathers melting into the brief twilight. Pain shot through my ankle every time I hit a bump in the path.

"What are you doing here, Miss Fili?" Shenay answered my knock.

"Fili?" Bo appeared behind his mother. "What's wrong?"

"Has your pumpkin been returned, Shenay?" I panted. "Was it put back on the roof?"

"Why ever would it come back, Miss Fili?" She giggled. "Like it was sorry it left? Your Ma bought me a new one, just like she said she would."

"Will you tell me if it ever comes back? Onto the roof? Then I'll know who stole it."

"Miss Fili!" Shenay flapped her hands dismissively. "What nonsense you talk! How can you know that, about a pumpkin that was stolen months ago? Now get on home. Bo will walk you back."

I felt Shenay watching us down the path and then heard the door close behind us. From the adjacent cottage Tannie Ellie shouted to one of her grandchildren to bring in the washing. I stopped and rubbed my foot. Lights blinked from Grand-mère's cottage on the far ridge.

"I think I know who did it," I said to Bo.

"*Ja*," he replied after a pause, "me too."

I stared at him. If Bo had seen Kula, then we had a witness. It proved you couldn't get away with stealing, there were too many watchful eyes. And here was my first test as a go-between: if I persuaded Kula to return the other missing items - the shears and the petrol - then his father and the others might be allowed to stay. Kula, of course, would have to leave.

"You saw him take it?"

"What do you mean?" Bo asked with a frown.

"Did you see Kula take it?"

"No!"

"So who did?" I shook Bo's arm.

The sun hovered on the shoulder of the mountains, then plunged behind it. The ibis were barely visible now, pale blots weighing down the tops of the willows by the dam.

"Bo!"

He turned to me. When we were alone, he often used to touch my cheek yet he didn't do so now. I couldn't make out the expression in his eyes but I could tell from the way he was holding himself that he was nervous. Bo gets skittish, he reminds me of a buck that senses a leopard and wants to bolt but can't resist staying to nibble one more mouthful of greenery.

"I don't know who took it, Fili. Or the shears. Or the petrol. But," he grimaced, "have you thought it might be someone who wants to put the blame on the squatters?"

His words were like pebbles thrown into the dam.

Ripples, steady and relentless, spread out far beyond their point of entry.

Not a deliberate attack like a stone hurled in anger, but something more subtle.

An inside job.

A village thief.

A deliberate casting of blame?

## CHAPTER TWENTY

Kula Mfusi liked to walk to the dam at night. He could go in up to his waist and clean himself better than washing in the stream. He kept to the shadows and so far had never met anyone on the way there or back. He liked looking at the water, seeing the way the light from the moon made a path. Moonlight didn't care who you were, the moon shone on you even if you were black.

He had only been there once during the day and that happened to be when Fili Du Bois was there, waiting for the Coloured boy. He couldn't remember what he said to her – it was one of those days – and she ran away and hurt her foot.

He felt bad and expected trouble from Du Bois, so he left the farm for a while and found a job at a warehouse in Paarl. But he wanted to see his father so he came back and started work again. He needed more money and his father wouldn't give him any if he didn't approve of what Kula was going to spend it on, so he returned to Paarl for two days a week even though it cost taxi money to get there and back. Du Bois didn't seem to mind him working part-time, apart from giving him a look on his first day back. The Coloured foreman ignored him, which suited Kula fine as long as he was paid every Friday.

One morning he went up to the house and left a note for Fili under the door. To say sorry.

He didn't like to think about that day anymore.

And what might happen next.

Adam had found a book on a rubbish dump outside town.
"Here," he said to Kula. "If you want to get ahead, you need to be better at English and numbers."
"How will I get ahead?" Kula had retorted. "Whites have all the best jobs!"
Adam shrugged. "You can hate the white man all you like but if you can't speak his words you can never fight him properly. Or work with him to get ahead."
Kula knew his father was right.
It was time to stop blaming everyone else and see what he could do on his own.
So he had taken the book. It was called A Guide to Running a Small Business, and it had pictures, too, which helped, although they only showed men in shirts sitting around tables, in front of computers. Kula could read and count a bit, but he'd left high school after only one year so his use of words was poor, and he couldn't spell. Instead, he'd learnt to use his fists when necessary and to swear like an adult. So far that had worked. But all around him, people were learning more and getting better jobs because of better English and use of tools like computers, so he should try, too. He'd seen young men like him at the warehouse, doing more than he could.
He read the book each night when he could manage to focus, slowly, by the light of a candle.

He found a dictionary in the same rubbish pile, to search for words that he couldn't understand.

The Guide book talked about the Law, and how to use it to protect what you had made, or get what you wanted. Or get others to get what you wanted.

His father was right. He needed to learn how to fight with words.

Maybe then, people would show him respect. Mandela had promised a better life for all. Kula wanted that life, wanted it so hard that it hurt and he needed to find a way to ease the pain. Especially after what had happened, and what might yet happen.

Maybe he could get that life if his threats were backed up by clever words.

Maybe, one day, there wouldn't need to be threats.

## CHAPTER TWENTY ONE

I hurried up to Grand-mère's cottage as fast as my sore ankle would allow. It was just after dawn but Grand-mère was a famously early riser. She liked to watch daylight creeping over the farm. From the dam came the squeak of coots calling their families for the first paddle of the day.

"Fili!" Grand-mère shaded her eyes. "Why so early? And so smart - how lovely you are, *chérie*!"

I kissed her and sat down. I was already in my uniform so I'd be ready for school.

"Grand-mère, it may not be the squatters who are stealing. The pumpkin, the shears, the petrol -"

She looked at me from beneath her broad sunhat. "Are you saying it could be an outsider? Someone unauthorised coming onto our property? But there's Blaze to warn us. And the workshop has an alarm."

I waited.

"You mean," Grand-mère's eyes widened in their cradle of wrinkles, "someone with legitimate access took them?"

"I can't prove anything yet. Bo says it would be a good way to cast blame on the squatters and get them evicted."

Grand-mère rocked in her chair. "How much of this have you told your parents?"

"Nothing. I don't want to say anything until I have the answer."

Dad would take me seriously but Mum, who'd once been sure of me, might cast doubt. It wasn't simply because she leaned in favour of the villagers over the squatters, but because I was starting to exercise a mind of my own.

"Ah, Fili," Grand-mère reached across and patted my hand. "You need to be cautious. Proof can be a slippery thing. Isn't this a matter for the police rather than a go-between?"

"But they won't come, Grand-mère! Not for a pair of shears and a can of petrol!" And, in the new South Africa, the police were less inclined to investigate theft where the victims could afford to buy replacements. "It's up to me."

"You know," Grand-mère mused, "you may not have found your mother via your birth church, child, but if she's looking down at you, like our old Du Bois forebears, she'd be proud."

I leaned over and gave her a kiss.

"I'm going to talk to Tannie Ellie after school. She sees everything that goes on. Don't tell Dad yet."

Grand-mère gave a snort and glanced towards the sun striking the cliff faces, leaving their clefts in deep shadow. "Be careful with that one. Ellie only sees what she wants to see."

I nodded and pressed her hand.

"Remember the honeyguide!" she called as I left. "Only point in the direction of the truth. Let your father or the authorities decide what to do about it."

"Where have you been, Fili?" Mum eyed me as I came through the front door ten minutes later.
"Just to see Grand-mère."
"Fili!" Jean-Pierre rushed from the dining room and launched himself at me. He had finally mastered his fs and rs. "Play after school?"
"Of course," I hugged him, ruffling silky hair that was as blond and smooth as Mum's.
"Only after homework," said Mum shortly. "And I don't want Jean-Pierre going anywhere he shouldn't."
I stared at her. I've become someone Mum no longer trusts. And it also turns out that my brother has far less freedom growing up than I had. I ran all over the farm on my own, but Mum won't allow him out of her sight. I can understand, given that Jean-Pierre is her unexpected triumph, as Grand-mère put it, her victory over nature's usual course, but it means he can't explore and discover -
"Where shouldn't I go?" Jean-Pierre shouted. "I want to go there!"
"The only place you're going, young man, is breakfast!" Dad swung Jean-Pierre over his shoulder in a fireman's lift and bore him, squealing, back into the dining room.

The heat was fading by the time I got back from school, checked my chardonnay block, finished my homework and glanced at my facebook page. I don't post much – unlike Petro – and I haven't tried to find my birth mother that way. But I suppose she might be able to find me, although I don't want to think about that. It might lead down a road I should rather avoid.

I climbed out of my window, muffled my voice in my hands and called to Jean-Pierre.

"Got you, Fili!" He flung his arms about me as he discovered my hiding place after a noisy search.

"Look!" I pointed out flocks of chittering white-eyes darting to their nests. "And there -" a pair of jackal buzzards, dark smudges against the luminous sky, circling for one last meal of the day.

"Come in for your bath, darling," Mum called, "then we'll play card games 'til supper."

I gave him a kiss and pushed him towards the house.

How I'll miss Jean-Pierre when I leave for university! Like I'll miss every row of vines, every crunch of gum leaves underfoot, every flash of Grand-mère's wisdom -

"Don't stay out long, Fili!" Mum shouted to me. "It'll be dark soon. I don't want you out late!"

But I won't miss Mum's scrutiny. Her constant surveillance. Am I cruel to say this? If she only worried about my safety, I'd understand. But it's more complicated than that. These days, Mum holds on to me with a mix of care and suspicion.

I turned towards the village. Tannie Ellie would be sitting on her step, watching her grandchildren. *Did someone arrange the thefts, Tannie? An inside job designed to cast blame?*

Perhaps I must not frame them as questions but as facts. Not allow her a way out.

Kula was lying just off the path to the village.

At first I didn't see him, I saw his phone. It was on the track, buzzing.

For a moment I thought it was simply a matter of a phone carelessly lost. But then I heard a groan. Kula was hunched on his side a few metres off the path, hidden beneath scrubby *fynbos*. I ran over. His hands were scratched and bloody. His jeans had a tear across the knee.

I knelt down and touched his shoulder. "Kula?"

His breathing was ragged.

A gasping and then nothing for a sickening while, and then another gasping.

"Kula!" I abandoned caution and shook him.

His head swivelled slowly and he opened his eyes. The whites were bloodshot, the pupils unfocussed. I pushed away the branches and leaned closer. "What's happened? Are you sick?"

"Why did it happen?" he muttered.

"What? Can you sit up?"

He turned towards me, wincing as his hands touched the earth. The phone stopped buzzing. I glanced around. There was no-one about. I could run to the camp and tell his father, or run to the village and get Bo to help me. Not Dad, because he'd have to tell Mum -

"Fili Du Bois," he said, smiling. I'd never seen him smile before. "Beautiful Fili."

"Come," I urged, "you must try and get up. It's will be dark soon -"

He began to laugh but it wasn't a happy sound or even an embarrassed one to acknowledge the state he was in. I felt a prickle of the same fear I'd experienced when he shouted at me at the dam. Forcing myself to grasp him under the shoulders, I tried to haul him to a sitting position. His eyes rolled back in their sockets and he slumped down. I scrambled to my feet and rushed up the path to the village, slowing down to a walk as I approached. It wouldn't do to advertise the emergency. Tannie Ellie was on her doorstep watching her grandchildren but also, presumably, watching for her slippery nephew who only ever came back when he had enough money to impress her with a shiny suit and a minibus taxi fare instead of walking down Gum Tree Avenue.

"So who is thieving, young Miss Fili?" she called to me.

"Bo!" I rapped on his door. "Bo, are you there?"

"Must be the squatters," Tannie Ellie spat out the word. "Something must be done! There aren't any thieves round here, Miss! Why would we steal from each other?"

*Ellie only sees what she wants to see,* Grand-mère had said.

"To make outsiders lose their jobs, Tannie?" I flung the words, recklessly, over my shoulder. I shouldn't have, but Kula's slack body was overwhelming everything I'd learned from Grand-mère about diplomacy, about waiting before I spoke, about being careful -

"Fili?"

"Bo," I fell into the cottage as the door opened. "Can you help me in the vineyard?"

"Now? So late?"

"It's almost dark," Tannie Ellie shouted, reaching for the knitting at her side. "Your Ma won't want you out in the dark!"

"Hurry," I muttered at Bo.

"Why? What's happened?" He pulled on his jacket. "Is it the chardonnay? The buds looked fine -"

"I'll show you when we get there. Bye, Tannie Ellie."

She wagged a knitting needle at me. "Don't say things you can't prove, young Miss!"

I hurried Bo along the path. "Don't run. Just walk fast. I found him, on my way here."

Bo stared at me, not understanding. When we arrived at the spot, Kula had turned over and was lying flat on his back, his eyes staring blankly up at the evening sky. His chest was barely rising and falling. Bo crouched down and put a hand on his chest.

"I tried, but I can't move him, " I said desperately. "We must get him back to the camp before anyone sees."

"Why didn't you fetch your father?"

"Because if he's been drinking then Mr Mfusi should deal with it."

"You're protecting him," Bo straightened up, staring up at me.

"Please, Bo, help me get him up! If I'm protecting him it's only for his father's sake."

It took both of us but finally we managed to raise Kula to his feet. I grabbed his phone. At least the gloom prevented us being seen from either the house or the village. Supporting him on either side, we began to stumble towards the squatter camp. Kula was much bigger than either of us but Bo has a wiry strength and he bore most of the weight.

"I should have kept quiet," Bo panted. "Or lied, Fili. I should have let you believe he was the thief after all. Then," Bo hauled him straight once more, "you wouldn't be so keen to help him."

About a hundred metres ahead, I made out the light from a small cooking fire. The squatter camp.

"Do you know what's wrong with him, Fili?"

I struggled to take the strain as Kula rolled towards me.

"No. Maybe he's sick, maybe he ate something bad."

Or maybe - I caught myself from crying out - it's AIDS. And that's why there's no Mrs Mfusi because she's dead from the disease and he caught it from her as a baby. All along I thought his rudeness was because of hunger but it could be because he was dying. Tears of shame stung my eyes. Kula hung between us like a rag doll, his head lolling, his feet dragging on the ground. I noticed he was wearing shoes, smart ones.

"Mr Mfusi!" I shouted. "Help! Mr Mfusi!"

Figures ran out of the darkness. They lifted Kula from between us with practised ease, as if they'd had to do so before. We followed the men into Mfusi's shack where they laid Kula down on a mat. I'd never been inside one of the shacks before. Peter Choba lit a candle. The wavering light played over the walls. There were pictures cut out from magazines pasted to the inside to make a crude wallpaper. An unlit paraffin stove sat in a corner, next to a cardboard suitcase being used as a table. A trickle of water dripped from one corner where there was a hole between the corrugated iron roofing. The other men muttered and disappeared into their own dwellings. The wind rattled in the nearby gum trees, delivering a chilly blast.

"Kula," his father growled, holding a cup of water to his lips. Kula opened his eyes and drank.

"Mr Mfusi," I whispered. "What's wrong with him?"

He looked at me and shook his head. "He just gets sick sometimes, Miss Fili."

"He's not drunk," asserted Bo. "I know what drunk looks like and what it smells like."

Mfusi nodded. "And it's not the *slim*, Miss Fili. Not AIDS."

Kula looked from his father to me. His lips moved.

I leaned closer. He was trying to say something and his brain was struggling to get out the words.

"Yes, Kula?" Mr Mfusi stroked his head. It was the first tender gesture I'd seen between them.

"Sorry," Kula mumbled before his eyes closed, "I made you fall."

I felt myself flushing but Mfusi and Bo didn't understand, they simply thought he was rambling.

"You must go home, Miss Fili, Mr Bo. Your family will be looking for you."

Bo nodded, and ducked outside.

But I couldn't leave them like that.

"Dad will call a doctor for Kula. Do you understand, Mr Mfusi? We'll pay for a doctor."

"He does not need a doctor, Miss Fili. He can cure himself. You must go now."

He got up and held open the flap of plastic for me. I stared at him but he wouldn't meet my eyes. He simply stood, holding open the makeshift door. I took a last look at Kula in the flickering candlelight and went outside to where Bo was waiting by the cut down saplings. It was completely dark by now and he took my hand as we ran towards the house. Warm light glowed from the inside. The shutters gleamed. The faint sound of Jean-Pierre's laugh reached us through the still night air.

"Not so fast, Bo!" My ankle was aching.

"You know what it is, don't you, Fili?"

"No," I gasped. "And why did Mfsui say he could cure himself? Wait, don't get too close -" I pulled him back as we reached the rose garden but we'd already been seen and heard.

"Fili!" Mum appeared in the doorway, hands on her hips. "Wherever have you been? Bo, why didn't you bring Fili back sooner? Come in at once!"

"Sorry Mrs Ray! It's my fault. We were walking the vines at the far end."

"I won't allow Fili out so late in future." Mum marched back inside.

"Bo?"

He bent his head and kissed me on the lips. Then he lifted his mouth and whispered in my ear.

"I love you, Fili. And it's drugs. Didn't you see his eyes?"

## CHAPTER TWENTY TWO

It was only while I was undressing after dinner that I discovered Kula's mobile phone in my pocket.
I sat on my bed and turned it over in my hand. When pressed, the power button lit up to show the missed call whose buzzing had guided me to his body in the bushes beside the path.
I could call the number back -
"Fili?" Mum's steps approached my door.
I shoved the phone under my pillow.
"It isn't wise to be out so late," she said, sitting down beside me in her cream nightgown and resting a hand on mine. Mum has taken on a finely-drawn look now that she's older, a kind of sharpened beauty. "You do understand that, don't you Fili? Philemon says Kula Mfusi has been seen down at the dam after hours. He's not safe -"
"You want them gone, don't you, Mum? Even though they've caused no trouble -"
She glanced away from me, her face revealing angles I don't remember from my childhood. I will never be as lovely as her, at any age.
"Yes, I do. And if your father won't act soon, I'll call the police myself."
I could feel her fingers squeezing mine, trying to influence me by physical pressure if not by words. Mum tries to rein me in, I try to break free. It's a curious

dance because all the while it is Jean-Pierre whom she most wants to protect, not me.

"You'll be eighteen soon," she said, relaxing her grip. "Stand behind me on this, Fili."

I pulled away from her and went over to the window. The oak tree where I've overheard so much that wasn't meant for my ears, loomed out of the darkness. The scrappy gums above the ditch where I'd been left, tossed in my imagination.

"It's not just the squatters," I turned back. "Why can't I be with Bo? Is it because he's Coloured?"

"No..." she smoothed the cover on my bed, "it's not about his colour." She hesitated, then looked up at me. "You're far too young to tie yourself down. You'll meet better-educated young men at university, Fili. Young men with whom you'll have much more in common."

Heat rose in my face and my hands bunched into fists. Tact flew out of the window behind me.

"So I might meet someone and settle far from Du Bois? Is that what you want? Me gone?"

"No!" Mum's voice rose to meet mine. "Of course not! I simply want you to have every opportunity!"

"I want my opportunity here! At Du Bois!"

Blood drained from Mum's face. I felt an upwelling of shame and covered my mouth with taut hands. I'd done it, I'd declared my competition with Jean-Pierre, and insulted my mother in the process.

"I'm sorry, Mum -"

Dad would be horrified, Grand-mère...

"Why are you and Fili shouting?" Jean-Pierre came through the door in his pyjamas, his hair mussed, a teddy bear trailing from his hand.

Mum jumped up and gathered him in her arms and smothered him in kisses. "We weren't shouting!"

"Yes, you were," insisted Jean-Pierre, pulling out of her embrace. "I'll tell Daddy when he comes home. Daddy doesn't like it when you shout."

"No, you won't," Mum soothed. "You'll keep it a secret, between you and me and Fili."

"Why must it be a secret? When will I know the secret?"

"When you're a big boy," I said, coming over to kneel beside him. "When you're a big boy I'll tell you. Come, give Mum a kiss and I'll take you back to bed."

I eased him out of Mum's arms and led him towards the door, stopping so he could wave at her. Mum waved back, but there was something breaking beneath her expression. It wasn't anger or fear, which I know causes her heart to pound and propels her to nervous generosity. It was a new thing, a coldness that came from deeper inside her than either of those.

"Fili?" murmured Jean-Pierre against my hand. "Will you stay while I go to sleep?"

"Yes," I whispered, and stroked his hair, the same texture as Mum's. "I won't leave you."

He climbed into bed and I rearranged the covers that he'd kicked off.

"Love you, Fili." He snuggled down, hugging his teddy, and closed his eyes. "Love you always."

"I love you, too."

I lay awake until late. The small lump of Kula's phone beneath my pillow pressed against my head. In a perverse way, it was a comfort. At least I could tell myself I was doing a good deed on his behalf: if the phone was with me, he couldn't call for more drugs.

"Who will you take to the matric dance, Fili?" asked Evonne the next day, linking her arm with mine during break time at school. "You have to decide soon!"
"What?"
"Wake up! You've been distracted all morning. You can't have my brother, Petro's bagged him."
I glanced about the crowded grounds. When it came to dating, none of the boys who'd whistled at me had ever asked me out. Neither had the watchful Joe Steyn, who Petro said liked to look at me during assembly. Perhaps Petro was right when she told me to wear more dresses.
"How about Bo?" Evonne eyed me.
"I don't think my Mum would want that," I managed to reply, after a pause.
"But why? You're friends, nothing's going to happen."
She stopped and clapped her hand over her mouth, recognition dawning in her eyes.
"Or has it? Has it already?"
I felt myself blushing.
"Fili?"
I shrugged and pretended not to care. "Mum says I can do better than him."
"What do you say?"

Tears suddenly pricked behind my eyelids. I rarely cry, and never in front of anyone but Dad - although I did cry when Mr Mfusi left the rattle for Jean-Pierre. And yet here I was, with potentially the whole school watching, about to weep. Evonne steered me towards a bench under a tree so we'd be less visible. She's more understanding than Petro, she tries to imagine what it might be like to be me. I wiped my face and stared up at the cleft peaks of the Groot Drakenstein.

"It doesn't matter what other people say, Fili." She nudged me. "Or what they believe. You taught me that. I was horrid to you in the past but you stayed my friend."

"Everything's changed since Jean-Pierre," I said, fighting back fresh tears. "Nothing I do ever seems to be right. Mum and I argue all the time."

"Well," Evonne considered, "you can't help what's happened. I've got an idea," her eyes sparked with mischief, "you should invite Bo to the dance and only tell your parents at the last moment! They'd never embarrass him by refusing to let you go when he comes to the door!"

I stared at her. Present ourselves as a couple without telling anyone first - not even Grand-mère? Strike out in the opposite direction to *politesse*...

"I can decide for myself," I said slowly, "can't I?"

"Exactly," Evonne opened up her lunchbox and offered me some of her dried fruit. "You're almost eighteen, after all! The bigger problem is how will we get you a dress?"

The days passed. I saw no sign of Kula, and Mr Mfusi made no mention of him when I stopped by where the men were working. Bo accepted my secret invitation to the dance. Spring began to deliver a scattering of showers and sunshine at the right intervals for my vines to burst into life.

"We don't need as much sun for chardonnay," said Philemon. "Not like that greedy cabernet."

"Why, Philemon?"

"Well," he sat back on his heels and scratched his head, "this grape doesn't make extra flavour because of the sun. We grow the flavour in the cellar. Out here we watch the sugar," he swept an arm around the *terroir,* "but we build the character - your character, Miss Fili! - inside."

I stared at the knotted trunks studded with fragile buds and found myself smiling. After testing my patience with a cabernet, Dad was now setting me the challenge of a short and sharp maturation to deliver the balance of fruit and crispness we were after.

And, all the while Kula was absent, his phone remained in my bedroom.

I kept it hidden at the bottom of my cupboard inside a pair of shoes - not out of spite or laziness, but more out of the conviction that he'd be safer without it. If the phone was his only means to buy drugs, I repeated to myself, then I was doing him a favour even though he might not see it that way. But imagine the furore if Mum came across it by accident! She'd see it as clear evidence of my slyness which, I suppose, it was. So I rearranged my shoes to make sure it was stowed far from a surprise inspection. And I tried to make peace with her.

"I'm sorry, Mum, I was rude the other day."

She nodded and smiled but the smile didn't reach her eyes or banish the cold that lurked beneath the surface pleasantries. When I reached towards her, she turned away, like she'd evade Dad's embrace after an argument. There was no reconciliation. We simply pretended the words I'd spoken had never been uttered.

"Fili!" she called one morning as I was getting ready for school, "we're having the neighbours around for dinner tomorrow night. Will you help Shenay with the table?"

"Of course, Mum."

"And you can eat with Jean-Pierre in the kitchen beforehand," she said over her shoulder, with breezy dismissal. "Your father wants to discuss business."

I opened my mouth to protest and closed it again. Dad was already discussing Du Bois business with me during our time in the cellar. Yield per acre, profit per bottle, the merits of one cultivar versus another. "You need to know, Fili. An informed decision is the best decision."

*But will I be making any decisions, Dad?*

It turned out that that the business Mum was referring to only began after dinner. Jean-Pierre was asleep, I was supposed to be in bed, and Shenay had washed up and left for the village by the time the group moved to the verandah with the dessert wine. It was a warm evening and pale, silky moths fluttered around the lamps Dad had lit. Blaze, after an initial sniff and snap, flung himself at Dad's feet.

"The valley must present a united front," Mr van der Weyden declared as soon as he sat down, rapping his hand on the arm of his chair. "If one farm continues to tolerate land invasions, our case is undermined."

The party exchanged glances.

Why, I wondered from my perch in the oak tree, don't adults say exactly what they mean?

*You, Martin, are undermining our case...*

"They didn't realise it was Du Bois property beyond the fence," Dad said in a neutral voice, "and we didn't spot them soon enough."

"I certainly want them gone," declared Mum, as she handed around coffee and mints, "before we find ourselves with an entire town on our doorstep! Coffee, Elaine?"

"Thank you, Ray. Just a dash of cream."

"They've proved to be reliable," Dad went on evenly, "and hard working. They haven't brought in any extra individuals. But I agree the situation is not sustainable. We've had some instances of theft, and our Coloureds are restless."

"Martin worries about the effect on Fili of getting rid of them," Mum said crisply. "She's allowed herself to get sentimental."

I leant forward. Mum was wearing a pale blue skirt and a midnight blue blouse that emphasized her delicate skin. In fact, all the ladies were beautifully turned out, Mrs van der Weyden in a peach dress and Mrs Newman in a green shift with a sparkling pendant. Grand-mère wore her usual black but she'd added Grand-père's wedding gift of a pearl necklace that glowed softly against her dress, like myriad Venuses against an evening sky.

"Oh, come now," said Mrs van der Weyden, "Fili's almost eighteen! She must realise the danger -"

"One moment," murmured Bert Newman, who always weighed his words with care. "I understand Martin and Ray's sensitivity so I think the question that must be answered first isn't about the settlement, but about Fili. And - forgive me for being blunt – whether she will inherit. If not, and the estate passes to young Jean-Pierre, Fili's reservations are of less importance. Indeed, perhaps of no import at all."

I found myself breathing in rapid, choking gasps and grabbed a nearby branch to steady myself.

"But surely you're going with Jean-Pierre?" Elaine van der Weyden turned to Dad. "You can't disown your blood line!" She raised her eyebrows and shot a glance at Mum.

"Elaine!" protested Mr van der Weyden, but it was a weak protest.

They all wanted to know.

I wanted to know.

"If we disown Fili," Dad said sternly, laying down his coffee, "it will betray everything we stand for. Our faith in the future of Du Bois, our faith in Fili herself." He paused and glanced at Grand-mère. "The children will jointly inherit the farm. We don't yet know if Jean-Pierre will be keen to take it on, whereas Fili most certainly is."

The group lapsed into silence but I could sense the fierce protest longing to burst out of Mum. Yet that would have exposed a private Du Bois fracture for all to see. The van der Weydens glanced at one another. The night sky seemed to darken around me, the ladies' jewels glowed brighter. I yearned for a nightjar's alarm call on Gum Tree Avenue or a caracal's bark by the dam, but no distraction would soften what was being said on the verandah.

"Our Fili has the drive and passion to take Du Bois forward," observed Grand-mère quietly from her corner chair. "With respect, Bert," she inclined her grey head towards him, "my grand-daughter's future is not the main issue here. Neither is her sentiment. Fili knows the risk of hosting squatters. She has spoken of her concern to me. I believe she could be persuaded to support their removal if," she shot a piercing glance at the group, "it's handled humanely."

"Do you agree that we can't allow indiscriminate squatting, Nanette?" Mrs van der Weyden put in.

Grand-mère smiled and looked out across the land towards the brooding mountains. I knew what she was going to say. Grand-mère has seen more history than any of us, she knows that the immigrants of today may become the owners of tomorrow.

"We must certainly try to safeguard our future. Equally, we have to allow for compromise along the way. Our Coloureds must learn that they don't have a divine right to undertake all work on the farm. The squatters must learn they can't squat forever. And we owners must learn patience and the value of influence - whether it's via the law or via a young messenger like Fili. If we don't, we will lose what we're most trying to protect."

Blaze woke up and growled, then ran off through the garden.

I strained to follow his bobbing shape in the dark.

"So can we agree a course of action?" Mr van der Weyden said, leaning forward. "Can you persuade your daughter to accept that the men will have to go - preferably of their own accord? Once she agrees, we can explain to them that their employment on Du Bois or any of our farms," he gestured to the group, "is over. We'll try and find them work elsewhere. Perhaps with the town council, on the road widening."

I strained into the darkness. Blaze hadn't barked.

"And if they refuse to leave?" Mum asked, twisting her hands together in the way I'd come to know. I longed to be able to reassure her that we would be safe even if the men stayed - but no-one can ever promise that. Not when beautiful, coveted land is at stake.

"In that case," Dad said, "we'll need to seek a court order for their removal. But we must do all we can to persuade them to leave voluntarily."

"The courts are reluctant," Mum put in, "given our history -"

Eviction, in South Africa, still carried the ugly weight of apartheid.

Dad reached across and touched her arm. He doesn't touch Mum as much as he used to, but perhaps it only seems that way because Mum avoids his tender gestures.

"I got an opinion from Tate and Partners," he said quietly. "If we persist, the law does allow it."

"It will cost, Martin -"

"One moment, Ray," Mr Newman held up his hand. "This would be a test case for the valley. It will benefit us all if you win, so it's only fair for us to contribute to the legal costs. Are we in favour?"

"Yes," said the van der Weydens.

"Well then, we're all set." He reached for his glass and raised it to the group.

Mum got up and embraced Mrs Newman who patted her back. Mrs van der Weyden rose too, and kissed both Mum and Mrs Newman. The men stood and stretched and poured the last of the wine, a glowing Sauternes-style from the Robertsvlei valley. Grand-mère watched them with a slight frown on her face.

And now Blaze was just visible, trotting back from where the garden gave way to the vineyard. A larger, human shape detached itself from the shadow of a nearby rose bush and crept away. There had been no interrupted nightjar alarm call. No barking from Blaze.

Kula?

He'd once crept up to the house and pushed a note for me under our front door without alerting Blaze... no-one else possessed that uncanny ability.
How long had he been there? How much had he heard?

## CHAPTER TWENTY THREE

Ray hung up her evening clothes, stroking the silk of her blouse, then pressed her fingers against her temples to ease the throbbing.

It was done. Even Nanette had agreed.

Now there was no excuse for Martin to avoid taking action.

Fili would have to toe the line and, later, accept she might need to give way to Jean-Pierre.

And the inappropriateness of Bo would surely become clear once she met other young men at university. It might be harsh to say so, but it was about time Fili learnt such lessons in life. Hopefully, she might even meet a suitor from another estate who could entice her from Du Bois, thereby leaving the way clear for Jean-Pierre to take his rightful place. That would be the most useful outcome.

And it would neatly resolve the issue of Bo at the same time.

Just in case, there was always the matter of changing her will in favour of Jean-Pierre, which would assure his position if Martin died before she did. Recently, at lunch with Elaine, she'd brought up the subject – hence Elaine's loaded glance earlier in the evening that she hoped no-one else had noticed.

Ray closed the cupboard door and seated herself at her dressing table and stared at her reflection. Hair still naturally buoyant, lips full, face slimmer but that only served to highlight her cheekbones.

It was a package that most women – and men – would fine attractive.

But outside opinion was not her priority right now.

She, Ray, must focus on achieving some kind of inner peace, some private closure.

And there needed to be a reconciliation with Martin.

But could she – could they? - go back to the way it was before?

She kept telling herself it was simply a passing phase, fluctuating hormones perhaps. After all, having a child later in life was bound to have consequences for her body, for her mind. Especially when paired with a dispute over land, and the need to harness a determined daughter.

The doctor kept urging her to relax.

He'd put her on extra medication but her pulse still raced.

No-one really understood. It went deeper than hormones, deeper than family disputes.

She'd always been more impulsive than was good for her, always felt her heart quicken when fearful or when tempted...

## CHAPTER TWENTY FOUR

When I think back on it now, I can see it was a turning point. Like when the north wind strikes early but you don't notice its potential bite until you see the leaves falling. At the time I was too taken up with the twists in my own life to detect that the air around Du Bois was shifting, too. And while I tell myself I couldn't have prevented what happened, I have to admit that, inadvertently, I set events in train. I must take responsibility for that.
"You choose, Fili," Dad said with a smile.
I scanned the rows of my cabernet bottles. A fine layer of dust had settled on them and I picked one from a central row and brushed it clean. *Treize ans,* my first vintage, born just before my brother. But now that the time had come and the waiting was over, I couldn't help feeling a strange reluctance, a nudging wish to leave the bottles for longer. While they remained unopened, building maturity, honing complexity, their promise was intact. My promise was intact.
"Here, Dad."
He peeled off the covering and inserted the corkscrew. Grand-mère put her hands together, and Bo and Philemon grinned. Mum, holding a wide-eyed Jean-Pierre firmly at her side, nodded to me.
"Good cork," Dad held it out and then sniffed the bottle and passed it to me.

"Blackcurrant and cherry?" I ventured, and passed it to Grand-mère.

She nosed it and smiled.

"I want some!" shouted Jean-Pierre.

"Not this time, young man," Dad said, pouring glasses for each of the adults and for me.

I swirled the ruby liquid, smelt the bouquet, swirled again and sipped and washed it around my mouth as I'd been taught. Grand-mère held her wine to the light, then drank. For a moment the cellar was quiet. Dust motes drifted in a shaft of sunlight from a high window. Philemon drained his glass. My tongue slinked about my mouth, savoured the lingering aftertaste. Tannins, but not too much of them, vanilla from the oak barrels, a hint of green pepper...

Dad met Grand-mère's eyes. He put down his glass and began to clap. Grand-mère joined in, then Philemon and Bo and Mum until the cellar resounded. Jean-Pierre jumped up and down, tugging on Mum's hand. "Brilliant, Fili!" Dad hugged me. "Full bodied, good notes, highly palatable!" He released me, stepped back and offered his hand. "Congrats, honey!"

We shook hands, my fingers trembling within his adult grasp, my heart struggling to realise that the miracle had happened: water, soil and *terroir* had indeed become wine. Were the ancestors watching, could they smell the bouquet? Grand-mère kissed me on both cheeks and wiped tears from her eyes. Philemon took off his cap and shook my hand - "You did it, Miss Fili!" - while Bo gave me a chaste kiss on the cheek. Mum passed Jean-Pierre to Dad and embraced me. "Well done, Fili." Her eyes briefly warmed before she turned back to Jean-Pierre.

The tasting lasted longer than I expected because Dad wanted to document our reactions, and also try a second bottle at random to check consistency. Then we had a celebratory lunch on the verandah, as was the tradition when a vintage was deemed ready to leave the cellar and find its way in the world.
"So," Grand-mère murmured, leaning towards me, "your first major hurdle leapt."
*Our Fili has the drive and passion to take Du Bois forward...*
"Thank you, Grand-mère, thank you, Dad," I raised my glass to them. "You believed in me."
"You're a wine-maker now," Dad grinned. "Not many of your fellow students will have a vintage under their belts by the time they start university!"
"*Bien sûr!*" laughed Grand-mère.
"Fili still has to pass her matric," said Mum with a sharp glance at Dad as she handed around plates of salad. "That's the priority."
"She will," asserted Grand-mère. "How can we doubt her, Ray?"
Once we'd finished our meal, I helped Grand-mère back to the cottage. Her steps were laboured and her body swayed as she favoured her hips. A jackal buzzard drew slow circles in the sky above our heads. The vines marched towards the mountains.

"When you were little, *chérie,* you said that you'd only be a true Du Bois once you'd made wine." She stopped on the path and gazed over the flow of vines. "Well, you have," she tapped her walking stick on the ground, "and now you are."

"Will it last, Grand-mère? Will I be a Du Bois forever?"

"Nothing is forever, child. No-one can predict the future, no-one can even guarantee the next harvest. But," she turned to me with a glint in her eye, "no farm would dare lose up-and-coming talent. Especially when it's home-grown."

It was late afternoon by the time I met Bo at the dam. Our resident pied kingfisher hovered, then dived into the water, emerging with a tiny fish caught in its beak. It flashed past us and settled on an overhanging branch to beat its catch.

"Do you really like my wine, Bo?"

"*Ja*, for sure." His brown eyes warmed me. "Pa says it's one of our best ever."

"I couldn't have done it without Philemon -"

"Next time, Fili, you'll do more of it on your own. That's how you learn."

A pair of egrets touched down on the far side of the dam and shook out their snowy feathers before stalking along the bank.

"I've still got his phone, Bo."

"What?" Bo sat up. "Whose phone?"

"Kula's. I put it in my pocket when we rescued him and I didn't give it back."

Bo's forehead creased in horror. The kingfisher swallowed the limp fish and bobbed its tail. An eddy flecked the surface of the dam and rippled towards the shore. Since we rescued Kula from the path, Bo is scared of what Kula can do to my head. He thinks I go easy on him.

"You're the one who found him, Fili!" Bo hissed. "So he'll know you've got it! He'll come for you -"

"Then why hasn't he?"

Especially after what he overheard at the dinner party. He'd surely told his father about the upcoming removal. Mr Mfusi wasn't afraid to come to the courtyard and speak to us. So why hadn't he come either?

"There was a missed call showing on the screen when I found it." I felt in the pocket of my jeans and pulled out the phone and switched it on.

"Fili!"

The screen lit up and the number appeared.

"Give it to me," Bo ordered, holding out his hand, "I'll throw it in the dam!"

I tapped and pressed the loudspeaker and watched Bo's face turn from concern to outright fear. Why did I risk it?

I still don't know. Whenever I do something that seems alien to me, I always wonder if it's been urged, invisibly, by my blood parents. But that's an excuse. The mother and father who made me eighteen years ago are not to blame. I'm old enough to be accountable for what I do.

"About time," a male voice boomed from the loudspeaker. "I've got the stuff for you, where've you been? I can't hang on to it when I've got other clients who'll take it."

Bo's hand closed over my wrist. He lifted his other finger to his lips to signal silence.

"Hello? Kula?"

We waited.

"Hello? Your phone's playing up. Call me again."

The man disconnected. I switched the phone off.

"What shall we do, Bo?" I found myself whispering, as if the man could still hear us. "Tell my father? Tell the police?"

Bo was silent.

He's angry, I thought. He feels my recklessness will reflect badly on him when the truth comes out.

"Bo? Talk to me."

"I know who that was," he said slowly. "I recognised his voice. It's Tannie Ellie's nephew, Blake. The one who went off the rails."

"He's supplying Kula?" I gasped. "Does Tannie know?"

"Maybe," Bo said grimly. "And maybe she set it up. Another way to get at the squatters. Plan for them to be caught with drugs."

*An inside job. A village thief.*

*Don't say things you can't prove, young Miss!*

We sat in silence as the dam reflected the stately passage of clouds across its surface. If it was true, and Tannie Ellie and her nephew had conspired to sell drugs on the farm, they could go to jail. Our close-knit village would be torn apart for Tannie was from one of the oldest and most respected families. Neighbour would turn on neighbour in the ensuing race to cast blame or claim innocence, even God would be invoked to bring damnation on all thieves and drug traders. And the next harvest would be a silent affair, the disgrace permeating the vineyards like the worst kind of virus... The kingfisher finished his meal and tried for more, hovering and diving, pulling up and trying again until he speared another silvery catch. I tried to recapture the euphoria of my triumphant cabernet but all I could sense was rising danger, as if Bo and I had waded into the dam, been caught by a hidden current and pushed to a place where we would lose our balance.

"I didn't find my mother at the church, Bo."

"No, you didn't." He put an arm around me and I leaned against him. "But this is your home, Fili. This is where you were really born. Not that other place."

I twisted in his embrace and looked up at him. Bo sometimes says things that don't sound right at the start but somehow become true when you say them again, under your breath.

*This is where you were really born. Not that other place.*

He let me go and stretched out on the grass, his once spindly legs now strong and muscled beneath his shorts. Village girls - some of Tannie's grand-daughters - flicked their hair out of their eyes or hiked their skirts a little higher as he walked by. They considered him a handsome catch with a steady job. Mum saw a boy who'd flunked school to work out his days in manual labour.

"Why don't you like Tannie Ellie, Bo?"

"She thinks I'm not good enough to take over from my father," he replied with a bitter twist to his mouth. "She wants one of her grandchildren in my place. But who cares about her and what she's done," he pulled me towards him, "when I love you, Fili! Even though you frighten me sometimes!"

I leaned over him and we kissed. His lips were urgent, his tufty hair felt crisp under my fingers. He smelled of Du Bois, of musky grapes and leaf sap and heat.

"I love you, too," I murmured against his mouth.

"Really? Like - like - forever love?" Bo's eagerness made him stumble over the words.

"Yes."

I felt the quickening beat of his heart.

Soon we will want to do more than kiss. I feel it in my body, I see it in his hungry eyes.

"Mum wants Jean-Pierre to inherit Du Bois" I said, when we stopped for breath.

"But your Pa and the *ou missus* have been teaching you! You're going to university to learn more!"

"If Mum wins the argument," I pulled out of his embrace and sat up, "I'd have to find a new farm, a place that will accept who I've become. But I won't go quietly, Bo. I've put a stake in this ground."

The dam winked back at me, placid once more. The vines I'd made my own stood proud in their rows. Surely tenure - the right to remain in a place you've made your own - confers the power to shape what happens next? And surely, with my *treize ans* cabernet, I'd won that privilege?

"Bo," I turned back to him and grabbed his arm, "we must make our mark like the first Du Bois! And run the farm alongside Jean-Pierre, not in competition with him!"

"They want someone better for you, Fili. I didn't even finish school."

"I don't care!"

"But they will." He stared down at his rough hands.

"Not forever! And they can't risk losing both of us! Look about -" I jumped up and flung my arms wide to embrace the glittering water, the *terroir* that had rewarded me, the brilliant, eternal sky. "Don't you see? It's ours, Bo! The future can be ours if we seize it now!"

Dad and Grand-mère were waiting on the verandah for me when I ran back from the dam, my feet dancing along the path without seeming to touch the uneven ground.

Did my face reveal I'd said 'I love you' to Bo? I wonder if grownups remember their first time -

"Fili?" Dad stood, his face serious. "We have a matter to discuss with you while Mum's in town."

"Is something wrong?" I shot Grand-mère a look, aware of Kula's phone dragging down my pocket. She nodded encouragingly and patted my arm. I followed them inside to the study where Dad and Grand-mère usually held their board meetings and planned for the future.

"There's been a development, honey, with our neighbours," Dad said, once we were settled.

Grand-mère took a chair alongside him behind the desk. I sat opposite, almost as if I was being interviewed and they were to judge my performance. I felt a jab of fear. The Newmans and the van der Weydens had brought disownment into the open, maybe my cabernet - and I – were not enough, maybe my brave words to Bo were only so much hot air...

"At our meeting the other evening, we jointly decided we could no longer allow indiscriminate settling on our land. Now I know," he held up his hand to forestall any protest, "that you want to help the squatters, and so did I. But it can't go on. The thieving - "

"I know who's responsible," I broke in, "and it may not be Kula."

"It won't make any difference," he replied sadly. "Our safety and security are at risk. We can't take any more chances. And those men need proper housing, with sanitation and water."

"But there's a shortage, it might take years -"

"It might, *chérie*," murmured Grand-mère. "So we have to press the government to act. If we condone squatting then we encourage the authorities to avoid their responsibilities. These poor settlements will become sinks. Places where unemployment and poverty are rife."

"And if they refuse to leave?"

Mum had asked the same question. I knew the answer but I wanted to hear Dad's response.

"We'll be obliged to go to court and have them removed."

An image of Mr Mfusi's tenderness towards his drugged son in the leaky shack rose before me.

I stared out of the window behind Dad's shoulder. The Drakenstein peaks were mantled with cloud spilling from the heights and dissolving in the warm air lower down. Should I explain about Kula and the drugs? No, that would shift the argument from squatting to crime. Mr Mfusi and the others didn't deserve that.

"Fili," Grand-mère leaned forward, her face creased, her eyes gentle, "we want to encourage them to leave. We don't want to be heavy-handed. But before we do so, we need to know you understand; that you will help us to persuade them if they refuse your father. Will you do this for us, Fili? For Du Bois?"

Like a bolt of sunlight piercing the clouds, the opportunity struck me, sweeping aside the drugs, the prickly stand-off between white, coloured and black, even the haunting memory of my own abandonment. It hovered in the air, waiting to be seized: the golden upland that I'd conjured for myself and for Bo.

Du Bois wanted my help.

And I wanted Du Bois.

I paused for a moment, wondering why I'd been so blind not to see it sooner. Dad and Grand-mère were watching me, Dad worriedly, Grand-mère shrewdly. *I wonder*, I could hear her speculating, *have I taught her well enough?*

"I tried to be a go-between," I began, picking my words with care, "but some of our Coloureds are suspicious. Mr Mfusi and the black men value me but Kula doesn't.

Here at home I know you and Grand-mère do, but Mum less so."

Dad flinched.

I clenched my hands until the nails dug into my palms. This was the moment, the route to a future for Bo and myself. *Be strong!* I urged myself. *Be the best vintage you can be!*

"I don't know if you want me back here when I finish university, even though I've made a good cabernet." My voice cracked but I pushed on, hoarsely. "I want to make my mark on the land and the vines, like Grand-mère says the early Du Bois did."

Tears sprang into Dad's eyes. He swallowed and brushed his silvering hair off his forehead.

Grand-mère smiled. "Go on, Fili."

"Am I a true heir of Du Bois, Dad? Along with Jean-Pierre?"

"Of course you are!" he replied quickly, glancing at Grand-mère who nodded. "It's in our wills."

I breathed deeply and struck, like a heron after its prey.

"Then I want to become a Director of the farm, Dad, when I turn eighteen. So everyone will see I have a place. And I'll be better able to persuade the men to leave if they try to hold on."

His eyes widened. A tremor ran through Grand-mère.

"I told you, Martin!" she exclaimed. "This child has the courage - the temerity - to renew us!"

"Dad?"

He got up from behind the desk and opened his arms wide. I sank into his embrace and felt myself held fast like all the times he'd rescued me.

"I love Jean-Pierre," I said, my voice muffled against his chest. "I'll be his faithful partner in the farm. And yours and Grand-mère's."

"So you will," said Grand-mère, struggling to her feet. "And you'll prove to your mother that you can be trusted, whatever challenges may arise."

I twisted out of Dad's arms and looked up into his face. "Will she love me again, Dad?"

## CHAPTER TWENTY FIVE

I lay awake most of the night after our meeting.

Mum returned from her trip to town and I heard murmuring behind their closed bedroom door. She didn't appear for supper and Dad said, with a glance at me, that she had a headache. I fed and bathed Jean-Pierre and read him a chapter from The Wind in the Willows.

"When will I know the secret, Fili?" he asked into the dark as I switched off the light. "The one when Mum was shouting? Ratty and Mole don't keep secrets."

"Soon," I replied, "Go to sleep, now. Mummy loves you, Fili loves you."

I went into the garden before bed, this time via the verandah door rather than out of my window. A quarter moon leaned drunkenly over the mountains which were now clear of cloud. Blaze pattered after me, and nudged against my hand. I'd brought a pair of scissors. I found a Fragrant Cloud rosebud just opening, its perfume heady on the still air, and I cut it and went back inside and put it in a slim vase and set it on Mum's place at the table.

"Why, Fili," she said the next day, her face composed. "How kind."

She took me in her arms and we hugged properly for the first time in a long while and I felt her heart racing against my body. Dad smiled his crooked smile at me. He looked weary, I don't think he'd slept much either.

Jean-Pierre jumped off his chair and pressed against our legs. "Let me in, let me in!"

Mum released me and bent down to embrace him.

"You'll have to put your private feelings aside, Fili," she said later, when we were alone. "Now you have no choice but to act in the greater interest of Du Bois."

"I will, Mum. I promise."

The news, announced officially by Dad and Grand-mère on my eighteenth birthday, shook the valley to its traditional core. The local newspaper interviewed us and took a picture of me that was later shared by my school friends on facebook.

*The youngest Director to take office at one of the oldest estates in the winelands.*

"Brilliant," giggled Evonne, ogling it on her computer.

People pointed to me in the street when I went into Franschhoek.

"Want to come to the dance with me?" Joe Steyn asked at the school gate.

I stared at my face in the mirror when I got home. Did my new-found admirers suspect the bargain I'd struck? Certainly, the timing can't have escaped the Newmans and the van der Weydens.

"Congratulations, Fili," said Mrs van der Weyden with an appraising glance. "What a surprise!"

"Perhaps," speculated Mr Newman - and relayed to me by a gleeful Evonne, "they'd been planning this all along for her eighteenth. It's just a coincidence it comes hard on our decision to act against land invasions."

"What's all the fuss about?" asked Petro, looking up from her phone. "You're there now, for as long as you want. But I can't think why it matters, Fili. Rather come to Cape Town after university. We'll get a flat together, with Evonne too."

"*Magtig*, Miss Fili!" chortled Philemon, throwing off his cap. "Must I call you Ma'am?"

"Do you still want me?" Bo whispered, when we kissed among my chardonnay vines. "Do you?"

It was Grand-mère who brought me back to earth.

"Be discreet," she advised from her rocking chair as the gossip swirled and the telephone rang with more requests for interviews. "Learn from your father, be humble with all you meet. But most of all, Fili, be discreet. Speak out only amongst we three."

"Do you still want me, Fili?" Bo asked again, as we met by the dam.

Does he know about Joe Steyn? Does he worry I've been tempted? But Bo knows he's my date - and my love - though we've told no-one yet. And we match on the inside, which is all that matters.

"Of course I want you!" I shook him. "We'll be partners, running the farm one day with Jean-Pierre. And after the dance, by the time the acorns set, everyone will know we're a couple!"

*And we'll make you proud*, I hissed at the sceptical ancestors. *Just watch us! The oaks and the gums will become our trees. When one falls down, we'll plant another in its place; when one block of vines yields too little, we'll plant for the next generation.*

"And what about Tannie Ellie's nephew, the drug pusher? We can't keep quiet forever."

"I know. But I have an idea what to do, how to use what we know -"

We both turned at a disturbance behind us.

Bo jumped up.

"*Ou missus!*" he offered his arm to Grand-mère who was edging down the slope towards our bench.

"Good morning, my dears," she sank onto the space he'd vacated and fanned herself. "I remember running down here as a girl. Old age is a terrifying business. Why so serious, you two?"

I glanced up at Bo. He nodded to me.

"We know Kula is taking drugs, Grand-mère."

She puffed out her cheeks and folded her hands in her lap. "And how do you know that?"

"We saw him, *ou missus*, drugged up to his eyeballs!" Bo blurted out, flexing his hands as if remembering the weight of Kula. "We carried him back to the camp."

Grand-mère's shrewd eyes moved from Bo to me.

"It's true, Grand-mère."

"Have you told your father?"

"Not yet."

"And why is that? Why didn't you speak up when we were in the study?"

I hesitated. Bo looked down at his feet.

"I thought I could use it as a way to get him to admit he'd been stealing. And make him leave."

"But if he didn't steal - and you've already said the villagers may be the ones responsible - how would you proceed? We've already decided that he and the others have to go."

I stared over the dam. The kingfisher was missing today but a grey heron stood motionless in the shallows, its sinuous neck and razor beak reflected perfectly in the water.

"I'd tell him that even if he isn't the thief, I'd say nothing about drugs to the police. But," I straightened my back, "if he refuses to leave Du Bois, I would."

"A bargain, child?" Grand-mère exclaimed. "It's dangerous to bargain where drugs are concerned!"

*But it wasn't dangerous to bargain about my future at Du Bois?*

"We'll tell Mr Du Bois," said Bo quickly. "And we'll ask him to offer help for Kula to go clean."

"Ah," said Grand-mère with a wag of her finger, "but you're too late, young man. Mr Du Bois is on his way to the camp this very moment, to tell them they have to leave by the end of the month."

"Why didn't Dad tell me?" I cried, jumping to my feet.

Grand-mère placed a restraining hand on my arm.

"He looked for you, Fili, but you weren't at home. And there was some urgency. There'd been trouble at the Newmans again and the police were called to remove some squatters by nightfall. Mr Newman has filed an emergency court order in case they refuse to leave. Your father felt Mr Mfusi deserved to be told without delay."

The ground was not as soft as on the day I ran away from Kula. Even so it was still a steep pull uphill and my breath soon burned in my throat. Blacksmith plovers took off from the side of the dam, trailing alarm calls. Did my birth mother face eviction and was that the reason she couldn't keep me?

"Fili!" Bo yelled, pelting after me.

"Careful what you say, child!" Grand-mère called in a tremulous voice.

Dad would be facing the men on his own without me at his side, and without realising that Kula was a drug addict - or that they might already know their fate and be prepared to fight for their scrap of earth. Do men in shacks have a breaking point? A needle moment when their quiet *Sho... sholoza* explodes into anger? The gums were in flower and silky blossoms sifted over me like crimson snowflakes as I ran, the breath catching in my throat. Why, in moments of danger, does nature offer up such beauty? Is it to make us pause before our fists ball and the blood runs too hot and hard through our veins? In the distance I could hear Blaze barking. Dad had taken him as protection. I crashed through thickets of proteas, scratching my legs, and found the path that the squatters had worn down to the stream. I could hear Bo behind me. He can run faster than me but today my feet have wings. I'm spurred by fear.

"Dad!"

"Wait, Fili!"

"Dad!" I blundered into the clearing. "Dad!"

He was standing in the centre of a small semicircle comprising Adam Mfusi, Peter Choba and Abraham

Phillips. Blaze capered at his feet, straining at the lead. Kula stood a little way off.

"Fili," Dad turned. "There's no need to shout."

"Why can't she?" Kula strode forward towards the group as if he'd been waiting for my arrival. "She knows - we know - what you've come to say! You're kicking us out!"

Mr Mfusi directed a volley of Xhosa at his son but Kula wouldn't back away.

Blaze wagged his tail and leaned towards Kula. Kula knows Blaze. He's not afraid of him.

Dad stood his ground. Bo and I were at his shoulder.

"We didn't make trouble, sir," Abraham Phillips spoke up in a small voice. Peter Choba nodded.

"No, you didn't," Dad managed a neutral tone, "and I'm really sorry. You've done good work for Du Bois. But we have no more jobs for you."

Adam Mfusi looked away from Dad and towards me.

"Is this true, Miss Fili? Is the work finished?"

"She doesn't know," muttered Kula. "She only knows what she's told to say."

"Kula!" growled his father.

"How dare you?" I cried. "I rescued you when you were high on drugs! I brought you back and said nothing so your father and Peter and Abraham wouldn't be fired!"

Dad gasped and put his hands on my shoulders and pulled me against him, tangling Blaze's lead between us. Kula's pale eyes burned at me and Mr Mfusi thrust out his arm to hold his son back.

"Fili's right," Bo said shortly. "I was with her."

The drumming of a woodpecker broke into the terrible silence. I looked up at Dad whose face showed shock but also bewilderment. Dad wants to believe the best of people. I understand more about this kind of world than he does.

"You know about this?" he gathered himself and asked Mr Mfusi, who nodded unhappily.

Behind Mfusi, I saw Kula's fists clench. If there was to be a spark, an impulse to propel the quiet *Shosholozas* into violence, this was surely it. If his father and friends chose to join in, Dad and Bo and I might be beaten and left for dead amongst the cut-down gum saplings that littered the clearing.

"Mr Mfusi -" I began.

Dad held up his hand to stop me.

"Bringing drugs onto our property is a serious offence," he addressed the men, deliberately ignoring Kula. "I must ask you to leave, please, by the end of this coming week."

Kula thrust his father's arm aside. Blaze wagged his tail. The wind picked up and the woodpecker shrieked. I caught a flash of olive and red feathers. The muscles in my legs tensed, ready to spring in front of Dad, to protect him -

"I would prefer not to involve the police," Dad said quietly, "but I will do so if necessary."

The wind rattled through the gum trees, a branch scraped against its neighbour.

"Sir," Mr Mfusi replied in a subdued voice, "there will be no trouble."

I felt a rush of shame. This was, after all, the same Mr Mfusi who'd woven a rattle for Jean-Pierre, who'd told me to go home because it was getting dark and my family would be looking for me. How could I believe he might harm us? Do we trust our fellow humans so little that we toss aside their previous good conduct at the first sign of disagreement?

"I'll give you references," Dad went on, "and I'll help you register with the town council for housing."

"I'm sorry, Mr Mfusi," I said, edging out of Dad's grasp. "We didn't want it to end this way."

Adam Mfusi looked at me with such sadness that I felt a sob gathering at the back of my throat, like when they'd put their hands together to thank me for making them sandwiches.

I held out my hand. "Thank you, Mr Mfusi."

"Miss Fili. And sir." He shook my hand, nodded to Dad and turned away, motioning Kula after him. Peter and Abraham shook our hands, too, and followed Mfusi. Kula stayed where he was, unmoving, legs astride, arms clenched at his sides. When he'd been lying in a heap on the path, he'd called me beautiful. When he was sober, he'd written a note to say he was sorry for making me fall. If he could redirect the anger, the pent-up intensity -

"We can get you treatment," Dad addressed him directly, "There's still a future for you."

The wind died for a moment. I could see rage and confusion jostle in his wild eyes.

"I don't need your help," he hissed, "and these Coloureds," he pointed at Bo with contempt, "they're not as honest as you think!" He turned and glared at me. "Where's my phone? I want it back or you're the thief around here!"

He stormed into the bush in the direction of the road to Franschhoek.

## CHAPTER TWENTY SIX

"I think you'd better tell me everything, Fili," Dad said tightly, as he strode away from the camp, "and you, too, Bo. I don't like to be ignorant of what's happening on our property."

I touched Bo's hand. "I'm sorry, Dad, I didn't mean to keep anything from you."

"We'll discuss it at home."

The sun was beating down on the vines and we hurried into the shade of the verandah. This year the heat had risen early and Philemon was already taking sugar readings. Harvest might come sooner than expected, especially as thunder clouds massed every afternoon, bringing the familiar risk of waiting too long. Shenay brought tea and lemonade and laid it on the low table. She threw an anxious glance at Bo who'd never before been invited to sit with us formally on the verandah. "Is Bo in trouble, sir?"

Bo wiped his hands on his shorts.

"Not at all, Shenay. There's nothing to worry about."

Only, I winced, a wider scandal that could escape from Du Bois to the newspapers and then onwards to the law courts. Hard on the heels of my elevation to Director would come an ugly story of drugs and eviction.

"Now, Fili," Dad folded his arms, "kindly explain."

"It started with Shenay's pumpkin, Dad. It was stolen, and everyone assumed it was the squatters."

"A pumpkin?" Dad looked at me in astonishment. "But -"

"Tannie Ellie put the word out, sir," interrupted Bo. "She said it was the squatters. But I thought maybe someone in the village stole it to put the blame on them so you'd evict them, sir."

Dad frowned and shook his head. "But what has this got to do with drugs?"

"Wait, Dad! Grand-mère said I should speak to you but I wanted to ask Kula first. Especially when the shears and the petrol disappeared. I thought," I swallowed, "that if he confessed and left Du Bois, then maybe you and Mum would allow the others to stay."

Dad leant forward and the sun briefly struck his face. He's aged since Jean-Pierre was born. I don't know why because I imagined a longed-for son would energise a father.

"So you thought you could resolve the thieving yourselves - you and Bo?"

"Yes." I felt my cheeks warm. "But it wasn't Bo, it was just me."

"Ah, Fili," Dad laced his fingers and gave a crooked smile. "You have a clever mind and a tender heart. You wanted to rescue the squatters because we'd rescued you. Life's not so simple, honey. One good turn doesn't necessarily guarantee another. But I still don't understand about the drugs."

I got off my chair and went across to him and knelt at his side.

"A while ago I was on my way to the village to ask Tannie Ellie if she had proof the squatters were stealing. I came across Kula on the path. I ran to fetch Bo."

"He was passed out, sir," said Bo. "Fili and I carried him back to the camp. I knew it was drugs, sir, because his eyes wouldn't focus and he didn't smell of drink. Mfusi had seen him like that before."

"Why didn't you come to me?"

I paused, torn between honesty and tact.

"Mum would have heard. She would've been even more determined to evict them."

"Go on," Dad's face tightened.

"That was the end of it. I didn't see Kula until today -" I stopped. That wasn't quite true, I know. But I wasn't going to confess I'd been in the oak, eavesdropping on the neighbourhood dinner at the same time as Kula had been listening from the garden.

"And the phone he talked about?"

"It was on the ground when we found him. I stuffed it in my pocket and forgot about it." I sneaked a look at Bo but he was studying his hands. "It's in my cupboard. I was going to give it back to him. If he agreed to leave the farm, I wouldn't tell the police about the drugs."

Dad shook his head in exasperation.

"You must let me have it, Fili. I'll return it to his father."

"Yes, Dad. And I'm sorry."

A pair of doves blundered out of my overhanging oak and flew towards the ranks of vines. Dad stood up and walked to the edge of the verandah. Pendulous clouds hung above the valley, painting static shadows on the land below.

"You're a canny negotiator, Fili," Dad turned back with a wry expression, "as I've recently discovered. But some things are too risky to trade over, honey. You need to learn that. And there are times when honesty and openness will take you further."

"There's more -" I went to stand alongside him.

He sighed. "Tell me."

"We think Tannie Ellie's nephew has been supplying Kula with the drugs."

I felt Dad's body tense beside me.

"Blake? The fellow who comes back every so often? How do you know?"

"I called back the number flashing on his phone."

"Dear God!"

"Bo told me not to," I muttered, "and I know it wasn't my business. Bo recognised his voice."

"Fili!" Dad wasn't often angry with me but he was, now. "If the drug dealers know they've been exposed, we could be in danger. All of us, your mother, Jean-Pierre, your grandmother, the villagers -"

"I never spoke!" I cried. "He wouldn't have known who was calling!"

"This must stop," Dad glared at me. "Please! No more private initiatives!"

I nodded and glanced across at Bo, who was wringing his hands.

"Let me think." Dad rubbed his forehead vigorously. "I'll forewarn Philemon now and then we must talk to the villagers tomorrow. It's a Saturday so they'll be home first thing in the morning." Dad ticked off the priorities on his fingers. "We'll increase security on the gates. I'll phone the alarm company and get them to extend their patrols onto Gum Tree Avenue and as far as the house. Don't forget to give me Kula's phone, Fili. And I don't want you wandering around the farm on your own, or into your chardonnay block. Bo, make sure she obeys me -"

"What's to obey?" interrupted Mum gaily, coming onto the verandah.

Bo jumped to his feet and sidled away.

"I've just been to the Newmans," Mum went on, with a triumphant glance at Dad. "Their squatters have left. The arrival of the police convinced them to go. Bo? Are you here to help your mother?"

"No, Mrs Du Bois. Fili and Mr Du Bois invited me for tea."

"Ah," said Mum, throwing her cardigan across the back of a chair. "Well then, will you run in and ask Shenay for two glasses? I think that Mr Du Bois and I will have some wine to celebrate. A sauvignon blanc. Fili, you can watch Jean-Pierre for me."

Bo hurried off, relieved to have escaped further questioning. Dad and I exchanged glances. I knew he wouldn't tell Mum about the drugs. He would keep it a secret so she wouldn't panic or be angry with him. And if the men left peacefully, there would be no reason to tell her even after the event.

Dad knows most of my secrets, now, but not all.

I didn't tell him about the oak, which has always been my vantage point for discovering what I might - or might not - be told about Du Bois and my place in it. There is a further secret I should have revealed, though, and I have double proof of it: Kula is not just a drug addict, he's a dog whisperer. One of those people who can pacify an animal without even trying. An essential talent when you want to eavesdrop without being discovered. Or go somewhere you don't belong, a place that's not meant for you.

\*

"It's done," said Martin over their sauvignon blanc. "I told them to go by the end of next week."

An expression he couldn't decipher flashed across Ray's face for a moment.

"Ray?"

She smiled and raised her glass. "At last! We'll be able to relax from now on!"

He leaned across and reached for her free hand.

"Can we make a fresh start, Ray? Take more care with one another?"

"Of course," she replied lightly.

He looked at her as she removed her hand from his in order to pat her immaculate blond hair.

"And," he went on, "I need you to reach out to Fili. She's feeling vulnerable."

"I don't see why," Ray shrugged and sipped her wine. "She's assured a formal role at Du Bois. What should she be feeling vulnerable about?"

Martin sat back in his chair. Since the announcement of Fili's appointment as a Director of Du Bois, Ray's tone had become increasingly brisk towards her daughter. He sighed. There was no manual to tell parents how to divide love – let alone inheritance - between adopted and biological heirs. Or how to behave when one parent supported the biological over the adopted.

And then there was Ray's mood, lately - whoever she interacted with. As if she couldn't quite make up her mind whether to be loving or cool, generous or self-absorbed; as if the pattern of her life had been fractured and was reluctant to be reassembled.

A pair of weavers chattered in the camphor trees. Pink cirrus clouds streaked the late afternoon sky.

Their marriage had almost foundered once before, until Fili arrived.

"Martin?"

If Ray gave her a chance, Fili might bring them back together again.

"Fili needs your love, Ray. And so do I."

## CHAPTER TWENTY SEVEN

"Fili? Is everything alright?" Petro's voice sounded unexpectedly anxious in my ear.
"Of course," I replied into my mobile phone. "Why shouldn't it be?"
"I heard there was trouble at Du Bois -"
"What sort of trouble?"
"Well, my Dad heard something in town. And then that rude young man – I can't remember his name - was nearly run over on the Franschhoek road this afternoon. Fili -"
I jolted upright at my desk. I'd been trying to finish my homework despite listening for interrupted cries, perhaps a caracal surprised during its hunt, or a nightjar flushed from Gum Tree Avenue. I'm expecting trouble. The curtains ballooned and I grabbed them with my free hand but it was only the breeze, drifting through the open window. Have I made a huge blunder in not handing the phone to my father sooner? Not involving the police over the drugs?
"I have to go, Petro. Everything's fine."
I cut her off, put down the phone and latched my window. All the lights in the house were off but I know my way in the dark. Even with my eyes closed, I can navigate through the lounge and wrap myself in the curtains behind the verandah.
A beam of light showed beneath the closed study door.
"Dad?" I knocked and went in.

"What are you doing up this late, Fili?" Dad looked up from his desk with a frown.

I breathed deeply and tried to slow my heart. "Kula was nearly run over on the Franschhoek road. If he's high on drugs, he could come back here – he's angry after what happened – "

Dad leaned back in his chair and regarded me.

"But he's never been to the house before. And Blaze wouldn't let him get anywhere near us. You're over-reacting," he came around the desk and put his arm about me and kissed my head with fond irritation. "It's been a difficult day for all of us. Go back to bed, now. I promise we'll sort everything out in the morning."

*Kula has been to the house before*, I wanted to say, but the words stuck in my throat.

"We're perfectly safe." Dad put his hands on my shoulders. "We've increased security. Go to bed, honey." He patted me and turned back to his papers.

Why won't Dad recognise danger when it's racing towards him, building like an invisible wave, its crest looming over Du Bois?

Or am I indeed over-reacting?

I didn't go back to bed. I waited in an alcove in the corridor until I heard Dad leave the study and make for the bedroom. The toilet flushed. The taps went on as he brushed his teeth. I edged closer and put my ear to the door and heard the creak of the bedsprings and a brief murmur with Mum. I wish I knew why Mum no longer seems to love Dad like before. I used to think it was my fault but she's sharp with Dad even on matters that have nothing to do with me.

I crept into the lounge and made sure that the two sash windows were closed. The ornate brass hinges on the front door shone through the gloom as I ran my hand along the wood to check that the bolts were thrown and the chain was on. The dining room window was already closed. Dad always latched the study window but I checked all the same. The route around the rear of the house was less familiar in the dark and I began to shiver even though it wasn't cold. Shadowed furniture leaned towards me from unexpected angles, the mirror in the spare bedroom reflected frightened eyes back at me. The bathrooms were next, then the kitchen windows that overlooked the courtyard. Finally, easing open Jean-Pierre's door, I tiptoed towards his bed. He was sleeping on his back with his arms flung out like an angel. I reached around the billowing curtains and fastened his windows.

Then I went back to my bedroom and sat on the sill and stared into the night. There was no moon and the Southern Cross hung on its side, suspended above the mountains amid a slew of stars. Mum's rosebushes sprouted from their beds like sentinels.

Grand-mère!

She loved to sleep with her windows wide open.

I pulled on shoes, grabbed a torch and my phone, unlatched my window and squeezed through, then pressed it closed behind me. It didn't lock from the outside - what if it proved to be the one he might climb through? - but I couldn't risk leaving Grand-mère unprotected. Blaze heard me from his kennel in the courtyard and ran over and pushed his nose into my hand.

"Come, Blaze," I whispered, "let's go."

The vines marched on either side of the path, a ghostly parade beyond the circle of my torchlight. I kept imagining a shape detaching itself from the dark mass and resolving into a man rushing at me. There'd be nothing I could do because Kula was bigger than me, and Blaze might not realise he was a danger until it was too late. Grand-mère kept a spare key hidden beneath a rock near her lavender. The cottage was in darkness but I knocked softly just in case - Grand-mère suffered from insomnia - but there was no response. I let myself in and went around the living area and the bathroom, fastening every window. Her door was ajar and I crept in, hooding my torch. She lay there, beloved Grand-mère, her chest rising and falling in deep sleep, her silver hair spread on the pillow, one arthritic hand clutching the covers. I watched her for a moment and then latched her windows.

There was a pad and pencil next to her telephone, and I wrote a note and propped it beside the kettle so she'd find it in the morning.

*Grand-mère*, I wrote, *I came in while you were sleeping and closed your windows.*

*I was worried about Kula.*

*I love you Grand-mère,*

*F*

Rain hung in the air as we drove up the dirt road towards the village the following morning. The car lurched over the uneven surface, crunching fronds of gum beneath its wheels. Dad and I could have walked but it was too far for Grand-mère, especially if the path turned slippery.

"I've put together an announcement," Dad had said to us in the study after breakfast. "We must clear the air before rumours take hold. Philemon knows, but I told him to say nothing."

Dad must have risen earlier than me because all the windows had been opened by the time I woke.

"Will you tackle Ellie, Martin?" Grand-mère asked. "About the drugs?"

"No," Dad glanced warningly at me. "I'll deal with her privately over that. But perhaps it won't be necessary. When Kula leaves, the problem will disappear. We could inform the police and leave them to deal with it."

"I'll bring the phone with me, Dad, in case Tannie Ellie does cause trouble. We can play the message to expose the drug-dealing, if we need to."

"Very well. I'll return it to Mfusi later. As regards security for ourselves, I've notified the alarm company. They'll patrol Gum Tree Avenue twice daily. I've ordered panic buttons for us in the house, and for you, Mum, in the cottage."

Grand-mère nodded and glanced at me. She'd made no mention of my night-time visit, other than a whispered

"Thank you, child," as she sat down beside me at breakfast.

"What have you told Ray?"

"I've said it's routine, and that we should've done it a while ago."

I stared outside. A pair of red-winged starlings scavenged at the base of the oak, their feet stirring tiny puffs of dust. I hadn't slept when I got back, I'd lain awake waiting for a pair of hands to rattle the windows, or an axe to smash down the kitchen door. Why am I so afraid? Is my uncertain heritage telling me to beware of something my adopted family can't see?

"But shouldn't we tell her, Dad? About the drugs? About Kula?"

Mum would turn on me if she later found out what I'd concealed. The tentative thaw between us would be destroyed in an instant and we'd be back to cold dismissal.

"I think not, honey. Let's try to fix this without worrying your mother. Now we should go."

I watched as he opened his desk drawer to collect his keys.

"One moment, Martin," Grand-mère raised a be-ringed finger. "I agree with Fili, and with her precautions. Given the circumstances, shouldn't Ray be made aware immediately?"

Grand-mère must have had beautiful hands as a young woman, I reflected. Long-fingered and elegant. I don't know why I'm noticing small, trivial things this morning, like Grand-mère's hands or the way Jean-Pierre flaps his hair out of his eyes at breakfast just like Dad does, or the dust the starlings are raising. Or Mum's extra bright laugh now she believes the squatters are leaving.

"Not yet," Dad's voice held a note of irritation, "leave this with me, please. When the time's right, I'll tell her."

I've begun to realise that Dad sometimes underestimates not only the impact of what he chooses to do – the brave courtyard handshake – but also what he chooses to let lie. He's bold enough to take hard decisions about the farm, and he was bold enough to rescue me. But when people around him begin to wrangle or diverge, every bit as dangerous as an outbreak of disease on the vine, he hesitates. Why am I permitted to understand more deeply than my father? Be wise to things he doesn't see?

We jolted along the road. The mountains were hidden, their peaks and saddles occasionally revealing themselves like photographs framed by the shifting cloud. On either side of the car, the vines that had frightened me the previous night were now etched in familiar green rows against the earth. Kula's phone weighed down my pocket, ammunition in case Tannie Ellie was already rousing the village to condemn Dad for employing black men who, according to her, were thieves. Our villagers might be angry at the competition for work but that didn't mean they would support Tannie's wickedness - and the wickedness of her nephew - if it was exposed.

My head began to ache with each thud of the chassis against the ruts in the road.

A small crowd was milling in front of the cottages. "*Ou missus!* Miss Fili!" the children shouted as they ran to surround us. A curtain twitched in Philemon's cottage and he hurried out, followed by Shenay and Bo. After the long and fearful night I longed to dash up to Bo and take his hand to show the watching crowd that he and I were the future, the face of a new Du Bois -

"Is everything alright, sir?" Philemon muttered. "I kept quiet like you asked."

"No trouble," Dad patted him on the shoulder, "but I'm pleased we increased our security."

"*Ou missus* will take some tea inside?" offered Shenay, glancing upwards. "It looks like rain."

"Thank you, Shenay, but I'll stay here."

"*Ou missus* must sit, then!" She bustled inside and collected a stool. Grand-mère gathered her black skirt and lowered herself down. Shenay patted her shoulder.

I stood beside Dad. The villagers would soon have Du Bois to themselves once more, I reflected. Coloured work, Coloured land...

"Gather round!" called Dad, clapping his hands. "Call your families! I have news!"

"*Meneer* Du Bois is here!" the youngsters ran from cottage to cottage, rapping on the doors that were closed. "*Maak gou! Daar's nuus*! Hurry! There's news!"

I glanced over my shoulder, down the path that led past the new vineyards. If someone wanted to reach the village from the squatter camp, that was the most direct route. Or, more cleverly, make a detour behind the cottages to remain hidden but still in earshot -

"Why the rush?" grumbled Tannie Ellie, emerging from her cottage and settling on her step. Mary Sammy flapped a hand at her and drew a passing toddler onto her lap. I studied the gathering crowd. I knew them all: Ellie's extended family, Mary Sammy's brothers and sisters and their children and grandchildren - Bo's cousins - and several families related to the van der Weyden and Newman villagers. They'd seen my arrival as a baby and accepted my conversion into a Du Bois. They were my family, too. But when they screamed *onse werk, onse werk* in the courtyard, I felt a rage that might lash me if I betrayed their trust. And as Dad stood before the growing semicircle, I could tell they were eager to hear his news but also unnerved by the presence of all three of us, especially Grand-mère who didn't often make it as far as the village these days. They began to whisper and point. It must be serious news for the *ou missus* to come.

"I know many of you have been worried about the squatters," Dad began. "You've been worried they'd take your jobs or threaten your families. Please," he raised his voice over the growing mutters, "let me finish. I've come to tell you they will be leaving."

A collective sigh - or was it a hiss? - broke from the ranks in front of us.

"I thanked them for their work," Dad paused, "and told them there are no more jobs on Du Bois."

"*Ja!*" came several shouts.

"About time," cackled Tannie Ellie.

"I hope," Dad went on, "you will allow them to leave with dignity."

There was silence. Folk looked at one another, and then at the ground.

"When will they go, sir?" Philemon asked loudly. Philemon wants everyone to hear that it will be soon. A swift exit will reduce the temptation of a parting skirmish, a rock thrown in defiance.

"By the end of next week. They've agreed to this."

Someone began to clap. Others joined in. Parents released their wriggling children and let them run off. I saw Shenay casting Philemon a triumphant look. There, she seemed to be saying, what did I tell you? We can manage fine on our own.

"One moment," Grand-mère laboured to her feet and the clapping died away. Dad glanced at her in surprise. "I know this has been hard, seeing strangers on Du Bois land, doing work you thought was yours." They darted looks at one another. "But remember," Grand-mère reached across to rest a hand on my shoulder, "we've learnt to value newcomers before. It may happen again one day. Will we be ready next time?"

There was silence.

"Grand-mère's right," I declared, stepping out in front of her and Dad.

There was a notable intake of breath.

"Mum and Dad made me a Du Bois and I'll always be thankful they saved me. I'll work every day for you and for the farm as long as I live." I stopped and took a breath. "But we must also help those who aren't as lucky as me. Or you."

They stared at me as I gestured to the neat, colourful cottages where they lived at minimal rent, the field where they played football, the row of trees we'd planted to give privacy and shade, and - invisible but most valuable - the interest in the farm that I'd learnt is awarded to the head of each senior family.

Was I foolish to speak out? Had I gone too far?

Bo locked eyes with me and gave a tiny nod.

"We won't allow squatting in future," Dad put in smoothly, coming to stand beside me, "but we need the right to offer temporary work from time to time to outsiders without upsetting what we've built together at Du Bois."

"Are our jobs safe, sir?" Mary Sammy's brother spoke up from the back.

"Yes," Dad nodded. "They are."

Grand-mère, leaning on her stick at Dad's side, raised a cautionary finger. "But it depends on you, my friends. If you go on working as well as you've always done, we shall go forward together happily. If there's trouble or laziness or drugs," she allowed her gaze to rest for a moment on Tannie Ellie, "then we can't protect your jobs."

Philemon gaped at us from his position in the centre of the crowd. Dad had chosen not to tell him about the drugs. And Bo had never revealed Kula's condition that day on the path. As far as Philemon was concerned, the squatters' accelerated departure was by mutual agreement.

"No-one does drugs here, *ou missus!*" Tannie Ellie called in mock outrage. "We drink a little, *ja,*" she nodded at the titter, "but who says we do drugs?"

I felt the crowd stiffen. Did they know what Blake was doing and chose to look the other way? Grand-mère lifted her hands as if to indicate she had no idea, and that her words were simply a warning. My heart began to thunder, Kula's phone bulged in my pocket. I could pull it out and fire it up and broadcast to the throng the sound of her nephew on the sell -

"Discretion, *chérie*," Grand-mère murmured to me. "Save your evidence."

I met Tannie Ellie's eyes. She knew that we knew.

Just then, a growling came from the side of the cottages and I whipped around but it was only a pair of dogs starting a fight. Bo and one of his cousins ran to separate them. The dogs were smacked with rolled up newspapers and ran off, squealing. A group of teenagers, among them Tannie's short-skirted granddaughters, turned away, bored that Dad's news was not something more lively like a party or a celebration.

"One more thing," Dad clapped his hands for their attention. "I've seen your children grow up and take their place on the farm. And we've helped those who wanted to train for other work."

It was true. Du Bois had paid for college for the brightest youngsters.

"For those who remain, our new vineyards will be ready to plant next year. That will bring more work for you and your families. We'll be relying on you to make them a success. For all of us!"

Mary Sammy began to clap once more and the rest joined in with whoops and shouts of relief.

They would reap the benefits of the land cleared by the outsiders. Perhaps this was justice after all. "Thank you, sir!"

"Thank you *ou missus*, Miss Fili!"

The Sammys came forward to shake our hands, and then the lesser aunts and uncles and cousins and the whole expansive family that made up our village. There were some tears and much laughter and I wondered how we could ever have doubted each other after so many years of working together. No doubt they'd speculate over Grand-mère's words later, and they'd gossip about me, too, but for now it was enough to rejoice that the competition for jobs was about to disappear along with the corrugated iron shacks on our fence.

"Will you take some tea now, sir? *Ou missus*? Miss Fili?" asked Shenay, blinking back a tear.

"That would be lovely," Grand-mère prepared to hoist herself up. I took her arm.

Shenay beamed and led the way.

Grand-mère leaned against me for a moment and I smelt her lavender perfume. She would surely have preferred to go home and rest but Grand-mère understands that taking tea is another way of paying respect, like offering roses after the harvest; an act worth more to the villagers than they will put into words. I glanced over the crowd, now dispersing cheerfully. Then I turned and stared down the path. It was empty.

## CHAPTER TWENTY EIGHT

"Fili," murmured Dad later, as the tea cups were being gathered up, "I'm going to drive your grandmother home and stay with her a while. Will you walk back with Bo?"

"Yes, of course," I glanced across the room to where Bo was entertaining a young Sammy cousin.

"Wonderful tea, Shenay," Dad stood up, "especially your shortbread. But we must get back."

"I know, sir," nodded Shenay with a glance at Grand-mère. "The *ou missus* needs her rest."

Grand-mère hobbled over to shake Philemon's hand and then embraced Shenay by the front door. "Thank you, Shenay dear. You and Philemon are our most loyal partners."

"Always, Ma'am."

I watched from the doorway as Dad led Grand-mère to the car. He helped her in, fastened her seatbelt and waved to me. They jolted down the road. I looked back at the crowded sitting room. It seemed that the entire village had stopped by for the chance to pay their respects to Grand-mère in person. But now that she and Dad had left, they were about to get started on the consequences of our visit. No-one would notice if I slipped away.

The sun was burning through the morning dampness as I set off. The mountains, hidden earlier, carved an unbroken line against a sky streaked with high level cirrus. A light breeze rustled the fynbos at the side of the path and shivered the leaves of the poplars on the ridge. I stopped for a moment. This was where I'd found Kula.

I pulled his phone out of my pocket.

I could drop it here, in the undergrowth, and leave it to be buried by the leaves and debris that mark each passing season. The rain and the alternating heat and cold would surely seep beneath its casing, destroying the battery, but would it also wipe out the record of whose phone it was and erase the evidence of its last call? That might be the best outcome… but I'd promised Dad to give it to him so he could return it to Kula's father.

The farm dam glinted in the distance.

A black-and-white butcher bird regarded me from the top of a nearby pincushion protea.

I thrust the phone back into my pocket and walked on.

Dad would spend time with Grand-mère before coming home and Jean-Pierre had gone to a birthday sleepover, so Mum and I would be alone for a while. I glanced at my watch. It was quarter past ten. I could tell her what had happened in the village. I could even tell her my part and perhaps she would understand that I only ever wanted the best for everybody - Du Bois, our villagers, the poor men on our fence. I picked up my pace. That was what I'd do. I'd speak to Mum privately and try to rekindle the warmth, especially since it would no longer be strained by events on our boundary.

I began to run, testing the ankle that had given way when I ran from Kula at the dam. The ground felt uneven beneath my feet. I could sense the earth forever pushing back, heaving the beaten surface of the path into ruts, allowing the rain to carve channels, defying our attempts to keep it smooth. A movement to the left caught my eye. I stopped and stared. Maybe a small buck, a duiker, flushed from the bush by the vibrations of my running feet? I listened for the clip of hooves, the thrash of branches whipped aside. But there was just the beating of my heart and the gentle sigh of the breeze. I ran on. Our house appeared, crouched beneath the expansive branches of my lookout oak.

"Mum!" I shouted. "Mum!"

I pushed open the kitchen door and ran through the house.

Mum doesn't need me, I once confessed to Petro. I'm surplus. You don't know what it's like.

So what! she'd responded with a shrug. You'll still be a Du Bois, wherever you go.

"Mum?"

Maybe she was in the bathroom? I knocked on the door but there was no reply. She wasn't in the bedroom either. A vase of scarlet roses, drooping slightly, sat on the dressing table in a shaft of sunlight. Of course! Mum would be outside, picking fresh.

I hurried through the lounge. The front door was open, hooked back against the wall.

"Mum!" I ran into the rose garden. "Everything's going to be fine!"

The familiar scent of Fragrant Cloud, Peace and Just Joey hung on the air like a promise. The roses had been good this year; Mum said it was due to the combination of a mild spring followed by steady but not searing heat. I could also tell her about Bo. Would she accept that I was allowed to love a boy from the village?

But there was no sign of her in the garden. And no sign of Blaze.

I ran round the side of the house and lifted the garage door. The family car was there. Maybe she'd gone for a walk to the dam? I dashed round the front of the house again and along the path that skirted my chardonnay block where the grapes hung plump in expectation of harvest. The sun was nearing its zenith and I could feel it burning the top of my head. Mum rarely went to the dam or into the mountains, she preferred her nature tamed rather than wild.

So maybe the vineyards.

In the distance I heard a yelp. Not one of our circling jackal buzzards, but a dog's yelp.

Or was it a howl, a low keening?

I ran into the vines.

"Mum!" I shouted. "Blaze!"

When you inspect at walking pace you don't appreciate that vines are small trees. Soft leaves and plush grapes conceal hard branches. As the rows whipped past, I felt the sting of a cut on my arm. A dark shape jumped at me, nearly knocking me over.

"Blaze!" I buried my face in his neck. "Where's Mum? Take me to Mum!"

He wagged his tail and leapt up about me and then raced back the way he'd come.

Mum was lying on her side in the narrow shade cast by an overhanging vine.

"Mum?" I crouched down.

She was asleep. But her position seemed odd, her legs crumpled as if she'd been walking and then collapsed. Perhaps she felt tired because of the heat and decided to lie down? Blaze whined and licked her arm but she didn't stir. Poor Mum, I'd stay here until she woke. There was a lock of blond hair falling over the side of her face and I lifted it away gently.

A trickle of blood had seeped below her ear.

My hands began to shake. I touched her cheek, moved her head towards me.

Blood stained my fingers.

Blaze whined and nosed against my arm.

"No, Blaze!"

I grabbed her wrist and felt for a pulse.

There was no pulse, not even a flutter beneath her skin.

I scrabbled in my jeans pocket for Kula's phone, flicked on the power. I'd charged it last night, in advance of our visit to the village. The screen lit up. My fingers struggled to hit the emergency numbers. Mum's face stared up at me, unmarked but for the small, rust-red meander below her ear.

"Hello? Please help! I need an ambulance - I think my mother's dying -"

The operator was speaking slowly as she asked me my name and where I lived. A grasshopper whirred down and perched on Mum's limp arm. I tried to flick it off but my movements were too shaky and I didn't want to hurt her -

"You must hurry," I screamed into the phone. "I've told you where I am! Du Bois Vineyards!"

I flung down the phone, put my ear to her mouth but there was no sound, no faint wisp of breath. I lifted her head back, checked her mouth was clear of obstructions, then pressed both hands against her chest.

One, two, three, four, up to thirty compressions.

Stop, pinch her nose, breathe into her mouth.

One, two, three, four, up to thirty.

A column of ants was crawling over her ankle.

Should I run up to Grand-mère's and fetch Dad? But I couldn't go, not when there might be a chance to save her. And I was the only one who knew where she was.

The sun is shifting.

How long have I been here?

I'm crouched over Mum, pumping her chest, listening for her to come back to life. But there is nothing. Just a random whine from Blaze and Mum's inertness beneath my hands. The blood from her neck has stained her white dress like the single crushed petal of a Fragrant Cloud rose.

I struggle to my feet.

There's a howl in my ears, like when a jet passes low overhead. But it wasn't a plane, it was me. I was standing in the middle of the vineyard with the musky,

sweet smell of grapes around me and the soft body of my mother at my feet and I was screaming.
"Mum! Mum! Mum!"
Over and over until the words merged into a bombardment that will never leave me.

## CHAPTER TWENTY NINE

The ambulance had no trouble finding where we were. I heard, afterwards, that the paramedics muttered amongst themselves that my screams could have been heard as far away as Franschhoek; and that they knew something suspicious was going on when they found a girl with blood on her hands standing over a dead woman.

Dad arrived at the same time as the ambulance.

He must have heard the siren on Du Bois land and then the shouts of the ambulance men directing their vehicle as close as possible to the vineyard. I won't ever forget his face as he looked down at Mum and then across at me. Dad has only ever shown me love and occasional exasperation but now his face seemed to have been stripped and left raw with horror. The sadness would come later, but it is the horror that I remember. Not shared, but directed at me.

The paramedics were thorough. They listened to Mum's heart and lungs, they tried to shock her heart into beating and all the while the sun moved across the sky and my screams retreated inside my head, battering against my skull.

The police arrived and took photographs.

Mum's temperature was recorded, and the temperature of the air sighing above her crumpled body. Then the senior man draped a sheet they'd brought out of the ambulance over her, covering her lovely face and the streak of blood below her ear. They lifted her on to a stretcher - "Careful," I cried, and Dad looked at me again with that expression of horror - and loaded her into the ambulance and took her away. Dad rode in the ambulance with her.

The last I saw of Mum was her foot in a blue sandal, dangling off the edge of the stretcher.

I don't remember a lot of what happened after that.

I watched the police as they continued to gather evidence at the scene, and scraped up samples of soil where Mum's blood might have dripped onto the ground.

They examined my hands and wrote in their notebooks.

They asked about the small cut on my arm and I told them it was from the vines.

"How did she die?" I asked, dully, from where I was sitting on the ground. I could see the depression in the soil where she'd lain; the long groove from her legs, the knuckles of her outflung hand, the deeper concavity of her head.

"Don't you know?" asked one of the policemen. "Where were you when she died?"

Grand-mère was waiting for me at home when the police brought me back. She embraced me and put her arm through mine and supported me through the front door. Our doctor was there and he gave me a tablet to drink and then a wide-eyed Shenay was washing the dry blood off my hands and getting me into my pyjamas. The police took away my clothes, my jeans, the shirt I was wearing.

"Close the windows," I said before the heaviness took over. "Shutters, too."

"Hush," whispered Grand-mère, stroking my clean hands. "Sleep now, *chérie*."

I don't know how long I slept. Perhaps I missed a whole day? When I woke it was early morning and for a moment I wondered if today was the day when Dad and Grand-mère and I were going to the village to announce that the squatters were leaving.

I looked around my room. The curtains were shifting gently in the breeze coming through the open window. I felt a familiar tightening in my stomach. No-one had believed me about the danger. No-one had closed the windows...

A light snoring was coming from the chair in the corner where Grand-mère slept, her hair tied into a scarf and her feet resting on a cushion from the lounge. Dear Grand-mère had watched over me, when all she probably wanted to do was retreat to her cottage to mourn in private.

Mourn...

I swung my legs out of bed. I had to see Dad.

I had to tell him it wasn't me, I had nothing to do with it, I don't know how Mum died -

I flung a gown over my pyjamas and crept out.

He wasn't in his bedroom. I found him on the verandah, wrapped up against the morning chill in a blanket. He heard me and turned around. His face was grey and he stared at me as if I was a stranger. I ran and flung myself at his feet.

"I came home and Mum wasn't here!" Tears, missing before, began to wash down my face. "I searched the house, I checked the garage and then I ran into the vines. Blaze found me and took me to her." I gripped my hands together. "At first I thought she was asleep! I didn't see the blood. I didn't notice she wasn't breathing."

Dad was staring at me intently. Then he reached out a hand and put it on my head. He didn't stroke my hair like he usually did, he just rested his hand on my head as if he had no energy for anything more. "It's alright, Fili. We'll go to the police station. You can tell them what you've told me."

I later learned that Dad was being kind. He didn't tell me that the police had insisted on my presence at the police station, instead he gave me the impression that we would go there of our own accord.

It was a quiet breakfast.

Grand-mère tried to make conversation, Dad said nothing.

The phone rang often. He answered it the first time and then unplugged it.

"The newspapers," he said shortly.

"Put on your school uniform, Fili," Grand-mère remarked as we got up from the table.

"I'm going to school?"

"No," she glanced at Dad, "but it will be a sensible outfit for you to wear."

The police station lay down a side road on the outskirts of town. Dad and I drove there in silence. Grand-mère had wanted to come but Dad said she should stay for when Jean-Pierre was brought home. There was no-one in attendance at the charge desk when we arrived, and the waiting room was empty. A burly policeman appeared and motioned for us to sit down, and then wandered off.

Dad's large hands fidgeted in his lap.

According to my watch it took twenty minutes for someone to emerge from the interior offices.

"How old are you, Miss Du Bois?" A tall officer came to my side, holding a clipboard.

"I'm eighteen," I replied.

He wrote on the clipboard and then addressed Dad.

"Do you want a lawyer present, sir?"

Dad didn't reply.

"Sir? Do you want a lawyer present for your daughter?"

"Dad?" I touched his restless hands and he looked at me. His eyes were wounded, now, rather than horror-stricken.

"Yes," he roused himself. "Yes, there must be a lawyer for Fili."

He felt in his pocket and took out his mobile phone. His fingers were clumsy, like mine had been when I struggled to dial for the ambulance. But mine were now, strangely, steady. I gently took the phone out of his hands and scrolled through his contacts.

"Tate and Partners," said a female voice at the other end.

"This is Fili Du Bois." I heard an intake of breath and hurried on in case the woman might want nothing to do with me and put down the phone. "My father would like to speak to Mr Tate."

I handed the phone back to Dad.

The policeman was watching me with interest. A younger man in plain clothes came into the waiting room. He had a holstered revolver on his hip. He inclined his head towards me and lifted an eyebrow at the man with the clipboard, who nodded.

"I need to you to come to the station, Ben," said Dad. "Fili is about to be questioned."

There was a pause while Mr Tate replied. Dad lifted a hand and passed it through his hair.

"Yes, of course. Whatever you require."

We waited.

The heat began to build up.

I took off my blazer and folded it on my lap. My school badge winked up at me. *Veritas et Justitia*. Truth and Justice.

They brought us water in paper cups.

After a while the plain clothes man sat down next to Dad.

"Your daughter is eighteen so she'll be questioned alone. With the lawyer present, of course. We need to take a statement from you as well. My men will visit the farm to question all the other parties to ascertain their whereabouts at the time of the -" he hesitated - "the tragedy."

"You think I hurt her?" I blurted out.

I felt Dad's body tremble.

The policeman leaned forward and looked at me.

"Ma'am we rule nothing and no-one out."

I could see they were wondering. I could see it in their eyes, in the eyes of each one of them. There were no witnesses and, for all the distress of my emergency call, I was found with blood on my hands. And, although they wouldn't say it out loud, they must know I was adopted. Within that gap might lie a motive for murder?

I stared up at the ceiling. A large spider was spinning its web across the corner. I watched as it detached itself and began to descend on a single thread towards the floor. I waited for the fragile silk to break -

"Miss Du Bois? Fili?"

Mr Tate was crouching in front of me. His face was red and he was breathing fast and clutching a briefcase. He must have rushed from a previous meeting. "I'm your lawyer, Fili. I'll be with you during questioning."

He straightened up and addressed the policemen. "I'd like to confer with my client before we begin. Do you have a private room where we can speak?"

They led us to a meeting room with plastic chairs and a stained table.

"I didn't do anything, Mr Tate, I didn't hurt my mother."

"Of course not," he said, putting on his glasses and taking a yellow pad out of his briefcase.

I stared at him. "But how can you know? I haven't told you what happened."

He took off his glasses and gave me a penetrating look.

"I am very sorry for your loss, Fili. We don't yet know how your mother died. In all likelihood it was from natural causes. But if there was foul play, my job is to prove you are innocent of involvement."

"But will you still defend me even if you don't believe what I tell you?"

Can I trust someone who may or may not believe me?

I need Grand-mère. I need her wisdom -

"I don't see that as an issue," he replied, uncapping his pen and looking down at his pad. "You've told me you're innocent and we will have no certainty about your mother's death until an autopsy is completed. Now, shall we start? I need to know exactly what happened on Saturday morning."

\*

Martin watched the closed door. He realised he was holding his breath and forced himself to exhale.

He would have liked to speak to Ben Tate first, but that might be considered improper.

And what would he have said?

That Fili could not possibly have killed Ray - and yet was he, Martin, certain about that?

Just recently, Fili had proved herself to be... not exactly deceitful... but worryingly secretive.

He though he knew her, this beloved child that he and Ray had rescued and nurtured as their own.
Now he was not so sure.

## CHAPTER THIRTY

The squatter camp was looking untidy when the police arrived. Only one shack remained standing, the others had been dismantled and most of the materials taken away. The hose pipe that had dangled over the bearded protea was gone. The clearing in front of the shacks that had always been swept clean – apart from the large stone - was now scattered with fallen leaves and gum fronds.
Adam Mfusi pushed open the flap of his shack and watched. The policeman in charge - presumably they'd come as a group in case there was trouble - poked a boot at the ashes of a recent cooking fire.
It wouldn't help to pretend he wasn't there.
"Can I help you?"
The men turned and hurried over. They were all black. That, at least, was something.
"What is your name?"
"Adam Mfusi."
"Where are the rest?" the man motioned at where the other shacks must have stood.
"They have left, sir. We were asked to leave by Mr Du Bois. They went before me."
The policeman got out his notebook.
"I need the names of everyone who lived in this settlement."
Mfusi regarded the officer carefully. There was no point in lying. They'd find out, anyway, from the farm. He had

insisted the others go as soon as he heard the ambulance. At the time, he didn't know what it meant but it was sure to be trouble. It was only later, when he rushed into Franschhoek looking for Kula, that he heard. He'd only ever seen Mrs Du Bois close-up once, that first day in the courtyard when she offered sandwiches. She seemed a nice woman, very pretty, very nervous, but kind. She'd written him a note, delivered by her husband, thanking him for the rattle for their newborn child. Later, Kula told him she hated the camp and wanted them out.

"My son, Kula, lived here. Also Peter Choba and Abraham Phillips."

Go, he'd said to Peter and Abraham. There may be questions. The best he could hope for was that they were already far away.

And Kula? His boy, so troubled, so unpredictable. If only his wife had lived -

"Why were you asked to leave?"

Mfusi hesitated. The less he said, the better.

"There was no more work for us here, sir."

The policeman stared at him. If they had checked, they would already know he and the others had been here for several years. If he, Adam, was a policeman, he would wonder why the work had come to an end so suddenly. And then been followed by -

"Do you know that there was a death on this farm on Saturday," the policeman asked.

"Yes, I heard so."

"Where were you on Saturday morning, Mr Mfusi?"

The other policemen were inside his shack, now, but there was nothing to see. Just his few possessions in a hessian sack, a pot and pan and a spoon and knife, a blanket, a bag of mealie meal.

"I was here, sir, helping to take down the shacks."

"Were the others with you?"

"Yes."

"Your son as well?"

"No. Kula went into Franschhoek the day before and I haven't seen him since."

"So who took down his shack?" this came from the officer who'd been poking around.

"I did."

"Where is the shack material, then?"

"I gave it to Peter and Abraham."

"So your son was not going to be squatting in the future? Where was he going to live?"

They were all gathered about him now, black men like him but with more learning than he had achieved with his Grade Four. They would have finished school and maybe gone to college.

"I don't know, sir. My son had friends in Franschhoek."

They were looking at him with expressions of pity mixed with suspicion. They were thinking that he wouldn't have stayed around if he'd been a murderer, so it must be the others.

"Do you know where we can find Choba and Phillips?"

"No, sir. Maybe Johannesburg. They wanted to find work."

It was a lie. Never again, they'd all agreed between *shosholozas* in the vineyard, even if there was plentiful work. A man could die in the mines like a twig snapped underfoot.

"How old is your son?"

"He is twenty two."

"We want to question him," the senior man said, closing his notebook. "When you see him, tell him he must report to the police station in Franschhoek straightaway. Do you understand? This is very important."

"Yes, sir."

"And when will you leave?"

"By the end of the week. Mr Du Bois told us we had 'til then."

The man tucked his pen in his top pocket. "You must report to the police station before you go."

"I will, sir."

They turned away. Amazingly, they turned away without pressing any harder, and without searching any further, perhaps noticing the three separate, small depressions on the edge of the clearing that marked the spots where he'd buried the dynamite, cap and fuse -

"Where will you go?" asked one of the younger officers hanging back, a thin fellow who hadn't said anything so far.

"I don't know. I have to go where there is work."

The youngster nodded and left, picking his way across the clearing.

Adam Mfusi watched them leave and listened for their van to start up. First the doors slammed, then the engine roared into life. The sound faded as they drove down Gum Tree Avenue.

Why hadn't they asked about the confrontation on Friday afternoon? Or the drugs?

Didn't they know? Hadn't Mr Du Bois or Miss Fili told them?

Or maybe pretty Mrs Du Bois had died from an illness that had taken her life at the very moment she happened to be walking among the vines. And yet -

He trudged back to his shack. He was shocked for the Du Bois family, especially for Miss Fili. She didn't deserve to lose a second mother. But he must be vigilant. He couldn't leave just yet. There might still be trouble ahead because he was fairly sure Kula had returned in the early hours of Saturday. He, Mfusi, hadn't actually seen him but he'd woken in the night to hear rummaging and cursing in the shack alongside. Then silence. And in the morning, an empty shack.

With Kula, it was often best to pretend to be deaf.

## CHAPTER THIRTY ONE

"Miss Du Bois, Mr Tate, I am Captain Dlamini. I'm sorry for your loss, Miss Du Bois."

He got up and shook our hands and motioned us to sit across the table from him where two chairs had been placed side by side.

"Thank you, sir."

*Be strong*, I reminded myself, *be the best vintage you can be.*

"I will be questioning you this morning," he said, opening a notebook. "Please answer honestly and clearly and tell me if there is anything you don't understand."

I could see that the left-hand page of his book was covered with writing, the right-hand page was blank. Perhaps he'd written down the questions he planned to ask with space across from them for nuances that couldn't be captured by the tape recorder he'd just switched on.

*Miss Du Bois's answer was too quick, too rehearsed.*

*She met my eyes.*

*She didn't meet my eyes...*

"Sir, how did my mother die?"

I needed to know as soon as they knew, but I also wanted my question to be recorded.

The policeman glanced at Mr Tate and then at me. He was a large man and barely fitted on the plastic chair behind the table.

"We're waiting for the autopsy, Ma'am. That will tell us."

I nodded and blinked back tears.

He looked at me kindly. "I know this is hard for you, but please will you describe the events of Saturday morning."

Give the facts, Mr Tate had said. No more, no less. Speak calmly and clearly.

"After breakfast I drove with my grandmother and Dad up to our Coloured village. My father told the villagers that the squatters were leaving by the end of the week. Everyone clapped. Then we had tea together. Dad drove Grand-mère home at about ten o'clock and I walked back."

"On your own?"

"Yes."

At my side, Mr Tate was scribbling nonstop.

"How do you know the time?"

"Because I looked at my watch, sir, when I left. It was quarter past ten and I thought I'd have some time with Mum at home before Dad got back."

He made a note in his book. *Alibi? Depends on whether time of death can be narrowed down.*

"The Coloureds were pleased that the squatters were going?"

"Yes. They'd been worried about their jobs."

Mr Tate leaned towards me and whispered in my ear. "Your father will deal with this."

"Were you sorry to see them go?"

I hesitated, and borrowed Grand-mère's words. "I knew they couldn't squat forever. They needed proper houses. But I felt sorry for them."

"Were they unhappy to be leaving?"

"Surely this is speculative?" Mr Tate put in. "Miss Du Bois can't be expected to know how they felt."

"I would say that she can, sir. And if the squatters didn't want to leave it could be a motive to hurt the farm, or a member of the Du Bois family."

I stared at the Captain. How much did he know? Could he already have visited the camp?

"Have you spoken to the squatters?" I hedged.

He smiled. "Why were you sorry for them, Ma'am?"

I glanced away from him. The floor was tiled with beige vinyl squares that had started to lose their adhesive. They were curling up where they met the side walls.

"Why were you sorry for them, Miss Du Bois?"

"Because they had nothing, sir!" I heard my voice rise. "Because they live in shacks that leak and I live in a house with a roof, with food on the table every day!" I found my fingers tightening into fists and tried to calm myself. "I've been lucky. They haven't."

Mr Tate put his hand on my shoulder. I reached for the plastic cup of water. The policemen was staring at me and I thought I detected a flash of respect.

"Let us continue. Did you see anyone on your walk home?"

"No -"

"No-one? Nothing suspicious at all? I want you to think very carefully."

Perhaps a duiker skipping through the bush, so well camouflaged I never actually saw him...

"Nothing."

I waited for him to write a note but he didn't. Maybe he knows I'm watching. Maybe he'll add to his notes afterwards. *She did see something. Or someone.*

"Your mother was at home when you returned?"

"No," I shook my head. "I looked for her in the house, I checked the garage in case she'd gone out but she hadn't because the car was still there."

"You have a dog, is that correct? Was the dog there?"

"No, Blaze was gone as well. So I thought Mum had taken him for a walk."

The Captain leaned back in his chair and folded his arms.

"Was this a regular event? Your mother going out for a walk with the dog?"

I glanced at Mr Tate. It wasn't a regular event. Mum never went out with Blaze on her own. But if I said so, would I be giving away information that could be used against me?

"Just answer the question as best you can, Fili," Mr Tate said.

"Mum never went out alone with Blaze. Never."

*So why did you, Mum?*

*Or did Blaze stay behind and only run to find you later? Did he hear you cry out?*

The Captain wrote down several sentences. Then he put down his pen.

"Miss Du Bois, will you please describe your relationship with your mother."

*My mother left me in a ditch, sir, when I was an infant so there was no relationship at all.*

"I love - I loved - my mother."

"Your adoptive mother?"

"Yes."

"And what about your real mother?"

I stared past his head towards a high window through which poked a tiny rectangle of sky. I suppose interview rooms are designed so there's nowhere interesting to look, nowhere to gain respite.

"I don't remember my real mother, sir. I don't know if I loved her or not."

There was a beat of silence.

"Is this relevant?" Mr Tate intervened gently. "That line of questioning has no bearing on the case."

The Captain looked down at his notebook.

"We have reason to believe there was tension between you and your adoptive mother."

I breathed in and out. Mum's heart used to throb when she was afraid.

"Yes. Mum sometimes didn't understand what it was like to be me."

"What do you mean Miss Du Bois?"

A cloud sailed across the tiny window.

"It was fine when I was little. But when I grew up, I started to believe in things that she didn't,"

I choked and swallowed, "and I felt sorry for the kind of people she didn't like."

"Did you father understand you better?"

"Oh, yes," I lifted my chin and nodded. "Dad loves me for who I am."

*Please, Dad! Don't regret me!*

There was a knock on the door and one of the other policemen poked his head in. "Sir?"

The officer turned off the tape recorder, picked up his notebook, excused himself and left the room.

I sank back in my chair and closed my eyes. Blaze was whining. Mum's crumpled body lay before me, the telltale trickle of blood tracing a path from her ear to her neck.

"You're doing well, Fili."

"What is well, Mr Tate?" I opened my eyes and took in the drab room. "Someone might have killed Mum. Maybe they suspect it's me."

"That is premature." He tapped his pad. "Firstly, they may ascertain that your mother died of natural causes. A heart attack. A stroke. Secondly, depending on the time of death, looking at your watch will have given you an alibi if need be. Witnesses from the village will also swear to the time."

But some of the villagers remain suspicious of me, Mr Tate, I wanted to say.

They may dispute my version.

If they do, then I have no choice but to implicate them - *an inside job, a village thief.* Everything will have to come out. The thefts. The drugs. My suspicion that the squatters were being framed for crimes they didn't commit. And what of the drug-addicted Kula?

The sky beyond the window was white with the midday heat.

"If Mum didn't die naturally, Mr Tate, and they don't find the killer, then people will always look at me and wonder."

They will see my surface, not my soul.

They will note the appearance of the wine, not the *terroir* that forged it.

I'll be condemned as surely as if I was in a prison cell.

## CHAPTER THIRTY TWO

In an interview room across the corridor, Martin Du Bois was being questioned at the same time as his daughter.
"Please sit down, Mr Du Bois. My condolences, sir, on your loss. I realise this will be hard for you."
"Thank you, officer."
"Sir, did you see any strangers on the farm from Friday evening through to Saturday morning?"
"No." Martin ran a hand through his hair. "I would have investigated if I had. And our dog would have barked, or the alarm would have gone off in the cellar if there was a burglary."
"There was nothing untoward," the policeman pressed, "nothing that made you suspicious?"
"No." He hesitated. "But earlier, I had told the squatters that they had to leave."
"This was the day before the death of Mrs Du Bois?"
"Yes."
"Were they angry?"
"It was more a case of disappointment." Martin stopped for a moment and chose his words. "Both sides had benefitted from the arrangement, but it was time for them to move on. I believe they realised that."
"Do you think any of the men would have hurt you or your family because they had to leave?"
"There was a younger man, Kula Mfusi. He was often angry but I never thought he was violent. Now please,"

Martin cleared his throat, "when will we know how my wife died?"

"Soon, sir. Could you describe your adopted daughter's relationship with your wife."

Martin gathered himself. Of course. They would have to ask him about that.

"Fili loved her," he replied hoarsely. "But it's no secret that Ray was very involved with our son, Jean-Pierre. I tried to make up for that but I think Fili sometimes felt left aside."

"Did your daughter and her mother argue often?"

"Only the way most teenagers argue with their parents." He gave a sad smile. "Fili is an idealist. She felt it was her duty to help the men squatting on our land whereas Ray wanted them removed."

"So there was friction between them?"

"Only for a while. The problem is over now. The men agreed to leave, before -"

The detective wrote in his notebook and then looked up. "I'm sorry, sir, I realise this is distressing."

Martin nodded and pressed his fingers briefly against his eyes.

"You said the squatters expressed disappointment when they were told to leave. Did the meeting became confrontational?"

"It wasn't a confrontation, officer, it was a conversation between the parties. We asked them to leave by the end of the week and they agreed."

"Was your wife aware of this development?"

"Yes, she was. She was relieved they were going."

"They'd been on your property for some time, sir. Why the rush to make them leave so soon?"

"What are you getting at?"

"I am trying to find out, sir, if these men felt threatened in any way by yourself and if so, whether one of them might have decided to attack your wife."

Martin stared at the officer. He was white whereas the other policemen on the case were black.

"They were decent men. The son was a drug addict but I'd only recently learnt of that from my daughter. In the light of Fili's information, we increased our security around the farm."

The officer sat back in his chair and raised his eyebrows. "Was your wife aware of that? Of the drugs?"

"No, I didn't want to worry her. They'd be gone soon enough."

The officer frowned and tapped his pen on the desk.

"Was the informal settlement a source of tension between you and your wife?"

"Is that relevant?"

"Yes, sir. I'm trying to find out if the discord over the squatters had any bearing on the tragic death of Mrs Du Bois."

"I sincerely hope not." Martin wiped a hand across his forehead. "Officer, we don't yet know how my wife died. Why is there a need to try and unearth a motive before we know the facts?"

*

Dad was waiting for me when they allowed Mr Tate and I to leave. "Fili -"

I reached up and kissed his cheek and squeezed his hand.

*You're my father. Always.*

"Ben?" Dad addressed the lawyer. "How was it?"

"Fili did well," Mr Tate glanced at me, "but we'll only know where we stand after the autopsy results are released."

"Thank you, Ben. I'm most grateful."

Mr Tate motioned to the front door and we followed him out. He stopped by his car and jiggled his keys in his hand. "I believe Fili played no part in Ray's death, Martin," he said quietly.

Dad looked down, his throat working.

"Stand together," Mr Tate put a hand on Dad's shoulder. "Du Bois will overcome this."

It was a silent journey home. I stared at every familiar landmark with wondering eyes. Would they still be mine at the end of this? Overhanging gum trees with their wispy fronds, pied kingfishers beating their catch by the dam, infant buds sprouting on the vine... even the endless sky, liberated from the small window through which I'd watched it all morning.

"I should have listened to Ray," Dad muttered finally, as we parked. "She was right all along. I should never have let them stay. She said I swapped our safety for a new vineyard -"

I stared across at him. His huge hands seemed helpless in their fidgeting on the steering wheel.

"You did it for the right reasons, Dad. We wanted to give them a chance. You were being fair."

"But what if I was wrong? Your grandmother too? What if one of them did it?"

"The squatters?"

"Yes," Dad nodded. "Maybe the world hasn't changed like we hoped. I thought we were doing the right thing by making Du Bois more representative. Giving those men a chance."

Fallen oak leaves eddied across the drive in a short-lived whirlwind.

"We looked too far forward, too soon -" his voice died away.

"Daddy! Fili!"

It was Jean-Pierre, banging on the side of the car with his hands. I caught a glimpse of Shenay, rushing towards us from the kitchen. I opened the door and Jean-Pierre flung himself into my arms.

"Why did Mummy die? Was she sick? Where have you been, Fili!" He pummelled me. "I looked for you all day -"

"She went to heaven, Jean-Pierre," I rocked him against me, "she went to heaven -"

"But why?" he cried, "why did Jesus need her there?"

I continued to rock him, and Shenay stroked his head and murmured *foeitog, foeitog,* shame...

Then Dad came around to my side of the car and bent down and lifted Jean-Pierre into his arms and walked off slowly, talking to him. "It's alright," I heard him say.

"We're home now. And Mummy is always in our hearts."

"Who did it?" muttered Shenay fiercely. She grabbed her apron and blotted her eyes. "Was it that Kula? I knew from the moment I saw him, Miss Fili!"

I watched Dad and Jean-Pierre. They were walking towards Mum's rose garden.

"Come inside, Miss Fili," Shenay's tone softened and she put an arm around my shoulder and helped me out of the car. Her eyes were red and swollen. She had loved Mum, loved her blond beauty and slender style. "The *ou missus* is here. She's staying in the guest room."

Dad had set Jean-Pierre down on the ground, and they were hugging.

Jean-Pierre's arms were around his father and Dad's face was buried against his son's thin neck.

"The police don't know anything yet, Shenay. We're waiting for the report to say how she died."

## CHAPTER THIRTY THREE

"Don't misunderstand me," Mrs van der Weyden said in a quavering voice when the police arrived at their farm, "we always admired Martin and Ray for adopting Fili. Of course we did! Yet I knew there might be trouble someday. Especially after Jean-Pierre was born."

"The youngster was ambitious," remarked Mr van der Weyden, folding his arms. "Mind you, ambition is no bad thing. But Fili was driven. She even talked them into making her a Director."

"Ray, God rest her soul, found Fili difficult." Mrs van der Weyden dabbed her eyes with a handkerchief. "There's a romance with Bo Sammy – from the Coloured village – that Ray disapproved of. And we know nothing about Fili's background, her parents could have been criminals for all we know! How do you escape your genes? Maybe they argued and things got out of control -" she covered her mouth with her hands.

"Calm down, Elaine. We don't yet know the cause of death," Mr van der Weyden put in.

"And Ray wanted Jean-Pierre to inherit. She was going to change her will -"

"Enough, Elaine!" Mr van der Wyden led his wife away. "It's not our business."

"Fili didn't do it," announced Petro, taking off her headphones as the policeman stood in her doorway. "She's not capable of murder. She's too soft. She wants to help everybody."

"My granddaughter," said Nanette Du Bois, offering the policemen a slice of lemon for his tea, "is an admirable young woman. I have no doubt as to her innocence of any involvement. I would like to see the doctor's report on the time of death. Fili was with us in the village until 10am."

"Would you say your granddaughter was jealous of her young brother?"

"Not at all!" retorted Nanette. "Fili adores Jean-Pierre. And vice versa."

"Excuse me, Ma'am, I meant jealousy over the inheritance."

Nanette leaned forward and fixed her gaze on the policeman's face. "Officer, let us be quite clear. Fili told her father in my presence that she wished to be Jean-Pierre's partner in the farm one day. There was no jealousy. My son was at pains to ensure both children would be equal beneficiaries."

"Where were you on the morning of the 15th, Mr Sammy?"

Bo stared down at his hands, then looked up. "She didn't do it, she couldn't do it. Fili loved her Ma, even though -"

"Just answer the question."

"I was here, in the village, listening to Mr Du Bois and then Fili and the *ou missus*."

"Did Miss Du Bois speak? I thought it was Mr Du Bois who made the announcement."

"*Ja*, he did. But then Fili, I mean Miss Du Bois, said we should be grateful for everything we had at the farm and that we were lucky we weren't poor like the squatters."

The white policeman wrote in his notebook.

"What was the response from the village?"

Bo shifted in his seat.

"Well, mostly people agreed. But mostly they wanted the squatters gone."

"Did you want them gone?"

Bo looked at the policeman. "*Ja*, I did. But not because I thought they'd take our jobs. I trust Mr Du Bois, he was loyal to us. If we worked hard, our jobs would be safe. No, I wanted them gone because they worried Fili."

"How did they worry her?"

"She felt sorry for them." Bo twisted his hands together. "She wanted to help them but helping would get her in trouble one day for sure."

"Did you tell her so?"

"Sort of. But I know why she did it."

"And why was that?"

Bo sighed and stared out of the open front door. In the distance, Fili's chardonnay block sweltered. What would happen to the harvest? Could any of them go into the vines where Mrs Du Bois died and pick the grapes and make a wine that would contain anything more than tears?

"Fili never knew her real mother, sir. So she helped the squatters because she'd been saved and they hadn't, and because she felt bad about hating her mother for giving her away."

The policeman frowned. Bo could understand that this tangle of real and adopted family must be confusing to anyone who didn't know Du Bois. It made solving the crime more complicated - if it was a crime. And they hadn't even got onto the drugs, yet. If only he could see Fili, kiss her lips and tell her everything would be fine. They still had a future... or did they?

"I will speak to the rest of your family, now."

Mary Sammy jammed her glasses on her nose the better to examine the policeman sitting on her flowered couch. "You should be ashamed! Miss Fili would never hurt her mother. Now go away and find the killer, if poor Mrs Du Bois didn't die from the heat. It'll be those squatters for sure."

"We have to look at all options, Ma'am."

"Miss Fili loves the vines and she loves Jean-Pierre like she loves her mother and father and the *ou missus,"* Philemon said, comforting a weeping Shenay. "Miss Fili doesn't have it in her to do a terrible thing like this,"

"Look for Kula Mfusi," shouted Tannie Ellie from her step. "He did it. He stole things all the time!"

"I'm sorry to trouble you again, Ma'am, but I have some more questions."

Nanette sighed. She'd called the station and requested someone more senior to continue the questioning or, at least, someone not prone to wild conjecture. But they'd sent the same man.

"You are a Director of Du Bois Vineyards, Mrs Du Bois?"
"Yes. Along with my son, Martin, and my granddaughter, Fili."
"Why wasn't the late Mrs Du Bois a Director?"
"She wasn't really interested in the business, officer. Ray's focus was the house and the garden and her family."
The officer consulted his notes.
"You spoke at the meeting in the village?"
"Yes, I spoke in support of my son and Fili."
"Was your granddaughter popular in the village?"
"Oh, yes. She was fully accepted as a Du Bois, with a role at the centre of the farm."
"Wasn't the late Mrs Du Bois keen for her son Jean-Pierre to inherit?"
Nanette smiled. The neighbours must have been talking. Elaine van der Weyden, no doubt.
"The Directors had decided that Fili and Jean-Pierre would share the management of the farm in due course, or, if Jean-Pierre was not interested, that Fili would take over in entirety."
"But that is not the same, if you will pardon me, Ma'am. Wasn't the late Mrs Du Bois keen for her son to inherit on his own?"
Nanette regarded the officer carefully. She probably shouldn't criticise the police. They were being scrupulous, if at times overly nosy or imaginative.
"Perhaps. But Fili had shown her ability as a winemaker and Jean-Pierre is still too young to decide his future."
She leaned forward and fixed the officer with her bright

gaze. "Legally, the farm is pledged equally to Fili and Jean-Pierre. And I think Ray had come to accept that Fili and Jean-Pierre would indeed share the management. Who will inherit after them is a choice for their generation to make."

"Do you think your adopted granddaughter hurt her mother because she feared she would lose her position on the farm to her brother?"

"No!" Nanette retorted. "You are quite wrong, young man. Fili has not the temperament for violence nor the calculation for it."

"So who do you think killed Mrs Du Bois?"

"Are you not jumping the gun - so to speak, officer? My daughter-in-law may have died of natural causes."

The policeman nodded and gathered up his notebook.

"We shall know soon enough, Ma'am. If a suspect is charged, it will probably be within the next 48 hours. And then the suspect will be detained or offered bail."

"You can't believe she did this? Did you see the state Fili was in? She is innocent. Furthermore, in the presence of her father and myself, she suggested warning Ray about one of the squatters taking drugs. She was concerned about our safety -"

"Oh, I'm so sorry," a voice came from the doorway. Mrs van der Weyden retreated slightly. "I'm interrupting. I brought you a casserole. Shall I leave it in the kitchen?"

"Thank you, Elaine," Nanette drew herself up. "How kind. I'm just finishing with the officer then I'll be with you."

"Please don't worry, but I wondered," she smiled at the policeman, "how the investigation is going? We're all so anxious -"

"The police are doing a fine job," Nanette put in swiftly, "and we're most grateful. Will you see yourself out, Elaine?"

"I can't talk right now," cried Mrs Newman, opening the door to the police later that week. "It's too upsetting. That poor child, and beautiful Ray found in the vineyards, it doesn't bear thinking about!"

"Fili isn't a murderer," Evonne threw over her shoulder as she led her mother away. "She's a victim."

The newspapers offered up both options, in bold print. They made no reference to the possibility that Ray Du Bois might have died of natural causes.

Did they already know something that no-one else did? Or maybe it was simply the case that death by violence always sells better than a heart attack.

**Murderer or Victim?**

**Gruesome events at Du Bois Vineyards point either to a premeditated attack or a random crime in which Ray Du Bois, wife of well-known farmer Martin Du Bois, died of her injuries.**

**Did Fili Du Bois kill her adoptive mother? Or is there an outside perpetrator? If so, Miss Du Bois, 18, becomes the victim of a heinous crime visited upon her family. Miss Du Bois was found beside the body of her mother after calling the emergency services, and is being**

questioned. Police are waiting for the autopsy report but sources close to the investigation say all possibilities are being considered.

## CHAPTER THIRTY FOUR

Kula threw the newspaper away.
His English had got better, to the extent that he knew the word autopsy meant tests to find out how Mrs Du Bois had died, so the next newspapers would surely say what had happened to her.
He pulled the hood over his head, heaved the rucksack onto his shoulder and set off.
His mind was clear, his eyes were clear. He wanted to keep them that way. All the time. But he must go fast, before they came for him and the others, because they would surely do so.
If you were the police, why wouldn't you?
After all, he and his father and Abraham and Peter had just been thrown off Du Bois land.
The police would suspect one of them hurt Mrs Du Bois out of anger.
He hoped that his father would understand his disappearance, and would cover for his absence, and would send the police in the opposite direction.
He intended to head for Cape Town, to the huge informal settlements that stretched across the Cape Flats. He could vanish there, he had connections who would help. And, if he missed seeing water like at the Du Bois dam, he could walk to the sea and watch the waves and see how the moon's path sliced across the swells.
He could become someone different.

But he didn't want to live forever in hiding. What sort of life was that?

He wanted something better. He wanted a real job, and to be respected for what he could say or do. He'd forced himself to be sober and properly-dressed on work days at the Paarl warehouse, he'd used the showers to keep clean and wash his clothes, and the foreman had promised that he could move up into checking orders, rather than packing goods.

But, after this, it was too risky to go back.

He needed to be somewhere new, a place where no-one knew him.

In another newspaper he'd found, it said that Fili Du Bois was being questioned by the police.

Why? She wouldn't have done anything bad to her mother. The Du Bois family had saved Fili, adopted her when no-one else wanted her.

None of this was his problem. In fact, it resolved a related problem for him.

And the longer the police wasted time with Fili, the more time they gave to him and his father and Abraham and Peter to get as far away from Du Bois as possible.

But where was the phone?

## CHAPTER THIRTY FIVE

The following day, apart from the usual police vans lined up in front of the station, there was a cluster of randomly parked cars out of which erupted a yelling crowd as soon as we arrived.

"What do you have to say, Miss Du Bois?" They thrust microphones at me.

"Did you see who did it?"

"Did you kill your mother, Fili?"

Dad ran around to my side of the car and tried to shield me.

"Over here, look this way! What do you have to say?"

Cameras flashed in my face like sheet lightning.

"Did you kill your mother?"

*Did you kill your mother...*

Dad held me close to his side and rammed his way through the front door like a rugby forward. A burly policeman shoved the door closed behind us and locked it. The shouting faded. I looked back. The reporters were clamouring against the door, their mouths opening and closing like fish. Dad reached down and pulled me against him again, then released me as Mr Tate appeared, accompanied by a policeman I hadn't seen before.

"Miss Du Bois? Mr Tate? This way, please." He ushered us into the interview room.

"Ignore them, Fili," murmured Mr Tate, following my backward glance towards the pack at the door.

"Do they know something we don't, sir?"

Before Mr Tate could respond, Captain Dlamini entered the interview room carrying a small case. From it, he first removed his notebook and laid it beside the tape recorder. Then he retrieved a clear plastic bag and placed it on the table between us.

Inside the bag lay a mobile phone.

There were red stains on the casing but even without those I would have known it.

I hadn't put it back in my jeans! I must have left it there, on the ground for the police to find -

He switched on the tape recorder, made the usual announcement of the date and who was present.

"Do you recognise this phone, Miss Du Bois?"

"Yes." I lifted my chin and met the man's eyes.

"Did you call the ambulance with this phone?"

"I did."

"Let the record show Miss Du Bois recognised this phone as the one she used to call the ambulance."

I stared through the small window. It was a beautiful morning and the sky was a shade halfway between peach and blue. I wanted to reach out and touch it. I wanted to run down to the dam and meet Bo and watch the peach sky reflect itself in the water.

"Is this your phone, Miss Du Bois?"

They would know already. Lying would only arouse further suspicion.

"No, it isn't. It belongs to Kula Mfusi, one of the squatters on our land."

I could sense Mr Tate shifting in his chair. He didn't know about Kula. It wasn't that I misled him by keeping quiet, rather it seemed to me there was no point in revealing something that would have no bearing unless Mum was murdered. And we didn't know that yet.

The policeman smiled at me and leaned forward. "Now why don't you tell us" - he glanced towards Mr Tate - "how you came to have Kula Mfusi's phone?"

I couldn't protect Kula or the village any longer. I had to protect myself.

"A while ago I came across Kula on the path near the village. He was," I hesitated, "high on drugs. Bo Sammy helped me get him back to the squatter camp. His phone had been on the ground and I put it in my pocket and forgot to give it back to him. Afterwards, I thought that if I kept it, he wouldn't be able to order more drugs."

The policeman frowned. "Why did you have it with you when you visited the workers' village with your father and grandmother?"

I could, perhaps, lie. I could say I picked it up only when I returned home on the Saturday morning, fully intending to run to the camp and return it to him after I'd chatted with Mum. That way, I could keep Tannie Ellie's - the village's - involvement in supplying drugs to Kula a secret. The *inside job* would be safe, even though it didn't deserve my silence.

"Miss Du Bois? Did you have it with you at the village meeting?"

I thought of Grand-mère. She would tell nothing less than the truth, wherever it led. And, in any case, she and Dad could tell the police they'd approved me taking it with us to the village.

"Yes, I did."

"Why?"

*You're a Du Bois*, she'd once whispered to me. *So act like one!*

"If the villagers intended to cause trouble before the squatters left, we'd expose the information I found via the phone to prove that one of them was arranging to supply drugs to Kula Mfusi."

Mr Tate's eyebrows climbed up his forehead. Captain Dlamini's mouth was wide open.

"Also," I went on, "the villagers had been blaming the squatters for stealing farm tools and petrol. But I think they were accusing the men in order to force my father to have them evicted."

Mr Tate had stopped writing on his pad.

"How did you discover about the drugs from the phone?" the Captain demanded.

"I turned it on, sir. And called the last number." Surely the police had also done so? Or at least found the number even if they hadn't called it. "Bo Sammy recognised the voice of the man who answered. He talked about supplying Kula. He's related to a village family who hate the squatters."

The Captain was silent, turning his pen over and over in his fingers.

If the phone had not been found or if I'd stuffed it back into my jeans in the harrowing aftermath, Kula Mfusi would be unconnected to Mum's death. The police would've assumed I'd called the ambulance from my own phone. Now, like me, he was implicated. My heart lurched. He could have whispered Blaze into surrender and then killed my mother in a drug-fuelled rage -
"May we take a break?" Mr Tate coughed into the silence. "I'd like to speak to my client."
The Captain put down his pen, turned off the tape recorder and left the room.
I got up and walked around the perimeter slowly, pressing the curling tiles down with my feet. It was mid-morning. There were probably still hours of questioning ahead but somehow, despite a jarring tiredness, I felt calmer than I had at the start. Perhaps honesty is liberating even if you aren't necessarily believed. Also, the baying from outside had faded. Perhaps the reporters, acting on their own information, assumed I'd be detained overnight and had left. The siege would resume the following day.
"Fili?" Mr Tate was leaning back in his chair, hands clasped over his chest. "Why didn't you tell me any of this? The drugs? The phone? The conflict between the villagers and the squatters?"
I sat down opposite him, taking the seat the Captain had vacated.
"If Mum wasn't murdered, would it help to bring that kind of rivalry into the open?"
He looked down at his legal pad and then back at me.

"Mr Tate," I pressed forward across the table, "we both know Mum and Dad saved me. They brought me to Du Bois and gave me an upbringing I can never repay. So while I see the world like they do, sir, I can also sense what it might be like if I hadn't been adopted."

His face flushed and I could tell it wasn't what he expected. But I will never be what people expect.

"Therefore you felt compelled to help the squatters?"

"I wanted to give them a chance. Also," I squared my shoulders, "I don't like one group undermining another."

He nodded and made a note on his pad, more to avoid my gaze, I think, than because I'd said anything he particularly wanted to record.

"And I didn't kill my mother," I added.

He regarded me for a moment. I doubt Mr Tate has ever had a client like me before. Dad used to say that Tate and Partners mostly concerned themselves with property deals or pricey divorces.

"I believe you, Fili Du Bois," he reached out his hand across the table and shook mine. "Now we need to convince the police."

*

"Mr Du Bois, we would like you to know, sir, that we accept you and the senior Mrs Du Bois were at the Coloured village or in each other's company at the time of Mrs Du Bois' death," the policeman announced at the start of the second interview.

"And I would like to know," demanded Martin, "where the papers are getting their information from! How dare they target my daughter?"

"I'm sorry, sir." The officer inclined his head. "It is the press. They jump to conclusions. We cannot control what they think."

"We don't have the autopsy results, we don't yet know how my wife," his voice cracked, "died."

"I'm sorry, sir."

"Well, you'd better make sure Fili is protected when we leave here today."

"We will, sir. Now, before we move on to the security arrangement at Du Bois Vineyards, I have a question regarding the late Mrs Du Bois." He hesitated. "It may be uncomfortable for you and I apologise, sir, but I must ask it."

"Very well."

"Did you notice any bruising on your wife's shoulders in the days before her death?"

*

When we returned home I found Grand-mère on the verandah, her foot propped up on a cushion.

"Don't get up, Grand-mère." I went over and knelt beside her. She was in her usual black but this time it was also for Mum. "I had to tell them about Kula and the drugs, Grand-mère."

She stroked my face. Her fingers were unsteady and they trembled against my skin.

"Be honest, child. And pray that your mother felt no pain."

"I don't think she did. When I found her," I swallowed, "it looked like she was sleeping. It was only when I moved her hair that I saw -"

Grand-mère allowed me to weep for a while and then shook me gently. "Enough, now. There are more questions to answer, more people to face. You need to be strong, Fili. The tears must wait."

Grand-mère may be close to ninety and her hands may shake, but her spine is made of steel.

Our evening meal was largely silent because, unlike the previous breakfasts, Grand-mère didn't attempt to make conversation. The three of us ate our lamb stew and probably never tasted it at all. Dad, weary from his interviews and then the strain of Jean-Pierre's unanswerable questions, excused himself before our simple dessert of fresh fruit. Earlier, Shenay had finally pacified Jean-Pierre and given him supper and read him stories until he'd fallen into an exhausted sleep.

"Go to bed too, Miss Fili," Shenay said in a voice thick with tears as I helped her carry the dinner plates to the kitchen. "You can't answer their pushy questions if you're tired."

My recent sleeps had been medically induced but tonight I'd be alone with the hammering in my skull, and Mum's crumpled body in front of my closed eyes. And where was Kula? A possible murderer at large -

I stared at myself in the bedroom mirror. Bruised eyes. Hollow cheeks.

"Fili!" came a whisper from beyond the window.

I stifled a scream.

"Bo?"

"Come outside!"

I pulled the curtains apart. He was standing in the shadows, shifting from foot to foot as if ready to sprint away at any moment. I opened the window wider and squeezed through.

He seized me as soon as my feet touched the ground.

"Why didn't you wait for me to walk you home, Fili? Your Pa told me not to let you go off on your own but I didn't see you leave!"

"Bo," I leaned back and looked into his distraught face, "it's not your fault."

"*Ja*, it is," he gritted his teeth. "If I'd been with you I could have *donnered* Kula before he got to your Ma. I could have saved her -"

"Come with me," I squirmed out of his arms, "let's climb the oak."

"Now?"

I wanted to be somewhere above the ugliness of the day, away from the stained earth. "Yes."

Even though there was only a sliver of moon, my hands and feet knew the way to my favourite vantage point. There was space for the two of us to sit close together where several branches met. The sky was ink-black through the tracery of leaves.

"Look at me, Bo. Look at me!" I put my hands on either side of his face. "We don't know if Mum died naturally or was killed. So we don't know if it's murder or not. The police think I could have had a hand in it -"

"What?" he cried.

"Ssh! We must be clear what we tell them. Bo, are you listening?"

"*Ja*," he said after a pause. "I'm listening."

"I used Kula's phone to call the ambulance. The police found it on the ground."

He gaped at me.

"I'd had it with me for the visit to the village, in case Tannie Ellie caused trouble. Dad was going to give it to Kula's father afterwards."

He clutched at his tufty hair. "How much did you tell the police?"

"I said we'd discovered Kula together and that he was getting drugs via a village contact. I haven't identified Tannie Ellie or Blake by name yet, but I will if they ask me."

A tiny gust shivered the leaves. I stared into the garden. Mum's roses were pools of shadow. They might have seen her killer. Or was it only the vines who were witness?

"You must be honest, Bo." I took his hand and squeezed it hard. "You must tell the truth. If you don't, they'll catch us out in a lie and we'll both be in trouble."

"A policeman came to the village," Bo said more slowly. "I told him you felt sorry for the squatters. He wanted to know why, so I said it was because of your real mother."

"Did you say anything about Kula?"

"No."

I lifted his hand and brought it to my lips. "I love you, Bo."

He gathered me close, bent his head and we kissed.

But there was fear in his lips, and his heart was racing. I could feel it as clearly as I'd felt Mum's heart when she told me I was adopted, and when she hugged me on the day the outsiders first made their presence felt in the courtyard.

## CHAPTER THIRTY SIX

Captain Dlamini arrived in the interview room accompanied by a women police officer.

"It's routine," he said, "when we take a DNA sample."

I've learnt about this at school, so I'm not unnerved as she asks me to open my mouth and she takes a swab from my cheek. It also means that they suspect me of some kind of involvement in my mother's death. The policewoman finished the job, gave me a shy smile and left. As she opened the door, the din from outside could be heard at greater volume. The press were back.

"Do we expect the autopsy report today, Captain?" Mr Tate enquired.

He shrugged. "It will come when it comes."

"Now Miss Du Bois," he switched on the tape recorder, "how long have you known Kula Mfusi?"

I hesitated. Mum's death was leading us down paths I didn't want to explore.

"Since the squatters arrived a few years ago."

"Is he your friend?"

"My friend?"

"Yes, did you make friends with him?"

I stared at Captain Dlamini. This was a new line of attack. And all the while the background noise from outside never wavered. Cars revved. Brakes squealed.

"No, he wasn't my friend. He didn't like me."

"And why was that?"

"I suppose he envied me. I'd been rescued and he hadn't."
"When did you last see him?"
"On Friday afternoon when my father told the squatters to leave."
"What was his mood compared to the others?"
I thought back to the needle moment, the spark that might cause him to rush at us and encourage the others to join him, rage unleashed -
"He was angry."
"Did you fear he would become violent?"
The woodpecker had squealed, the gum leaves rustled and Kula's eyes burned into mine.
"Maybe."
"Could you tell if his behaviour was because he was drugged?"
I hesitated. I'd resolved to tell the truth wherever it led. If I lied, it might implicate him even more.
"Kula wasn't drugged, sir. His eyes and speech were clear. He ran off into the bush without falling."
"Miss Du Bois, how long have you had Kula Mfusi's phone?"
This was more dangerous.
"Miss Du Bois?"
"I can't remember exactly," I said. "Not long."
If they discover I've had the phone for weeks, their suspicions will multiply. Why would I keep a phone that wasn't mine? The police will gnaw on this bone until they find the marrow. Or press Dad and Bo for the information -

"You kept Kula Mfusi's phone even when you heard he was being supplied with drugs?"

"Yes."

"Why did you keep it, Miss Du Bois? And why didn't you tell the police? Or your father?"

"I did tell my father, sir."

"And what did he say?"

"He said to give it back to him so he could return it to Adam Mfusi."

"And why didn't you?"

"Because we agreed to take it with us to the village meeting, like I told you yesterday. Then I was going to give it to Dad."

There was silence as the Captain looked down at his notebook. He had scribbled nothing on the right-hand page. That could either mean he believed me - or had no need to make notes because he thought I was lying. But at least I'd managed to shrink the time between finding the phone and potentially giving it back. Only Bo knows exactly how long I've had it. And, of course, Kula. I should have warned Bo to be vague -

"Do you have a phone of your own?"

"Yes, sir. But I didn't take it with me that morning."

"Do you normally take it everywhere with you?"

"Yes," I choked up suddenly. "Mum used to insist I had it with me all the time."

*Take your new phone, Fili,* she'd call, when I took sandwiches to the men. *For an emergency.*

"Do you want a break?" Mr Tate asked me, with a glance at Captain Dlamini.

"No," I replied. "I want to finish so I can get home and look after Jean-Pierre."

"Miss Du Bois, are you jealous of your brother?"

"No!" I shouted. "I'm sorry -" I lowered my voice, "no, I'm not jealous of my brother."

"Why did my question upset you, Ma'am?"

*But Martin! We'll have a biological child!*

*We'll treat both children the same...*

"Because it's a question people have been asking ever since Jean-Pierre was born."

"And it makes you upset?"

I looked at him. He was only doing his job. It must be hard for an outsider to unravel the web of love, adoption and land that has enmeshed me since the day Mum and Dad brought me home.

"It makes me sad, Captain." I felt the prick of tears. "I'm tired of having to tell people over and over that I love my brother. And that he loves me."

The newspapermen began to bang on the door to the station. They think I killed Mum, so there must be evidence she didn't die naturally. They must know something that I don't. I felt myself begin to shake in time with the beating of their hands on the door.

"We should take a break, Captain." Mr Tate touched my shoulder.

Captain Dlamini nodded and switched off his tape recorder. "Twenty minutes."

I admit that I didn't answer his question truthfully.

Am I jealous of Jean-Pierre? Of course I am - or was. Wouldn't you be?

But now I'm a Director, the envy has faded. We can run Du Bois together one day, Jean-Pierre and I, alongside Bo. We can create a farm where competition for ownership – and work - has no place; a farm where there can be several stakes in the ground. And each of them will matter equally.
Or am I being naive?

I only heard afterwards what happened during the break that Mr Tate insisted upon.
"I want to see the person in charge," the young woman at the front desk announced. "I've fought my way through those horrible reporters and I'm not going outside again until I've seen someone."
"You'll have to wait, Miss," said the junior officer. "They're all busy."
She sat down gingerly on a plastic chair and hauled out her phone.
"I'm at the police station," she said loudly. "They're making me wait. I think I might call our lawyers, maybe that will hurry them up." After several more loudly-voiced comments involving time-wasting and incompetence, the junior officer scurried away to find someone who would deal with the situation.
"Your name, please, Miss?"
"Van der Weyden. Petro van der Weyden."
"Come this way."
Petro found herself in a sterile room with a large black policeman in a tightly fitting uniform.

"I am Captain Dlamini. I don't have much time, Ma'am. What is it that you wish to tell us?"

Petro smiled. Most men, even black ones like this, were malleable.

"I've come to tell you it was Kula Mfusi who killed Ray Du Bois."

"What evidence do you have of this, Miss van der Weyden?"

"Well, it's cumulative, officer, so you must hear me out. First of all, my father saw him on the Franschhoek road soon after the squatters had been given their marching orders on Friday afternoon. He was wandering in the middle of the carriageway, clearly drunk or drugged up. He nearly caused an accident. I phoned Fili and told her. Fili was always upset on behalf of the squatters," she confided, leaning forward, "it comes from being abandoned herself, of course."

"So what is the evidence that you have, Miss van der Weyden?"

"I saw him, myself!" she declared triumphantly. "I saw Kula Mfusi."

"When was that?"

"Why, first thing on Saturday morning. I was driving into town to go shopping for a party dress and I saw him heading for Gum Tree Avenue. Towards the farm, Captain, towards Du Bois Vineyards."

"And what time was that?"

"Oh, "Petro stared at the ceiling, "eight thirty-ish. I wanted to get to the shop right on opening time, you see. I had a particular dress in mind and I didn't want anyone getting there before me."

"How did you know it was him?"

"I've seen him before, of course. First, when Fili showed me the camp. Terrible place. And then he was often in town, hanging about. Quite good looking, actually. And quite well-dressed. But a lot of attitude."

"Did he seem drunk, like your father noticed the previous day?"

"No, not at all. He was walking straight down the road. So you see, he was heading for Du Bois in the morning, right when Mrs Du Bois was about to be killed."

"We don't yet know the cause of death, Miss van der Weyden."

"Oh, it will surely be murder. People don't just fall down and die."

"Why didn't you tell all this to our officer when he came to speak to you and your parents?"

Petro smiled sweetly. "I forgot, sir. I was too taken up with my purchases. But I didn't forget to tell the policeman that Fili is innocent. She could never have hurt her mother. She's always been hopelessly grateful to her parents, even after Jean-Pierre was born."

She twirled her fingers and departed.

"Shall we continue?" Captain Dlamini re-entered the room.

"Yes, but I must ask you to allow my client regular breaks, this is harrowing for her."

The Captain inclined his head.

"Now, Miss Du Bois, was Kula Mfusi aware that you were in possession of his phone?"
"Yes."
I must keep my wits about me, he is indeed like a dog with a bone.
"You say that you kept it in order to potentially expose the drug supplier to the village."
"Yes. And to stop Kula Mfusi ordering more."
"But if your visit to the village only came about as a result of your father's decision to evict the squatters on Friday, then that must mean you only rescued Kula Mfusi from his drugged state within the last day or two. Not 'a while ago', as you said yesterday."
It was a plan that had evolved as I held onto the phone, a multiple trade I thought I could pull off via my role as go-between. A play, if you like, between the villagers, a drug supplier, Kula, the remaining squatters - and Du Bois Vineyards. But events had moved ahead of my scheming.
"I kept the phone for another reason," I said, deliberately veering away from the timing. "I thought it could be used as a bargaining tool to get Kula to leave, but allow his father and the others to stay."
"To stay?" Captain Dlamini took the bait, frowned, and shook his head. "Please explain, Miss Du Bois. I thought you kept the phone primarily to expose the villagers."
"That was what you said in yesterday's testimony," Mr Tate reminded me in a low voice.
"You're right, sir. But I also wanted to use it to confront Kula. If he agreed to leave the farm, I wouldn't call the

police and tell them about the drugs. And if I told Mum and Dad that he was leaving - and had been unfairly framed for the recent thefts - then my parents might let the others stay. They were hard workers, they'd been with us for a while, they didn't deserve to be evicted."

There was silence apart from the furious scratch of Mr Tate's pen on his yellow pad. Captain Dlamini stared at me in exasperation, then rubbed his face and switched off the tape recorder.

"We will bring you some sandwiches. We must carry on after lunch."

"Yes, sir," I replied. "I'm sorry if this is confusing. It made sense to me at the time."

But I'd ignored a crucial piece of Grand-mère's advice: that go-betweens, like honeyguide birds, only point the way. They leave the action, the heavy lifting, to those more qualified.

Instead, I tried to engineer an outcome on my own.

"The timescale around the phone does not make sense to me, Miss Du Bois," Captain Dlamini said when he returned. "It seems that you had the phone for some time. If you were planning to negotiate the squatters' position with your parents, why did you not do so straightaway? Before your father evicted them? Before the meeting with the villagers?"

He waited as I folded up my paper serviette and put it into a bag that had carried the sandwiches. The clamour from outside had faded so presumably the press had gone off to find their own lunch.

I didn't answer. I couldn't answer.

He leaned back in his chair and stared at me. "I believe there may be another explanation for all this - in fact two possible explanations."

Yesterday I thought he'd felt some respect for me, today was different. Maybe he'd read the evidence collected by his colleagues who'd fanned out across the valley to talk to our neighbours, the villagers, the squatters... and it was unfavourable to me.

"Firstly, if your mother did not die of natural causes, you could be Kula Mfusi's accomplice. You wanted your mother dead because she favoured your brother to inherit Du Bois Vineyards, and, we believe, may have considered changing her will to that end."

I found myself gasping for breath.

"Kula Mfusi, for his part, wanted her dead because he believed she was the driving force behind the eviction of the squatters. I suggest to you, Miss Du Bois, that you conspired with Mfusi to kill her."

"I did not!"

"And your second theory, Captain?" Mr Tate put a restraining hand on my arm and deliberately kept his voice calm. "Even though we do not yet know the cause of death?"

"Your client is trying to cover for Mr Mfusi. He met Mrs Du Bois, perhaps while he was in a drugged state. There was an argument, and he attacked her. When Miss Du Bois found her mother, she was frightened and by mistake called the ambulance with the phone Mfusi had dropped in the struggle."

"That's not true! I'd already told my father and grandmother about the phone!" I jumped up. The room swam before my eyes. "Why would I cover for Kula Mfusi?"

"Captain," Mr Tate retorted, "may I repeat: the cause of death is still unknown. These accusations are improper and speculative. They can have no bearing at this time."

"Miss Du Bois, is Kula Mfusi your lover?"

The floor tilted towards me. The patch of sky in the tiny window revolved. My chair fell over by itself and I was aware of Mr Tate reaching for me but he wasn't fast enough.

The Captain shouted faintly.

The beige tiles met my head in an explosion of stars.

## CHAPTER THIRTY SEVEN

"Do you know anything about your adopted daughter's parents, Mr Du Bois?" the officer asked.

"No, she was left at a church. The minister tried to trace them but no-one came forward."

"Has your daughter ever exhibited violent tendencies?"

"What are you suggesting?" Martin rose to his feet. "How dare you?"

And yet the officer had talked of bruises on Ray's shoulders... He hadn't been able to bring himself to ask Fili. And somehow the press had got wind that Ray's death might not be due to natural causes. Someone from within the police or forensics must have leaked, so the papers had splashed their suspicions across the front pages -

"Please sit down, sir. I am wondering whether the tension between your wife and daughter enlivened a violent inclination in Miss Du Bois. She has been seen to clench her fists under pressure. If you don't know her background, sir, how can you be sure this wouldn't happen?"

Martin sank back onto his chair. It was the very thought that had flashed into his mind as he looked down at Ray's body on the ground, with Fili standing over her, a streak of blood on her hands. He'd forced it away. No. Surely she couldn't - and yet it persisted, sowing doubt ever since that terrible night he'd spent on the verandah staring at the vines, mute witnesses to his wife's death.

"Mr Du Bois," the policeman looked at him with pity, "you did a brave thing to adopt. And you gave your daughter everything to equip her for success. But, under pressure, do we act from our upbringing or from our genes, sir?"

Martin leaned his elbows on the table and rested his head in his hands. To imagine that Fili could have turned on her mother was too extreme to contemplate. So he shouldn't.

But the bruising?

He straightened up. He wouldn't.

A rapping sounded on the door.

"Sir?" a young constable burst in and beckoned to Martin. "Mr Du Bois? You must come with me."

"Why?" demanded the officer, frowning. "We're busy. What's going on?"

"The station chief says to come, sir."

"Fili would never harm Ray," Martin flung over his shoulder as he rushed out, "wherever she came from!"

\*

It took a while for the room to resolve itself into a floor and a ceiling and a high window.

People were bending over me. The policewoman from earlier was cradling my head while someone in the distance was shouting.

"A doctor, I said. Right now!"

I lifted my hand and felt my forehead. It was swollen and my fingers came away red. Mum -

"No!" I screamed. "Not again! Mum!"

"It's not your mother, Fili," said Mr Tate. He was on his knees. He was my lawyer and yet he was on his knees. "You fell and hit your head. You've got a small cut but it's not serious."

Someone rushed into the room and I heard the sound of tearing. The woman police officer reached up for something and pressed it against my head.

Dad took my hand. He was crying.

"Don't, Dad. Please don't."

"How did this happen?" He shouted at the other people. "How could you let this happen?"

"Martin," Mr Tate put a hand on Dad's arm. "Fili stood up in reaction to a question and fainted."

"You're her lawyer," Dad's voice choked up, "your job is to protect her, not to let them goad her! Who is in charge?" He struggled to his feet. "Who did this?"

Dad must stop. If he makes them angry, they will come for me even harder.

"I was, sir." Captain Dlamini stepped forward. "I apologise, sir. I did not realise -"

I heard a door open. It must have been the station's outer door because the roar of raised voices swept inside and then ceased as the door banged shut.

"Stand back please," came a woman's firm tone. "Clear the room so I can examine the patient."

The group of concerned faces melted away. Dad hesitated, and then followed them.

"She will be fine, sir," said the woman, before closing the door behind him. "I won't be long. Now," she squatted down beside me, "I am Dr Saunders. Can you tell me what happened to you?"

I swallowed and tried to remember. She took my wrist and looked at her watch.

"The policeman said something, I stood up and then the room started to blur, the floor came up towards me -"

*Miss Du Bois, is Kula Mfusi your lover?*

The doctor was pretty like Mum, with blond hair. She let go of my wrist and took a pen out of her bag and asked me to focus on it as she brought it close to the bridge of my nose. She did it a couple of times, and also from the side of my face, all the while examining my eyes closely.

"What is your name and how old are you?"

"Fili Du Bois. I'm eighteen."

"And when is your birthday, Fili?"

I looked at her. No-one really knew for sure. They picked a date when they thought I'd been born.

"21st of August."

She lifted the bandage off my forehead and wiped something liquid over the skin. Her cool fingers probed my head gently.

"Were you at school earlier? Is that why you're in uniform?"

"No. My grandmother said it was the right thing to wear to the police station."

She smiled. "Grandmothers can be like that." She reached into her bag again. "I'm putting on a butterfly plaster. It's going to help the skin knit together. Do you have a headache?"

"A little."

"Well," she sat back on her heels, "it may last for a day or two so you must rest. You're also going to have a very impressive black eye." She cast me a faintly mischievous look.

"Thank you," I said. "Thank you for helping me, Doctor."

"Shall we get you into a chair?" She put her hands under my armpits and levered me up slowly until I was back in my seat.

"They need to fix their tiles," I said, pointing to the curling edges on the perimeter.

"They do indeed. Fili, do you know why you're here at the police station?"

"Yes. They think I might have killed my adoptive mother."

I saw the alarm play across her eyes and then subside. She drew up a chair and sat beside me. She was wearing a white coat over a red dress. And smart, flat, red-and-white shoes. If I ever got around to wearing dresses all the time, I'd like to wear them with matching flat shoes.

"You'll be at home resting for the next two to three days, with no further questioning. We need to watch that headache and make sure it doesn't get worse."

I stared out of the small window. The sky was hazy.

"I feel my real mother when the seasons change."

She nodded. "It's not unusual to have feelings like that. Our brains are very clever, Fili. They take their own course, they surprise us sometimes."

"Is the autopsy report out yet?"

She looked at me. I wondered how much she knew, whether she believed the newspapers, if she had an opinion like everyone else in the valley.

*Fili did it...*

*She was jealous of Jean-Pierre...*

*She never got on with her mother...*

*You couldn't mix up blood from different families and always expect a smooth dessert.*

"Fili," she touched my hand, "if you'd like me to, I will ask the police to brief me when the findings come out. Then I can bring them to you and explain what happened to your mother."

My mother... whom the Captain said might have changed her will to disinherit me.

## CHAPTER THIRTY EIGHT

The police did not return to the squatter camp fast enough. By the time they went back, the only sign that the area had been inhabited was a clearing beneath the trees and a ring of cut down saplings at its margins. Adam Mfusi's shack was gone. The embers from previous cooking fires had been raked away.

"Check for pieces of fabric, anything that might carry DNA," instructed the officer in charge. "Look by the stream as well."

But they found nothing. It was as if the place had been swept clean.

"There was also rain last night," the officer said to Captain Dlamini when he returned to the station. "It must have washed away any bits of material."

"And Mfusi? The old man?"

"Gone."

Have you ever been wrongly suspected of murder? Probably not.

I can tell you what it feels like: it feels like drowning. And there's nothing you can do because the weight of apparent evidence and outside opinion pushes you into the depths until there's no breath or space left for escape.

The doctor gave me some pills to take for my headache. They also made me sleepy - or perhaps it was the motion of the car as Dad drove me home.

"I can manage," I heard Dad murmur when we stopped. I felt myself being lifted up in his arms.

"Dear Lord!" came Shenay's horrified whisper, "it's a disgrace, sir -"

I opened my eyes. The mountains resolved into crisp outlines. The oak stood tall and proud.

"Rest, *chérie*," Grand-mère said once I was in bed. She tucked the blankets around me. "Give that poor head a chance to heal."

"How's Jean-Pierre, Grand-mère?"

Her bright eyes clouded. "He's sad and confused. But not for long. Children bounce back, and so will he. We're keeping him busy, Shenay and I. Many card games."

"I can read to him," I said, my eyes closing.

"Not yet, only when you're better. Rest now, child."

I dreamed that I was back at the church, only this time I saw my mother. She was small and frightened, glancing over her shoulder, carrying me in an open cardboard box with a pink shawl draped over the top so I wasn't visible. She looked around again and then bent down and wedged the box into the ditch. She lifted the pink shawl and wrapped it around me. I looked up at her. She had the same shape to her body as I had. And the same black eyes. She said something but I couldn't hear. The gum trees were tossing, the sun was aiming yellow beams into my eyes -

"No!" I screamed, rearing up, "don't go! Don't leave me!"

The bedroom door opened. A shaft of light, not as bright, carved through the darkness.

"She hasn't gone, honey," Dad gathered me in his arms. "She'll be with you always."

Who? Which mother?

Dad's heart beat steadily against mine.

"I'm sorry, Dad." I buried my face in the chest.

"We'll get through this, Fili."

Has he forgiven me? Does he believe I'm innocent? Dad was rocking me against him as I'd rocked Jean-Pierre - was it yesterday... I'm losing my grip on the days. I need to hear the morning piping of coots on the dam and the evening churring of nightjars on Gum Tree Avenue, otherwise I'm disconnected. The only sound I can hear is the howl of reporters. The only view I have is a square of sky through a high window.

"Is your head sore?" Dad whispered. "Do you want another pill?"

"No," I slid down under the covers. "I just want to go back, Dad. To where we were before."

He looked down at me and gave the ghost of a smile.

I think I only slept for a single night because the dawn came not long afterwards. Pale light grew behind my curtains and the first doves began their *werk stadig, werk stadig* in the oak. My door creaked open and a tiny figure ran in and flung himself onto my bed.

"Fili!" he pushed under the blankets and I folded him in my arms. "What happened to your head?"

"I fell over," I murmured against his hair. "Silly Fili!"

He giggled and then his face crumpled. "Will Mummy never come back?"

"No, she'll never come back. But she's looking down on us, Jean-Pierre. Like all the ancestors."

"Like Grand-père?"

"Yes, just like him."

He struggled upright. "But I want her here, not there!" he pointed heaven-wards.

"I know, Jeanie. But sometimes sad things happen and we don't know why."

"That's what Mrs Newman said. She came to visit and gave me a chocolate. Shenay said I mustn't eat it all at once."

"That was kind of her. I hope you said thank you."

"Jesus mustn't take you, Fili, because I don't know the secret yet. Remember?"

The secret of me loving Bo, to the disapproval of Mum.

"I'll always be here. With you and Dad and Grand-mère."

Yet do I have the courage to stay and face the stares, even if I'm declared innocent? There will surely be speculation that, despite my innocence, I'm still in some way to blame...

Jean-Pierre picked at his sleeve. He was wearing pyjamas patterned with aeroplanes. Ever since he received a model plane as a gift, he's been less interested in earthly toys. And now Mum is up there, not in a plane but lost in the upturned blue bowl above his head and he's been left behind.

"Promise," he whispered. "Promise you won't go!"

"I promise," I said, hoping that he'd forgive me if it turned out to be a lie.

"I'm pleased to see you resting," Dr Saunders said when she came into my bedroom later that morning. Today she was in trousers under her white coat. I peeked downwards. Her shoes were cream with black toecaps.
"How is your headache, Fili?"
"Much better. I haven't taken any pills today. Why are you worried about a headache?"
She sat down on the side of the bed. "You could have been slightly concussed when you fell. A post-concussion headache could be an indication you've hurt the inside of your head a little bit. If it carries on, then we need to investigate further."
She got out her pen and made me follow it with my eyes. She took my pulse and my blood pressure. She felt the swelling on my forehead.
"Sometimes," she went on, "when we bang our heads, it can cause a subdural haematoma. A bleeding beneath the bony cage of our skull. It can be dangerous if we're not alert to it."
"Have I got one of those?"
She replaced her blood pressure meter back in her bag and looked me straight in the eye.
"No, Fili. But your mother had something similar. She died from what we call an aneurism."
I fell back against the pillows. That trickle of blood near Mum's ear, down her neck... and my voice screaming 'Mum' over and over again.

Dr Saunders took my hand.

"Let me explain. When your mother fell to the ground, she may have hit her head at a particular angle which caused a rupture, a serious haemorrhage on the brain."

"Did it make the blood run from her ear?"

Dr Saunders shook her head. "No. That came from a cut as she hit the ground."

"I don't understand," I whispered. "How could she die, but I didn't?"

What game is God playing with us that He could allow both of us to fall - but only one to die?

Dr Saunders paused before responding.

"Some people are more likely to suffer injury when they fall. I spoke to your family doctor, Fili. He says your mother had complained of severe headaches. He put her on medication to lower her blood pressure some time ago. It seems she may have had a weakness. There was potential for a fatal aneurism."

I stared out of the window. The curtains blew in the breeze. Mum's heart used to throb. I thought it was fear.

"Why did she fall?"

Dr Saunders flexed the hand that was not holding mine.

"There is some evidence of an argument. She may have been pushed."

The darkness that had blurred my vision in the police station began to encroach. I was aware of the doctor stroking my hand and speaking but I couldn't hear what she was saying.

"So it was murder?" My voice was shrill in my ears. "Not natural causes - the heat - the weakness -"

Again she paused, waiting for me to calm myself.

"It's hard to say for certain. There are bruises on her shoulders that indicate she was held firmly and perhaps shaken. But she may have fallen to the ground of her own accord, Fili, because there are no serious attack injuries. And the aneurism could have ruptured before she fell, rather than because she fell."

I felt Dr Saunders hand slide towards my wrist. She was taking my pulse again.

"Breathe, Fili," she said.

"Who did it? Do they still think it was me?"

"There's no evidence to suggest you were involved. The time of death is estimated to be during the period when you were in the village with your father and grandmother. The small smudges on her dress are consistent with where you did chest compressions to try and revive her. And DNA has been recovered from under your mother's fingernails which does not match yours."

I looked down at my hands. "What do you mean, Doctor?"

"She scratched someone, Fili. And that person was not you."

An attacker grabbed her by the shoulders, shook her and pushed her? Mum fought back, she scratched and tried to escape and then fell and hit her head. Life began to bleed out of her brain. The attacker saw - or feared - she was dead and ran away.

"So it wasn't me?"

How silly, to ask the doctor if I wasn't a murderer.

"It's unlikely that you killed your mother, Fili. There's no evidence to support it."

I've tried not to cry, like Grand-mère told me, in order to stay strong. But it was as if a wall had been breached because the tears began to flood down my face. Dr Saunders let me weep and didn't say anything, just kept hold of my hand and looked at me with an expression of understanding such as I haven't seen in recent days.

"Do the police know that?" I choked. "Does Dad know? And Grand-mère?"

"Shortly, yes. The police will need to ask you some more questions once I allow them to, but you are not a prime suspect."

The tears continued to flow and she reached for a box of tissues. "Here, dry your eyes." She was back to being business-like. "There is something else I need to mention."

Kula.

They've found Kula.

"The police may no longer consider you to be directly responsible for your mother's death but they will still investigate whether you encouraged someone else to commit a crime."

She was watching me carefully. She's surely heard talk of inheritance disputes, and tension between Mum and me over the squatters.

"So they will ask me if I put someone up to it? If I commissioned a murder?"

"Yes," she nodded, "they will."

*Miss Du Bois, did you conspire with Kula Mfusi to kill your mother?*

The tears dried up and I felt a stream of ice enter my veins and isolate my heart.

*Be strong. There is no choice.*

"I did not, Dr Saunders. I did not arrange for my mother's death. We sometimes disagreed but she's the only mother I've ever had."

## CHAPTER THIRTY NINE

"Take a seat, Martin," said Ben Tate, ushering him to a chair beside a low table on which lay a manilla folder. "Coffee? Tea?"

"No thanks, Ben. I need to get back soon. I'm not happy leaving the family alone at the moment."

Tate nodded. Nanette Du Bois, while of stout disposition, would not be able to handle an emergency, Jean-Pierre might hurt himself playing outside, and Fili – He settled into the chair alongside Martin and picked up the file. This was a conversation he would have preferred to avoid. Martin was his friend as well as his client. He, Ben, had been uneasy about the whole business, especially when he was later asked to be Fili's lawyer. It represented, if not exactly a conflict of interest, then an awkward entanglement. To counter this, he'd decided that a formal approach to proceedings was the only option.

"We are here today to read the will of your wife, Ray Du Bois."

He paused. Martin nodded.

"I am authorised to declare that you, Martin Du Bois, are the sole beneficiary of this will. There are no other beneficiaries or dispensations. As executors, Tate and Partners will complete the necessary probate arrangements and declarations to the authorities in this regard to wind up her estate. We will keep you informed at every stage of the process."

Martin nodded again. "Thank you, Ben."

Tate hesitated. Martin would need a copy of the will. It couldn't be avoided.

"Having said that, I must inform you that Ray approached me privately a while ago with a specific request for a change, which was incorporated but has no bearing today, as you will learn."

Martin raised his eyebrows. "Go on."

"As you know, once you and Ray have passed on, your wills were set up to leave Fili and Jean-Pierre as co-heirs to Du Bois. Ray wished to change this arrangement so that if you passed away before she did, she wished to leave the majority of her estate to Jean-Pierre."

Martin gave a jolt and Ben put out a hand, then withdrew it.

"I counselled her that such a move could drive a rift between Fili and Jean-Pierre which would be to the detriment of Du Bois going forwards. But she was adamant."

There was a moment of silence. From outside came the shout of workmen repairing a culvert.

"Why didn't you tell me? At the time?" Martin rose to his feet, face ashen.

Tate regarded him with sympathy. A daughter suspected of a crime, a wife who wished to disinherit her…

"I was bound by the confidentiality that must be preserved between client and attorney, Martin. My hands were tied. I asked her to reflect on it but she insisted the change be made." He opened the folder. "I must therefore tell you that, if you had pre-deceased Ray, upon her death a seventy percent share of Du Bois would have been left to Jean-Pierre, via a special trust if he was a minor at the time."

Martin remained standing, his hands flexing and unflexing. Tate was hit by the memory of Fili clenching her fists - in imitation of her adoptive father rather than via wayward genes, as the police were inclined to suspect?

"There are, as I've indicated, no implications to this. Ray has tragically pre-deceased you and therefore you are her sole beneficiary. The clause she inserted will never be invoked. No-one needs to know it existed. Your daughter," he emphasized, "need never know."

Martin fell back into his chair. The industrial sounds from outside stopped. Birdsong intruded.

"This cannot become public knowledge, Ben."

"It will not."

"But what about the police? Can they ask to see the will? Use it against Fili?"

"They may choose to ask about it. We will have to comply if they have the correct authority. Having said that," he paused, "I must caution you that Captain Dlamini raised the possibility of Ray changing her will during the interview when Fili fainted. He also postulated that Fili might be romantically involved with Kula Mfusi."

Martin stared at him in horror. "But that's insane! With Mfusi? Surely this is intimidation, Ben, quite aside from being complete nonsense! I will go and speak to Dlamini myself – tell him so -"

Ben reached out and placed his hand on Martin's arm.

"You need to be careful, Martin. Leave this with me. Don't antagonise the police."

The noise from outside returned. Men shouted, a truck ground its gears.

Tate waited.

Martin fought for composure.

"Fili must never know for certain, Ben, that Ray did indeed change her will. Kindly tell that to the Captain." He glanced out of the window, then back at Tate. "If he reveals this to her, he will gain nothing but the crushing of a young woman whose mother has abandoned her. For a second time."

## CHAPTER FORTY

**Du Bois Murder Latest: Police seek outside suspect in farm death.**
**DNA evidence will be crucial.**
**No arrests yet.**

"So my daughter is not a suspect? She is no longer implicated?"
"Not directly, no," said the Captain over the phone to Martin. "But we still need to question her. She may have more information that will be useful going forward."
"So who is your suspect?"
"We're working on several leads, sir. I can't say more at this time."
"I trust you will treat my daughter more carefully in the future, Captain, and not make wild claims about her and Kula Mfusi. Or the nonsense over the phone. I was intending to return it to Mfusi's father after our meeting with the villagers. If Fili hadn't had it with her," Martin's voice broke for a moment, "she wouldn't have been able to call the ambulance – and perhaps save my wife -"
There was silence at the other end.
"My daughter deserves an apology, Captain."
"I cannot know what questions will distress Miss Du Bois, sir."

"Just be sensible, please." Martin tried to keep his voice civil. "My daughter is eighteen. If you were an eighteen-year-old implicitly accused of murder, wouldn't you also lose your balance?"

"Fili?" Dad tapped on the door. He came and sat down on the side of my bed. He was wearing a smart shirt and he'd combed his hair carefully. Shenay said he'd been at the church, arranging the funeral. "Can you forgive me for doubting you?"
I reached over and hugged him.
"Ben Tate was right," he muttered, "we must stand together. Du Bois will get through this."
*Du Bois will survive*, I wanted to reply. *The land will survive. But will my stake, my tenure...*
He straightened up. "Mum's funeral is to be on Friday, honey."
Fresh tears welled into his eyes. It's hard to see a grown man cry, especially when it's your father.
"Jean-Pierre will stay home with Shenay. You don't have to come if you don't want to, Fili."
"But I must," I gripped his arm. "I must be there for you and Grand-mère. Can I speak in church?"
It would be my chance to make everyone see I wasn't cowed by the stares and the mutters about genes and how you could never be sure of someone whose parents you didn't know. "Can I talk about Mum? I want to honour her. And you, Dad."
"Yes," he hesitated, his eyes showing a strange confusion, "yes of course you can."

He buried his face in his hands and I pulled him against me once more and held him like he'd held me at my birth church while the seagulls soared above us and the salty breeze stung my nose and my real mother remained unknown.

"Daddy!" Jean-Pierre raced in. "Daddy, the doctor's here! Why's the doctor here when Fili's better?"

I handed Dad a tissue and he quickly wiped his face and turned and caught Jean-Pierre in his arms.

"The doctor's here to make sure. Off we go, young man," he swung Jean-Pierre into his arms and bore him out.

"Fili?" Dr Saunders came in. "How are you today?"

"I'm fine. I'd like to get up, please."

She went through her usual routine, making me focus on her pen, taking my blood pressure and asking questions that required some logic and memory so she was sure my brain was still working.

"I want to go to Mum's funeral on Friday, Dr Saunders."

She put her pen in her bag and looked at me coolly.

"You're physically well enough, Fili. But are you well enough emotionally?"

"You mean will I be able to last without breaking down or fainting?"

She regarded me with a slightly reproving smile. "No, I think you'll be fine in that respect. I'm more concerned about how you'll respond to the other mourners. There will be lots of people looking at you. Are you prepared for that? Are you prepared for some," she hesitated, "some hostility?"

"Yes, I am."
Can't she tell I have ice in my veins? No hostility can hurt me if I don't let it reach my heart.

Mr Tate and I met Captain Dlamini in Dad's study. He sat in Dad's chair and Mr Tate and I sat opposite him. Through the window behind his head, the branches of my oak spread against the sky.
"Are you feeling better, Miss Du Bois?" he asked before he turned the tape recorder on.
"Yes, sir. My head is fine."
"I wish to state for the record," Mr Tate pointed to the recorder and the Captain switched it on, "I wish to state for the record that I reserve the right to stop the interview at any point if I feel my client's health is being compromised by the nature of the questioning."
The Captain made no reply, only opened his book and found where we left off. Perhaps he was disappointed that I was no longer the suspect because it meant searching for someone else.
"Miss Du Bois, you are aware of the findings of the autopsy?"
"Yes, sir."
"With the evidence of bruising on her shoulders and the presence of foreign DNA under her fingernails, Mrs Du Bois's death is now being treated as a potential murder."
A gust of wind eddied through the oak, making its leaves flutter. Did Mum's soul fly up to heaven like that? As an eddy? A shimmer, disappearing into the blue?

"These findings, plus the indication of time of death, means that you are not suspected of murder."

"Thank you, sir."

"But," he looked up from his notebook, "this does not necessarily exonerate you from involvement."

"You still think I had something to do with my mother's death?"

At my side, I could sense Mr Tate shifting in his chair. Whenever he feels I'm being provocative or swerving into territory that should be avoided, he shifts in his chair.

"I think you may be hiding more than you are telling about your relationship with Kula Mfusi."

"I have no relationship with Kula Mfusi. As I said before, he didn't like me. My father also knows this. He heard Kula Mfusi being rude to me."

"But the phone, Miss Du Bois, the phone," the Captain sighed and shook his head and looked back in his notes.

"Sir," I leaned forward, "if I planned to hurt my mother, if I planned to do so with Kula Mfusi's help, wouldn't I have returned the phone to him straightaway so that we could keep in touch? I kept it to stop him ordering more drugs. I kept it to expose the village connection. I kept it so maybe I could put pressure on him to leave."

"Miss Du Bois makes a valid point, Captain," Mr Tate intervened smoothly. "I believe the phone is no longer the key to this tragedy. It contains no incriminating evidence apart from the number of a drug dealer, therefore it cannot have been involved in the commission of this crime. I must ask you to move on."

"But what if Miss Du Bois planned her mother's death in person with Kula Mfusi?"

"What evidence do you have for that, sir?"

Captain Dlamini made no reply, but rather turned back in his notebook to an earlier page written on both sides. He scanned down to a particular spot and then looked up at me.

"Miss Du Bois, I need to go back to the subject you became upset about. I asked you if Kula Mfusi had been your lover. I asked you the question because I wanted to find out if your judgement may have been affected by your relationship with him. Even if you did not actively conspire with him to kill your mother - and this remains a line of investigation - it is possible that you were a witness to events that are relevant. Or to their aftermath."

"What do you mean, sir?"

Stall him. Remember Grand-mère's advice about not rushing in.

"You may have had no intention of hurting your mother but came upon Kula Mfusi after he had confronted Mrs Du Bois over the eviction. Mrs Du Bois had been pushed or fell. Kula Mfusi ran away and left you to deal with the tragedy on your own."

There was a knock on the door and Shenay pushed her head around.

"I have tea, sirs, Miss Fili."

She came in, casting an indignant glance at the Captain sitting in Dad's chair, and set the tray down on the desk.

"Will you pour, Miss Fili?"

"Yes, thank you, Shenay."

"Thank you, Ma'am," said the Captain.

It was a useful intervention for me. I think both men realised it, too, because by the time I'd poured tea, offered sugar and lemon, passed around Shenay's shortbread - plain, this time, presumably Mr Tate and the policeman didn't warrant Shenay's speciality - the Captain's theory had lost some of its fire and I had had time to formulate an answer.

"Sir, I never conspired with Kula Mfusi to kill my mother." I forced my tone to be even. "I'm already a Director of Du Bois Vineyards." Mr Tate nodded at my side. "I've always had the right to stay here, sir, alongside my brother. And I didn't come across Kula that morning. I never saw him."

"Do you believe Kula Mfusi killed your mother?"

"This is a speculative question, Captain Dlamini," Mr Tate said.

"Yes, it is. I am asking Miss Du Bois for her opinion and her answer will be recorded as such."

The Captain is a clever man. And he is persistent, worrying away at the bone in order to find the prize at its centre. I dare not even give him an opinion because he may find a way to turn it into fact and an innocent man may be tarnished. As I have been.

"I don't know if anyone killed my mother. Dr Saunders says she could have died of the aneurism at any time. I have no opinion about Kula Mfusi and whether he could commit a murder. I can't help you, sir."

But I have a private opinion.

I think he did it. Perhaps it was the drugs, perhaps it was rage over the eviction. Perhaps it was a combination of the two, a poison that fed into his brain and forced him to grip Mum by the shoulders...
And she fell.
Only he knows. And he is gone.
Or perhaps he didn't do it at all and we're looking in the wrong place for the killer.

## CHAPTER FORTY ONE

"I brought you a dress," said Petro, coming into my room with Evonne. "I didn't tell my mother, but I know you need a dress for the funeral -"

"Oh, Fili!" Evonne rushed to my bed and flung herself at me. "I'm so sorry, all these horrid stories -"

"Shut up, Evonne!" Petro hung the dress in my cupboard and came and sat on the other side of the bed. "Fili's had enough crying. When are you coming back to school?"

"Next week." I couldn't help smiling. Not even a murder would change Petro. "I want to come back but everyone will stare."

"We'll make sure they don't," Evonne asserted. "Won't we, Petro?"

"We can try," Petro shrugged, "but it's mostly up to you, Fili. The police say you didn't do it, so show everyone that you're confident. Defend yourself if you have to." She got up and marched over to my dressing table mirror and examined her complexion, tilting her head from side to side. "People must be made to feel sorry for you, convinced that you're been unfairly treated. Instead of being suspicious of you."

"What do your parents say?"

The girls glanced at each other, just a swift glance but enough to tell me that their belief in my innocence was not necessarily shared by their parents.

"How are you, Fili?" whispered Evonne, "really?"

"I'm sad," I said, trying not to cry. "I'm sad for Jean-Pierre and for Dad and for the whole farm."

"So who did it?" Petro perched once more on the side of the bed. "Was it Kula Mfusi? I saw him, you know, on Saturday morning."

"Where?" The words burst out of my mouth.

"On the road to Du Bois. I told the police. I actually went all the way to the police station and fought my way through that mob of reporters," she rolled her eyes, "to let them know."

"The papers said there were leads," Evonne whispered.

"I don't know," I said. "I don't know who did it."

Better to give nothing away than compromise myself or anyone else. I'm learning to hold my tongue. Grand-mère would say that was no bad thing, but to me it feels like suffocation.

"We'll be at the funeral," said Petro. "Will your head be better by then?"

"Now you two must shoo!" Shenay bustled into the room. "Miss Fili has to rest. Doctor's orders!"

No-one knew where Adam Mfusi, Kula Mfusi, Peter Choba or Abraham Phillips had gone. It was as if they'd vanished into the summer heat like a mirage that was there one moment, gone the next.

"Have you tried the informal settlements beyond the railway line?" Captain Dlamini demanded.

"Yes," said the young constable who'd been put in charge of the search operation. "I spoke to the community leaders, I spoke to the spaza shop owners, I asked at the shops in town. I told them that if they saw any of them, they must tell them to come to the police station."

"You were there when we found old man Mfusi, weren't you?"

"Yes, sir, I was. I asked him where he was going next and he said he didn't know. He also said that he'd stay until the end of the week."

"He changed his mind," Captain Dlamini snorted. "Of course he would! Police asking questions. He wasn't going to wait around. Probably packed up the minute he heard our van start."

"Yes, sir. I felt sorry for him, sir. I don't think he hated the Du Bois's."

The Captain regarded the junior man with pity. Poor fellow. He had a lot to learn. Imagine what he'd make of the grieving but devious Miss Du Bois. Now there was a puzzle still to be fully solved. Just because she hadn't killed her mother with her own hands didn't mean she was innocent.

"Keep at it, constable."

The day of Mum's funeral dawned bright and warm. The mountains shed their early morning mist and rose above the valley, turning from pink to grey as the sun wandered across their face. The vines had never looked so lush, the roses were opening fresh blooms that Mum would never see.

"Very smart, Miss Fili," approved Shenay, noticing my borrowed navy dress. "Ma'am would like it."

The dress was a little long for me but perhaps that was just as well because it was rather tight over my curves. Petro is slimmer than me. Shenay herself was firmly trussed into a shiny black jacket under her apron even though she was staying at home to look after Jean-Pierre. "I've got to, Miss Fili," she muttered, wiping away a tear, "your Ma deserves it."

"We should go," said Dad, his normally tanned face pale against his dark suit and black tie.

"Fili," Jean-Pierre looked up from his toy planes, "can Mummy hear me in heaven?"

"Be good, listen to Shenay," Dad bent down to kiss his son. Grand-mère fondled his hair. Jean-Pierre jumped up and ran to me and buried his face in my skirt.

"Can we play hide-and-seek afterwards?"

"Yes," I forced a smile. "We'll play whatever you want."

The church was the one I'd known since I was a baby, when I used to sit in Mum's lap and look up at the soaring roof, or over her shoulder at our curious neighbours. Today, every pew was full. Dad led Grand-mère in and I followed. I could hear the murmur as the congregation spotted me, I could see their mouths opening as they whispered amongst themselves.

*Poor child, what an ordeal.*

*The papers said she fell at the police station.*

*They say she's still a suspect...*

"We are gathered here today to celebrate the life of Ray Ellen Du Bois. Friend, companion, wife, mother, and daughter."

A sigh rolled through the church. Mum's parents were long dead, but at least that meant her soul would not be lonely in heaven. The organ began to play and we stood for the first hymn.

*Abide with me, fast falls the eventide...*

I don't remember much about the service.

I think the minister spoke about Mum's life, I caught snatches of her childhood in Stellenbosch and her meeting Dad as a young woman. Clearer to me was the sense of the congregation being a living thing, a massed body of subtle shifts, whispered words, synchronous movements as we stood or sat. At any moment, at some unknown signal, might they throw off the ritual and rise from their seats as one... and drive me out of the church?

By my side, Grand-mère sat with a bowed head, and a hand firmly clasping mine.

On my other side, Dad was unnaturally still; he stood when he had to, he opened his mouth during the hymns but no sound emerged. His hands did not fidget. It was as if life had temporarily left him.

*All things bright and beautiful, All creatures great and small...*

"And now, Ray's beloved daughter, Fili, would like to say a few words."

The background murmur stopped. The silence roared in my ears. My feet were glued to the floor.

"Thank you, Fili, please step this way."

They were waiting for me.

"Go, *chérie*," whispered Grand-mère, nudging me. "Make her proud."

I have never stood in front of a congregation before.

They were mostly white, apart from Philemon and Bo and the group of villagers who'd squeezed into three minibus taxis to get here. Their group formed a tight, brown block in the centre of the church. I searched for Evonne or Petro but I couldn't see them. Dad and Grand-mère were looking up at me from the front row. Or rather Grand-mère was, Dad was staring down at his hands.

"Mum and Dad saved me," I began, "like Jesus saves us all."

I turned and glanced at the statue of the crucified Christ at the altar.

"They rescued me from a life of poverty and brought me to Du Bois and made me their daughter -" my voice ran out and I breathed deeply.

"Mum explained one day why I was different from her."

Dad looked up.

"She told me there are many proteas in the world and they all look a little different. And that was why there was nothing strange about me being a little different from her."

They were listening. They weren't moving or whispering, they were listening - as one - to me.

"Mum did her best for me. She tried to get me into dresses like this," I waited for the titter to abate, and I think I heard a giggle that sounded like Petro's, "and she let me hold my baby brother, Jean-Pierre, on the day she came home from the hospital. We became a complete family that day. I would never harm my family, especially the only mother I have ever known. The only mother I have ever loved."

Dad was staring at me from the front row. Grand-mère was dabbing her eyes with a black lace handkerchief. I could hear crying, from further back.

"After her family, I think Mum loved her roses the most. She cared for them, she pruned them, she picked them and they filled the house with perfume. They were as beautiful as Mum. Fragrant Cloud. Peace. Just Joey."

The congregation were nodding, the tension was unwinding.

"I'll look after her roses for her. I'll make sure they stay healthy and I'll pick them in the summer and fill the house with them. Mum showed me what beauty is, but also that it could be found in different places."

I stepped down and rejoined Dad and Grand-mère.

And then I was the only one sitting. The congregation had indeed risen as one - and they were clapping. Dad stroked my head. Grand-mère nodded to me through her tears. Still they clapped, and their warmth swept over me and lifted some of the ice from around my heart.

## CHAPTER FORTY TWO

**Murder Victim Buried.**
**Ray Du Bois, of Du Bois Vineyards, was buried yesterday after a funeral service attended by hundreds of mourners led by her husband, Martin Du Bois. No arrests have been made so far but this newspaper understands that police are looking to question four men who lived in an informal settlement on the edge of Du Bois Vineyards. Miss Fili Du Bois, the victim's adopted daughter who discovered her mother's body, delivered an emotional eulogy which was well received. Police say investigations are ongoing and all possibilities are being pursued.**

I walked around the farm today for the first time in over a month. The vines are looking good. I don't need to measure the bunches, I can tell that they're the correct size for this time of the year with the sun we've had and the rain that's fallen. Next year, when I'm at university, I'll learn about the latest science on bunch sizes. But here, as I felt the berries between my fingers, I knew they were doing well. I stopped at the end of the row. On a patch of grass a few metres away, a rakish hoopoe strutted and pecked for insects. It spotted me, spread its showy crest, and swooped away.
"Miss Du Bois?"
I turned.
Captain Dlamini was puffing along the path towards me.

"Miss Du Bois? Can I ask you something?"

"Don't I need my lawyer present, sir?"

He stopped and caught his breath and gave a shame-faced smile.

"Yes, you always have the right to a lawyer. But I don't have my tape with me," he cast me an embarrassed look, "so you could always deny saying anything."

I found myself smiling back at him. He was doing his best. He hadn't intended that I should react to his questioning by falling to the ground and hurting my head. But I mustn't allow him to lull me into a confession of any sort because we happen to be out in the open and the farm is wrapping me in its seductive beauty. He's not the sort of policeman who gives up when a murderer isn't conveniently found.

"What do you want to know, sir?"

"Why did you want the windows and shutters to be closed on the night of the murder?"

I racked my brain for the memory. Who had told him? Shenay helped wash the blood off my hands, she changed me into pyjamas, the doctor gave me a pill that made my eyes heavy, I asked someone to close the windows, Grand-mère said hush, sleep now...

"I don't remember why."

I felt darkness creep across my vision and I sat down on the grass where the hoopoe had been.

"Miss Du Bois?" he squatted down beside me. "Are you feeling sick again?"

Beads of sweat were gathering on his forehead. He was feeling the heat, too.

"No," I gritted my teeth. "I'm fine, it's just hot."

"You see the issue here. If you asked for the windows and shutters to be closed, you must have been worried about an attack on your home. At that stage we did not know if Mrs Du Bois had died from natural causes or not. But it seems to me that you, Miss Du Bois, already knew. You were afraid the murderer might strike again."

I stared into his eyes. Normally we were across a desk from one another. But now he could see every fleeting emotion in my face as clearly as I could see the sweat on his brow.

"I'd been given a pill to make me sleep. I could have been rambling."

The grass was pricking the back of my legs below my shorts. The sun was beating down like an avenging force.

"Miss Du Bois, how did you know it was murder before anyone else did?"

A black-shouldered kite hovered over the nearby ridge. How do kites hold so still in the air? Do they calculate the exact number of times they must beat their wings, or is it down to the strength of each beat? Who teaches them or is it embedded in their bodies from their parents?

How did I know it was murder?

I didn't, I just assumed the worst.

Captain Dlamini lumbered to his feet and held out his hand to help me up.

"I want you to think about my question, Miss Du Bois. If you know something you aren't telling me, then you could be obstructing justice."

Yet if they don't know what I'm hiding, they won't know if it is relevant. Maybe they have a theory? Maybe they believe I saw Kula - the disturbance in the bush wasn't a buck, it was a man fleeing a murder - but without a second witness or the discovery of his matching DNA, they're helpless. I am their only lead. But how can I implicate him if I'm not sure?

*Proof*, Grand-mère once said, *can be a slippery thing.*

"Is there anything else, sir?"

"No." He looked at me. "Are you coming back to the house, Ma'am? You should get out of the heat."

"I'll go in later. I have to look at my vines. I'm responsible for this year's chardonnay."

He raised his eyebrows and began to walk down the path. The dust was caking his boots.

"Be aware, Miss Du Bois," he turned back for a moment, "you're remain a person of interest in this case. You could still be charged as an accomplice."

I went back to school two days later.

"Are you sure, Fili?" asked Dad quietly over breakfast when he saw me in my uniform.

"Yes. I have to go, my exams are coming soon."

"I'll take you," he said, "and fetch you."

"No, Dad," I put a hand on his arm. "you can take me in the morning but I'll get the bus home. I need to show I'm not afraid."

Evonne was as good as her word. I'd sent her a text, and she and Petro were waiting for me outside the school gates. They stayed at my side all day, talking to me, shielding me. It turned out that their vigilance wasn't necessary.

"It's because of your speech at your mother's funeral," Evonne said triumphantly. "Petro took notes, she wrote some of it up on a facebook post. Everyone read it, Fili."

"Thank you," I turned to Petro who was immersed in her phone.

"I thought people should know," she looked up. "Pity I couldn't take a video. Then they would've seen you in my dress!" she giggled. "Mum nearly choked when she saw you - didn't you notice?"

"The thing is," I leaned towards them, "the police still think I could be involved. They say I might be an accomplice."

Evonne frowned. "How come?"

"They think I'm protecting Kula Mfusi."

"Well, you'd be crazy to do that," said Petro, snapping her phone shut. "You need to get over this loyalty, Fili. The squatters have gone. Kula will probably never be found. So there's no point in holding back. Why don't you give the police more than they can deal with?"

There was a beat of silence.

"She's right," breathed Evonne, eyes lighting up. "Distract them with detail!"

"Exactly." Petro beamed. "Overwhelm them. Tell them Kula hated all whites, remind them he was a drug

addict, say he didn't get on with the others. Tell them whatever is true. Full disclosure."
*You don't make it easy for anyone to be friends with you,* I'd said to him at the dam.
*I don't need friends,* he'd replied. *They let you down. And your mother wants to kick us out.*

Bo was waiting for me after school. He stepped out from the shade of a gum tree and began to walk alongside me as the bus pulled away.
"Fili?"
"Not yet. Wait until no-one can see us."
We went a little further, then he grabbed me and kissed me briefly.
"Is it true? They've stopped questioning you? Are we safe, Fili?"
I leaned back in his arms. Of all of us, Bo has actually been the most afraid. Not of being accused of murder - his alibi is rock solid - but because he fears being caught between a drug addict, outraged villagers, relentless police, the girl he loves, his father, my father...
"They won't stop yet, Bo. But we have nothing to hide."
He shook his head violently. "You're wrong. We do."
"What?"
He groaned and pulled away from me.
"I love you, Fili," he said, his brown eyes intense. "But when the police find that out, they'll think we planned this together, with Kula."
"Why? Why would they think that?"

"Remember," Bo seized my hand, "when you said we could run the farm alongside Jean-Pierre one day? Your father wouldn't mind, or the *ou missus*. You thought you might even persuade them, and the villagers, to let Mfusi and the others stay."

"So?"

"Think, Fili!" He beat our clasped hands gently against his chest. "The only person who'd say no to that would've been your mother. She would never have agreed to that sort of plan."

The gum trees swayed above me, the sun shafted through their sparse canopy. Mum could have been the potential stumbling block to our golden future, and to the men remaining.

"But if she was gone," I murmured, "we'd have free rein."

"The police might think we did it for that," Bo's voice almost failed. "The three of us. You, me and Kula. Together."

It would be a motive for murder that went beyond a drug-fuelled rage or an individual grudge.

And Bo and I would be co-conspirators.

Potentially, co-accomplices?

## CHAPTER FORTY THREE

Adam Mfusi decided to go to the police station.

He had set up a shelter near an outlet pipe on the edge of town but he'd had to walk into the centre to buy bread and it was there that he heard his name, along with Kula's and Peter's and Abraham's, and also the speculation that Mrs Du Bois had not died from a disease but had been murdered.

The police wanted to speak to all four of them.

It had been on the radio and in the newspapers.

Unless he left the area, sooner or later they'd pick him up. He prayed Kula had gone far away.

"I am Adam Mfusi," he said to the constable in the charge office. "You want to see me."

The young man's eyes widened at his name.

"Yes, Mr Mfusi. Please sit down. The Captain wants to talk to you."

But it turned out that the Captain was more keen to wipe out his mouth with a swab.

"Why do you want to do this?" he asked, keeping his lips resolutely shut.

The fat Captain looked at him carefully and spoke in Xhosa, which made it easier. The police had evidence of who killed Mrs Du Bois and they could compare his saliva with that evidence to prove he, Adam Mfusi, was not the murderer.

And they wanted to do the same thing with the other three, especially his son.

Adam felt a chill. Was there a way, even if his saliva was not the same as the evidence, they could tell that Kula's might compare better?

"My boy is not a murderer, sir," Adam said, after they'd put the swab in a tube and sealed it up.

The Captain shrugged. "Maybe. But you knew he was a drug addict?"

Mfusi nodded. How had they found out? That business with Miss Fili? He supposed they would have insisted she tell them. Poor Miss Fili. Caught up in a death when all she wanted to do was help.

"Have you seen your son since we were at the informal settlement?"

"No, sir. I have not seen Kula. I don't know where he is. I don't know if I will see him again."

It had happened before.

Several times.

Kula disappeared, Mfusi himself was forced to move on and despaired of ever seeing his son again, but eventually Kula always reappeared. He seemed to have an instinct about where his father would be. He'd turn up, sometimes with blood shot eyes but more often completely normal, bearing a bag of food and no inclination to reveal where he'd been and what he'd done.

Adam Mfusi had learned to welcome him back and be grateful. Kula, when sober and not enraged by white privilege, had a rough charm that was hard to resist.

## CHAPTER FORTY FOUR

Bo and I have decided we must no longer meet. It's too dangerous to give the police the chance to wonder if our closeness indeed has a more sinister nature. I don't meet him at the dam any longer, and I can't take him to my dance, even if I wanted to go. But I don't. How could I manage to laugh and enjoy myself when Mum is so newly buried? And Joe Steyn, who asked me to be his date in the aftermath of my elevation to Director, seems to have changed his mind. He slinks away, pretending he doesn't see me.

But I have a new set of admirers. Petro's facebook post about my funeral speech has gone viral, reaching beyond the valley and into a world where everyone feels they know me.

*Be strong*, strangers tell me in an unconscious imitation of what I've so often told myself.

*Don't let them take you down.*

*I know you, you could not have done it.*

*#Filibestrong* gathers thousands of supporters on a new messaging system.

Yet instead of making me feel better, I have the sense that I'm losing my identity. It's being splintered into tiny pieces that other people are picking at and examining. They're answering for me. They're speaking as if they have special access to who I am.

How dare they?

At home, the telephone rings constantly, especially now that the press have decided that I didn't kill my mother but may still have something worth revealing.

**Filli Du Bois... in her own words**, they propose for an article.

**Growing up as an adoptee - the real story,** for a women's magazine.

Even those who don't get through still write opinion pieces about my state of mind at the time of my mother's death as if they were with me, looking down at the blood trickling past her ear. Dad refuses to allow the telephone callers to speak to me. Captain Dlamini warns me that I'm still part of an active investigation.

"Ignore all this," murmurs Grand-mère, peering over my shoulder at the hundreds of messages that crowd my screen, "they know nothing of you or Du Bois. Remember what I said, child. Be discreet. Speak out only amongst we three. The rest is merely noise."

I present myself at the police station after school. Mr Tate is at my side - which is as well because Captain Dlamini remains convinced I'm hiding something and will keep probing, while Mr Tate will call a halt if he worries about what I might say.

But I have to change the game. I need to take back the identity I fear I'm losing amid the noise.

And I must steer the police away from Bo and the possibility of a three-way collaboration.

"I asked for the windows and shutters to be closed because I was afraid Kula Mfusi might attack us," I announced before Captain Dlamini could ask the first question.

The Captain raised his eyebrows. "And what made you afraid?"

"Because he'd been to our house at night before."

Would Grand-mère approve of my new approach? This is surely similar to being a go-between, pointing the way but leaving the hunter to decide what action to take. Or perhaps it is a dangerous initiative, as Dad might call it, and a game I should never play.

Mr Tate leaned towards me and murmured into my ear. "Should we discuss this first?"

"No, Mr Tate. I saw Kula Mfusi in our garden one night, when my parents and their friends were on the verandah, discussing the squatters' eviction."

Overwhelm the police, Petro and Evonne had said. Overwhelm them with detail.

The Captain leaned forward. "This was before your father told the squatters to leave?"

"Yes, sir."

He looked at me for a long moment.

"Why didn't your dog bark, Miss Du Bois? Was he inside the house?"

"No, Blaze was in the garden. I saw him."

"Are you saying that Kula Mfusi was able to approach your house without arousing the dog?"

"Yes, sir."

Kula is a dog whisperer. I know it, and now the Captain does, too.

"That's why I was afraid he could come, sir, and no-one would know until it was too late."

I didn't tell Captain Dlamini that Kula had also come in daylight, to leave a note for me. I didn't want him to know that Kula had shown any remorse for his past behaviour. If Kula did kill my mother, why should I show him any sympathy?

But what if he didn't, the voice in my head needled. What if he's condemned because of you...

"Thank you, Miss Du Bois. We'll call you again if we need anything further."

He switched off the tape recorder and stood up, ushering us out of the room.

"Fili?" Mr Tate asked, as we stood outside the station. "Is this a new tactic?"

Tiny clouds scudded across the sky. My exams were starting the following week. And then it would be Christmas - we'd have to put on a show for Jean-Pierre – and, soon afterwards, the hardest of harvests. But after that, hopefully, I'd be one of thousands of students at university, one of those scudding clouds indistinguishable from the rest. I could disappear - and find myself again.

"Fili?" Mr Tate repeated. "You do realise you're implicating Mfusi? You tried to shield him earlier on but now you're implicating him."

I stared up at the mountains. They look down on us, they know who killed Mum.

"I'm just giving as much information as I can, Mr Tate. That's what the Captain has always wanted."

"Indeed," Mr Tate nodded. "But he's no fool. He'll wonder at your sudden eagerness to help."

A car pulled up. I made ready to run back into the station in case it was a reporter, but it was only a pair of uniformed policemen. They piled out of their car, nodded to us, and headed inside.

"I've been accused of protecting the squatters, sir. I did try, because they were good people. But Kula was different. He hated me. He hated all of us."

"Be that as it may, I would suggest," Mr Tate said quietly, "that you discuss any further revelations with me before you present them to the police. You're my client, Fili," a note of irritation crept into his voice, "and my brief is to prove you innocent of any role in the sad death of your mother. I can't do that if I'm constantly being thrown on the back foot."

"I understand, Mr Tate. I'm sorry."

"Let's get into the car." He opened the passenger door for me and then went around to the driver's side and got in.

"I didn't hurt my mother, Mr Tate. And I didn't conspire with anyone else to hurt her."

He turned to look at me and gave a tense smile.

"It doesn't matter, Fili. It's what they," he pointed at the police station, "find out."

"And what do they know so far?"

"They suspect there's a fair chance it's Kula Mfusi's DNA beneath your mother's fingernails. But until they find him - or an alternative culprit - they'll have no proof. You are the only connection between the crime scene

and the suspected perpetrator. You could be an innocent party, or you could be an accomplice. Even if you played no part in the actual crime, any piece of corroborative evidence that shows you conspired with Kula in a way detrimental to your family may be sufficient to charge you as an accessory."
"When will I be in the clear?"
"If the perpetrator is arrested and either confesses he acted alone or the police can prove his guilt while finding no evidence that you helped him, then you will be clear." He started up the car. "I'll drive you home."
Our car journeys away from the police station have tended to be silent and this one was no different. I could understand why. If you were her lawyer, how would you manage to find light conversation to bridge the gap between police suspect and normal eighteen-year-old girl?
The valley's orderly sweep of vineyards flowed past my window. A labourer heading out of town waved at us, hoping for a lift.
"You can drop me at the gate, sir. I'll walk up the avenue."
But he ignored me and drove up to the house.
"Thank you for the ride, Mr Tate."
He lifted a hand, reversed and drove off.
*What if the perpetrator is never found, Mr Tate?*
*For how long will I live in this limbo of being neither guilty nor innocent?*

\*

Martin had started taking late-night walks with Blaze.

He told himself it was to make sure the property was secure, that no-one was lurking near his mother's cottage, for instance, or on Gum Tree Avenue. Blaze, of course, would bark, and that would surely scare away any would-be intruders.

But in reality Martin walked because it seemed to be the only way to get his thoughts in order.

Ben Tate had said that, in her most recent interview with Captain Dlamini, Fili had implicated Kula Mfusi in Ray's death. She suggested that Mfusi had come to the house in the past, and that she feared he would do the same on the night of Ray's death and attack them while they slept.

At first Martin put this down to the trauma of finding her mother's lifeless body, she'd been given a sleeping tablet, she had allowed her imagination to take over...

But then he'd started wondering how Fili could have known that Kula had come to the house before.

And, if so, why hadn't she raised the alarm?

Martin had been proud of the way she'd tried to help the squatters. But she'd kept quiet about the drugs for too long, and the phone. Why didn't she confide in him sooner? She said she wanted to use the phone as evidence to get Kula to leave, but was that entirely true?

Yet how could he doubt her? His precious daughter?

Martin stared down the dark avenue. The gum trees stood like sentinels in the still air.

Blaze whined and pressed his nose into Martin's hand.
He turned and headed back.
And then there was Ray's intention to disinherit her daughter. He could hardly bear to think of it. He had never imagined his wife to be so cruel. Misguided at times, yes. But never this cruel.
As a result, every word of Fili's eulogy at Ray's funeral had stabbed at his heart. Over and over.
Please God she never finds out for certain -
Sometimes his solitary walks did not serve to order his thoughts.
Sometimes they threw up possibilities and challenges that he would prefer to avoid.

## CHAPTER FORTY FIVE

"Miss Fili?"

I turned, startled. Tannie Ellie beckoned to me from the path.

"Will you take some water, Miss? In our place? It's very hot."

I looked at her warily. Tannie Ellie had never invited me into her cottage before. Maybe, in the light of the tragedy, she wished to make peace. Or use me to pass on a message to Dad and Grand-mère that there would be no more trouble now the squatters were gone.

"Thank you, Tannie," I said, coming out of the vines. "That's kind of you."

We set off along the path, not far from the spot where I'd found Kula. Tannie shuffled ahead of me without saying anything further. Since the murder, the village had been unnaturally quiet, too. Folk went about their duties in silence, there weren't even any shouts from the pitch because the children had been told that noise was disrespectful.

"You're back at school, Miss Fili?" she asked as we neared her cottage.

"Yes. I start my exams next week."

"You should be at home, learning," she observed, "not fiddling about in the vines."

I hid a smile. Tannie couldn't be emollient for long.

She pushed open the door. "Sit down, Miss Fili."

A sharply-dressed man in his thirties rose from the couch. It was Blake, Tannie's nephew.

"Hello Fili," he gave me a broad smile and offered a hand encrusted with rings. "I haven't seen you for a while. I'm sorry about your mother."

I shot a glance at the front door. Closed but not locked. I could get out -

"Please sit, Miss Fili," repeated Ellie as if she could read my mind.

"Why are you here? And Tannie," I rounded on her, "how dare you lure me in? I won't sit!"

I turned back to Blake. "What do you want?"

"Fili," he adopted a wheedling tone, "please. I need to know what you've told the police."

He settled himself on the couch and motioned me to do the same but I stayed on my feet.

Who else had seen him? How much did this compromise me? I should leave -

"Look," he said, spreading out his arms, playing the reasonable man, "you've got Kula's phone. He told me. So you might have told them about me."

I felt my body tense. "You've seen him? Since my mother died?"

"Why do you want to know? So you can tell the police?"

Tannie Ellie poured a glass of water from the jug by her side and handed it to me.

"Kula Mfusi is bad, Miss Fili," she sniffed, "and my Blake has been caught up in his badness."

I drank it down, then placed the glass on a nearby table.

"You supplied drugs to Kula," I said to Blake, "and you, Tannie Ellie," I pointed at her, "knew about it - probably even encouraged it!" The words and gestures were rude, I know, but I haven't spent days under interrogation without learning that boldness often gets results that reticence doesn't.

"Fili, "Blake leaned forward and forced a smile, "I don't want trouble. I need Kula's phone back, that's all. That's what I've come for."

For all the smart clothes and easy grin, I could tell he was nervous. He kept twisting his rings.

"I haven't got it."

He darted a look at his aunt. "Then where is it?"

"I used the phone to call the ambulance when I found my mother. The police have it."

Their gasps were stifled by the moan of the wind through the shade trees. A southeaster was picking up. By tomorrow it would be in full voice.

"Did they look at it?" he rasped.

I made him wait. I wanted to unnerve him further.

"If you're asking whether they know you supplied Kula with drugs, I don't know. But they'd be able to find your number, and who it's registered to. I didn't tell them your name," I paused and then added, deliberately, "but you called Kula. It's in the phone's memory."

He looked at me hard, wondering if I was lying and what it would mean if I was.

"Why didn't you tell them, Miss Fili?" Tannie's Ellie's voice was harsh. "You could've made trouble for my Blake. Set the police after him straightaway."

Again, I made them wait.

"My father was planning to evict the squatters." I looked from her to Blake. "I decided not to add drugs to the mix. I tried to protect the village. You should be more grateful. Both of you."

I turned towards the door. Blake got up as if to stop me.

"Thank you for the water, Tannie. And don't forget," I proffered the glass, but kept hold of it for a moment before letting her take it, "I know everything. The thefts. The drugs. Everything."

I could tell she was angry but I could also sense fear, like I learned to sense Mum's fear.

"My respects to the family, Miss Fili," she said in a small voice.

Blake walked to the door beside me. His early swagger was gone. "I haven't told Tannie," he muttered, glancing over his shoulder as Ellie went into the kitchen, "but I've moved. Just as well, if the police are after me. And I always use separate phones for my customers," he opened his jacket and showed me pockets bulging with devices. "I threw Kula's away as soon as I heard he was in trouble." He grimaced and opened the door.

"Goodbye," I said. "Stay away from Du Bois in future."

"I suppose I should tell you," he added casually, as I stepped out, "Kula wants to see you. I told him it was stupid, but he wants to see you."

Do you know what it means to be an 'accessory-after-the-fact'?

It means you've assisted a perpetrator to evade detection after a crime. A kind of accomplice, but only after the event - in this case a potential murder. Even if the perpetrator is never found, you can still be charged as an accessory-after-the-fact if there's proof you helped the murderer escape the law and the punishment that should have come his way.

No, I told myself as I strode down the path, you will not meet Kula.

If he didn't kill Mum, he should give himself up to the police and they can test his DNA and it won't match and he'll be beyond suspicion. But, the voice in my head whispered, what if he knows something that's important to the investigation but can't come forward?

"Fili!" Dad was waving at me from the verandah.

Jean-Pierre raced through the roses to meet me. "Fili, come!" He grabbed my hand and dragged me along. "Hurry, they're here! Grand-mère's got them!"

A hand clutched at my heart.

They?

The police knew about Blake? I'm already compromised?

"Come inside, honey," Dad said. His eyes were bright with unshed tears. I opened my mouth to cry out, to say that we couldn't survive another blow, that our family had been tested enough -

Grand-mère was sitting at the dining room table with a set of documents spread out before her.

"Ah, *chérie*," she got up with difficulty and held out her arms, "you're a winner, child."

"A winner?"

"Yes," Dad grabbed one of the papers and waved it. "Your cabernet's been awarded five stars!"

I felt for a chair and sat down.

My wine.

My *treize ans* cabernet was a winner.

Grand-mère clapped her hands, Jean-Pierre climbed onto my lap and wrapped his arms about my neck.

"Miss Fili!" Philemon stood in the doorway, holding his cap in his hand. "Congratulations, Miss!" Bo was standing behind Philemon. I set Jean-Pierre down, went to each of them, and we hugged. It wasn't really my triumph, even though they were being generous enough to give it to me.

"Thank you, Philemon. It's actually your award, your five stars."

He twisted his cap. "My pleasure, Miss Fili."

"Mum would be proud," Dad murmured in my ear. "She really would."

"Well done, Fili," Bo pecked my cheek and whispered, "I'll be at the dam tomorrow, before supper."

Dad and Grand-mère began discussing how to make an announcement. An interview? A statement? Perhaps, Grand-mère was suggesting with a twinkle, the papers that have so besieged us may be persuaded to report a slice of better news. I watched them. This was the boost Du Bois needed. Jean-Pierre clutched my hand and giggled at the noise. Somehow we've managed to keep him busy and surrounded with enough love to distract from what he, and we, have lost. I leaned down and hugged him. We need more giggles, it's been too quiet of late.

But this trial, although not yet in court, is not over. Not for me.

*Kula wants to see you.*

*I told him it was stupid but he wants to see you.*

At what point do I become tainted by meeting him?

Yet if Kula confesses he acted alone and there's no evidence I helped him either as an accomplice or an accessory, then I'll be clear.

As will Bo.

## CHAPTER FORTY SIX

"She doesn't have the phone," said Blake. "The police have it."

Blake hadn't wanted to meet Kula again, but he reckoned it would be the last time.

Did Kula kill Ray Du Bois? In a drug-induced mood, maybe he did. But Blake didn't intend to ask. He didn't need to know. The whole thing had become messy and he wanted to put distance between himself and anyone involved with what had happened at Du Bois Vineyards. He planned to move to Johannesburg. It would mean more competition, but he had a friend up there who had a thriving business and needed a partner. He was finished here, whatever happened. He'd said nothing of this to Tannie Ellie, of course. She could never keep her mouth shut.

"Did she tell you what she told the police? About me? About you?"

Kula, Blake noted, was looking better, despite the pressure of being hunted. He hadn't ordered any drugs, although maybe he'd found another dealer. Or maybe he'd reckoned he needed to have his wits about him in the circumstances. Blake had seen what drugs could do and wouldn't touch them, himself. His reputation as a partying, boozing ladies' man was a carefully constructed lie in order to acquire clients. Business was business. Pleasure would come afterwards, on his own terms.

"Fili said nothing to them about who supplied the drugs, Kula. And I believe her. But my message to you is on the phone, so the police will guess from that."

"What about Fili? Will she see me?"

Blake wondered why Kula wanted to see the girl. Ellie said she was keen on Philemon Sammy's boy. Surely seeing her would serve no purpose?

"She wouldn't say if she'd meet you or not. She's angry, and upset about her mother, and being questioned so much."

There was silence. Kula stared outside the hut, towards the ocean.

Blake rose and punched Kula's shoulder lightly.

"Get away while you still have the chance."

## CHAPTER FORTY SEVEN

"So, Captain," began the Prosecutor, regarding Dlamini across his desk, "you have a middle-aged woman with a history of hypertension and headaches, who dies of a brain aneurism while walking in the vineyards of her wine estate. She is found by her adoptive daughter who attempts resuscitation. There is bruising on the body, and the DNA under the dead woman's fingernails belongs to a close relative of squatters who had taken up residence on the edge of Du Bois Vineyards. You have a search warrant out for the prime suspect, Kula Mfusi, but as yet you have not found him. Am I correct so far?"

"Yes," said Dlamini. "Please be assured that the search for him is our main focus. But there are others involved, who may have had a motive."

The Prosecutor regarded Dlamini and then lifted his hands in light protest.

"A motive for what, exactly? Any defence lawyer will produce expert witnesses to testify that Mrs Du Bois's death was the result of an underlying medical condition. The unfortunate lady could have dropped dead at any time. The fact that there seems to have been some sort of altercation does not prove that she was murdered, Captain."

There was a silence.

Dlamini glanced at his notebook and then at the Prosecutor who was leaning back in his chair.

"I suggest, sir, that a case can be made for Fili Du Bois, the victim's adoptive daughter, conspiring with one or more persons to cause harm to Mrs Du Bois."

The Prosecutor raised his eyebrows.

"Really? Why, Captain? What would be her particular motive?"

"I believe the motive has been building for several years, sir."

"Very well," the Prosecutor gave a half-smile and settled into his chair, "enlighten me."

Dlamini had rehearsed how he would present the case. The Prosecutor was a sharp man – unlike some of the lazier ones - and he would leap on any mistake. Dlamini would have to be precise.

"Miss Du Bois was known to have a tense relationship with her adoptive mother. This sprang from two issues: a dispute over inheritance of Du Bois, and a difference of opinion over the informal settlement – Mrs Du Bois wanted the men evicted, Miss Du Bois felt they should be allowed to stay and encouraged her father to employ them."

"Please begin with the inheritance angle, Captain."

"Thank you, sir. Miss Du Bois was adopted as an infant because her parents were unable to have children. However, a biological child was born when Miss Du Bois was a teenager and already established – so she thought - as sole heir to Du Bois Vineyards. She was determined to retain her position, or at least retain an equal share with her new brother, Jean-Pierre. Her mother preferred her son to inherit the majority of the estate."

"What evidence do you have to support that, Captain?"

"Interviews with neighbours and friends of the family confirm the dissent and the tension between the two. We also requested a sighting of the late Mrs du Bois' will, which confirms that it was changed in favour of her son. It is possible Miss Du Bois was aware of this change some time ago."

The Prosecutor nodded. "Interesting. Please continue."

"Let me move on to the situation of the informal settlement, sir. On the day before the death of Mrs Du Bois, the squatters had been given notice by Martin Du Bois that they had to leave. This was brought on by pressure from neighbouring land owners, from the resident Coloured workers, and the revelation – by Miss Du Bois to her father - that Kula Mfusi, our current suspect, was a drug addict, being supplied by a village contact. We believe Mfusi's reason for attacking Mrs Du Bois was in revenge for the upcoming eviction."

"Go on, Captain."

"The following morning, after a meeting at the Coloured workers' village to announce the closure of the informal settlement, Miss Du Bois discovered her mother's body in the vineyards. A key point here is that she had Kula Mfusi's mobile phone with her and used it to call the ambulance. Miss Du Bois was found to be distraught at the scene and had to be sedated. Upon later questioning, she stated that she did not see Mfusi that morning, but could give no logical explanation for why his phone had been in her possession for, it turned out, several weeks prior to her mother's death."

"How did she explain it – illogically?"

Dlamini allowed a small smile. It was always best to acknowledge a Prosecutor's attempt at humour.

"Miss Du Bois claimed she had picked up the phone upon finding Mfusi unconscious from drugs. She said she intended to return it to him, but discovered that it had been used to order his supplies and therefore justified keeping it to prevent him doing so. She also planned to confront Mfusi and threaten to expose him to the police if he did not leave Du Bois. With his departure, she said she hoped to persuade her parents to allow the remaining squatters to stay and continue working at Du Bois."

"A convoluted - but not unreasonable – explanation, if I may say so," the Prosecutor frowned. "What is your position on this?"

"While Miss Du Bois has claimed she wanted Mfusi to leave Du Bois, we suspect a different sort of connection between the two. When questioned as to whether this was possibly of a romantic nature, Miss Du Bois became agitated and fainted." Dlamini paused for emphasis. "Throughout her questioning, I must report that Miss Du Bois has been devious, or failed to provide information that might have led to an early arrest of the suspect."

"Anything further?"

"Yes, sir. We know for a fact that there is a romantic relationship between Miss Du Bois and Bo Sammy, the son of the Coloured foreman at Du Bois Vineyards. The pair intended to play a leading role in the estate going forward. We have evidence Mrs Du Bois disapproved of this relationship and spoke of it to a friend."

"So, in the light of what you have told me, what is your case against Miss Du Bois, Captain?"

There it was. The most crucial part. Dlamini stopped and arranged his thoughts.

"We accept that Miss Du Bois did not personally kill her mother. But a case may be made that she conspired with either one or both of the young men – Kula Mfusi and Bo Sammy – to arrange the attack. Her mother's death would offer a significant benefit: the freedom to pursue her relationship with Bo Sammy and cement their joint role at Du Bois."

The Prosecutor viewed Dlamini with some sympathy. The police were taking heavy criticism for the apparent tardiness of the investigation, and the failure to arrest the likely perpetrator. And yet he was uneasy about them charging a young woman who had been trying to revive her dead mother; a young woman who was a model student and loving sister to her step-brother, and a keen promoter of her father's estate while being understandably ambitious for her own position. She was also, clearly, somewhat naïve regarding land invasions, an opinion that should not be held against her. But the police needed results, and Fili Du Bois was all they had - as a potential accomplice or co-conspirator. Be that as it may, it was necessary to haul the Captain back to the fundamentals.

"This is a difficult case, Captain. Even if you arrest Mfusi, the underlying health condition of Mrs Du Bois will always be a powerful weapon for the defence."

"Yes. But we will continue to search for more evidence, sir. The drug dealer, for instance."

"Indeed. As regards Miss Du Bois, I doubt you have enough at this time to charge her as an accomplice. I realise the anomalies in her statements; I note her utopian desire to encourage a mixed workforce at Du Bois and pursue a multiracial relationship with young Mr Sammy but come, Captain," he lifted his hands again, "these are traits many South Africans now happily share with her. I cannot see this young woman going as far as to commission a murder."

Dlamini inclined his head and played his final card.

"Sir, if we discover she later assisted the perpetrator or perpetrators to escape justice, then we could charge her as an accessory. That might unlock the case."

"Indeed it might." He stood up and extended his hand to Dlamini. "Thank you, this has been a useful update. Forgive me for rushing you, I'm now due in court."

They shook hands. Dlamini closed his notebook.

"Captain," the Prosecutor glanced up from gathering his papers, trying to give the man some comfort, "you may be onto something with the devious Miss Du Bois, as you called her. Or you may not. My advice would be to pursue Kula Mfusi, your prime suspect, with all the resources you can bring to bear. I recommend you keep an open mind on Miss Du Bois, ignore the media, follow the evidence and come back to me when you have something stronger."

## CHAPTER FORTY EIGHT

So often in my life, I find myself trapped.

Trapped between Coloured villagers and black squatters, between a real and an adoptive mother, between the knowledge that if I decide to meet Kula to establish his innocence or guilt, I will myself risk guilt by association.

I put off a decision. Perhaps, in fact, I should never reach a decision. There is a current, valid excuse.

"You have three hours," said the vice principal on the first day of exams. "May I remind you that electronic devices are not allowed, and there must be no conferring or communication between students. Turn over your papers. Good luck to you all."

I turned my paper over and scanned it.

Read the questions carefully, it says at the top. Make sure your name is on the front of your paper.

Check your work carefully. Marks may be lost for spelling and punctuation errors.

There was a multiple-choice section and then a choice of essay.

*Describe the impact of the re-unification of Germany on Europe, with particular emphasis on trade, politics, culture and the balance of power on the continent.*

*or*

*Trace the establishment of liberation movements in Africa, their supporters and detractors, and their successes and failures over the past half-century.*

To my right, Evonne flashed me a quick grin before settling down to write. She was clever, she'd have no trouble getting top marks. Petro would slide through, doing just enough to gain the pass required for university but not sufficient to make her parents over-ambitious. She wanted to party for a few years and then snap up an eligible man who could easily provide for her comfort.

I could tackle either topic. I've learnt about Germany, how the barriers between east and west came down and a nation was renewed. I also know about the African liberation movements and their fight for freedom. I should write about them. They're part of my heritage.

But I think I'll write about Germany.

And I will mention, in an aside I hope the examiner won't mind, that by an almost unbelievable coincidence, Nelson Mandela was released from his prison a few months after the crowds were chipping away at the wall that had separated the two Germanys. I won't say I'd probably been born around that time, too. The examiner will have no interest in my private history. Or that my Du Bois parents were about to take the biggest decision of their lives to adopt a stray child.

**Better news for Wine Murder Estate.**
**Du Bois Vineyards, site of the recent murder of farmer's wife Ray Du Bois, received some welcome news. The vineyard's Treize Ans Cabernet Sauvignon was awarded a five star rating at the recent wine**

awards. Du Bois could not be reached for comment but sources close to the family-run estate say that the recognition will help to heal the wounds of the recent tragedy. Pressure is growing on the police, who have made no arrests yet.

"Have you seen?" Petro chortled over the phone. "It's not just #Filibestrong, it's now #Filifivestar!" You're a celebrity! Who'd have thought?"
I logged on. Hundreds of messages of support from strangers who were also, it appeared, newly emboldened to share their theories about Mum's death:
*Is a serial killer on the loose in the winelands?*
*A rival wine farm wanted to stop Du Bois's rise...*
*I know you, you could not have done it...*
*Reverse apartheid is alive...*
*The police already know who did it...*

"Take a break from studying," said Grand-mère, casting a disapproving look at my screen, "and help me in my garden. I've rather neglected it. And it will be good for you to get outdoors, *chérie*."
We headed for her cottage, and I gathered her tools and eased her onto the folding stool she liked, so she could get down low enough to work the soil. Grand-mère always wanted to feel the earth between her fingers. There were no roses in her patch, she preferred squat plants that relished dry ground, like lavender and

succulent *vygies*. Plant for the hard times, she'd say. That way you'll always win.

"I love Bo, Grand-mère," I blurted, as we worked the tiny garden.

"I know, child," she snipped a spent clump. "I've been waiting for you to tell me. So what are you going to do about it?"

I raked up some fallen leaves and dumped them into the wheelbarrow to take to the compost heap. Nothing ever surprised Grand-mère. Or else she was well-skilled at masking her expression when it mattered most. I leaned on the rake and stared towards the village.

"Mum felt Bo wasn't good enough for me. She wanted me to meet someone else at university."

"That's not what I asked." Grand-mère adjusted the brim of her hat to protect her eyes from the lowering sun. "I asked what you, Fili, are going to do about it."

I glanced at her over the mounds of fragrant lavender. Bees hummed above their purple, filigree heads. It felt peculiar to be here, in the open, talking about regular things like love and the future. Petro and Evonne talked about them constantly but, since Mum died, my future has been held hostage by the present.

"I told Bo that I want us to run Du Bois together one day, alongside Jean-Pierre."

"That would be fitting, *chérie*." Grand-mère smiled. "A union that would take Du Bois forward. But what will happen if you grow in a different direction at university?"

"What do you mean, Grand-mère?"

She struggled to her feet, stripped off her gloves and let me help her to her chair on the verandah. "Your mother, God rest her, tried to tell you something important, Fili, but she went about it the wrong way." She paused, drinking in the hazy outline of the mountains, cocking her head at the harsh croak of a pair of crows in the poplars on the ridge. "It's not about Bo being inferior to you. It's about who you will become after engaging with a wider world. Be aware, child," she leaned towards me, "while your horizons will expand, Bo's may very well stay the same. Will he struggle being in your shadow, rather than an equal partner? Will you, in turn, be drawn to a man who's taken an academic path as you have? Who seeks new horizons?"

She paused again and gestured at the undulating farm. "Like the seasons, we grow and change. We leave behind those who don't. It's the dance of life, Fili."

"But I love him, Grand-mère! Surely that can't fade?"

"Only time will tell, *chérie*."

It has always been about time, I reflected, as we went back to work in the garden. Time for me to be old enough to make my first vintage. Time for a new vineyard to produce its first harvest. And time — alongside smart detective work - for justice to be delivered to Mum's killer and hopefully sweet release to me.

And Bo? What would the passage of time mean for him?

How destructive would it be if I outstripped him when we were already tied together?

Grand-mère reached across and took my hand. A black-and-white fiscal hopped onto the grass in front of us, grabbed a worm, and returned to perch on Grand-mère's plum tree.

"There's always a middle way, *chérie*, as I've tried to teach you before. In this case, it means waiting a while. Make no commitment just yet. Be close, but don't limit yourselves - either of you. Go to university, meet cleverer people than you, learn about the world. If, at the end of it, Bo is still the man for you, and you the woman for him, then marry him with the blessing of all Du Bois."

## CHAPTER FORTY NINE

"The DNA you found," I overheard Dad say through the half-open study door after I returned from Grand-mère's. "It matches no-one on your files?"
I listened from the corridor.
"Have you investigated the drug angle?"
I held my breath.
"No, I don't know where he can have gone. His aunt lives in our village, she may know."
There was a further silence. Then -
"I see. Well, thank you, Captain. Please don't give up."
The telephone went down. I waited a moment and then knocked on the door and pushed it open.
"Dad?"
He looked up at me with weary eyes. Sometimes I hear him leave the house after dinner with Blaze, sometimes I find a blanket on the verandah where he's spent the night instead of in bed. He seemed to rally after the funeral and the five-star award, but he's sad once again. And the nights are his worst time. I know. I'm often awake too, fending off the familiar yellow nightmares. The gums toss above my head, the sun burns my face, and my mothers walk away from me.
"Do they still think I had something to do with it? As an accomplice?"
"They aren't saying," Dad ran a hand through his hair. "But neither are they making any progress in finding the

murderer. They want to talk to Blake, but he's left the address they have for him."

*Yes,* I wanted to say. *I know he's left.*

*And he's already thrown away the phone he used to communicate with Kula.*

*Blake may be bad but he's not stupid.*

But I said nothing, just went around to Dad's side of the desk and put my arms about him.

"I'm at sea, Fili," he muttered. "I need you to be steadfast for me, steadfast for Du Bois."

"I will, Dad. I promise."

Mr Tate phoned later to say that the police had informed him that there was no clear match between the DNA found under Mum's fingernails and the sample provided by Adam Mfusi, who had gone to the police of his own accord.

"But," Mr Tate's voice took on a guarded note, "Captain Dlamini said that there was sufficient of a match to make it likely that an offspring of Adam Mfusi was involved."

I sat down on my bed.

"Will they announce it to the papers?"

"Not yet," Mr Tate replied. "They want to keep it under wraps for the moment. But there is a warrant out for his arrest. Therefore, Fili," his tone hardened, "I cannot stress how vital it is that you have absolutely no contact with Kula Mfusi until he is apprehended."

So... Kula did it.

I wanted it to be him because that would make sense - but I didn't want it to be him, either. I couldn't bear to imagine his eyes burning at Mum, I didn't want her to have felt the kind of fear he'd aroused in me. Better it be an unknown perpetrator and a random crime, rather than the knowledge of how it might have been for her - or that I might have prevented this murder if I'd acted sooner, exposed the drug-taking, involved the police -

"Fili? Did you hear me?"

"Yes, Mr Tate. I heard you."

Yet what if Kula attacked her but did not kill her? What if the aneurism was her murderer...

"I will speak to your father as well, Fili, but I thought you should know straightaway."

"What happens if the police never find him?"

"The warrant will remain in place. If they don't find him, the case will remain open until a decision is taken to close it."

"And what about me? How long will I be under suspicion?"

There was a short silence.

When Mr Tate replied, I could tell that he was choosing his words carefully.

"You are not a suspect in the murder, Fili. And there's no evidence you're an accomplice or an accessory-after-the-fact. Provided you do not imperil that status, you have nothing to fear."

"Can't they announce I'm innocent? Please?"

He gave a short laugh. "I'm afraid that won't happen. You need to be patient."

I stared outside. I haven't climbed the oak since the night Bo appeared at my window. There is no longer any need to eavesdrop on verandah conversations. In due course the harvest will come and go, Mum's roses will droop for winter, I'll watch my chardonnay's fermentation, and I'll be watched in turn by the valley and by the police in case I put a foot wrong. The leaves on the poplars will turn yellow and orange, and drift to the ground.

"The longer it goes on, the harder it will be for me, Mr Tate."

"I understand it's frustrating, but you'll be at university next year. A fresh start."

I must aim to lose myself amid the masses. I must be just another scudding cloud in a packed sky. Or will everyone already know who I am - and steer clear of me?

"Thank you, Mr Tate."

I put down the phone and stared at my face in the mirror. The black eye has faded but there are new hollows beneath my cheekbones. My hair has grown longer than I usually let it, and it surrounds my face in a billow of curls.

Do you remember when I said I was caught in a tug-of-love?

From the day Jean-Pierre was born, it's lurked beneath every hug, every uncertain glance, every celebration. Mum moved to Jean-Pierre's side of the rope, Dad tried to be a neutral referee, Grand-mère was supportive of both sides and the valley watched from the flanks, agog at the prospect of a dispute for control of Du Bois. The rope has now gone slack - not because my position has been cemented as Director but because any argument seems distasteful, overwhelmed by the weight of Mum's death and also by the awkward place where I now find myself: I may not have killed my mother, but my innocence is not yet guaranteed. My position – my tenure? - will only be settled when there is a resolution of the crime.

Social media is awash with speculation.

One phrase begins to stand out. It's appeared many times and become imprinted in my mind.

I don't look for it, instead it seems to leap out at me.

*I know you, you could not have done it...*

Could it be her? My birth mother?

I try to find out who is posting the message but the sender is anonymous. I consider asking Petro, who's an expert on all platforms, but I don't want her to suspect what I'm up to. And I can't confide in Dad or Grand-mère because that would seem like a betrayal rather than curiosity. The minister at my birth church promised to pray that I would free myself from my past, so do I want to find my real mother now, in the glare of my adoptive mother's death?

"You need to get more sleep, Fili," Dr Saunders observed, when she called in. She's taken to doing so in the late afternoon after her surgery closes. I enjoy her visits. We talk about things that have nothing to do with the murder or the police or my origins. "If you like, I can give you something to help you rest but it may make you drowsy for your exams."

"I need to learn to sleep on my own."

"Yes, in time." She regarded me. "I think older generations dealt with grief better than we do, Fili. Wearing black, for instance, helped to acknowledge mourning, not suppress it. I believe we try to be resilient too soon. If you need to cry, then you should do so."

"I need to be strong for Dad. For Grand-mère."

"You cannot carry them on your shoulders, Fili. They, too, have to find a way through. And remember," she paused and tapped my hand, "your mother died of an aneurism. Possibly caused by an altercation, possibly by natural causes. And there is nothing you could have done to prevent either scenario. Hold on to that."

"Get in," ordered Petro the following day, winding down the window of the car she'd received for her eighteenth birthday. Evonne giggled and ran around to open the door for me with a flourish.

"Where are we going?"

"We're celebrating being halfway through exams. I've made an appointment for you to have your hair cut. Then we're taking you shopping afterwards. No arguments, please!"

An hour later I sat in front of a hairdresser who was a stranger. She didn't seem to know me, either, because she talked only about hair. I treasure being unknown. And the salon was filled with ladies who chatted amongst themselves, taking no notice of me. I closed my eyes, sank into anonymity, and let her get on with it.

"Brilliant," Petro and Evonne chorused as they picked me up later.

"Now you must change your facebook picture." Petro pulled out her phone. "I'll take a photo and send it to you. You need a new image, Fili."

"No more the victim," Evonne linked her arm through mine, "it's time to move on. Break with the past and think of yourself as a winner. Because," she gave me a quick hug, "that's what you are."

## CHAPTER FIFTY

Adam Mfusi sat outside his crude shelter and watched the clouds gather over the mountains. He hadn't been back to du Bois, hadn't risked unearthing the dynamite, cap and fuse. It was too risky to be caught with them and, until he had somewhere more certain, where would he bury them? So why not leave them there? He had no wish to exact vengeance on behalf of his son or anyone else, not anymore. That time had passed. And Kula was old enough to fight his own battles.

He, Mfusi, had been in this place for more than a month now, although it was difficult to be sure. When he'd been living at the camp at Du Bois, it was easy to tell the passage of time from the rhythms of the farm.

The once weekly delivery from the farmers' supply store.

The wages he and the others had collected from Mr Du Bois on Friday afternoons. The change in the colour of the vines that heralded the change in the seasons.

He'd been there through almost four growing seasons. At first he'd thought they'd be pushed out when the first vineyard was dug, but Du Bois kept them on to do more work because they'd proved themselves and also because of the influence of Miss Fili.

Four seasons was a long stretch.

Kula hadn't been there throughout that time, of course. He'd come and gone.

Those years, Mfusi realised, had taken him from an angry teenager to an angry young man. It wasn't the fault of the farm or the Du Bois family. Kula was simply angry at his lot and there was nothing he, Adam, could do other than to try and limit the damage he left behind him.

It began to rain and Mfusi drew his ragged jacket around him and retreated under his plastic shelter.

He'd found the odd piece of work, but nothing that would last. A bit of gardening from a man who stopped and offered him a lift. A few days of loading rubble from a construction site into wheelbarrows. He should move on. He'd heard, on one of his trips into town, that there were jobs further north, on a bridge that was being built. But he was reluctant to move.

Kula would surely find him here.

If he moved away, it would be harder.

He hadn't told the police where he was, and they'd written 'no address' on the form when he gave them his saliva. He'd been told to report back to the station to get the results of the test. He'd done so. They'd told him he was innocent of poor Mrs Du Bois's death but that they wanted to do the same test on Kula and that if Mfusi saw him he must tell him to come to the station otherwise he, Adam, would be in trouble. And they asked if he had any other children but of course he didn't. Kula was his only child.

"Mr Mfusi?" a figure appeared through the drizzle. He squinted. How did the person know his name? He couldn't tell if it was someone he knew because the man was covered by a raincoat and had a hat pulled down over his eyes.

"It's me, Mr Mfusi. Fili Du Bois."

The figure came closer, and he could see it was indeed Miss Fili, swamped by the raincoat and almost hidden beneath the hat.

"Miss Fili" He rose to his feet. "You should not be here, Miss!"

She came closer and squatted down at his side. He pulled a flap of plastic over her to try and shield her from the rain. She looked different. Older, thinner, sadder.

"I am sorry for your loss, Miss. It is a cruel thing for a child to lose a mother."

She nodded and wiped her face. Maybe it was rain or maybe it was tears, he couldn't tell.

"How did you find me, Miss?"

"Someone at the spaza shop told me. The outlet," she gestured to the concrete pipe. He didn't take water from it, he fetched his water from higher up, but it was a useful landmark.

He waited for her to go on, to say why she was here, why she had come, but she said nothing. Maybe she was here to say that Mr Du Bois had changed his mind and that he needed the men to come back and do more work. Mr Du Bois - and the Coloured foreman Philemon Sammy - had valued what he and Peter and Abraham had done. Was that what Miss Fili was here to offer? Or might they take him back, just him, on his own?

"Why have you come, Miss?"

"You can't stay here, Mr Mfusi. It's not healthy. The water from that pipe isn't clean."

"I know that, Miss. I will leave soon. Why are you here, Miss?"

"I want to know if you've seen Kula." She glanced around suddenly, as if she'd heard something, but there was nothing and no-one to be seen or heard, just the patter of the rain on the plastic and the mountains disappearing behind a lowering mist.

"He's not here, Miss Fili," Mfusi said, wondering if the police could have forced her to get information that he, Mfusi, might be hiding. So it wouldn't do to tell her he was staying in this miserable spot for the very reason that he hoped Kula would find him here one day soon.

"Have you seen him since -" she hesitated and then went on, "since my mother died?"

"No, Miss, I haven't. That is the truth."

And it was. But if she visited him in the future he might have to lie.

"The police think that Kula killed my mother."

He felt the rain trickle down his neck and settle, coldly, near his heart. The police hadn't said those words to him but he could see it was what they thought. Especially when they said that his saliva contained ingredients nearly the same as what they'd found on Mrs Du Bois's body. It was what he had feared. He didn't understand how they discovered such things, it was too hard to understand. But these were people who had school and university and something called science that could tell these things.

"Do you think he did so, Miss?"

She met his eyes. Miss Fili had lovely dark eyes and he'd always seen honesty in them but this time they were clouded, as if she couldn't let them show what she was thinking.

"I don't know. Only Kula knows."

The rain that had been gathering on the plastic suddenly reached a weight that couldn't be borne any longer and sluiced down in front of them, sprinkling Miss Fili's raincoat and thoroughly wetting Mfusi's already damp trousers. She scrambled up.

"I need to know!" Her eyes threw off their dimness and blazed at him. "I need to know if he did, Mr Mfusi and why. Not just for the police but for me."

"Why, Miss? What good will it do? It will not bring back your mother, Miss."

She stood there in the open, the drips gathering on the brim of her hat and dropping to the ground in a circle around her. She was brave. She was the sort of girl Kula needed, the sort of girl who would take no nonsense, who would show him what could be done with his life.

"Don't you see, Mr Mfusi? They think I might have had something to do with it. If Kula killed my mother, then I'm more likely to be innocent."

He felt the rise of a sudden anger. She wanted his son to confess to the murder to get herself off the hook. He wouldn't do it. He'd thought she was better than that -

She saw the way his mind was working and stepped closer again.

"It's not what you think, Mr Mfusi. This isn't just about me. If Kula didn't do it, he can prove his innocence by going to the police. They'll do a DNA test and agree that he couldn't have done it. I will be happy for him and for you if this happens."

Mfusi nodded.

"But if he did do it," her voice shook, "and he escapes, I'll pay the price. I'll never be free of suspicion. The police will find evidence I might have helped him. That I wanted my mother dead. I could go to jail."

Mfusi looked at her, this small, busy girl who'd tried so hard to help. She'd persuaded her father to employ them, she'd soothed the annoying Coloureds, she dragged Kula to the camp when she could easily have called the police. And he was more certain that Fili had never touched her mother in anger than he was about his own son.

"Why do the police think you wanted your mother dead?"

She looked at him with a sorrow that seemed to crumple her face.

"Because she wanted my brother to inherit the farm."

Mfusi looked away from her. Land. It always came down to land. And if you were lucky enough to own it, was hard to share.

"If I see Kula, I will tell him what you told me. But I can't force him to do what he doesn't want to."

If Kula was sober, he'd be reasonable and honest. If he was out of his mind, he would storm off with no thought for his father, for this girl, or for anything beyond the desperate need to attack the world around him and stay high.

"Thank you, Mr Mfusi."

She was crying now, it wasn't the rain. And she didn't wipe her face, she just stood there in front of him, weeping as if her heart could not contain all its tears.

He lurched to his feet and did something he would never have dreamed of doing even just a few minutes ago. He reached out through his tattered sleeves and hugged her.

## CHAPTER FIFTY ONE

"As you go out into the world," the Principal intoned through the fresh morning air, "we know that you will carry with you the lessons and values we have taught you during your time at this school."

He paused. Petro fidgeted by my side. A flock of pigeons circled overhead, looking for space to land but it had all been taken by the audience for our outdoor Speech Day.

"There will be challenges ahead - for you, for our country - but I'm confident you will rise to meet them with courage, with fortitude and with compassion. Let us never forget the compassion, ladies and gentlemen, boys and girls, for that is the building block of a worthy society."

He gathered his notes and stepped away from the lectern. Applause rang out. Some of the parents stood up as they clapped. The pigeons wheeled away. The crowd began to disperse. I glanced about me. Joe Steyn caught my eye and looked away.

"That's it!" Petro exulted. She undid her school tie and waved it above her head. "Freedom!"

"Don't be silly," Evonne giggled, weighed down with prizes.

"Fili?" I turned at the familiar, precise tone. It was Mr Tate, standing on his own a little way from me. His son was to be Head Boy the following year. I went over to him.

"I wanted to congratulate you on your award, Fili. I know how hard it's been."

"Thank you, Mr Tate. I'm looking forward to next year."

"Indeed." He inclined his head and made to walk away.

"Mr Tate, did my mother plan to disinherit me?"

He stopped, and regarded me carefully. Mr Tate rarely speaks without due consideration.

"Your parents are my clients, Fili, as are you. I never betray a client's confidence." He paused. "Your mother's choices are in the past. They should not - and will not - define your future."

The kind minister at my birth church would agree. So would Dr Saunders.

I turned and ran over to Dad and Grand-mère, who was struggling across the uneven grass.

"We're so proud," Dad said, sweeping me into his arms in the old way.

"Bless you, child," Grand-mère murmured, propping herself against her stick.

I didn't cry. It was too beautiful a day for tears and, in any case, I think my well is empty. The last of them flowed for Adam Mfusi in his grim shelter, awaiting - dreading - news of his son; and there are none left for Mum's betrayal, or for my birth mother, maybe hoping I'd find her, forgive her…

"Let me look," Grand-mère motioned to the small trophy that was poking out of my side pocket. Not an academic prize, like Evonne's haul, but one given at the discretion of the headmaster and staff.

I handed it to her. She traced the words engraved on the side.

*For Valour.*

And, underneath, *Veritas et Justitia*, our school's motto.

"This award," the Headmaster had said, "is not one we confer every year. It is not for any skill or attainment achieved within these walls or on any field of sport. It goes, instead, to a student who has shown courage and strength outside of the school, someone who has overcome personal challenges while embodying our core values. This year, the award goes to Fili Du Bois!"

It was like being in church for Mum's funeral and the minister inviting me to the pulpit: my feet remained fixed to the ground, the silence roared -

"Go!" Petro dug her elbow into my side. "Get up there, Fili!"

I walked to the lectern. The headmaster smiled. A murmur rose from behind me.

"Stay true to yourself, Fili," he said as he handed the silver cup to me.

I turned to face the audience. They were on their feet, applauding. Boys from my class whistled, Petro waved her arms in the air, Grand-mère was dabbing at her eyes.

Does this mean I'm innocent?

Innocent in the eyes of my community if not yet in the eyes of the police?

I went down to the dam before supper.

More than a month had passed since Bo whispered to me to meet him there, but I never did. It was still too soon. Instead, we exchanged glances in the vineyard as we worked alongside Philemon; we stood near each other in the dimness of the cellar; he touched my hand when we parted at the door. Anyone watching us closely might have noticed but been unable to say for sure that we were accomplices.

I stood at the top of the slope and looked down. A pair of white-faced ducks were idling on the water while our familiar swallows swooped above their heads, taunting them with their agility.

"Fili!" a figure uncurled and stood up.

I ran down the slope and into his arms.

"Fili!" he covered my face with kisses, and strained me to him. "I've waited so many times!"

"I know. I'm sorry," I gasped and laughed against his cheek. "But we had to be careful -"

"*Ja*," he released me and sank onto the ground, pulling me with him, "but I don't think I can take this anymore. Let's run away, Fili, just for a while - you and me, no-one else -"

I leaned over to look into his face.

"We could go to Cape Town, walk on the beach," he propped himself up on his elbow, "I know someone with a flat -" he blushed a little and took my hand. "Marry me, Fili! Marry me before you go to Stellenbosch!"

The setting sun was gilding the water in veins of pink and silver.

*Make no commitment yet*, Grand-mère had warned. *Be close but don't limit yourselves.*

"Fili? You want it, too, don't you?"
Bo reached for me.

I asked Dad to take me to the police station a few days later.
"But why, Fili?" he shot me a quick glance as we drove. "You've told them everything, haven't you?"
"Yes, but I want to find out if I'm still under suspicion. I want to know before I go to university."
Dad nodded. I sense he believes in me once more. He's also been swept up in the euphoria around my silver cup for valour, and he can't imagine a cloud still hanging over me after I've been exonerated by the valley, in public, on two occasions.
"I asked Mr Tate to come, too."
"Very sensible."
But Mr Tate, I suspect, was deeply alarmed at my call. He hated me springing surprises. Or posing a question he was not in a position to answer.
"Is there anything I should prepare?" he asked over the phone.
"No, sir. I have no new information to give the police. I want something from them."
"They may not be prepared to reveal the state of the investigation."
"I understand."
We pulled into the station car park.
I got out. Only Mr Tate was waiting. There were no reporters, no microphones in my face.

*Did you kill your mother, Fili?* they'd yelled, and then pounded on the station door.

"Miss Du Bois, Mr Tate." Captain Dlamini shook our hands and led us into the interview room.

I glanced up. The sky poked through the small window. In the corner, a spider was weaving a web.

Captain Dlamini turned on the tape recorder and announced the date and who was present. He did not open his notebook but it was at his side, on the table that separated us. I wondered at that. Did it mean he believed there was nothing further I could give him? Nothing that might contradict or expand on a previous entry?

"What can I do for you, Miss Du Bois?"

I felt an insane desire to laugh. What could he do for me...

"If she didn't die of natural causes, do you know who killed my mother, Captain?"

Mr Tate turned to a blank page on his yellow pad and uncapped his pen.

"We have a suspicion, Miss Du Bois, based on DNA evidence. But we haven't been able to locate the suspect, Kula Mfusi. We think he may have left the country."

"How do you know that, sir?"

"His father, Miss. His father hasn't heard from him since the night before the murder but he believes Kula's gone north. Mfusi says he has family in Zimbabwe."

Zimbabwe?

Adam Mfusi had said nothing about that to me. Maybe he was trying to divert the police. In any case, Kula had probably left the Cape after Blake revealed I no longer had the phone in my keeping. Perhaps they left together, running hard before the police got wind of Blake's new place.

"Can you apprehend him there?" this from Mr Tate.

"Unlikely. The country is in turmoil. A man like Kula Mfusi could disappear and never be found."

"So, sir, where does that leave me?"

I still don't know if the Captain trusts me, and believes what I tell him. To him I'm a witness who won't give him what he most needs: the culprit.

"You're still a person of interest, Miss Du Bois. It remains possible you colluded with the killer. If we find evidence that supports this, you could still be charged."

"But surely that is unlikely?" put in Mr Tate smoothly. "It's three months since the tragedy. Your prime suspect has disappeared. There's no evidence my client was involved. Indeed, it is possible that there was no foul play at all, and Mrs Du Bois's death was a tragic accident. It's surely time to let this young woman," he nodded at me, "get on with her life."

Captain Dlamini gave a faint smile.

"You're a persuasive lawyer, Mr Tate. But Miss Du Bois remains the vital link between what we believe was a murder, and the suspected perpetrator."

I stared down at the floor. They hadn't repaired it. The tiles still curled up at the edges.

"Have you ever been under suspicion, Captain? For something you didn't do?"

I felt Mr Tate shifting in his chair. Careful, I told myself.

"No, I have not."

I remembered the moment by the dam with Bo, the sound of Blake's voice on Kula's phone, the sense of being swept into the deep by a hidden current, unable to escape -

"It feels like drowning, sir. Without the strength to get to the shore. With the water pressing down and filling your mouth until you can't breathe."

Mr Tate put a hand on my arm.

I nodded to him and forced myself to speak the words I'd rehearsed calmly, and with respect, and not allow the anger that was boiling in my throat to smother them.

"I've lived with this near-drowning since my mother died, sir. Sometimes I've felt forgiveness, even though I've done nothing wrong. Like I felt from the congregation at the funeral, or at my school speech day. Or when my wine won an award. But suspicion still follows me like a shadow, sir. And I don't want it to follow me anymore."

Mr Tate looked down at his pad. He'd written nothing.

The Captain clasped his hands and leaned his elbows on the table. I stared at him. He looked at his hands, then back up at me. I didn't look away. For the first time, I wasn't wearing school uniform. Instead, I was in a dress that Petro and Evonne had chosen for me on our shopping trip. And matching shoes that I'd insisted on buying, to their surprise.

"Will I become an accessory-after-the-fact if I happen to come across one of the men from the informal settlement on the street? Or greet one of the villagers who knew about the drugs?"

*Hello Miss Fili. I haven't seen you for a while.*

Would he concede that a chance meeting would not be grounds for collusion after the event?

Mr Tate glanced from me to the Captain. "I think what Miss Du Bois is saying is that she cannot control a random meeting with a person on the periphery of the crime. She can report it to yourselves, of course, but she should not be viewed with suspicion as a result of an encounter she did not initiate."

Captain Dlamini shrugged. "This investigation is still live, Miss Du Bois. We have to proceed on that basis. Your conduct will still be examined as new evidence comes to light."

I let a silence build.

Mr Tate waited. I think he knew I wasn't finished.

"I need more than that, sir."

The Captain leaned over and switched off the tape recorder. I suspect he thought I might assume that the interview had ended and get up to leave, but I didn't. Mr Tate stayed seated as well.

Clouds processed slowly past the small window.

"We don't have any evidence that suggests you conspired either before or after the death of Mrs Du Bois," he said, when the silence began to grow awkward. "You have, at times, tried to protect those you thought were innocent. Going forward, we will not hound you, Miss Du Bois - provided you do nothing to attract our curiosity."

He stood up and offered his hand to Mr Tate and to me.

"We need nothing further from you at this time. Thank you for your cooperation. May I say again, Miss Du Bois, how sorry I am for your loss."

Mr Tate put the Captain's words another way, as we left the station.

"Stay under the radar, Fili, and they'll leave you alone."

## CHAPTER FIFTY TWO

Christmas arrived in a blaze of heat and thundering southeasters. The poplars swayed on the ridge and our blacksmith plovers shrieked as they took refuge in the undergrowth.

"Will Mum see us?" Jean-Pierre demanded as he unwrapped his presents. "Even through the wind?"

"Of course!" said Grand-mère, patting him. "There's no wind in heaven, child."

"She sees you, Jean-Pierre," I whispered in his ear, "and she sends you her love, every day."

"But I want to see her, Fili."

"I know," I pulled him close. "But you must make her proud by being brave."

Yet instead of trying to be brave, perhaps we should have followed the ancestors' customs and worn black, as Dr Saunders suggested, and as Grand-mère did for Grand-père; allowed ourselves to display our loss in public and find some comfort. Even Jean-Pierre. Not forever, but just for a while...

Life, though, has a way of re-asserting itself. No sooner had the festivities of Christmas and New Year wound down than the harvest approached. I got into a pressed shirt and my best shorts, and tolled the brass bell on the appointed day to summon our workers. You might have expected that the weather would have conspired against this saddest of harvests, but conditions were perfect. The wind abated, the grapes were plump, and the temperature set fair for the week.

"Let's get the job done," said Dad, wearing his ringmaster face. "We can't afford to lose focus."

The grapes were duly picked and sorted; the older women checked the bunches; the de-stemmer and crusher roared into action. Yet there was no singing, no joy. It would forever be remembered as the silent harvest, the pickers departing at the end without their usual sense of tired triumph.

"I can't force them to sing," Philemon scratched his head. "They're too upset, Miss Fili."

"The spirit will come back," murmured Grand-mère from her verandah. "One day. But not yet."

I patrolled the cellar, watching the fermentation, mindful of the fruit notes we wanted: apple, pear, leaning towards citrus with a lightness and crispness that Mum would have enjoyed. And I sensed she was there, hovering over the process, her bright hair and slender frame flitting through my imagination and between the steel tanks: Mum, as I wanted to remember her. For me, this vintage did not have a date, it simply became Mum's vintage. And between themselves, our villagers called it Mrs Ray's wine.

Compared with the marathon process required for my *treize ans* cabernet, chardonnay was a sprint. Much of the early hard work was done by the time I was ready to leave for university.

"Just as well," observed Petro. "You can't be forever running back home to fuss over wine."

"I wish you all the best, Fili," said Dr Saunders on her last visit. This time she was in a pink sleeveless dress, cut loosely for the heat. "It's time to look forward."

"That's what Dad always used to say," I stared out over the cropped vines. "When he and Mum adopted me, he said they were looking forward rather than back."

"Did he tell you that?"

"No," I glanced at her. "I overheard them. From up there." I pointed into my oak.

Her lips twitched. "No more secret listening, Fili. Face the world on your own terms. Look ahead with confidence, with enthusiasm."

But it is hard not to be drawn back. Both of my mothers haunt me.

"I think my birth mother has been trying to reach me."

"She's been in touch?" Dr Saunders' forehead wrinkled with alarm. "By telephone? In person?"

"On social media. In amongst the messages of support.

"Show me, Fili."

I fired up my computer.

*I know you, you could not have done it."*

The same message, over and over, interspersed with random ones telling me to be brave, or congratulating me on my five star vintage, or asking me to donate to special causes.

"Ah, Fili," she relaxed and took my hand. "That is a well-known ploy, sadly. I have patients who've received similar personal messages for a variety of reasons. All are anonymous. None can be traced." She squeezed my hand. "It can be a psychological condition. Vulnerable individuals align themselves with someone they perceive to be a victim - or a winner! They want to be part of the publicity, they yearn for the attention that you are receiving."

Dr Saunders is wise. And she may be correct.

"Look forward, Fili," she repeated, "not back. Seize your future."

As she left, I handed her a bottle of my *treize ans* cabernet tied with a bow. "For you, Dr Saunders."

"Why," she turned delighted eyes on me. "How kind! It's in demand, I believe."

We walked towards the front door.

"You taught me something, Doctor, that day you arrived at the police station."

She stopped on the threshold. "And what was that?"

"That it's possible to find calm in the midst of chaos. Then, and now."

She smiled, leant forward and kissed me lightly on the cheek and stepped outside. "Essential for doctors, and presumably for wine farmers? Take care, Fili. Keep in touch. And," she tapped me lightly on the arm, "ignore provocative messages from unknown sources."

I glanced into the hall mirror after she'd gone. I'd bought two more dresses in the same style as my friends chose for me. And I'd been back to the hairdresser. My dark hair curled tightly about my face, emphasising the hollows beneath my cheeks. Perhaps they were a permanent mark, now, and that was as it should be: we should all be altered in some way by our loss.

"Show them what you can do, Miss," said Shenay fiercely, up to her elbows in flour for the mammoth batch of shortbread she was making for me to take along to university. She worries that I won't be getting enough to eat in my hall of residence. "Philemon says you know more than all those smart teachers for sure. And don't forget to eat a proper breakfast."

One more incident took place before I left for university.

It happened when I woke up one morning and opened my curtains. A note fluttered to the floor. It must have been pushed through the fanlight while I was sleeping and lodged in the folds of the curtain. It was creased, as though it had been in a pocket.

I didn't want to open it.

After all, university awaited within days and I was excited about going. The police had left me alone, there'd been nothing more from Blake nor any trouble in the village, and Dr Saunders' words had grounded me. I no longer scanned my social media messages with trepidation. She was right. I didn't need to be drawn back. The future was beckoning, ready to be seized -

I sat, turning the paper over and over in my hand, while the house and the farm woke up about me. The rattle of the frying pan in the kitchen as Shenay prepared scrambled eggs; the *werk stadig* chant of the doves in the trees; the random shouts of village children heading down Gum Tree Avenue to pick up the school bus.

I unfolded the paper.

*I know what happened to your mother*
*Im sorry*
*I will find you*

Feet scampered down the corridor.

"Fili!" Jean-Pierre launched himself through the door. "Why must you go?"

I shoved the note under my pillow, as I'd done with Kula's phone.

"Today is registration day, Jeanie. Like when you went to school for the first time."

My voice sounded hoarse to my ears.

"I don't want you to go," he buried his face in my shoulder. "I don't want you to leave me."

"I'll be back at the weekends," I whispered into his ear. "And you'll have Dad and Grand-mère and Shenay all to yourself. Lucky boy!"

"It won't be the same," he lifted a tear-stained face. "What if they take you away again?"

"No-one's going to take me away."

He wiped his face and regarded me. Jean-Pierre has Mum's beauty but also Dad's persistence. Whether it's card games or anger at being left behind, he doesn't give up.

"Was it the same man who hurt Mum, who hurt you?"

I stared into his blue eyes, the exact shade of his mother's.

"I fell, remember? At the police station. Silly Fili!" I smiled and tickled him.

"I know who hurt you!" he twisted away from me and pointed through the window. "You came inside with a sore foot. And I saw him again. Here. He talked to Mum. Was he also at the police station?"

Shock tore through my body.

"Listen, Jean-Pierre," I grabbed his hands, "can you keep another secret? Can you?"

"Maybe," he pouted.

"If you tell no-one what you've just told me, then I'll tell you why when you're a bigger boy."

I know it sounds clumsy but I was already off balance from Kula's note.

None of us ever imagined Jean-Pierre might have... evidence?

But of what? He was at a sleepover on the day Mum died.

Oh God, what should I do? Is this a time to follow the truth wherever it leads - or wait?

"Can we play outside before you go, Fili?"

Jean-Pierre's a child. And a fanciful one. He may know the identity of the killer, or he may not.

And Mum's death may not be murder, as Dr Saunders has been at pains to point out.

I can't possibly let Jean-Pierre be a police witness. They will destroy what tentative recovery he's made.

Is this an obstruction of justice?

## CHAPTER FIFTY THREE

"Welcome," the Professor said, shaking my hand. "Over at that table you can pick up your lecture schedule. Classes start on Thursday."

"Thank you, sir," I said, willing him not to look at the name on my registration form and say it out loud. Luckily, he moved on down the line of new students, greeting others at random. I glanced about. Hundreds of young folk were milling about the hall, and none of them were looking at me. The Department of Viticulture and Oenology promised a busy schedule of lectures and practical sessions which would leave its undergraduates little time for idle gossip. Hopefully, I could indeed disappear, a face in a crowd, a background of no particular significance.

Not all students were so well occupied. Petro found time for a whirl of dates, interspersed with a little light study. "You should have chosen Art History, girls," she announced on her way to yet another night out. Evonne, by contrast, was almost as busy as me. She'd switched from wine studies to mathematics. "I love numbers more," she explained. "Just think, Fili, I can help you with your maturation calculations."

"Fili Du Bois?"

"Yes?" I turned round. It was Joe Steyn, the boy who'd asked me to our matric dance and then changed his mind. "Will you come with me to the undergrad ball?"

"I'm sorry," I said, smiling at him sweetly. "I've already been invited."

It wasn't true - but if I was going to meet young men who'd be competition for Bo, I intended to look further than a cowardly schoolmate.

"It's wonderful, Dad!" I laughed down the phone after my first week. "Wait till I tell you and Philemon about the latest inoculation techniques. How's Grand-mère? And Jean-Pierre?"

"Slow down, Fili. Jean-Pierre's doing better but he misses you." I heard Dad's sigh over the phone. "He worries you won't come back, poor boy."

*Was it the same man who hurt Mum, who hurt you?*

"Tell him I love him." I paused. "Anything from the police?"

"No news. Let it go, Fili."

*And let Mum go too, Dad,* I longed to say in response. I'd been granted the luxury of distance but Dad had to walk in Mum's footsteps around the house each day, touching the furniture she chose, sitting on the chair where she'd once nursed their son. He lived with Mum's phantom presence.

"I love you, Dad. Tell Jean-Pierre I'll be back soon."

"This is your time, honey. Make the most of it."

"Are you a Du Bois from Du Bois Vineyards?" a tall young man approached me one day.

"I am," I glanced about cautiously. "Why?"

"I read your cabernet won an award. My name's Steven Glover. Do you want a coffee? You called it *treize ans* - did you really make it when you were thirteen?"

"Yes," I laughed, "although my father and our foreman held my hand the whole way."

"My family owns a fruit farm, so I'm doing Agriculture." He pulled out a chair for me. "Not quite as glamorous as wine."

"Where's your farm?"

"The Elgin valley. My ancestors originally came from Germany. We grow apples and pears."

"I'm making a chardonnay at the moment. Those are the fruit flavour notes we're after."

"Well then," he grinned, "I can be your sounding board."

Was this what Grand-mère intended? A young man to provide competition to Bo? And it turned out that Steven Glover was not the only student who sought me out. Some were classmates, others were young men who met me in hall or happened to fall into conversation over lunch or while watching a sports match. I hadn't realised university would be so informal and that my new admirers would be so unconcerned with where I came from, at the start.

*Baby drop-off. Ages up to 3.*

Or that I was a person of interest in a murder investigation.

"Are you seeing other boys?" Bo asked when I came home for my first break.

"Only as friends." I squeezed his hand as we sat by the dam. He kissed me, cupping my face between his hands. None of the others made my heart race - at least not yet. And none of them shared my history as Bo did. But Grand-mère was right. I should explore new friendships if I was to be sure that the one which survived would be the one I truly wanted. In the interim, Bo was determined not to lose me, and he sent me text messages every day.

*We racked from the lees yesterday. I love you Fili.*

I put my phone away and looked up from the secluded bench where I was sitting.

Unlike the farm, the campus was forever busy and sometimes I needed to find a place to be alone. Not to brood but to relish slipping beneath the gaze of the police, as Mr Tate hinted was possible.

A paradise flycatcher flew into a nearby bush and draped its ribbon tail over the foliage. Why do I love birds so much... is it because they can fly away? Or because they see the world from high up, the stark lie of the land, the silver curve of rivers, the path of love and loss?

"Don't turn around."

*I will find you.*

I sprang up.

"Don't go."

My hands clenched into fists. I'd fooled myself into believing he was gone, that he'd never track me down, that his note was a final thrust, a last salvo, before he disappeared.

But it was not.

He eased out of the shrubbery. No-one would suspect he wasn't a student, his tee shirt and jeans fitted right in with the dress code.

We stood - I tensed, ready to sprint away - with the bench between us. He must have been watching me and knew I liked to come here. Would Captain Dlamini classify this as a chance encounter -

"I have something to tell you."

Why did I stay? Why didn't I run?

"You killed my mother." It came out of me like an animal's growl.

"I did not." He didn't look away from me, as he used to. He met my eyes squarely.

"Did you push her? Did you see her fall?"

People were coming. I could hear their voices.

He came around the bench and in one swift move clamped a hand over my mouth. I twisted away from him but he was too strong and he held on to me and wrapped me in his arms as if we were a couple, pressing my face against his neck so I couldn't scream.

We stayed like that, clasped together, as the group walked past. Couples embracing were nothing unusual on campus.

Their voices faded.

"I'm going to let you go," he muttered into my ear, "but you have to be quiet, Fili."

He released me slowly and sat down on the bench.

I lifted my hands, forced open my fists and watched my fingers shaking. I don't want to clench my fists any longer, I don't want to fear that one day I might strike someone -

"I have something to tell you," he repeated.

"You're a wanted man," I hissed. "I could be accused of collusion, of obstructing justice -"

"You could," he nodded. "But unless you listen to me, you'll never know what happened."

"I already know. Tell the police," my voice strengthened, "don't tell me."

"It will take some time," he said. "Come and sit down."

I forced myself to look at him more closely. There was something new in his manner. Kula always breathed menace, but this was less threatening, more calculated. He knew I was desperate to find out, he calculated I wasn't going to run away.

"Why did you have my phone with you? On the day your mother died?"

For a moment, I was thrown by his change of direction - the sort of tactic Mr Tate said I often used.

"How dare you question me?" I ground out the words. "I've had days of questioning and you think you can come here and ask more?"

He looked at me with what could almost be sympathy. "It's not what you think."

"I don't believe you," I retorted. "You're a drug addict. You hate me and Du Bois, you hated my mother enough to kill her -" I edged away but once again he was too quick for me. He shot out a hand and closed it about my wrist and pulled me slowly, painfully, down on to the bench.

"I don't want to hurt you, Fili. But you must listen to what I have to say. And I'm off drugs."

He made me look at him. His eyes were completely clear. But I won't be seduced by his guile.

"I have to go," I said. "I have a lecture."

"Then I'll wait for you here." He motioned around the garden with the hand that was not imprisoning mine. "Once you've heard what I have to say, you can decide if you want to tell the police or not."

He let go of my wrist.

I stood up.

"How do you know I won't call the police right now? Let them come and arrest you?"

He smiled.

And that's when I became truly frightened. Because he seemed too calm, too sure of himself to be guilty of having attacked my mother and left her for dead.

## CHAPTER FIFTY FOUR

People have told me I look different. They don't say it's since Mum died but I know that's what they mean. And it's not about the new dresses and the smart shoes and the haircut – they're only surface changes. I've left behind two mothers. That's what shows in my face.
Kula Mfusi looked different, too. And it wasn't because he was sober.
We are both altered.
Is that why I didn't call the police?
I walked around campus for an hour. Every sound seemed eerily magnified. My footfalls exploded in my ears, the doves in the oaks screeched rather than cooed, the laughter of passing students became shrill cackles. I visited parts of the university I'd never seen before, specialities I didn't know existed. The Centre for Chinese Studies. The Faculty of Military Science. The School of Public Leadership. Above me, the mountains I've gazed at from the Franschhoek side, looked down on me and wondered why I didn't pull out my phone and call the authorities and be done with it.
*Captain Dlamini, Kula Mfusi is here. I will lead you to him.*
There would be no downside.
If he had disappeared, I could say I'd done the right thing by calling the police. If he was still there, they could arrest him and take him away.
Either way, my innocence would not be at risk.

"Fili!" Evonne ran over to me. "What are you doing around here? This isn't your usual patch!"

"Just taking a walk."

"Are you alright?" She shifted her books and linked her arm through mine.

"Yes," I forced a smile. "I'm fine. I sometimes just need to walk."

"Of course," her face softened. "I tell you what! I'll meet you later, we'll have coffee and a slice of cake at the Pear Tree Cafe. At four? Must run." She waved a hand and raced into the Maths building.

I'm alone with this.

Truly alone.

I can't speak to Dad. I can't run up to Grand-mère's cottage to ask for wise advice. If I phone Mr Tate, he'll waste no time in ordering me to call the police.

Kula Mfusi was sitting on the bench when I returned.

He didn't look past me to see if the police were following in my wake.

A party of yellow weaver birds whizzed over my head, chattering amongst themselves. In the lush surrounds of campus they wove their intricate nests wherever a dangling branch presented itself.

"You knew I'd come back." I sat down at the opposite end of the bench. "Alone."

"Yes."

"Why? How could you be so sure?"

I waited but he said nothing, just looked at me.

I should take the initiative, set the agenda and the pace. Give a little at the start, to get more at the end. He might have found me, but that didn't mean he should dictate the outcome.

"I kept your phone so I could accuse the villagers of supplying you with drugs via Blake." I paused. "And then also persuade my parents you weren't necessarily responsible for the thefts on the farm, because you'd been framed."

He offered no reaction, no appreciation for the fact that I believed he wasn't a thief.

"You dropped the phone at the place where your mother died," he countered instead, as if accusing me of negligence.

"Yes." I found myself choking back a lump in my throat. "I used it to call the ambulance."

*Hello? Please help! I think my mother's dying* -

A car backfired on a nearby street. I jumped. The weavers flew up in fright.

"Why did you want to help me?" he demanded. "Why did you care that I wasn't a thief?"

I was suddenly back at the police station facing Captain Dlamini, trying to explain how I live between different worlds; then I was sitting with Grand-mère on her verandah, hearing her story of the honeyguide's agile role as go-between, and vowing to follow its example...

In this public garden, though, there's no time for a lengthy explanation. I'm putting myself ever more deeply at risk as the moments tick by. I could end up in jail for failing to alert the authorities.

"Tell me what you know," I snapped. "Otherwise I'll leave."

He reached into his pocket and pulled out a piece of paper. He turned it over in his hand and then passed it to me. "This is a copy," he said. "The real one is in a safe place."

I took it from him.

There was handwriting on it, handwriting that I recognised.

*I must see you again. Just one more time.*

*Then I will leave you alone.*

*I know it's wrong but I can't help myself. I have never felt like this before.*

*R*

## CHAPTER FIFTY FIVE

Kula Mfusi first saw Fili Du Bois when he was eighteen and she was about fourteen.
Why was it that every time he saw her, he behaved badly?
I don't need friends!
Don't tell me what to do!
Sometimes he blamed it on the drugs, or rather the lack of drugs when his skin was on fire and his tongue couldn't be trusted unless he found another fix. Other times, it was because she was rich and he was poor and only luck had delivered her to Du Bois and a life of privilege. So, in a moment of soberness some while after the incident at the dam, he found a piece of paper and wrote on it to say that he was sorry he'd made her fall.
He glued the sides together and wrote her name on the outside.
He could speak English quite well by then but he still couldn't spell so he hoped she'd understand.
He already knew the farm routine. He knew when the maid, Shenay, went home for lunch. He knew when old man Du Bois was out on the land, when the small boy slept, and when Fili got back from school. He always made it his business to case out the places near where he lived. People were surprisingly casual about their possessions. He never broke in, he'd only take something if it was on display. There was a gap of about

an hour when he could go to the house and leave the note and no-one would see him. The dog, of course, was no problem. Animals were never a problem. If only he could charm people like he could charm animals.

He kept close to the tree line along the avenue, then darted across the courtyard and round the side of the house past the bedrooms and across the verandah to the closed front door.

He slid the note underneath and sneaked back the same way.

"What are you doing?"

He froze and turned around.

Mrs Du Bois was standing in the kitchen doorway. She was wearing a blue dress.

"I'll call the police -" she began to retreat and was about to slam the door shut.

He raced across the space between them and thrust his foot against the door.

"No," she shouted, her face flushing, "How dare you?"

He kept his foot there. "Why are you afraid?"

She stared at him. "You're a thief. You've come here to steal from us."

"No," he said, "I came to see if Fili was home. I came to say sorry for yelling at her one day."

He took his foot away from the door and stepped back. She stared at him, open-mouthed.

"I know you hate us," he said. "But we're not thieves."

It was as well that he'd had a pill earlier that morning because he was calm. The words often came out better, but only if he hadn't taken too much. And he'd washed himself in the dam the previous night, which always made him feel better. She really was very beautiful.

"Do you love your husband, Mrs Du Bois?"

He didn't know why he said it.

She gasped. "Yes. He's the best man in the world."

"Then you're lucky, Ma'am."

He hadn't had a conversation like this with a white woman ever before.

Usually, they only said things to him like... dig that trench, paint that wall, get off our land.

"Why am I lucky?"

"Because most people don't get love like that."

His father might have felt it once, with his mother, but she had died when Kula was born and so his father had not felt anything like it for all of Kula's life. The thought of his father always stopped Kula in his tracks. Adam had spent every waking moment since Kula was born, trying his best for his son. And he, Kula, had repaid his father's care by taking drugs and getting into trouble.

Mrs Du Bois was looking at him.

He could see something odd in her eyes. She was staring at him but also beyond him. He began to get nervous. He should go. The Coloured woman, Shenay, would be back soon and she would shout if she saw him and then the boy would wake up, if he hadn't woken up already. And the villagers would spread more lies.

Yet he found himself moving towards her, pushing the door open.

She backed away but she didn't protest or cry out. It was almost as if she wanted him to come in -

What would it be like with a white woman?
He couldn't believe he was even thinking of it -
He wouldn't do it unless she wanted to, he wasn't an animal.
And they'd have to be quiet because of the boy -
So he waited. It would have to come from her. He remembered how, in the carpark, when he'd loaded her shopping, he'd caught her staring at him like this. As if surprised that he could actually be normal and not a savage.
Her cheeks began to flush pink.
Her eyes met his and, to his surprise, there was no fear. Curiosity, perhaps?
He reached out and touched her hand.
She didn't snatch it away. She looked down at their hands and then back up at him. Maybe, for all her white privilege and sheltered life, she wanted to be a risk-taker?
He should have turned around and left but instead he reached behind him and closed the door.
Why? Why didn't she scream? Or run away into the house –
He waited again, but she just kept looking at him. And beyond him, in that strange way.
Maybe she was tired of her husband. Or maybe she just hadn't had it in a long time. Neither had he.
And she was beautiful. No-one need know.
He leaned forward, she didn't pull away, and he kissed her on the neck.
She did not protest, or retreat.

"Why?" he found himself saying.
But she didn't say anything back.
Just let her eyes wander across his face and settle on his lips.

Afterwards, he tried to remember but it happened so fast, they were both suddenly so urgent after the waiting by the door, and it was so extraordinary and so horrifying that his mind refused to relive it in any detail. He remembered only the cushiony feel of her lips, the longing in her body, and her frenzied delight at the end.
And he remembered his fear.
He tore himself away from her and sprinted home, wide-eyed with horror.
This was the end.
She would come to her senses, she would say she'd caught him snooping and had chased him off.
Du Bois – who she'd called the best man in the world - would have no choice but to evict them, if he didn't come around with a shotgun and shoot them all first.
He'd messed up the best job his father had had in years. And she'd got her way. He'd been used, and then discarded.
Just like he and his father and the others had been used, and would be discarded.

He didn't dare tell his father what had happened.
But, strangely, the eviction he was expecting didn't follow straightaway. And there was no change in Du Bois's attitude. Adam and Abraham and Peter continued

to do whatever chore was set for them on the farm. But he couldn't go back to the way it was. So he found a part-time job at a warehouse in Paarl, and started working there. And he worked on reading and understanding books that he found, and he practised talking to men at the warehouse with better language than him.

At night, he went up to the house to see what was going on. Mostly it was nothing, just Fili doing her homework and playing with the small boy and the parents arguing in their bedroom and sometimes the grandmother coming for supper.

He was getting drugs from Blake. Good quality stuff that helped him with his studying, as he now called it. He'd make a pickup in Franschhoek, arranged by phone. It was easier than with some of his previous suppliers who were unreliable.

He saw Mrs Du Bois in town one Saturday after he'd collected.

She saw him, too.

They stood on opposite sides of the road with the sun beating down and the air utterly still, and he was tempted to cross over and confront her - he'd already taken, so he was feeling bold - but she turned away and went inside a fancy shop.

He wanted to shout her deceit to the skies, to the careless passersby. They'd surely spread the word. By nightfall she'd also know the shame of disappointing someone she loved.

He took too many pills and woke up on the path with Fili Du Bois leaning over him.

He'd never seen such a pretty thing in his life.

She dragged him back to the camp, helped by the boy from the village that she hung around all the time. She didn't call the police, but she did keep his phone.

And that made him angry.

And nervous.

So he went up to the house and waited outside her window but he couldn't bring himself to climb into her bedroom and demand the phone back. If she came outside and into the tree, he'd grab her.

And that's how, one night, he overheard the party on the verandah, when the Du Bois and their neighbours drank wine and talked about getting rid of all of the squatters in the valley... as if he and his father and Peter and Abraham were simply tools that were blunt or no longer needed. He hid amongst the rose bushes - nasty, thorny brutes - and listened and patted the dog to soothe the rage in his heart.

*I certainly want them gone*, said Mrs Du Bois, who'd been unable to contain her lust for him.

*We can't allow indiscriminate squatting*, said the mother of the girl who'd gawked at the camp.

He stole away.

Again, he said nothing to his father. There was no point. The eviction would come whenever it came.

The next day, a letter was thrown into his shack. He didn't know how it got there.

*I must see you again. Just one more time.*

*Then I will leave you alone.*
*I know it's wrong but I can't help myself. I have never felt like this before.*
*R*

## CHAPTER FIFTY SIX

Martin paused before leaving the cellar, and rested a hand on the steel tank. Fili's chardonnay. Ray's vintage. Perhaps it was fitting that Fili should be in charge of the wine that would always recall her mother, even if Ray's name didn't appear on the label. He'd thought about commemorating Ray in this way but then felt it would be like profiting from a tragedy.

He turned away and locked the cellar door.

His doubts about his daughter had vanished since the DNA recovered from under Ray's fingernails was found likely to be Kula Mfusi's. Dr Saunders had also made it clear that Ray's death could have been natural causes, perhaps exacerbated by a confrontation with Mfusi. As a result, the police had quietly shelved their suspicion of a violent streak in Fili, and any implication that she had attacked her mother - or collaborated in some way with Kula Mfusi to do so. Provided, of course, as Ben Tate was careful to point out, that Fili gave them no reason to revise their position.

The police's entire focus was on finding Mfusi.

It was now time, Martin reflected, for the commotion surrounding Ray's death to be tempered.

Public suspicion of Fili also appeared to have faded and she was happily settled at university. The valley was keen to return to the business of viticulture rather than gossip. Jean-Pierre had recovered much of his previous zest, and even the mood among the villagers was improving. Despite the silence among the vines, he sensed that the picking of the grapes and their conversion into wine had finally laid Ray to rest. His mother had been right: the spirit would return, the next harvest would be better.

Did it matter, now, whether Ray had died of natural causes or foul play?

And was there any merit in dwelling on the change in her will? Surely it was best to draw a veil. Ben Tate had said nothing further and, apparently, the police had failed to pursue that angle or confirm it to Fili, for which he was grateful. He, Martin, should also let it go, but keep the secret.

Perhaps, if they'd been able to re-kindle their love properly...

Personally, he was convinced Kula Mfusi was guilty of murder. But his capture and conviction would not bring Ray back, nor answer the two questions that still troubled Martin, especially at night when the stars poked through the leaves of the gum trees on the avenue, where he went in search of some kind of incriminating evidence that Kula Mfusi might have left behind, and that the police might have missed.

Why was Ray wandering among the vines that morning? Why didn't Blaze defend her?

## CHAPTER FIFTY SEVEN

It was getting dark. The weavers had long gone and the only sound was distant traffic and the overhead cries of hadedas flapping laboriously to their roosts. I'd forgotten about meeting Evonne, but she'd probably think I was tied up with work or a practical.
My chest, I realised, was aching.
I'd been holding myself so rigidly, so tightly, that it was painful to breathe. I wanted to get away, to fill my lungs and run down to the glittering dam and laugh with Bo at the antics of the kingfishers and then climb up to Grand-mère's cottage to take another lesson on *la politesse*.
"You haven't told me if you killed her," I said, still clutching the note in Mum's handwriting.
"No. That will come tomorrow."
I stared at him and nodded. He had the upper hand.
"You can see that it's not the way you thought," he said.
"Yes, I see that now."
The last few months have taught me a lot about manoeuvring around the truth - and what shows on people's faces when they lie. Even if he hadn't produced the note, I might very well have believed him. He told his story slowly, sometimes frowning when he couldn't find the right word and trying it out in Xhosa in case I might understand. The piercing eyes were directed inwards, as if he was searching inside himself. There was no trace of the rage I would have expected, and which had been directed at me so often in the past. And

he wasn't embarrassed in the telling, but rather gave off a sense of mute outrage, as if he'd been a pawn in someone else's game. That he'd always been a pawn.
If there was any rage, it was mine - on behalf of Dad.
"You can keep the note," he said. "But maybe you want to destroy it."
*Destruction of evidence, Miss Du Bois, is a chargeable offense.*
"I'll decide when I know what happened to Mum."
Beautiful, reckless Mum.
Betraying her husband for a quick thrill with a young man she claimed to despise. And then wanting more.
This was a Mum I never knew.
"I'll be here at the same time tomorrow."

I don't know where he went because I left the bench first. Maybe he slept there overnight?
My phone chirped in my pocket as I walked away.
*Yr chard'y into oak. Love you, call me. Bo*
I found my way back to my hall of residence through the darkening streets. One or two people greeted me but I didn't reply. I'll have to make amends tomorrow.
Or the next day.
I closed my door and locked it and pulled the curtains and turned off the light. At one point someone knocked and called my name but then went away.
I didn't sleep much that night.
Images of Mum, some real, some imagined, played across my closed eyelids.

Mum glowing in her pastel dresses, Mum cradling Jean-Pierre, Mum reaching for a man other than Dad.
Jean-Pierre had been right. *I saw him again. Here.*
How much had he seen? Heard?
And there was more to come. For if I believed Kula today, I'd probably believe him tomorrow.
I'm alone with his revelations, like I was alone with her body in the vineyard. There's no-one I can confide in.
No-one I can call.
Because if I did, they might also become accessories-after-the-fact.
*Be calm*, I urged myself, remembering Dr Saunders' poise. *Be calm in the midst of chaos.*
The sky was already brightening by the time I fell into a thin sleep. In recent dreams, I often see my two mothers but this time my birth mother was at the outer edge of the dream and Mum was at the centre, in the vineyard, and she was running after someone who had Dad's body, tall and rangy, but when he turned around and laughed at her, his face was Kula's.
My telephone woke me.
Brilliant sun was poking around the sides of the curtains. I fumbled and took the call.
"*Bonjour, chérie!*" came Grand-mère's warm voice. "Wonderful news to start your day! Your father and I tasted the chardonnay yesterday and decided it was ready to go into oak! It's a real tribute," she hesitated and I could tell she was struggling to control her emotions, "it's your dear mother's sort of wine. She'd be so proud of you, Fili. Be in no doubt of that."

"Thank you, Grand-mère."
"Bless you, child."

## CHAPTER FIFTY EIGHT

If he, Kula, hadn't lost his temper during the confrontation over the eviction from their camp, things might have been different. After all, Du Bois was trying to be fair. He could see that. But Du Bois's hand had been forced by his neighbours, by the yapping Coloureds, by his two-faced wife.

But not by his daughter, which made Kula's response all the worse.

"She doesn't know," he'd shouted. "She only knows what she's told to say!"

He'd seen the outrage in Fili and he'd been ashamed, but his blood was up and he couldn't stop.

"I want my phone back otherwise you're the thief around here!"

And then he ran into the bush and kept running until he reached the main road. The cars raced by, no-one cared who he was, he could end everything by running into the middle and lying down on the tarmac and someone would drive over him and it would be over.

Part of the problem was that he was coming down off a high. He was actually sober but the craving always made him mad. Only this time, he told himself, as a car swerved around him and the motorist leaned out of the window and yelled at him, this time he'd sweat it out and get through the cravings and the tremors and he'd come out the other side. He'd find his father and say sorry and mean it, and then set about getting a job and living like a normal person even if he had to scrounge at the start.

And he'd remember Fili Du Bois.

And hope that, one day, she might understand why he'd always behaved badly around her.

He wandered through town, drinking huge amounts of water from the free street fountain and eventually made his way back to the camp. Adam and the others had already started taking the shacks down. He tossed and turned on his thin mattress, got up and headed back out.

It was better being under the stars.

He fell asleep on the grass by the side of the road.

It rained at some point, but he didn't mind because it cooled him down.

The noise of the traffic woke him and he again headed back to Du Bois. His mind was clear and he felt better. Maybe the worst was over.

He'd go down to the dam and have a swim if no-one was there, and then leave for good. Clouds were swirling over the mountains. Kula liked this place, he liked the farm. But it wasn't safe anymore. Too many people knew too much about him. He skirted the house and headed through the vines. He sometimes saw Fili here, among the grapes. He envied her, having a proper future mapped out and the means to make it happen. He always hid away so she wouldn't see him, so he wouldn't be tempted to be rude to her again.

"Kula!"

He turned.

Mrs Du Bois was running towards him. He turned and walked faster. But she kept shouting and he thought someone might hear so it would be better to stop. The dog loped up ahead of her and nuzzled against his side.

"Kula!" she gasped and pushed her pale hair out of her eyes. "Why didn't you come? You got my note? It was dangerous to write to you, but I had to see you -"

She put out a hand and touched his arm.

He pulled it away.

"Don't be like that. You liked it, I know you did."

He said nothing.

"Do you want money? I could give you some," her voice took on a cajoling note, "it would help you get started wherever you want to go."

He felt disgust but he forced himself to be calm.

"I don't want money, and I don't want to do it again with you."

The beautiful eyes hardened. She was, he realised, made crazy by her desire.

"No-one will see," she whispered, coming closer, "they're all at the village, and Jean-Pierre's staying with friends. Take me here, among the grapes." She gave a short laugh. "I sometimes think my husband and daughter love the grapes more than they love me."

She lifted her face to his. She smelled of flowers.

He grabbed her by the shoulders and lifted her bodily away from him. "I won't do this!" He shook her, for emphasis, but she laughed and fought against him as if it was a game, as if he just needed a little rough persuasion. Blaze pranced about them and gave an excited bark. He kept hold of her, hard, and waited for her to realise he wasn't going to yield.

Then she twisted and began to scratch his arms, raking her nails against his skin.

He let her go and she stumbled backwards and steadied herself, watching him with a sly curve to her lips. "Imagine what our neighbours would say," she murmured, "if they could see me now?"

He backed away.

She began to smooth down her white dress, over and over, and her eyes again took on that expression from the kitchen doorway. She seemed to be seeing something far away from him, beyond his shoulder. The previous time, that expression had been the point at which her initial fear seemed to dissolve. This time, it seemed to signal a loss of interest. Or a distraction.

He turned quickly. Had someone spotted them?

But there was no-one there, only the ranks of vines and the dog sniffing about.

He turned back.

"Mrs Du Bois?"

And then she crumpled like a rag doll, her legs giving way until she collapsed gently onto the ground, coming to rest on her side. A fine dust rose about her. The dog whined and pressed his nose against her leg but she didn't notice. Her eyes drooped and closed. She seemed to sigh although that could be his imagination. He realised, with a shock that made his heart jerk, that this is what he, Kula, must have looked like when Fili found him on the path.

But he'd been drugged.

Mrs Du Bois had simply fainted.

And she hadn't fallen hard. He bent over her. There was no blood that he could see, so she'd wake up soon. When she did, he'd better be far away.

He turned on his heel, the swim in the dam forgotten, and ran.

## CHAPTER FIFTY NINE

"You didn't kill her," I said.

I remember crouching down beside Mum, also convinced she was simply asleep.

*Perhaps she felt tired because of the heat and decided to lie down?*

"No, I didn't kill her. And I didn't push her over. I wasn't standing near her when she fainted." He looked across at me. "But I can't go to the police and tell them that, they'd never believe me."

*With the bruising and the presence of foreign DNA, Mrs Du Bois's death is now classified as murder.*

No, they wouldn't believe him.

After all, Mum was a respected member of the community. What would possess her to embark on a risky affair with a young man half her age, who lived in a shack?

"You have the real note," I said slowly. If I tore up my copy, he could still produce the original.

He smiled. I've never seen him smile when he's been sober. But there was no warmth in it.

I felt my chest begin to tighten once more. He wasn't stupid or naive, he wouldn't have come here to tell me the unwelcome truth about my mother unless he knew I would have no riposte.

"The note is with a reporter I know. If you tell the police, or if I disappear, it will be published."

The full force of his cleverness hit me with a blow that was physical, pinning my body against the hard slats of the bench, pressing the air out of my lungs.
*Breathe*, I told myself. *Breathe and think.*
I had imagined I was in control, and that I possessed the right to expose him or not.
But it turns out he was in charge all along. And the consequences if I spoke out would be devastating. Mum's death was a single, lightning bolt compared with the storm that would overwhelm Du Bois if it was revealed that Ray Du Bois had an affair with a squatter while simultaneously trying to get him evicted.
"Dad will be broken," I tried to keep my voice steady, "he doesn't deserve this. He loved Mum. And my brother will find out."
Will every happy memory become tainted with bitterness? Will Mum and Dad's marriage, their love, become a sham to be maintained for Jean-Pierre until he discovers his mother's treachery?
"I don't hate your family, Fili," Kula said quietly. "But I won't - how do you say - sacrifice myself?"
I turned to him. He face was implacable.
"Do you know the findings of the autopsy? That DNA was found under Mum's fingernails?"
He nodded. "Yes. It was in the papers. And it will be mine."
"It will. They tested your father and they found enough of a match to suspect you."
"And that makes me a murderer, in the eyes of the police."

"That, and the bruises on Mum's shoulders from where you held her."

But it was not the full story.

*She died from what we call an aneurism,* Dr Saunders said. *It seems she may have had a weakness.*

I stared up through the tree canopy. Clouds were racing across an overcast sky. Kula Mfusi knew he didn't kill Mum - maybe she was still alive when he left her. Can you imagine his horror when he discovered in the news that she had died?

*Tell the truth,* Grand-mère said, *wherever it leads.*

"There's something you don't know. Mum didn't necessarily die from her fall."

He frowned. "What do you mean?"

"She died because she had a rupture of blood vessels that caused her brain to bleed. She'd been suffering from headaches, she was on medication for high blood pressure."

He didn't react. Despite the number of times I've seen him lash out, he also has a talent for being completely still, like he'd been in the garden that night when he eavesdropped.

"If there was a weakness," I went on, "the rupture - the aneurism - could have happened at any time. Maybe it was the stress. Maybe it was the fall. Or maybe it was her time to die."

He moved then, grabbed me, his hands digging into my shoulders, his eyes piercing mine. No wonder Mum bruised, he was stronger than he realised.

"So I didn't make it happen?"

"We'll never know. Maybe you did, by shaking her. Maybe she did, by running after you."

His fingers relented and he let me go, as he'd let Mum go.

*Think!* I implored my brain. *Explanations aren't enough. You need a way forward.*

"Do the police know about her condition?"

"Yes, they know she died of an aneurism. And that it can happen suddenly, with no warning."

"But they need a murderer," he muttered. "The evidence demands it."

Voices approached. He shifted along the bench and draped an arm around me. Once they'd passed, he moved back to his end of the bench.

"We're at a stalemate," I said.

"Explain that, please."

I turned to face him.

"Kula, neither of us can do anything or say anything without causing more trouble. More heartache." I reached out - tentatively - and touched his arm. "Or a miscarriage of justice."

"So you believe me."

"Yes, I do."

A silence fell between us. The distant sound of traffic swelled and faded.

"My father always says we should look forward, not back. That's why he and Mum adopted me. They wanted to give a stray child a chance. They looked to the future."

Perhaps Kula had overheard Dad say the words?

Or perhaps this was where he'd been hoping to lead me all along, for he got up and walked across the grass, stopping before the path that led back to campus.

"Let's keep the stalemate in place, Fili Du Bois." He flashed me a warning glance. "I will trade my silence for yours. You'll never see me or hear from me again. Neither will my father. Or the police. Your mother's murder will never be solved. And you will say nothing of what I've told you."

I nodded. It was a fair exchange. I think Grand-mère would approve.

And it was the only course open to us.

Our eyes met for a long moment. I hope he saw gratitude in mine. He turned away.

"I won't ever speak your language," I called after him.

"You don't need to," he replied over his shoulder. "Truth is the same in any language."

And he was gone.

The murder — if it was murder - of Ray Du Bois was never solved.

I learnt to live with waxing and waning suspicion. Every five years or so, an investigative reporter in search of a scoop sifts through the evidence - and the conjecture — to advance a new theory. There's a brief revival of interest and then it fades like the vines in winter.

I give no interviews and admit to no public or private suspicions - or the truth.

Not even with those closest to me.

For the rest of his life, Dad mourned Mum and revered his untarnished memory of her. Jean-Pierre grew up and forgot about the secrets I'd asked him to keep, and we never spoke about the man he said he'd seen. Does he know something that he later decided should be kept quiet?

Captain Dlamini was promoted and moved to a senior position in Kwa-Zulu Natal, where the murder rate is high. Adam Mfusi disappeared into the informal settlements around Cape Town. I tried to find him - I thought I might give him some oblique reassurance about his son - but he'd vanished. Tannie Ellie's nephew, Blake, also disappeared but I saw a photograph in a glossy magazine some ten years later of a well-dressed man who resembled him closely, posing beside a sports car. Speaking of money, Petro found a millionaire and went to live in New York. Evonne remained at the university where we'd both studied and became a professor of mathematics. Dr Saunders married and kept sufficiently calm to combine a thriving practice with the arrival of three children. Grand-mère – beloved Grand-mère – attained her century and then lay down one evening and slipped away before morning.

Our valley, our country, edges forward but it's hard.
Graft swirls about our leaders and homelessness still stalks the poorest among us. At Du Bois, we employ a rainbow workforce who live in an integrated village. It's not popular, but we keep at it and one day it will be

normal for all colours to live and work alongside one another. Sometimes, in a crowd, I find myself looking for Kula Mfusi. The fierce eyes. The unnerving stillness. But I never saw him again. Or heard from him.

Years later, on the anniversary of Mum's death, there were different flowers on her grave from the roses we all traditionally brought - copper Just Joey, creamy Peace, scarlet Fragrant Cloud.

There was no card. No indication of who they were from.

Just a sheaf of white lilies, to match the dress she was wearing on the day she died. No-one remembers the colour of her dress. Only someone who was there that day? Or a stranger who happened to choose white flowers? *I know you, you could not have done it...*

But I refuse to speculate.

I look forward, rather than back.

"Someone from her schooldays, perhaps," suggested Dad fondly. "In memory?"

He walked away slowly. Dad doesn't have complete use of his arm since his stroke, but enough to be able to manage a stick. We don't let him do too much but he likes to wander through the vineyards, feel the soil between his fingers as Grand-mère used to do - *this special dirt* - and hear the pickers singing when they bring in the harvest, and watch the jackal buzzards as they circle.

"Come," said Bo, putting a gentle arm around me. "The kids will be waiting."

I smiled up at him. Bo and I make magnificent, award-winning wine, and we've made two lively children as well. Jean-Pierre comes back whenever he can but he's very busy in his role as an airline pilot. When the winds over the valley are in the right direction, and the flight plan is favourable, he will fly over the farm and, very gently, dip his wings. Not enough to alarm the passengers, but enough to let me know that he's up there, like the ancestors, looking down on our stake in the ground. And on what we've made.

Water, soil, and *terroir* into wine...

And into life.

## ACKNOWLEDGEMENTS

This novel took five years to research and write. Along the way, I learnt that wine-making is a magnificent, complex process. I am therefore grateful to the owner of an estate in the Cape Winelands who, along with his winemaker, gave of his time and knowledge to educate me. I hope that I have done their teaching justice! And I also gleaned knowledge from other estates that I visited during the research phase of this project.

Adoption, and the challenge of integrating adopted and biological children into a family, was a poignant reminder of how fragile human relationships can be. Thank you to those parents and children who described their personal experience.

The beautiful cover of the book was designed by Heather Thomas, for which many thanks. The layout, production and marketing were managed by my husband, without whose expertise it would have been impossible to bring Fili Du Bois to a global audience.

Barbara Mutch
2024
www.barbaramutch.com

OTHER BOOKS BY BARBARA MUTCH:

The Housemaid's Daughter

The Girl from Simon's Bay

The Fire Portrait

Printed in Great Britain
by Amazon